P

GHOSTHEART

'This compelling novel, with its shock dénouement, is both beautifully written and skilfully crafted and confirms Ellory as one of crime fiction's new stars' *Sunday Telegraph*

'Genuinely heartbreaking . . . an extremely vivid, moving picture of the human condition, *Ghostheart* is a superb tale of tragedy and revenge' *Big Issue*

CANDLEMOTH

'An ambitious first novel . . . incisive, often beautiful writing' *The Times*

'You know you're on to something from the opening line . . . compelling, insightful, moving and extremely powerful' *Sydney Morning Herald*

A QUIET VENDETTA

'With exquisite pace and perfect timing, R. J. Ellory has given us a piercing assessment of the nature of love, loyalty and obsessive revenge, not to mention a deep understanding of la cosa nostra' *Guardian*

'A sprawling masterpiece covering 50 years of the American dream gone sour . . . [A] striking novel that brings to mind the best of James Ellroy' *Good Book Guide*

CITY OF LIES

'Ellory writes taut, muscular prose that at its best is almost poetic . . . *City of Lies* is a tense and pacy thriller taking the reader into a world of secrets, betrayal and revenge'
Yorkshire Post

'A gripping thriller with many twists and turns'
Woman's Weekly

A QUIET BELIEF IN ANGELS

'*A Quiet Belief in Angels* is a beautiful and haunting book. This is a tour de force from R. J. Ellory'   Michael Connelly

'This is compelling, unputdownable thriller writing of the very highest order'   *Guardian*

'Once again R. J. Ellory shows off his special talents . . . it confirms his place in the top flight of crime writing'
Sunday Telegraph

R. J. Ellory is the author of four other novels: *Candlemoth, A Quiet Vendetta, City of Lies* and *A Quiet Belief in Angels*. Twice shortlisted for the Crime Writers' Association Steel Dagger for Best Thriller, Ellory's books have been translated into Italian, German, Dutch and Swedish. Having originally studied graphics and photography, he intended to pursue a career in photojournalism, but for many reasons this never came to fruition. He started writing more than ten years ago and hasn't stopped since. He is married with one son, and currently resides in England. Visit his website at www.rjellory.com.

By R. J. Ellory

Candlemoth
Ghostheart
A Quiet Vendetta
City of Lies
A Quiet Belief in Angels

Ghostheart

R. J. ELLORY

An Orion paperback

First published in Great Britain in 2004
by Orion
This paperback edition published in 2005
by Orion Books Ltd,
Orion House, 5 Upper St Martin's Lane,
London WC2H 9EA

An Hachette Livre UK company

Reissued 2008

A CIP catalogue record for this book is available
from the British Library.

Typeset at The Spartan Press Ltd,
Lymington, Hants

Printed and bound in Great Britain by
Clays Ltd, St Ives plc

The Orion Publishing Group's policy is to use papers that
are natural, renewable and recyclable products and
made from wood grown in sustainable forests. The logging
and manufacturing processes are expected to conform to
the environmental regulations of the country of origin.

www.orionbooks.co.uk

Beyond the writing of a book,
there are those who make it happen.

In this case, the usual suspects are as follows:
My agent, soundboard and co-conspirator, Euan Thorneycroft.
My assistant editor, compadre and text-buddy, Nicky Jeanes.
My editor, my friend, the modest genius, Jon Wood.
And to Robyn Karney (aka Thelma),
for her balanced eye and faultless precision.

To all those whose words captivated my imagination:
Raymond Chandler
William Carlos Williams
Walt Whitman
Jerzy Kosinski
Rene Lafayette
Anita Shreve
William Gay
Stephen King
Tim O'Brien
and an unnamed hundred more . . .

To my wife and son, constant reminders
of all that makes life worth living.

My surface is myself.
Under which
to witness, youth is
buried. Roots?
Everybody has roots.

William Carlos Williams – 'Paterson'

ONE

The sound from the street was bold, bellying up against the breeze like a bright colored streamer, and from the sidewalk vents the smoke and steam crawled like tired ghosts from the subway below. It was early, a little after eight a.m., and from the boulevards, from the junctions and corners and storefronts, people emerged to meet the world as it surfaced from sleep.

Manhattan came to life, here on the Upper East Side. Columbia University, Barnard College and Morningside Park, bordered to the west by Hudson River Park, to the east by Central, and then the West nineties and hundreds, roads that skipped out in parallel lines – a mathematician's archipelago. Here was academia – the students and bookshops, the Nicholas Roerich Museum, Grant's Tomb and The Cloisters – and wrapped around it the smell of the Hudson River, the sound of the 79th Street Boat Basin and the Passenger Ship Terminal to the south.

Amidst these things was the haunt of freshly baked bread and donuts, frosted sugar and frying bacon; the sound of bolts being drawn, of voices merging one into another like the murmur of thunder somewhere along the horizon; the rumble of traffic, of cars, of wagons, of delivery vans bearing fresh fruit and ham hocks, newspapers and cigarettes and new-drawn churns of cream for the coffee houses and delicatessens: all these things, and more.

And into this ripe medley of life's small pleasures, rough edges, and sharp corners a young woman walked past the steps that climbed from the tunnels below, her movements swift

1

and deliberate, her windswept hair clouding her face, her hand clutching her coat up around her throat against the bitter fists of wind that seemed to lunge at her from behind doorways, from around corners. Her skin pale, her features aquiline, her lips rouged with aubergine, she hurried forward until she reached the junction between Duke Ellington and West 107th. Here she paused, glancing left and right and left again like a child, and stepped from the curb, hurrying across the hot-top to the other side. Here, almost unnoticeably, she paused again and, turning left, she made her way along a sidestreet to a narrow-fronted bookstore. Pausing there in the doorway she searched her coat pockets, found keys and leaned into the lee of the frame to unlock the door. Once inside she turned on the lights, flipped the sign and hurried into the back room where she filled a coffee jug with water. She switched on the antique percolator, filled the glass reservoir, set the jug beneath, and with the deft motions that came from endless repetition, lined the bowl beneath the reservoir with paper and coffee grounds and slid it home. She removed her coat, tossed it nonchalantly onto a chair beside a small deal table, and made her way back to the front of the shop.

She looked around the room, a room not unlike some narrow closeted library, the ceiling-high bookshelves racked from left to right with not so much as breathing space in between, and in no order, and with no formality, and discounting any such thing as alphabet or barcode, these books, these battered hand-worn, dog-eared, musty-smelling books, challenged her with their totality of words, with their myriad silent voices, with the pictures that each paragraph and sentence, each phrase and clause inspired. These were her words. Her books. Her life. Here on Lincoln Street, in the backyard of nowhere special, she had created a brief oasis of sanity. Her name was Annie O'Neill. She would be thirty-one come November. Sagittarius. The Archer. With her hair a rich burnished auburn, her features clear and concise, her eyes almost aquamarine, she was beautiful, and single, and often a little lonely. She wore open-necked blouses and cumbersome sweaters, constantly tugging the sleeves up above her elbows and revealing a man's wristwatch, given to her by her mother. The watch had belonged to her father, and it was too big, and the leather strap was drawn to its tightest hole, but still that watch ran up and down her forearm like a mischievous child. Her eyes were sometimes clouded and quiet, other times bright and fierce, and her temperament unpredictable – often mellow, sometimes challenging and thunderous and awkward. She read poetry by Carlos Williams and Walt Whitman, and prose too – Faulkner's *As I Lay Dying*, and Shapiro's *Travelogue For Exiles*. And other things, many things, and though not all the books that lined the shelves, perhaps a thousand of them, or two, or five.

This was Annie O'Neill's world and few people came here, the majority because they did not know of it, others because they did not care, because they were rushing to some other place that bore greater importance than the written word. And there were things that did not belong here: vanity; ostentation; falsity; cowardice; greed; superficiality.

And there were things that did: love; lust; magic; definitiveness; compassion; empathy; perfection.

Idealistic, passionate, decisive – fingers grasping for life in handfuls too broad to be held – Annie O'Neill wished for something. Something unspecific, but dangerous. She wanted to be loved, she wanted to be touched, she wanted to be held. She desired; she longed; she ached; she hurt.

These were her feelings, her emotions, her thoughts. These were the unfolding patterns of her unsettled and brooding life. These were her colors, her deliberations, her emptinesses.

And this was Thursday morning, a Thursday in August towards the closing chapters of summer, and even as she considered her life she knew she was an anachronism, a woman out of time, out of place. For this was the beginning of the twenty-first century, and she knew, she *knew*, that she didn't belong here. She belonged with Scott Fitzgerald, with

Hemingway and Steinbeck, with *To A God Unknown* and *The Outsiders*. That was where her heart could be found, and she struggled with this, struggled with each new dawning day as she went about the business of her narrow life, turning in ever-narrowing circles and centrifugally spiralling away into the hollowness of solitude.

Something had to change. Something had to be *made* to change, and she was pragmatic enough to realize that she herself would be the fulcrum of any change. Such changes did not come unprecipitated, nor did they come through divine intervention. They came through decision, through action, through example. People changed with you or they stayed behind. Like Grand Central. You took the train, the 5:36 for Two Harbors, nestling there beneath the Sawtooth Mountains where, on a clear day, you could almost reach out and touch the Apostle Islands and Thunder Bay, and those that walked with you came too, or they did not. And if not, they were content to stand and wave, to watch as you rolled away soundlessly into the indistinct distance of memory. And if travelling alone you packed only sufficient for your needs and did not burden yourself with things too weighty, like lost loves, forgotten dreams, jealousies, frustrations and hatred. You carried with you the finer things. Things to share. Things that weighed next to nothing but held the significance of everything. These were what you carried, and in some small way they also carried you.

Annie O'Neill would often think such things and smile, alone with her thoughts.

The coffee was ready. She could smell it from the front. She went out back, washed a cup in the sink in the corner, and took a small carton of cream from the refrigerator, upended the last half-inch into a cup, and filled the cup with coffee. She stayed a while in the back room, and only when she heard the bell above the door did she venture once more into her world within worlds.

The man was elderly, perhaps sixty-five or seventy, and

4

beneath his arm he carried a brown paper-wrapped bundle tied with string. His topcoat, although heavy and once expensive, was worn in places. His hair was silver-grey, white over the temples, and when he saw her he smiled with such warmth and depth Annie couldn't help but smile back.

'I intrude?' he asked politely.

Annie shook her head and stepped forward. 'Not at all . . . how can I help you?'

'I don't wish to disturb you if you are busy,' the old man said. 'I could perhaps come back another time.'

'Any time is as good as any other time,' Annie said. 'Are you after something specific?'

The old man shook his head. He smiled once more, and there was something about the way he smiled, something almost familiar, that put Annie at ease.

'I'm just visiting,' he said. He stood for a moment surveying the store, glanced once or twice at Annie, and then turned to look again across the racks and shelves that surrounded him.

'You have an impressive collection here,' he said.

'Enough to keep me occupied,' she replied.

'And to serve the needs of those whose taste runs beyond the *New York Times* bestseller list.'

Annie smiled. 'We do have some odd and unusual items here,' she said. 'Nothing too rare or intellectual, but some very good books indeed.'

'I am sure you do,' the man said.

'Was there something you were hoping to find?' she asked again, now somehow slightly uneasy.

The man shook his head. 'I suppose you could say that,' he replied.

Annie stepped forward. She had the unmistakable sense that she had missed something.

'And what might that be?' she asked.

'It is a little difficult . . . '

Annie frowned.

The man shook his head as if he himself were questioning

5

what he was doing there. 'In all honesty, I have come for no other reason than reminiscence.'

'Reminiscence?'

'Well . . . well, as I said it's a little difficult after all these years, but the reason I came down here was because I knew your father –'

The old man stopped mid-flight as if he'd anticipated a reaction.

Annie was speechless, confused.

The man cleared his throat as if in apology for his own presence. 'I knew him well enough to take books,' he went on. 'To read them, to pay him later.'

He paused again, and then he laughed gently. 'Your father was a brilliant man with a brilliant mind . . . I miss him.'

'Me too,' Annie said, almost involuntarily, and was gripped by a sudden, quiet rush of emotion at the mention of her father. She paused a moment, gathering herself perhaps, and then walked a little further into the shop.

The old man set down his package on a stack of hardbacks and sighed. He looked up, up and around the shelves from one wall to the next and back again.

He stretched his arms wide, a fisherman telling tales.

'This was his dream,' he said. 'He seemed to want nothing else but what he possessed here . . . except of course your mother.'

Annie shook her head. She was having difficulty absorbing everything that she was feeling. A sense of absence, of mystery, and a sudden reminder of a huge hole in her life which, even at this moment, she was trying desperately to fill with half-forgotten memories. Her father had been dead more than twenty years, her mother more than ten, and yet in some way her memories of her father were stronger, more vivid, more passionate. In that moment she could almost see him. Right now. Standing where the old man was standing with his worn-out expensive topcoat.

'How did you know my father?' Annie asked, the words

clawing their way up out of her throat. There was tension in her chest as if she were fighting back tears that had long since been spent.

The old man winked.

'That, my dear, is a very long story . . .'

Annie O'Neill's mother had listened to Sinatra. Always. The mere fact of hearing his voice so often as a child had enchanted Annie O'Neill long before she saw his films or read his biographies. And she couldn't have cared less *who* the world believed he was. She didn't care that Coppola called him Johnny Fontaine in *The Godfather*, or that he introduced a girl called Judith Exner to both Sam Giancana and John Kennedy, or that he underwent extensive investigations regarding his alleged involvement with the Mafia . . . man, he could *sing*. From the first bars of 'Young At Heart' or 'I've Got The World On A String', whether the orchestra was led by Harry James, Nelson Riddle or Tommy Dorsey, even if it was Take #9 or Take #12 with Frank's irritated demands left intact on the master, it didn't matter. A man could sing like that, didn't matter if he'd been the one behind the grassy knoll smoking a cigarette and waiting for The Man to come to town. Hoboken, New Jersey, 12 December 1915, the world was given a gift from God, and God deigned to leave him here long enough to enchant a million hearts.

And it was to Frank that Annie O'Neill would go when she felt she was losing herself inside the anonymity of her own life. And it was within the timbre and pace of his voice that she would find some small solace; find refuge in the mere fact that this had been a love she had shared with her mother. Inside her third-floor Morningside Heights apartment – four rooms, each decorated with care and consideration, each color labored over, each item of furniture selected with a complete ambience in mind – she would sequester herself from reality and find her own reality that was so much more *real*.

It was from this same safe haven that she had ventured that

August Thursday morning, a walk she made each and every working day, and it was within those ten or fifteen minutes that she would habitually re-design her life into something more closely approximating her desires. For all the hundreds, perhaps thousands of people who passed her in the street, it was nevertheless a lonely walk, a methodical passage from one foot to the next with little of consequence in between. And in arriving she would see much the same people. There was Harry Carpenter, a retired engineer who'd once worked down at the Rose Center for Earth & Space: a man who talked endlessly of his Spiderman comic book collection, how he'd found a mint copy of *The Amazing Spider-Man*, March 1963, *#14* of July '64 when The Green Goblin first appeared and, to cap it all, a *#39* from August '66 when Norman Osborn's real identity was revealed. Harry was perhaps a little lost, sixty-seven years old, his wife long since gone, and he trawled through the shelves and selected books that Annie knew he would never read. And then there was John Damianka, a lecturer from Barnard, a kindred spirit in some sense. John and Annie had been neighbors an eternity ago, and when she'd moved to Morningside John had kept right on visiting like it was something that would happen for the rest of their lives. Once upon a time, sitting on the stoop, they had talked of life's inconsequentialities, but now he came to the store, and however well he might have seemed there was always something about him that reminded Annie of the quiet sense of desperation that accompanied all those who were lonely. He talked endlessly of the trials and tribulations of finding *a decent girl* these days. *I don't need Kim Basinger* he would say, *I just want someone who understands me . . . where I'm at, where I'm coming from, where I'm going.* Annie held her tongue, resisted the temptation to tell him that it might be a little easier if he knew those things for himself, and she listened patiently. *Irony of it all*, he would say, *is that the only letters people like me receive are Dear John letters.* He would laugh at that, laugh each time he told her, and then he would add: *But you know, the only girl that ever dumped me by* *mail called me J.D. And that was how it began. Dear J.D. So the only real Dear John letter I ever got wasn't a Dear John letter at all.*

People like this. Lost people perhaps. Lost enough to find the little bookstore down a narrow sidestreet a short walk from Ellington and West 107th.

She welcomed them, all of them, because she was still idealistic enough to think that a book could change a life.

And thus her first thought when the old man in the expensive but tired-looking topcoat had mentioned her father was that he had come to reminisce, to select a book perhaps, to consume a few minutes of their lives shooting the breeze and skating the differences. And then her second thought, her third and fourth and fifth also, was that this man – whoever he was – might be the key to understanding something about her own past that had been forever a mystery. The urgency she felt could not have been explained any other way; he represented a line to the shore, and she grasped it with both hands and pulled with all she possessed.

'You are busy?' the old man asked her.

Annie held her arms out as if inviting him to survey the crowds that were even now jamming their way into the store. She smiled and shook her head. 'No,' she said. 'I'm not busy.'

'Then perhaps I can take a few minutes to show you something.'

He collected his package from the stack of hardbacks as he came towards her, and when he reached the counter he set it down and untied the string that bound it.

'I have here,' he said quietly, 'something that may intrigue you.'

The brown paper unfolded like dry skin, like a fall leaf once again unwrapped from its own multi-hued chrysalis. Within the package was a sheaf of papers, and on top of the papers a blank manila envelope. The old man took the envelope, and from within it he drew a single sheet of paper. He handed it to Annie.

'A letter,' the man said.

Annie took it, felt the coarse and brittle texture of its surface. It felt like the page of an age-old volume, a first edition left somewhere to hold its words in breathless perpetuity. At the top of the page, faded now but still legible, was a scrawled heading. *From the Cicero Hotel* it read.

'No longer standing,' the old man said. 'They tore it down in the sixties and built something strange and modern.'

There was something clipped and too articulate in his voice, something that made him difficult to place.

Annie looked up at him and nodded.

'It's a letter your father wrote,' he went on. 'He wrote it to your mother. See . . . '

The man extended his hand, then his index finger, and the index finger skated over the letter and rested above the words *Dear Heart*.

Annie frowned.

'He always started his letters that way . . . it was a token of his affection, his love for her. Shame, but I believe the letters never actually reached her . . . '

The old man withdrew his finger.

Annie watched it go like a train leaving a station with someone special on board.

'If there was one thing your father knew how to do,' he whispered, almost as if for effect alone, 'it was *how* to love someone.'

And then the old man nodded towards the letter, and the hand with the index finger made this small flourish, like someone introducing a minor act in vaudeville.

'Proceed,' he said, and smiled.

'What's your name?' Annie asked.

The man frowned for a second, as if the question bore the least possible significance and relevance to the matter at hand.

'My name?'

'Your name?' she repeated.

The man hesitated. 'Forrester,' he said. 'My name is Robert Franklin Forrester, but people just call me Forrester. Robert is too modern for a man my age, and Franklin is too presidential, don't you think?'

He smiled, and then he bowed his head as if a third person had made a formal introduction.

Once again she felt a twinge as he smiled. Was there something too familiar in the way he looked at her?

She was possessed then, compelled to consider something that at once excited and terrified her. She found herself scrutinizing his face, looking for something that would serve to identify who he might be. She shuddered visibly and turned her eyes back to the letter.

Dear Heart,

I am lost now. More lost than I ever imagined I could be. I am sorry for these years. I know you will understand, and I know that your promise will stand whatever happens now. I trust that you will care for the child, care for her as I would have had I possessed the chance. I feel certain that I'll not see you again, but you are – as ever – in my heart. I love you Madeline, as I know you love me. Love like ours perhaps was never meant to survive. A moth to a flame. A moment of bright and stunning beauty, and then darkness.

Always, Chance.

Annie frowned; she felt her heart tighten up like the fist of a child. 'Chance?'

Forrester smiled. 'He called her Heart, she called him Chance . . . you know how love is.'

Annie smiled as if she understood. She did not question the feeling, but nevertheless the feeling came. She believed – all too unwillingly – that she did not know how love was.

'He died soon after,' Forrester said. 'I believe, though I could never be sure, that even though she never received it, it was in fact his last letter to her.'

Annie held the page in her hands, hands that were even now beginning to tremble. Emotion welled in her chest, a small,

11

tight fist in her throat, and when she looked back at Forrester she saw him blurred at the edges. Blurred through her own tears.

'My dear,' he said, and withdrew a silk handkerchief from his pocket.

He handed it to her and she touched her lids gently.

'I did not mean to upset you,' he said. 'Quite the opposite.'

Annie looked at the page once more, and then back at the old man. They became one and the same thing – the old man standing beside her and the letter she held in her hand, and in that brief second they represented all she had ever wanted to know about her own history.

'I came, you see, with an invitation,' and then he smiled once again in that strangely familiar fashion.

Of her parents' relationship Annie O'Neill knew little. Her father had died when she was seven, and in the years that followed, when she'd lived alone with her mother, Madeline, there was little said of him. Of course he would crop up in their conversations, perhaps her mother mentioning something about the shop, about a book they'd read . . . but the intimate details, the whys and wherefores of life before his death – these things went unspoken. Madeline O'Neill had been a woman of character, self-possessed and intuitive. Her intelligence and culture defied description, and time and again she spoke of things that Annie believed no-one could have known. She knew books and art, she knew music and history; she spoke the truth directly and without hesitation. She had been Annie's life, a totality, a completeness, and for the years they had been together Annie could never have comprehended existence without her. But time marched, and it marched with foot-soldiers, and the footsoldiers carried weapons that weakened the heart and frayed the nerves. They arrived one evening a little after Christmas 1991, and they brought with them Madeline O'Neill's call-to-arms.

After her mother's death, after the funeral, after people she barely knew had come and gone with their words of sympathy and regret, Annie was left with almost nothing. The house where they had lived all those years was sold, and with the proceeds she bought ownership of the shop and paid a deposit on her apartment. Aside from that there was a box of papers and oddments beneath her mother's bed which Annie knew were meant for her. Among those things was a book. A single book from all the many thousands that had passed through the family's collective hands over the years. It was a small book called *Breathing Space* by Nathaniel Levitt. Printed in 1836 by a company called Hollister & Sons of Jersey City and bound by Hoopers of Camden – companies both long since vanished into the tidal wave of conglomerates – and Annie had no real understanding of its significance. The book came to represent her father, and thus she had never investigated its significance, never searched out other works by its author. These things did not matter, and seemed in some way to challenge the memory of her father. Inscribed inside the cover were the words *Annie, for when the time comes. Dad.* and the date: *2 June 1979*. It was a simple story, a story of love lost and found once more, and though the places and names and voices were dated, there was something about the rhythm of the prose, the grace with which the slightest detail was outlined and illuminated, that made the book so special. Perhaps it meant nothing of any great significance, but to that book she had granted character and meaning far beyond its face value. It had been left for her. It had come from her father. And though she would perhaps never understand the time to which he referred it didn't matter. It was what it was, but most of all it was hers.

Nevertheless, it struck Annie O'Neill that for the first time in many years she was thinking of her father as a real person: a person with his own life, his own dreams and aspirations. What had Forrester said? That if there was one thing her father had known *how* to do it was to love his wife, Annie's mother. And love seemed now such a tortuous path, such an un-known territory. Navigating the arterial highways of the heart. And even how it sounded. *Falling in* love. Surely that said everything that needed to be said. Like a headlong pitch forward into the hereafter. Why not *rising into love*? Hey, you never guess what happened? I *rose* into love . . . and man, was that a feeling. A feeling like no other.

Annie's mother had always looked a certain way when they spoke of him. Annie would beg her to talk of him, to tell her what he was like, but there was something there, something so driven and powerful that seemed to prevent Madeline from expressing her heart. Losing her husband had devastated her, something that was evident in her eyes, in the way her hands tightened when his name was mentioned. Madeline O'Neill had possessed a strength of character that Annie had rarely seen in anyone else. Her wit and intelligence, her compassion, her *passion* for life, were things that Annie had always aspired to but always seemed to fall short of. It was that character that had made her mother so special to her father, of this Annie was sure, and from this single, simple fact she knew that her father also must have been a remarkable man to capture her mother's heart.

Annie held the letter. *From the Cicero Hotel*. Why was he in a hotel? In a hotel and writing to his wife? She believed she had experienced more emotion in this single moment than she had in the last year. Emotion for her father, the man who had given her life, and almost as soon had disappeared from that life. Emotion also for her mother, for these few words seemed to say everything that could be said about the depth of their love for one another. There was a vacuum within her, as wide as the building within which she stood, and never had she discovered anything that could erase that emptiness.

She looked at Forrester. He looked back – unabashed, direct. He possessed a lived-in face, warm and generous. His features were neither clumsy nor chiselled, but somewhere in between. This was the face of a man who would reach the end of his life, sitting somewhere in a hotel lounge perhaps, or in a rocker on a porch stoop, and with unequivocal certainty declare that it had in fact been a life. A *real* life. A life of moment and significance, a life of loves and losses and calculated risks. Here, she thought, was a man who would never ask himself *What if . . . ?* Sadly for her, but nevertheless realistically, the antithesis of her own quiet existence.

Annie smiled. She handed back the letter.

Forrester raised his hand. 'No, it's for you to keep.'

She frowned, but didn't question how or why this stranger possessed the letter in the first place.

Anticipating her unspoken thought Forrester smiled. 'Frank . . . your father and I, we shared a room together many, many years ago. I have been away, have recently returned to the city, and in preparing my things to move I came across this letter, some others also – '

'Others?' she asked.

Forrester nodded. 'Other letters yes, all of them from your father to your mother . . . also I found some snapshots, old snapshots . . . even one or two of you when you were younger.' Forrester smiled. 'That was how I knew you were Frank's daughter when I came in.'

'You could bring them?'

Forrester didn't answer her question at first. He merely nodded, and placed his hand on the stack of papers on the counter. 'This is my invitation,' he said. 'Your father and I, we started something. We started something special here in Manhattan many decades ago. It was soon after he leased this store – '

Forrester raised his hand and indicated the room within which they stood.

'I met him here, and here is where it all began.'

Annie placed the letter on the counter. 'Where all of what began?'

Forrester nodded and winked as if imparting a tremendous secret. 'The reading club.'

Annie frowned. 'A reading club . . . you and my father?'

'And five or six others . . . closet bohemians, poets, even some writers . . . and every week we would gather here or in

15

one of the apartments and we would share stories and read poems, even letters we had received. It was a different time, a different culture really, and people wrote so much more . . . had so much more to say if the truth be known.'

Annie smiled. Here was a facet, an angle of her father's life she had never seen before. He founded a reading club.

'And as I am here for some time, weeks, months perhaps, I felt we should revive the tradition.' Forrester smiled. He once again performed the small introductory fanfare with his hand, indicated the shelves that stood to all sides: literary sentinels. 'After all, we have no shortage of material.'

Annie nodded. 'You're right there.'

'And this,' Forrester said, taking the sheaf of papers from its wrapping on the counter, hesitating for a second as if a little awkward. 'Well Miss O'Neill, I thought that this might perhaps be the first subject of discussion.'

He handed the papers to Annie. She could smell their age, feel the years that had somehow seeped into the very grain of the pages. Perhaps it was her imagination, but it was almost as if her history was here, a history her father had been part of, and thus she might find something that would contribute to her own. An open door beckoned her and there was nothing she could do but walk right through it.

'It is a novel I believe . . . at least the start of a novel. It was written many years ago by a man I knew for a very short time, all things considered. He was a member of the club, and while he was there he possessed all of us in some small way.' Forrester smiled nostalgically. 'Never met a man quite like him.'

He paused quietly for a second or two. 'This is the first chapter . . . reads like a diary I suppose. I would like you to read it, and then next Monday I will come and we will discuss it.'

He smiled, and there was something so warm, so genuine about his face, that Annie O'Neill never questioned intent or motive or vested interest; she simply said, 'Yes, of course . . . next Monday.'

'So there it is . . . signed, sealed and delivered.' Forrester held out his hand.

Annie looked at his hand, then up at his face, and his eyes were looking at the silk handkerchief that she still clutched in her hand. 'Of course,' she said. 'Sorry . . . ' and returned the handkerchief to him.

'It has been a pleasure,' he said, and once again he bowed his head in that strange clipped European fashion.

'Mr Forrester?'

He paused.

'Could you . . . would you tell me about my father? I know that it seems a strange thing to ask but he died when I was very young . . . and . . . and well – '

'You miss him?'

Annie could feel that tight fist of emotion again, threatening her ability to breathe. She nodded. She knew if she tried to speak she would cry.

'I will come on Monday,' Forrester said, 'and you can ask me all the questions you like and I will tell you what I know.'

'Could you . . . could you stay a little now perhaps?' Annie ventured.

Forrester reached out and touched her arm. 'I am sorry my dear,' he said quietly. 'There is, unfortunately, something I must attend to . . . but I will be here on Monday.'

Annie nodded. 'You will come . . . you promise you will come.'

'I will come Miss O'Neill . . . of that you can be certain.' And then he turned, and Annie watched him go, and though there seemed to be a confusion of questions and noises inside her head she said nothing at all. The door opened, the breeze from the street stole in to gather what warmth it could, and then the door closed and he was gone.

Annie carried the sheaf of papers to the counter and set them down. She turned over the first blank page, and then started to read:

17

A friend of mine once told me something about writing. He said that at first we write for ourselves, then we write for our friends, last of all we write for money. That made sense to me, but only in hindsight, for I wrote these things for someone I believed I would never see, and then I wrote them for money. A great deal of money. And though the story I will tell you has more to do with someone other than myself, and though this thing began long before I met him, I will tell you about it anyway. There is a history here, a history that carries weight and substance and meaning, and I write of this history so you will understand how these things happened, and why. Perhaps you will understand the reasons and motives, perhaps not, but whichever way it comes out . . .

The bell above the door rang again. Annie paused mid-sentence and looked up. The wind had pushed the door open, and the chilled breeze hurried in once more to find her where she stood.

She closed the door, closed it tight into the jamb, and walked back to the counter. There were things to do, a new delivery to log and inventory, and the sheaf of papers would have to wait until she returned home.

She wrapped the papers carefully inside the package that Forrester had brought, tucked the letter he had brought in the package too, put it into a bag, and carried it through to the kitchen at the back of the store. She set the bag on a chair, and in the event that she might absent-mindedly hurry from the store for some reason, she covered it with her coat. She would not forget it; *could* not forget it.

Annie O'Neill thought of the papers throughout the day, like a promise waiting, a sense of anticipation and mystery surrounding them, but even more so she thought of the man who had visited. Robert Franklin Forrester. A man who had known her father, and in the few minutes she had spent with him had given her the impression that he'd known her father far better than she had. And the reading club. A club for only two it

18

seemed. First meeting evening of Monday, 26 August 2002, right here at The Reader's Rest, a small and narrow-fronted bookshop near the junction of Duke Ellington and West 107th.

TWO

Seemed to all who knew him, and those indeed seemed few enough, he was called Sullivan. Just Sullivan. To Annie O'Neill he was Jack, the man who shared the third floor of her apartment building and the suite of rooms that faced hers. Jack was, like Annie's mother, an anachronism, a man out of time and place, and perhaps the greatest living storyteller Annie had ever had the fortune, or misfortune perhaps, of meeting. He was there when she moved into the apartment back in 1995, standing at the top of the stairwell as she heaved and humped boxes and bags up the stairs. Never once offered help. Never really said a word until finally she came to rest and introduced herself.

'Annie O'Neill,' he said. 'And how old are you Annie?'

'Twenty-five,' she'd replied.

'Fuck it,' he said. 'Wanted someone closer to my own age . . . figured there might be a little housewarming, if you know what I mean?'

Jack Sullivan had been fifty then, was fifty-five now, and possibly had lived the most fascinating life that Annie could have imagined – fascinating, that is, if only from the standpoint that she could never comprehend why he'd chosen the life that he did. His father had served in the US military in the Pacific and returned home after the Japanese surrender in August of 1945. His wife, Jack's mother, was pregnant by Christmas, and come 14 September 1946 Jack Ulysses Sullivan was born. The early part of his life, his childhood and teens, had been regular enough. An only child, a loved child, he attended school, took College, studied photography, and at age twenty he followed in his father's footsteps and joined the army. His photographic qualifications got him assigned to the Press Corps, and this duty took him out to Vietnam in June of 1967. He stayed there until December of 1968. Came back with a bullethole in his right thigh, hadn't walked straight since, and though he was invalided out of the army he never lost the taste for his work. That taste took him to Haiti in March 1969, and there he stayed until the death of Papa Doc Duvalier and the accession of his son Jean-Claude to the presidency in April of 1971. After Haiti came El Salvador – February 1972, just before the failed revolt in March that year – an assignment that lasted until January of 1973. In August of '73 Sullivan flew out to Cambodia and photographed the atrocities perpetrated by the Khmer Rouge as they attempted to oust Lon Nol; he witnessed first-hand the vicious guerilla warfare tactics employed after the US officially ceased its bombing, and when he was shot once again in September – the same leg and almost the exact same place – he returned to the US. He stayed for five years, working freelance for UIP and Reuters, and other smaller syndicates and franchises of the media network, but always he was pulled by the war zones of the world. By October of 1979 he was back in El Salvador after President Carlos Romero was ousted in a military coup; was there in March of 1980 when Archbishop Romero was murdered; there when the American nuns and missionaries were killed, as Jose Duarte returned to lead the new junta, and fled home once again in January of 1981 when martial law was declared. And it was from such places as these that the stories came, the haunted painful stories and, as Jack Sullivan spent much of his time the better part of drunk, he would spill those stories out to anyone who might listen.

And Annie listened. Listened good. There was something about the horrific brutality of all he had witnessed that made his ramblings almost intoxicating in their intensity.

The night she'd moved in Jack Sullivan had come knocking on her door with a bottle of Crown Royal and two glasses. She invited him in, it seemed the neighborly thing to do, and he stayed until three or four in the morning regaling her with his horrors. There was an image, a moment perhaps, that had stayed with her through all the things he'd said that night. He had talked of his return from Vietnam in December '68. He spoke of something called the Tet Offensive, the attack on the Khe Sanh firebase, of hills called 101S and 881N. He spoke of a man he'd befriended, a member of the Langvei Camp Special Forces Unit, a young man of twenty-two who'd been shot through the side of his face.

'Could see his teeth through his cheek,' Jack had told her, 'and when he tried to speak the blood just came running out like someone had turned on a faucet.'

Annie, never a drinker, drank more that night than she had in the previous year.

'January '68 the Vietcong came all dressed up in South Vietnamese uniforms and stormed the US embassy in Saigon,' he told her in his slow and languorous drawl. 'US troops were helicoptered in onto the roof and they went through that place room by room and killed every last person inside. I was there, took some snaps of our brave boys doing Lyndon B.'s work. Took six hours . . . and Christ, I can't even begin to count how many they killed.'

Jack smiled as if reminiscing about a family barbecue some warm Savannah Sunday afternoon.

'In February we liberated the Citadel of the Imperial City of Hué. That was one helluva blow for the commies. That was the jewel in the crown for the Tet Offensive. There was a river there, the Perfume River, and alongside it a park that separated Le Loi Avenue from the riverfront. I was there, me and a few others, and we waited in the rain until we could get inside the Citadel compound. The guys we waited with were called the Citadel battalion . . . tough bastards, fought every hard battle throughout the previous six months between Hai Vanh Pass and Phu Loc. Anyways, the Americans and the South Vietnamese went in there and killed every last man standing, replaced them all with their own people. Place was awash with blood. And in the middle of all that, this flock of white geese came down and settled in the compound. Splashed around in the puddles . . . been rainin' all night . . . and some asshole says we should catch one and eat it.'

Jack laughed, a dry grating sound that seemed to fill Annie's new and empty apartment.

'Sergeant said if anyone so much as touched one of those geese they'd be court-martialled. Place went quiet. Everyone knew he was no joker. Geese stayed there the whole time we did . . . have some pictures somewhere . . . perfect white geese splashing in puddles of bloody rainwater, and around them the dead bodies of a hundred or more men.'

Sullivan paused, drank, refilled his glass.

'Then in April Martin Luther King got himself shot, and then in June they killed Bobby Kennedy, and by the time they elected Nixon in November I'd sure as shit had enough of standing in three feet of mud and blood taking pictures for the military. I came back in the middle of December . . . figured I got myself shot in the leg so's I'd have a good enough reason to come home, and I remember sitting in a bar, half-drunk out my mind, and the radio comes on. It's a week before Christmas and the guy on the radio says John Steinbeck died, and then they play 'What A Wonderful World' by Louis Armstrong and I start crying like a high school cheerleader done lost her boyfriend. I'm sat in a bar . . . a bar no more than a mile from where we are now, and I'm sobbing my heart out like a kid. No-one says a word, not a thing, and they just leave me there weeping like a baby for the best part of an hour. Hell, I must have drunk half a bottle of something, but when I goes to pay the barman says to keep my dollars, that he understands where I've been, and though he never agreed with the war he still respected me for going out there to protect the innocent and the American way of life. Didn't tell him I was crying for John Steinbeck . . . wouldn't have seemed right, but sure as shit I was. Sat there crying while Satchelmouth sang about what a wonderful world it was, and considered the fantastic irony of it all.'

Jack paused, drank some more, set his glass to balance on his knee.

'The Earth was not capable of swallowing all that we took to Vietnam. We dropped bombs and food parcels . . . fucking bombs and food parcels . . . and then Nixon got us out of there with our tails between our legs and we're still asking ourselves what the fuck we went out there for in the first place. Helluva thing Annie O'Neill . . . helluva thing.'

And then he'd smiled, raised his glass, and Annie had raised hers, and he whispered: 'To the blessed crazy irony of everything eh?'

She smiled, drank her glass empty, and closed her eyes.

She didn't remember falling asleep, but when she woke he was gone and the bright new light of morning was peeling apart the shadows in her empty apartment.

That had been her welcome to Morningside Heights, Manhattan, and Jack Ulysses Sullivan had never stopped talking to this day. They became close, they shared their time, their apartments almost – each possessing a key for the other's door, each letting themselves in whenever the other was home to share coffee or insignificant details of insignificant days – and though there was never anything but a platonic relationship, there was still a closeness that Annie could only ever measure in terms of family. Jack, in some small way, represented the father she'd never known, and thus Jack, drinker though he was, could only ever be forgiven for his idiosyncrasies and irritations.

Jack was there when she returned home that Thursday evening, the sheaf of papers clutched in her hand, thoughts of her father and who he might have been in her mind, and when he asked if she'd like to come in and 'share a cup of coffee with the drunken fuck opposite' she smiled and said she would like such a thing very much indeed. She took off her coat, set her papers down, and busied herself making a pot in his kitchen.

'Someone came in today,' she told him, as they sat at the small table in his front room. He looked back at her with the fifty-five-year-old face that never ceased to amaze Annie with its depth of character and life; a face created with origami and then carried through a storm. He was a handsome man, had been blond she figured, and now his hair was a salt-and-pepper gray turning white at the temples. His eyes were deep set, his nose thin, almost Roman, and when he spoke there was a light and a fire within the shadows beneath his brows that said everything that could be said without needing to say anything at all.

'Someone came in,' he repeated. 'You had a customer?'

She shook her head. 'No, not a customer . . . an old man, a man who said he'd known my father.'

'The mysterious and irrepressible Frank O'Neill no less,' Sullivan said.

Annie had spoken with Sullivan about her father before, had shared the little she knew and the less she remembered, and Sullivan had always perceived that deep sense of longing. She missed the fact that she had never really known him. Missed it like hell.

'He brought something for me,' Annie went on. 'And he made me an invitation.'

Sullivan looked up and frowned.

'Robert Franklin Forrester,' Annie said. 'That was his name, and he told me that he knew my dad many years go and they had founded a reading club.'

Sullivan turned his mouth down at the sides and nodded. 'Seems logical, him owning a bookstore an' all.'

'He said he was back in Manhattan for a while and he figured we should revive the tradition . . . start the reading club again. He's coming over Monday.'

'Just the two of you?'

Annie nodded.

25

'Hell of a club you have there.'

Annie smiled. 'He seemed okay, lonely I think.'

'And you said it was okay for him to come?' Sullivan asked.

'I did.'

'You want me to come protect you . . . he may be a serial killer or somesuch, preying on beautiful young women working in run-down bookstores.'

Annie waved Sullivan's sarcasm away. 'He brought something for me to read . . . my first assignment for the club, and he also brought a letter my father wrote for my mother.'

Annie rose and walked to the door. She took the sheaf of papers from the chair beneath her coat and returned to the table. She set the papers down.

Sullivan lifted the pages and leafed through them.

'It's a novel I think . . . something like that,' Annie said. 'This man Forrester said that one of the members of the original club had written it.'

'Big novel.'

'I'm sure there's more,' Annie said. 'I thought he might bring it one chapter at a time or something.'

'You've read it?'

Annie shook her head.

'You mind if I read it too?' Sullivan asked.

'Read it with me now,' she said.

'The whole thing?'

'Sure, it's not that long.'

Sullivan nodded. 'Fetch my glasses from the dresser will you?'

Annie fetched Sullivan's glasses, took a moment to refill her cup, and then pulled her chair around to sit beside him.

The room was warm, and beyond the front windows she could hear the wind sneaking its way around the eaves of the building as if it were gently pleading to come in out of the cold.

She looked down as Sullivan turned to the first page, and they started reading together, page for page, line for line

26

almost, and there was something special about their closeness that made her feel that this – once upon a time – might have been something she'd have shared with her father:

A friend of mine once told me something about writing. He said that at first we write for ourselves, then we write for our friends, last of all we write for money. That made sense to me, but only in hindsight, for I wrote these things for someone I believed I would never see, and then I wrote them for money. A great deal of money. And though the story I will tell you has more to do with someone other than myself, and though this thing began long before I met him, I will tell you about it anyway. There is a history here, a history that carries weight and substance and meaning, and I write of this history so you will understand how these things happened, and why. Perhaps you will understand the reasons and motives, perhaps not, but whichever way it comes out I believe that these things are better spoken than left silent. I carried years of silence, and sometimes silence seemed all that I possessed, but once I realized that you existed my life meant something else. So read, read all of this, and make of it what you will. This was my life, and because of who you are it is to some degree your life too. As Whitman once said, 'My surface is myself, under which to witness youth is buried. Roots? Everybody has roots.'

These are my roots, diseased and broken though they may be, but they are my roots. Read on, and I trust you will understand.

This thing begins with a child born of a tryst that could never have survived. His history begins with the peasants and gypsies, once Polish by birth, who occupied the Sudeten and Carpathian Mountains beneath Krakow and Wroclaw along the Czechoslovakian border. It was from this lineage, these wild-eyed, dark-haired gypsy wanderers, that this child, Jozef Kolzac, was born, a breach beneath the filthy shrouds of a hand-stitched canvas shelter in the bitter winter of 1901. His mother, an itinerant, illiterate seventeen-year-old, impregnated by a man she neither knew nor remembered, died in childbirth.

Kolzac, taking his name from the warrior myths that had passed down through age after age, legends that were spoken by the Silesians who camped along the River Oder long before Jagiello and the Saxony accession, grew into a small, weak child, narrow-shouldered and pale-skinned, scrimping for nourishment amongst the scraps and offal that were thrown from the tents and coverings where his people slept and ate and raped and killed one another. He was shunned perhaps, this runt, this stripling child, this half-minded semi-animal who possessed no rights.

Jozef – surviving through childhood, this in itself a miracle, and astute enough to know that succor and support were not to be found here – left his place of birth and took to the deeper Carpathians. He fell in with a wandering musician, an old man seeking an apprentice, and here Jozef learned his trade, the one skill that would in time serve to sustain his life, to feed him, to bring him some small comfort in a country that was barren and loveless and cold.

Following the old man he headed west, back towards Krakow. Camping by night, walking by day, they became friends as well as journeymen and compatriots. Jozef learned of music, his fine fingers dextrous and agile across the instrument the old man carried, a bell-shaped violin, seven strings, balanced across the knees and plucked with one hand while the other strummed. The music he played was beautiful, flowing and melodic, and through and amongst the small encampments they would pass, and there find rugged wild-eyed people, as much animals as Jozef had been as a child. These people would grow calm and listen, and feed the minstrels, at night lighting fires and dancing, singing their songs – ancestral voices rolling down the years – while Jozef Kolzac, now in his teens, now a strange and oddly featured youth, played as if the Devil possessed his fingers and God his soul.

The proclamation of independence for Poland in 1918, the Treaty of Versailles which redrew Poland's borders and led to the war with Russia in 1920, brought the nineteen-year-old Kolzac back to the real world. The same year saw Poland advancing as far as Wilno, the capital of Lithuania, and then onwards far into the Ukraine. Armed Russian soldiers rolled their heaving tonnage of cannons and horses across the barren landscape of this country, sweeping through and killing these people, these wild-eyed gypsies, until the Treaty of Riga gave Poland a new frontier a hundred miles further east.

The old man, teacher, his apprentice ever following him, fled again to the Carpathians. They left behind them a land ravaged and desolate with war, its people starving, its aristocrats clinging desperately to their estates and refusing to share or divide their concerns. Foreigners came – Ukrainians, Ruthenians, Germans – and in 1926 Marshal Pilsudski – a man who had refused to contest the presidential election in 1922, a man who had led Polish forces to victory in the 1920–1921 Polish-Soviet war – took his army, overthrew the government, and declared a dictatorship.

Jozef Kolzac and his master stayed in the south, the heart of the Carpathians, for close to ten years. The old man died, was mourned, a pyre built, his body burned, and his ashes scattered across virgin snow by the young man who had followed him. And then that same young man returned to civilization as the dictator Pilsudski was succeeded by a military junta following his death. Kolzac journeyed west, out along the Czechoslovakian border, north again to Krakow, and finally to Lodz in central Poland.

Kolzac was there in 1936, and here the pattern of his life changed. Here he played for people who had never seen such a man, who had never heard such music, who stood and stared as the tousle-haired, wild-eyed gypsy cavorted and danced and struck such chords upon this instrument. They fed him, they threw him coins, these people who believed that Chopin and Paderewski were the true geniuses of their homeland, and yet found themselves enraptured and breathless as this errant mongrel Paganini serenaded them through their streets and squares.

Kolzac, never having witnessed such wealth, such seeming extravagance, believed that here he would find what he had been looking for: a patronage, a sufficiently generous person to support him. He was thirty-five years old, ageless and indefinable, and he believed he would never travel nor hunger again.

It was in the winter of that year, three years before Germany, citing maltreatment of its own nationals within Poland, rolled her tanks and troops across the borders and started World War Two, that Jozef Kolzac saw Elena Kruszwica, a sixteen-year-old Polish Jewess. She stood in the doorway of a butcher's store, holding her provisions, and watched as this crazed Rasputin figure, his eyes brighter than any jewels, his hair wilder than the mane of any lion, flipped his body through gambols and cartwheels, his stringed instrument dancing such fine melodies, performing with such panache and abandon for the townsfolk, that she was enchanted, mystified, excited. She returned to watch him time and again, and he felt her presence each time she appeared, sometimes so bold as to dance towards her, to watch her shrink back in the doorway, her laughter, her face beneath her scarf, her hands clapping in thick woollen gloves as he bowed and stepped back, collecting the coins and applause of these people.

Understanding little of what she felt, Elena Kruszwica became fascinated, enamoured by this man, this wild gypsy creature blown down from the hills into Lodz.

Her parents asked of her whereabouts, why she took so long to collect the provisions and she, embarrassed, or fearful perhaps, answered with white lies and half-truths that seemed in some way to bring her closer to this crazed genius Kolzac.

In November of that year she stopped coming. Kolzac played in the streets, the squares, but his music was hollow, performed with the obligation of self-preservation, having somehow lost its magic, its real enchantment. He searched for her, asked of her, and found that she had only been sojourning in Lodz, that her hometown was Tomaszow, a handful of miles south. He walked there at night, running much of the way, his instrument roped to his back, his pockets filled with coarse black bread and a fistful of cheese wrapped in linen, a blanket around his head and shoulders against the bitter, bone-freezing cold.

He was there as she walked to her piano lesson the following morning, there in the street as she turned the corner, and these people – Elena, a mere teenager, understanding little of life, little of being a woman – and Jozef, knowing nothing of life but the music the old man had taught him – stared at each other for minutes before speaking.

They believed in one another it seemed, for she never took her lesson that morning, and he never played through the streets of Tomaszow, and for the hours until evening they walked and talked, laughed and sang together in the fields and woods beyond the town.

Perhaps love, perhaps fascination, perhaps none of these: it did not seem to matter. For three days they were together but for the hours that they slept, Elena telling her parents that she was studying in the house of a friend, and he content to do nothing but be there for her. They spoke of life and love and laughter; they spoke of dreams and aspirations; they spoke of a future yet unrevealed and a past which now seemed to bear no significance to the present. The present was what they had themselves created, and it was within this present that they cared little but for one another. Elena was a girl of passion and spirit, a spirit constrained by the etiquette and protocol of a life to which she believed she did not belong. She sought freedom: freedom from the person she was expected to be, freedom to be whom she chose. Jozef granted her that freedom, granted it without payment of penalty, and this – perhaps above all – was the reason she loved him.

And then life reached them, and Elena – having no coins, having given all of her laughter and applause – gave everything

31

else she had. Beneath the roof of a barn, within a tumbled-down mountain of straw, she lay down for Jozef Kolzac, and Jozef – tears in his eyes, an emotion filling his heart that he had never before experienced – gave his virginity and took hers. He was thirty-five, she was sixteen, and perhaps no greater well-meant love ever breathed or spoke or walked the earth.

Elena turned seventeen in January of 1937, and it was in this same month that she became aware that her monthly cycle had ceased, became aware of her condition, and ran from her home to Jozef. He understood, took her away, and the pair of them walked, taking assistance offered by itinerant journey-men, wanderers and travelers on horseback or with carts.

They reached Lublin to the east by February, and here Jozef Kolzac, a father-to-be, fully cognizant of his responsibilities, played for two, bringing money and food to his pregnant Elena where she worked as a maid, a cook and a cleaner for a family related to the town's mayor.

And it was in Lublin where her parents found her, where they brought the menfolk of Lodz who had heard word of this dreadful act of depravity and kidnap. Kolzac was taken by his hands and feet, he was beaten and whipped, and then he was hung from a tree in the nearby woods, his body left for the birds and the wolves.

Elena Kruszwica was returned to Lodz, insane with rage and grief, and in the care of the town's doctor she was retired until the birth of her son in August. She was seventeen, and once her strength had returned she took her son and fled from Lodz into the Carpathians, the home of her child's father. Her parents searched for her in vain, searched until the Germans invaded in September of 1939, and when the Russians came less than a month later, once again to rape and assault their country, Elena's family understood that they had lost her, that they would never see her again. Her mother took her own life as the Russians stormed into Lodz, and her father – a strong and stubborn man – ran from the house screaming and was cut down in a hail of communist gunfire that left his body decimated and bloody, lying there in the snow much as the body of his only grandson's father had done in Lublin.

Elena, finding only solitude and poverty in the mountains, returned to seek work and shelter in Krakow. It was here, towards the summer of 1941, that she was seized and questioned by Nazi troops. Proclaimed a Jew, a belief and faith that had dissolved in the moment of her lover's death, she and her four-year-old son, Haim, were transported by cattle truck to the town of Oswiecim, thirty-three miles west of Krakow.

Here they found their home for the next four years: a place called Auschwitz I.

To describe the horrors, to feel the suffering, to understand the depth of pain . . . These things we cannot comprehend; only observe, withdraw, perhaps pretend that such events do not belong to the same humanity as ourselves.

Those summer months – July, August, on into September – became the birthing ground of true revelation for Elena and her four-year-old son. A ranking officer, Wilhelm Kiel, a man indoctrinated with the Nietzschian concept of Man and Superman and the birth of the true Aryan Race, took this twenty-one-year-old Polish Jewess to his quarters, a wooden barrack room separated from the junior officers by a gravel walkway. Here, she was subjected to barbaric acts of sexual depravity, subjugated and overwhelmed, forced to the limits of sanity as he vented his sadistic fervor. He was tall, broad-shouldered, blond-haired, a Gestapo prodigy, and sexually insatiable. He would return from his duties to find her cowering beneath the bed, her son clutched in her arms, past tears, past screaming, and he would stripe her back with heated wires, tie her down and sodomise her, beat her across the back, the shoulders and the breasts with the flat of his hand, burn her with cigarettes and a crude brand fashioned from a length of metal into the word *JUDE*. Laughing, spitting, shouting, holding her by her hair as he bent her backwards over the table, raping her time and time again as her son crouched in the corner and watched, wide-eyed and confused.

She fell pregnant, he beat her into a miscarriage; she became infected with lice and swellings upon the skin that burst and seeped, and Kiel threw handfuls of salt over her; he cut her hair to the scalp, branded the back of her head, and as he thrust himself into her he would shout 'Jude! Jude! Jude!'

Such things as these, daily, week after week, running into months, years it seemed, and beneath this torture and abuse her memory of Poland, of Jozef Kolzac, of Lodz and Tomaszow, of everything she had been and possessed and believed before Oswiecim, faded into a distant blur. She became a non-person, feeding her son with scraps of blackened filthy bread, sucking moisture from the threadbare carpet into which rain had leaked through the bare wooden floor, nursing her wounds, her shame, her debasement. She ceased to consider herself a human being, and though more times than she could recall she had challenged the justice and equity of God, it was during these times that she realized with utter certainty that God could not exist. Her spirit broken, the freedom she had once sought with Jozef now shattered beyond repair, she breathed solely because she could not stop herself; she slept because her body could stand no longer, and she survived each hour, each minute, each second, simply for her son.

Elena endured her ignominy and anguish in silence, a shell of who she once was. She watched as her fellow Jews and Poles were shipped out to Birkenau, Treblinka, Sobibor, and perhaps – had it not been for her son – she would have run to them, clung to them in her despair and begged to be taken in the trucks, in the horse-carriages to something that could only be better than this. At least silent, without agony, a vacuum of pain.

But her son kept her alive. She watched him grow in stunted inches, watched his eyes deepen, hollow out, perhaps the only future conceived that of taking him away from this, if only beyond the gates, the wires and the sentry towers into the woods, the fields that stretched out as far as the eye could see. Somewhere out there was a world, a world she had lost, had been torn from, her voice shredded with pain, her heart thundering with fear and a profound lack of comprehension. Sometimes she believed she had died, and for her sins with Jozef she was consigned forever to this hell, but somehow, through this blackness of pain and humiliation she remembered his eyes, his genius, his imagination, and understood that a love such as this could never have sentenced her to such a term of punishment.

Kiel did not speak with her, he barked, he ordered her to her knees, onto her back, her stomach. He pulled her by her hair, often tearing clumps from her scalp when it grew back over the seared brand, and then he would sodomise her once more, burying his fingernails in her breasts and gritting his teeth as he hurt her, causing pain that at last left her insensate and numb.

April of 1945 found the Allies in Berlin, Americans and Russians meeting at Torgau on the Elbe, troop carriers and tanks rolling onwards in the heart of the Reich. With these events came the liberation of Belsen, Dachau, Buchenwald, and the full realization of what had taken place. The soldiers – victorious, elated – grew subdued, stunned, silent and sickened as they drove through the corridors of bodies, saw a heap of unclothed women prisoners eighty yards in length, thirty yards wide and four feet high. Belsen housed forty thousand prisoners, many of them beyond all help – stick-thin, suffering from typhus, starvation and tuberculosis. In the days that followed, despite every effort from the Allies, more than six hundred human beings were buried daily. A wheeled scaffold stood against the skyline, from which hung a dozen beaten and broken bodies; the air was thick with the stench of rotting corpses, dead of disease and starvation, gassing and slaughter.

Soldiers in their late teens and early twenties liberated Auschwitz. Soldiers who walked amongst the dead with the eyes of men three times their age. Piles of human ashes, unburned bones, hair shorn from the newly dead, toys taken from children as they were led to the 'showers' – the gas chambers into which men, women and children had been herded in their tens of thousands – and 'sound machines' built to mask the horror of screaming. The Allies had discovered the Final Solution, the attempted extinction of a race.

Elena Kruszwica was there to see the soldiers, standing ankle-deep in mud in the small garden behind Wilhelm Kiel's barrack, there as her now seven-year-old son clung to her leg, asking her who these people were as she fell to her knees, as she heard the screams and shouts of the SS troops being herded into the central square of the camp for surrender to the Americans. Kiel was there, his uniform – and his rank – discarded now, believing he could be filed away with the rest of his men. Elena ran towards him, ran through the American soldiers who tried to hold her back, and lunged for him as he cowered and fell to his knees. With her hands she clawed at his face, tore at his eyes until his features were spattered with blood, gouged and tormented.

The Americans did nothing, watching in horror and disbelief, and when she turned and stared at one of them, holding out her hand, her eyes demanding, her face filthy and grim and resolute, the soldier could do nothing but unclip his gun and hand it to her.

Elena Kruszwica held the gun against Kiel's face, and Kiel – screaming at her, begging for mercy, pleading for his life until he was hoarse – fell into shocked silence as she spat at him, and then pulled the trigger.

These soldiers, these young men – so valiant, so victorious – were welcomed to Auschwitz I by a woman their own age who looked twenty years their senior, a woman with the word *JUDE* burned into her flesh, into the back of her head, into her breasts.

Elena turned as trucks filed through the gates, as the earth trembled beneath her feet, and then she saw her son, her Haim running towards her, running straight towards her across the path of a jeep. Screaming, she charged out, her feet sliding through the mud, her voice audible over the sound of the engines, reaching him just in time to catch him and hurl him forward away from the jeep's wheels. And in this moment she understood: understood that her willingness to die to give him freedom had arrived, for the jeep skidded away from the boy and hit her. Had she been strong and healthy, had she not suffered four years of mental and physical torture at the hands of the Nazis, perhaps she would have survived. But she was not strong, she was emaciated and weak, a broken spirit, a battered body, and the impact of the vehicle killed her within moments. She died with her eyes open, having seen, and then reflecting the sight of a United States Army sergeant picking up her son and holding him close. She died with something resembling a smile on her face, knowing that somehow the boy would see beyond these wires, out into the fields, the woods, the world she remembered before the death of the boy's father and the rape of her country.

The soldier who held the boy was a Jew himself. His name was Daniel Rosen, and the jeep that had killed the boy's mother was his own, driven by his aide. Stunned and shocked, he held the boy closer, watching as his fellow soldiers picked up the woman's body, carried it to the back of a truck and wrapped it in a blanket. Rosen walked with the child, held him carefully, listened to his breathing, understood that nothing could be said to reach this soul, and they stood together at the tailgate of the vehicle. Rosen lifted the corner of the blanket, revealed the almost angelic expression on Elena Kruszwica's face. The child – wide-eyed and drawn, his cheeks sunken beneath his bones, his forehead high, his hair thin on an almost translucent skull – said nothing; merely reached out and touched his mother's mud-spattered face. It was said that Daniel Rosen cried for the child, but no-one was sure.

Rosen, commanding an infantry unit, did what he could before medical battalions arrived, before the doctors and nurses stepped from the trucks and administered watered milk, penicillin, sulfa-based immune system fortifiers – whatever they could to stem the tide of dying that continued for weeks after the liberation.

At the beginning of June Rosen left. He took with him the child; though they had never spoken, Rosen only whispering to the child in Hebrew, the child watching him with that same open, vacant expression, they had found some sense of unity, formed a silent bond that surpassed the need to speak. Perhaps Rosen felt responsible for the death of the child's mother, perhaps he felt an obligation to salvage one battered soul after having witnessed the atrocities of Auschwitz, this small Polish town where thousands upon thousands of human beings had been destroyed.

The unit returned to Berlin, Rosen smuggling the child through the border patrols and checkpoints inside a worn blanket, at one point laying him beneath the seat of a jeep while Russian soldiers searched the vehicle. Germans were escaping into Czechoslovakia, into the Carpathians, into Silesia and the Sudeten Mountains; the Russians were hunting them down and killing them, often torturing them, and some of the German women – knowing this – had gathered around the fences of the camps to plead with the Allies to capture them before the Soviets came. Desperate and distraught, these young women pleaded for their lives, but the Allies could not take them, they were too involved with the vast operation of liberating and saving the lives of the thousands of Jews who remained.

From Berlin Rosen took the child to the US airbase at Potsdam, and from there they flew out, on through Magdeburg, Eisenach, Mannheim, and then across the French border to Strasbourg. From here they drove by night to Paris, to the European victory celebrations, and once there Rosen took a hotel room and stayed for seven weeks, feeding the child, strengthening him, clothing him, walking him back to life through the streets, the boulevards, the parks, sitting in cafés in the sunshine – saying nothing, watching him, eventually sharing some words in a strange mixture of German, Hebrew and Polish. Haim Kruszwica began to learn English, and the first question he tried to ask Rosen was 'Where is my father?' Rosen, thinking that Haim's father must have been one of the many thousands murdered in the camp, questioned him further, and came to the unwilling and unwanted realization that the child was speaking of a tall, blond uniformed man who had shared his mother's bed. Rosen had seen the woman kill the soldier, and understood that this man must have been an officer, hiding his rank for fear of the consequences should he be discovered. He told the child that this man was not his father, that he did not know where his father was, and the child asked if Rosen would now be his father.

Rosen, tears in his eyes, said that he would do his best. The child smiled, for the first time in eighteen weeks he smiled, and Rosen cried openly, his face in his hands, there at the street table of a café while passers-by stared at him, his uniform, the child with him, and understood that, of all things, war tears the soul apart and reveals pain of such depth it cannot be fathomed.

At the beginning of September, three weeks after Haim Kruszwica's eighth birthday, he and Sergeant Daniel Rosen set sail from Calais for New York. They arrived in mid-October, among hundreds of returning soldiers, to the celebrations of victory still ringing throughout the free world.

Daniel Rosen, a forty-six-year-old bachelor, took the child to his widowed sister, a devout Jew, generous and worldly-wise, and suffering her protestations to the contrary he calmed her and spoke with her for more than an hour while Haim was bathed and dressed by the housekeeper and taken to the kitchen where he was fed rich chicken broth and homemade bread. Rosen's sister, Rebecca McCready, having left Palestine in the thirties and married an Irish-American despite her family's threat of disavowal, stood in the kitchen doorway and silently watched the thin, wraithlike child: his wide almond eyes drinking in the sights, his ears thirsty for the sounds of other voices, for the music that played in the parlor, his mouselike eating habits as he picked mere crumbs from a heel of bread and chewed them as if they were steak.

'Yes,' she eventually said to her brother standing beside her. 'I will take him.'

Haim Kruszwica became Haim Rosen, Rebecca's maiden name, and though he was a Pole, though he knew nothing of the Jewish faith, he was taken across the East River into Brooklyn, to the Rosens' synagogue, and was presented to God as a child of this family.

They possessed a relationship of such quiet and measured stability. Daniel taught the child the alphabet, taught him to read, to write, to spell his own name. He enrolled him in school and would sit for hour after patient hour coaching the child through his assignments. Haim asked questions, Daniel would answer them as best he could, for though he had never had either the will or the inclination for fatherhood it came more easily than he'd believed it would. The child would take his hand as they walked, would hug him when he left for school, would run with him in the park come Saturday, and on Sunday evenings, in the warm sanctuary of the Rosen home, Haim would carry Daniel's newspapers, his cigarettes, and sit at his feet with his picture books and crayons. Rebecca, watching them, would never cease to be amazed at the resilience and compassion of the human soul. Such a thing could not be measured or fathomed, or ever truly understood. She believed such a thing was a reflection of God, and God alone would know the words with which it could be described.

Daniel Rosen was demobilised from the army in June of the following year. He lived to see Haim in school, one day sitting and watching the child run and laugh through the playground for more than an hour, his heart elated, his eyes filled with tears, and when he walked away he believed that if this act had been his life's sole purpose then it had been worth it.

In August of 1951 Daniel suffered a stroke, became paralyzed down the left side of his body, and for eight weeks he lay in a bed in his sister's apartment in Manhattan's Lower East Side district, the child beside him, saying nothing, holding his hand, sometimes reading to the man who had brought him out of hell and back to America. Haim Rosen was fourteen years old, and though he had spoken with Daniel about his mother, though he had described what he had seen in Auschwitz, it still seemed that he did not understand death. At least not as something that eventually came to everyone.

On 9 November 1951, Daniel Elias Rosen, Sergeant-At-Arms, twice decorated for valor above and beyond the call of duty, passed over. Haim was there when he died; he sat with him for three and a half hours as the body cooled, as the eyes became glassy and reflective, and this was how Rebecca found him. She remembered entering the room, remembered stepping towards the bed, understanding what had happened without speaking or asking anything of Haim, and when he heard her he turned to her, and he smiled – angelically, she recalled, an expression of such peace, such complete serenity – and said in pigeon Hebrew: 'I understand how bad the world can be, Mama. I see that our lives mean nothing at all to God. I give back my faith, for what use is faith against God? I give back my faith and belief, and I will live my life without Him.'

She remembered saying nothing, remembered hearing the words, only later understanding their import, but by that time Haim Rosen – once Haim Kruszwica, before that Kolzak, son of the errant Rasputin from the Carpathians – had become the product of a disordered mind, amoral and detached.

Haim Rosen, now less a Jew than he had ever been, left Manhattan's Lower East Side in July of 1952, fifteen years old, and crossed the East River into Queens. Rebecca McCready did not see him again, and when she died in the summer of 1968 the last words on her lips were a blessing for her adopted son. By then, sixteen years after his departure, he had become something she would never have recognized.

And perhaps would not have wished to.

Sullivan turned over the last page and sat back in his chair.

'Whoa,' he sighed. 'Not exactly "Green Eggs And Ham" is it?'

Annie was silent for a time, a little disturbed by the feelings and images the text had evoked in her. She looked towards the window; again the sound of the wind pushing at the glass beyond, and she turned and looked at Sullivan.

'Perhaps you should come,' she said. 'Come to the store Monday night . . . '

Sullivan nodded. 'Perhaps I should.'

THREE

Annie O'Neill woke on Friday morning, sweating in the cool half light of dawn. At the edges of her thoughts was something she had dreamed, something half remembered. Sullivan's voice was there, slow and languorous, soothing almost.

'There were three types of people in Vietnam,' Sullivan had said. 'Those who thought a lot about why they didn't wish to kill anyone, those who killed first and thought later, and lastly there were those who just killed as many as possible and never thought about it at all. They were either frightened kids, Midwestern schoolteachers or homicidal maniacs.'

Even now she could remember the way his face had looked when he'd told her, the face of a man carrying ghosts.

Annie turned over and buried her face in the pillow. It couldn't have been later than five a.m. The room was chilled, and she could see her own breath in the cold air. She shuddered, buried herself deeper into the mattress, and though she fought with wakefulness it had arrived with best intent, and after ten or fifteen minutes she rose and switched on the thermostat.

She pulled on a sweatshirt and some pants, busied herself making coffee in the kitchen, and when she sat down at the table, her hands clasped around the mug, she closed her eyes for a moment and wondered what had caused such dark aspects to fill her mind. She thought of the manuscript Forrester had brought, and instinctively glanced towards where it lay on the kitchen counter. Images came back, and with those images a sense of panic and apprehension.

She could hear Sullivan's voice in her head.

'Body bags all lined up waiting for the choppers to come down. Crew of guys collecting the dead. Killed In Action Travel Bureau we called 'em . . . and they used to douse those bags with Old Spice of all things. Could feel the decay in your throat . . . the stench of warfare, and above and beyond all of it the overpowering smell of Old Spice . . . made you sick like a dog Annie, sick like a dog.'

She thought of Daniel Rosen, a man no different from those Sullivan had fought alongside in Southeast Asia. Sergeant Daniel Rosen who witnessed the liberation of Auschwitz and brought a child back to America as if in atonement for the sins of others. And what had happened to the child? What was it he'd become that his foster mother would have been so unwilling to recognize? And who was writing of these things, and who was it they had written them for?

She thought of Forrester, and for a second wondered if there was any possibility in the world . . .

Why had he come? What did he want? Why did he want her to read these things? What, if anything, could it have to do with her father?

Annie shook her head and rose from the kitchen table. She walked barefoot to the bathroom, stripped her clothes off and stood for some minutes beneath the pounding heat of the shower. The feeling didn't leave for some time. The feeling that something ugly had gotten inside her and was damned if it would leave without a fight . . . but it did leave, eventually, and as she dried herself and dressed again she believed the tension of the nightmare, the thoughts that had crowded her mind afterwards, were passing. She was relieved. Her life was simple, too simple perhaps, but sufficiently full to permit no room for the horrors of which she'd read. Perhaps she would tell Forrester that she wanted no part of his club, that it had been good to meet him, that she'd been happy to receive the letter he had given her, but of his manuscript, of the things it contained, she wanted no part. All she wanted to know was what he remembered of her father. That was important, perhaps the most important thing in the world, but everything else that he carried with him he could leave beyond the door.

Seemingly resolute in her decision, she made breakfast, and then she listened to Sinatra, and by the time the sun finally peeled away the shadows within her apartment she felt at least somewhat settled.

She checked on Sullivan before she left for the store, found him sleeping the sleep of a dead man on his couch, and leaning forward she touched his salt-and-pepper hair. She could smell the alcohol even now, wondered how a man could drink such a quantity and not die of liver failure. She smiled, closed his door behind her, and made her way downstairs to walk the same fifteen minutes to The Reader's Rest on Lincoln by West 107th.

John Damianka brought her a sandwich a little after twelve, told her that his first lecture that day wasn't until quarter after one.

'Be a miracle if more than a dozen show up,' he said, and she could hear the bitterness in his voice.

'How you doing on the girlfriend front?' Annie asked.

'Had a date last Tuesday,' John said. He smiled broadly, a child at show-and-tell who brought the best thing going. A *real* salamander. An *honest-to-God-hand-on-heart* rock from the moon.

'It went well then?'

'Sure did,' John said. 'Took her to that Italian place on Park near the Drake Swissôtel.'

'And what's her name?' Annie asked as she leaned across the counter.

'Elizabeth . . . Elizabeth Farbolin.'

'What does she do?'

John shook his head. 'Something at the International Center of Photography, research or something.'

'John, I told you . . . you have to know everything it's possible to know without taking away all the mystery. You

45

have to pay attention. You want to have someone interested in you then you just ask them questions about themselves and shut the hell up.'

John shrugged. 'I know, I know Annie, but – '

Annie shook her head. 'But nothing John. I'll tell you the most interesting guy I ever went out with let me talk about myself for the best part of two hours, and I came away from the date thinking he was the most fascinating person I'd ever met.'

John looked down at his shoes, a little sheepish.

'So when d'you see her again?'

'Week Monday . . . we're gonna go see something on Broadway.'

Annie reached over the counter and punched John's shoulder. 'That's my man. You listen to her now . . . ask half a dozen questions and let her do all the talking and she won't be able to leave you alone.'

John nodded, reached for his ham and swiss on whole, pushed the bag containing Annie's sub towards her and talked a little about a weekend football game he was planning on attending.

He left fifteen minutes later, told her he was lecturing nineteenth-century drama, focusing on Goethe's *Faust* and its influence on twentieth-century European television melodramas.

Annie frowned, smiled, and said, 'Knock 'em dead John, you go knock 'em dead.'

He came in as she was halfway through the sub, mayonnaise on her cheek, her hands sticky with salad oil.

He came slowly through the door, tentatively almost, and when he paused in the shaft of light that flooded in through the dusty front window she believed for a moment it was Forrester. He turned then, turned and looked right at her, and though he did not smile, and though his gaze was direct and unflinching, there was nothing menacing or disquieting about his silence.

He walked towards her then, between the waist-high stacks

46

of battered books, around the central shelves that reached for the ceiling and could never have released their uppermost treasures without the assistance of a stepladder. He seemed lost, as if he'd wandered into The Reader's Rest by mistake, and even now would open his mouth to ask her for directions, for help with something he was trying to find.

But he didn't. He merely stopped and said, 'Hello.'

'Hi,' Annie replied.

'So many books,' he said.

Annie shrugged. 'We're a bookstore.'

He looked at her for a second, tilted his head, and then he reached with his hand and touched his cheek with his finger.

'Mayonnaise,' he said.

Annie frowned.

'On your face . . . here.'

Annie smiled, a little awkward. 'Oh,' she said, and reaching for the serviette she touched the smear of mayonnaise away and then set her sub aside. She wiped her greasy fingers on the serviette and dropped it in the trash can beneath the counter.

The man looked slowly around the store, and then turned once again to Annie. 'This is alphabetized, right?'

Annie shook her head. 'No, not really.'

He frowned. 'Not really?'

She laughed, a gentle echoey sound in the emptiness. 'Some of it sort of hangs together around the same sort of bit of the alphabet, and some of it doesn't.'

'So how d'you find anything?'

She shrugged. 'You wander, you look, you take your time . . . if you're really stuck you ask me, I look in the inventory, and if we have it then we try and find it together, or I find it for you and you come back tomorrow.'

'And this system works?' he asked.

'Well enough,' she replied. 'This is a bookstore for people who just love reading books, people who don't really have a thing for a particular author or genre. We have regulars, quite a few of them, and each fortnight a new crate comes in and I

47

stack them by the front door. They come in and go through the new stuff before I put it somewhere else.'

'Well, if it works it works,' the man said.

Annie smiled. She looked at the man more closely. She placed him at thirty-five, thirty-six perhaps. He was five-ten or eleven, reasonably well built, his hair a sandy color, his eyes gray-blue. He was dressed casually, a pair of jeans, a worn-out suede jacket over an open-necked blue shirt. His clothes were expensive nevertheless, and he wore them as if they had been cut exclusively for him.

'You after something in particular?' Annie asked.

He smiled. 'Something to read.'

Annie nodded. 'Sure, something to read. Well, something to read we can do.'

She waited for him to say something, but he stood there in silence, still surveying the semi-organized chaos around him.

'So what do you like to read?' she prompted. 'And don't say books, okay?'

The man laughed, and there was something meaningful in that sound. The sound of a man who had learned to laugh because he had to, because he'd realized it was therapeutic.

'Pretty much anything,' he said, 'except for sci-fi . . . don't get on fire for sci-fi.'

'What was the last thing you read?' Annie asked.

'I read *The Weight Of Water* by Anita Shreve on the plane,' he said. 'I enjoyed that.'

'Plane from where?'

'Northwest Territories in Canada.'

The man seemed to relax a little. He put his hands in his coat pockets and took a step towards the counter.

'That's where you're from?'

He shook his head. 'No, I'm from here . . . originally I'm from here. Moved into this neighborhood a month or so ago but I've been away working since.'

Annie resisted the impulse to ask the man what he did. She

48

believed she had a right to ask him – an odd thought, but her thought all the same. She was sharing her time with this man, and more than likely he would be one of those that browsed and never bought, and thus she felt she should at least come away from this moment knowing something. She didn't ask him about his work however, and instead asked him where he'd moved from.

'East Village,' he said. 'Born in East Village. Work has taken me every place I can think of, but this has always been home.'

'And you're out surveying your new neighborhood?'

The man smiled, nodded. 'Yes, surveying my new neighborhood,' he replied, and then once again he took a step forward and extended his hand. 'David,' he said, 'David Quinn.'

Annie instinctively wiped her hand on her pants before extending it in return. 'Annie O'Neill,' she said.

'And this is your store?'

She nodded. 'Was my father's . . . now it's mine.'

David Quinn took a few moments to look up and around the racks and shelves of books once again, and then said, 'Hell of a place Annie O'Neill . . . hell of a place.'

He stayed close on an hour. He bought three books. *Provinces Of Night* by William Gay, *A Confederacy Of Dunces* by John Kennedy Toole and *Cathedral* by Raymond Carver. The total was thirteen dollars; he gave Annie a twenty and told her to keep the change.

'You know something?' he said as he started towards the door.

Annie looked up.

'Apparently the average book passes through twenty pairs of hands in its life.'

Annie shook her head. 'I didn't know that.'

David Quinn held up the bag with his three books inside. 'Sixty lives will connect with what's in this bag . . . makes you think huh?'

And with that he smiled, nodded, and then turned and left the store.

Annie came from behind the counter, crossed between the stacks of hardbacks and reached the window just as Quinn disappeared at the junction.

She shook her head and sighed. She thought of every person who'd ever wandered into The Reader's Rest over the years, every person who'd browsed, who'd asked for help, who'd perhaps been looking for nothing more than someone with whom to share a few moments of their life before they moved on. And she'd let them move on, every single one of them, and had never once considered that there might have been something in those moments for her. She had created her own loneliness, and but for Sullivan she could go from one week to the next without ever sharing anything but the time of day or the cost of a second-hand paperback with a real honest-to-God human being.

But why? she asked herself as she turned from the window and made her way out back to prepare coffee. *What am I afraid of? Of gaining something only to see it slipping away? But then isn't it better to have loved and lost than never to have loved at all?*

She smiled at her own clichéd thoughts and busied herself with the percolator.

She closed a little before five. After David Quinn there had been two other customers – one who bought a dog-eared and battered copy of *Being There* by Jerzy Kosinski, the other who asked if she had any early edition Washington Irving. She did not.

She walked quickly, the wind was cold, and she was home by quarter after five. Jack was out, more than likely playing chess with a couple of guys from his bar, and once inside her apartment she made a salad, doused some cold chicken in vinaigrette, and sat in the kitchen with a glass of white wine and Frank singing from the front room. 'Chicago, Chicago . . .'

She smiled. She thought of her father, she thought of

Forrester, and once again she sensed that fleeting moment of identification when she thought of them together. She shook her head. It could not be . . . surely it could not be. She shrugged such a consideration aside, and she remembered the events of the afternoon, the moments after David Quinn had left.

I will meet with Robert Franklin Forrester on Monday, she thought. *Jack can come down there to protect me . . .*

She stopped mid-flight.

Protect me from what? An old man in a worn-out topcoat who wants to ease his own loneliness by reading stories and bringing letters written by my father?

And with that she considered the possibility that Forrester might bring another letter . . . that he would open up something of her own life by sharing a little of her father's. And that was what clinched it, clinched the decision that whatever vacillation and uncertainty she might experience over the weekend, she would have Forrester come down on Monday and she would talk about the manuscript he had brought, ply him for further details of her father's life, and see what came of it. She had to do it if only to somehow keep alive the memory of her father. Her parents were her past, they were her life in some way. He deserved that much. At least that much.

Live a little Annie O'Neill, she told herself. *Live a little before you die.*

FOUR

From her bedroom window she could see Cathedral Parkway and the Nicholas Roerich Museum, beyond that Hudson River Park, and further on the water. Late at night, restless, perhaps seeking some sense of connection to the outside world, she would stand with her nose against the cool glass and wait until her eyes grew accustomed to the dark. Then she would catch the reflection of the mainland lights against the underbelly of the sky. She imagined the source of that light – a hundred thousand homes, a million streetlights, alongside them the shops and stores and malls and hotels. And then she would hear the sound of the boats slipping effortlessly out of the 79th Street Basin and wonder who was on those boats, where they were going, and why. A billion intricate patterns of life, and in amongst all of this the six degrees of separation: the theory that each and every one of us is in some way connected to someone, and they to someone else, and on and on six times over until a map could be drawn between every single human being to show how they relate. But there were some, it seemed to Annie, who had fallen through the loop. The exception that proved the rule. The odd one out. And such an exception was she. Or so she believed. Sometimes.

These were her thoughts in the early hours of Saturday morning and after a while, after returning to her bed and sleeping fitfully, she once again woke up as dawn water-colored the sky. She showered, she breakfasted, and then she walked out of the apartment. She did not take her usual route, did not approach The Reader's Rest, and though a clock could have been set against Annie O'Neill's tracks, though there had never been a Saturday in the last God-only-knew-how-long that the store had not been open for the hours between nine a.m. and one p.m. each Saturday, that morning – for no other reason than some sense of necessity – she walked the other way. Down Cathedral Parkway onto Amsterdam, out towards Columbia University and St John the Divine; slower than usual, a little hesitant perhaps, and had you seen her, had she passed you in the street, you would have seen nothing more than an attractive brunette, petite, her aquiline features almost implacable, and yet her eyes bright and inquisitive and searching. She would have appeared to be looking for something. Or someone.

Annie stopped after a little while, went into a delicatessen and ordered coffee. She sat at a small table on the sidewalk and watched the world pass her by. Some people numbed with sleep, others purposeful and direct, and yet more of them seemingly absent-minded and without direction, a little like herself. The coffee was good and strong, and for the first time in as many years as she could remember she wanted to smoke a cigarette. She'd quit some eternity ago, had been determined never to start again, and yet always there seemed to be something vaguely romantic about it. The brunette at the sidewalk café, her coat pulled up around her throat against a bitter breeze, men walking by believing that such a woman as this *must* be waiting for someone. A rendezvous. The beginning of an affair. He's late. She is wilful and certain enough not to care that he's late. She is sufficiently single-minded to amuse herself with her own thoughts, and if he comes . . . well if he comes he comes, and if he does not, then there will always be someone else who can amuse her for a while. Very Marlene. Very Ingrid.

And very imaginative, Annie thought, and smiled to herself.

'Annie O'Neill,' a voice said.

Snapped from her reverie she looked up. The sun was behind him, and with a step he moved forward. David Quinn stood no

53

more than five feet from her. He was smiling. Smiling like a child who'd found a long-lost friend.

'David?' she said, surprise evident in her voice.

He didn't hesitate to take the seat facing her. 'What are you doing up here?' he asked.

She shrugged, felt a little awkward. 'Just took a walk.'

'You don't open the store on Saturdays?'

'I do, yes,' she said, 'but today . . . well today I just didn't feel like it.'

She thought then of coincidence, and before the thought had even half-formed in her mind she remembered that he'd mentioned his move to the other side of Morningside Park. From East Village to the north-western edge of Harlem.

From his jacket pocket he took a pack of Marlboros.

'Cigarette?' he asked.

She smiled. 'I quit a long time ago,' she said.

'You mind?'

She waved her hand nonchalantly. 'Have some coffee too,' she suggested.

He smiled, seemed so at ease in that moment, as if they had indeed been long-lost friends. A chance meeting after so many years.

How've you been?

Good . . . very good. And you?

Fine. Working hard.

And what do you do now . . . seem to remember you always wanted to be an architect.

I am, yes, and actually I'm down this way working on a plan to level some of these tenements and build a godawful mirrored monolith . . .

Annie smiled to herself as David Quinn rose from his chair and went inside to order coffee.

He came back with two cups, set one ahead of Annie, and then he sat again, was quiet for a time as he poured cream, as he stirred, as he lit his cigarette.

'You have nowhere to be?' she asked.

54

He shook his head, his hand around his cup as if to draw warmth from it. 'Nothing special,' he said. 'I was going to get some groceries.'

She didn't say anything in response, and for a little while there was silence between them. She felt strangely at ease. She sipped her coffee, her third cup of the day. *Living on the edge Annie*, she thought, and then *Well, you know what they say . . . if you're not living on the edge you're taking up too much room.*

And it was then that she asked him. 'And what is it that you do? If you don't mind me asking.'

'Not at all,' David said. 'What I do is marine insurance.'

She frowned. 'Like boats and things?'

He nodded, smiled a lazy half-smile with an undercurrent of warmth she found immediately appealing. He wasn't what she would have called a handsome man, not in the classic sense of the word, but his face had that lived-in feeling, the same way that Jack Sullivan carried his whole life in a single expression.

'Like boats and things yes,' he said. 'Especially the things.'

Annie smiled. His humor was dry, a little caustic. 'So what *is* marine insurance?' she asked.

'Commercial stuff mainly, cargo ships, ferries, things like that . . . we cover the insurance, and then when they sink or go aground I go out and investigate, make sure it wasn't scuttled just to claim the insurance money.'

'And that's why you were in Canada?'

He nodded. 'An icebreaker went aground in the Amundsen Gulf, a boat that does the trip round Sachs Harbor, Cape Prince Alfred and back down the Prince of Wales Strait. Tore its belly out and sank like a stone.'

'You don't dive, do you?'

'Out there, minus three thousand degrees, God no. If it's a big enough contract they'll haul it up. If it's not so big we send underwater cameras down.'

'And the icebreaker?' she asked.

'Was driven ashore intentionally, at least there's every indication that was the case.'

Annie frowned. 'How can you tell?'

David smiled. 'The same way I'm sure you can tell if a book's gonna be good from the first paragraph. There are all sorts of signs you look for.' He paused for a moment to drink his coffee. 'Anyway, enough of work . . . what are you doing today?'

Annie shook her head. 'Nothing much of anything really.'

'So let's take a walk, go see something, have some lunch.'

Annie O'Neill looked at the man facing her, this David Quinn, marine insurance investigator, and she remembered the thoughts she'd woken with – the exception that proved the rule, the one that fell through the loop. Perhaps the loop was closing, and even now she had a choice: step through it and allow the loop to close behind her, or stay and be closed within it.

What had she to lose? A few hours, perhaps nothing more than that.

'Okay,' she said quietly.

'Sorry?' he asked.

'Okay,' she said. 'Okay, let's do that.'

Later – that same evening in fact – when she had left him after the walking, the talking, the quieter moments when neither of them had anything much of anything to say, she would remember a small thing. Always the small things. It was the way he would pause every once in a while, and reaching with his right hand he would sort of massage the back of his neck, like there was a tension there, something psychosomatic, something neither physical nor muscular, but nevertheless as real as any ache someone might feel. He did it several times, even as they ate lunch together in a small bistro off Riverside Drive, and she'd wanted to ask him if he was in pain, if there was something she could do. But she did not. She did not reach too far, for to reach too far was to lose your equilibrium, and the weight of a rejection could only serve to cause a fall. She did not wish to fall, not this time, not any time, and prevention was always better than cure. Her mother would say that. But then her mother would say a lot of things.

She had wondered if she would always be the anachronism, the odd-one-out, the incongruous literary recluse who spent her life in a bookstore.

Until that Saturday afternoon. And it was during that afternoon, as she walked and talked with the stranger that was David Quinn, as he smiled and made her laugh, as he showed her things in the neighborhood that she had never seen before, that she realized that perhaps there might be hope. Not necessarily with David, for David seemed *complete*, a word that came to mind without searching for any description. He seemed like a whole person, a person without attachments and appendages, without all the emotionally complex baggage that so many men seemed to carry as if it was their life's purpose. Here, she believed, was a man who would take the 5:36 for Two Harbors, nestling there beneath the Sawtooth Mountains, where on a clear day you could almost reach out and touch the Apostle Islands and Thunder Bay, and if there were those that cared to walk with him he would let them. And those that were not . . . well, he would leave them standing on the platform and never give them another thought. They would wave perhaps, and then watch him roll away soundlessly into the indistinct distance of memory. He did indeed appear to travel alone, packing only sufficient for his needs, not burdening himself with things too weighty, like lost loves, forgotten dreams, jealousies, frustrations and hatred. He carried with him the finer things. Things to share. Things that weighed next to nothing but held the significance of everything. These were the things he carried, and in some small way they also carried him.

She appreciated his independence, his sense of balance and closure, and when he spoke of himself he spoke humbly, as if there were no great matters to understand, no great depths to fathom. He was neither pretentious nor vain nor ostentatious. He seemed neither possessive nor jealous nor quick to rebuke. He listened well, and in speaking she found a silent mouth and a receptive ear. He was there – and that was enough.

A little after four they had parted company, he heading north to the other side of the park, she heading south towards home. They had shaken hands, nothing more than that, and though in itself such an action seemed almost incongruous, it also seemed so right. They were not yet friends, merely acquaintances at best, and to read anything further into their meeting was to read into fiction.

He said he might come by sometime, perhaps to get some more books, and she had nodded and smiled and said he was welcome anytime.

And so, later – Saturday closing itself up around the night-people that haunted the streets of New York, the theatergoers, the clubbers, the drinkers, the hookers – she watched from the same window as the night before, and yet her thoughts were still. For once they were still. Sullivan was out there some-where, out among the six degrees of separation beyond her window, and she wished he were home. It was a moment to share. She wished her father were there. Her mother had always been the one with which to share such things, but now, after Forrester's visit, with her memories stirred, she was acutely aware of how absent he was. Her mother had been there for so much longer. They had talked and laughed and cried together. She possessed a suitcase of memories of her mother, but of her father she possessed nothing. That, of all things, was the thing that hurt most. She did not think of him long, for to do so was to feel once again the irresolute sense of loss that accompanied such thoughts. He was gone, gone for ever, and somehow, some way, she had to come to terms with that.

And then Annie slept, neither fitful nor restless nor agitated, and when she woke it was Sunday, and in amongst her feelings was a quiet sense of reassurance, as if the world had ventured to return a little of that which she had lost: faith in basic human nature, perhaps, something such as a belief that somewhere out there things made sense, and she would no longer be the only one to miss the point.

FIVE

Sunday morning Annie did not wish to be alone. Such a desire was new, a little strange, and yet she did not resist it as she would ordinarily have done. She crossed the hall and told Jack Sullivan to come have breakfast with her, and he – ever the one to take a free meal when it was offered – came willingly.

She made eggs and hash browns and bacon, fried some mushrooms and brewed fresh coffee. She had Sullivan squeeze a dozen oranges and set the jug in the freezer to chill while she cooked, and then they sat together in silence and ate well.

'Something has changed,' Sullivan ventured as they sat drinking coffee. He frowned, tilted his head to the right. 'You didn't go out and get laid, did you Annie?'

She smiled, laughed. 'No Jack, I didn't go out and get laid.'

'So you stayed home and did it, right?'

She shook her head. 'No, I didn't stay home.'

'So tell me.' He pushed his plate to one side, rested his elbows on the table and set his chin on his steepled fingers. He looked down his nose at her. 'Tell Doctor Sullivan my dear . . . tell me your secret.'

Annie paused, silent for a moment. 'I've been thinking,' she began, then waved her hand in a dismissive fashion. 'Not too hard, don't worry,' she added. 'Just thinking about what I want I s'pose.'

'What you want?' Sullivan asked. 'You have the store, you have this apartment, and you have me . . . what the hell else could a beautiful single thirty-year-old New Yorker want?'

'A relationship?'

Sullivan closed his eyes and exhaled. 'Oh shit,' he said quietly.

Annie laughed. 'Oh shit. That's what you have to say? Christ Jack, you didn't expect me to stay single for the rest of my life did you?'

'Hell no Annie, I was hoping you'd fall head over heels for me.'

Annie reached out and closed her hand over Jack's. 'You, you old warhorse . . . you will always be the one.'

Sullivan opened his eyes and smiled at her. 'So tell me his name.'

'What makes you think there's a someone?'

'His name,' Sullivan repeated.

Annie looked away towards the window. 'It's nothing,' she said. 'Nothing happened, nothing at all.'

'He's married?'

Annie shook her head. 'No . . . well, at least I don't think he's married.'

'So what's his name?'

'Quinn . . . David Quinn.'

'And you met him where?'

'He came to the store on Friday,' Annie replied.

'And he bought a book – '

'Three,' Annie interjected.

'Well fuck it Annie . . . marry the guy.'

She laughed. It felt good to be talking about real things with a real person, perhaps the realest person she'd ever known.

'And then?'

'And then yesterday morning I woke up and thought to hell with it. I didn't go to the store, I walked uptown, the other side of the park, and there I was, sitting outside some place drinking coffee, and he shows up. Just like that.'

Sullivan shook his head. 'You believe in coincidence?'

'Sure I do,' she said.

Sullivan shook his head. 'Coincidence, my dear, is bullshit.'

'Bullshit,' Annie said matter-of-factly.

'Your thoughts are almost exclusively responsible for the situations you get yourself into.'

'My thoughts?'

Sullivan nodded.

Annie frowned. 'You've lost me.'

'Okay,' he said. 'Ask yourself this . . . you get up in the morning and you feel like shit off a griddle, bad hair day, bad everything day, right?'

Annie shrugged. 'Right.'

'So you don't feel good about yourself, you don't feel good about the way you look. Well, from that perspective you're going to have a negatively biased view about yourself. That viewpoint will communicate in what you say, how you say it, your body language, agreed?'

'Agreed.'

'So how do people judge people . . . generally on first impressions in this day and age? Well, their first impression is going to be of someone who doesn't think very much of themselves, someone who's perhaps reserved, withdrawn. That will then influence the way they respond to you, what they say, how they say it. You project something and people are aware of it, if it's negative or positive. And thus someone comes along with an idea, they're all eager to tell someone . . . who are they gonna tell? They're gonna tell someone they feel might be receptive to their idea. You're with me so far?'

Annie nodded.

'So this guy comes to the store, he buys some books, you share a few words, and there must have been something about the way you responded to him to make him feel that he could come and talk to you when he saw you outside drinking your coffee. If you had been cold and aloof he perhaps would have pretended not to see you or something.'

'Okay,' Annie said, 'and after lunch we do world hunger and the AIDS crisis.'

'Be facetious,' Sullivan interjected, mock indignation in his eyes. 'What I say is true . . . whatever you said and however you said it made him feel safe enough to come and speak with you again.'

'So what now?'

Sullivan frowned. 'What d'you mean what now?'

'What do I do now?'

'Well, hell Annie, you call the guy up, have him come over, make him some dinner and then fuck him six ways to Sunday.'

Annie laughed, embarrassed perhaps. She held her hand to her mouth and closed her eyes.

'You *do* know what that means, right?' Sullivan asked.

'Enough,' she said, and stood up. She started to clear plates from the table.

Sullivan reached out and took her hand. He tugged at her until she sat down again.

'Listen,' he said quietly. 'I'm only half joking Annie. I see you come and go every day, I see the store, the way you're so wrapped up in yourself and what *you* feel and I worry about you. You need to be out there, out there talking to people . . . and sure there are rough edges and sharp corners, that's just the way it is, but hell, if you never actually live a life then you'll wind up more bitter and twisted than if you get kicked a few times.'

Annie O'Neill couldn't think of anything to say. He was right, right enough to empty her head of any reply. She looked at him. She hated him, but in the same moment she cared for him as much as anyone she'd ever known. She reached out and pressed her hand against the side of his face.

'And you can stop drinking so much,' she said.

Sullivan nodded. 'I'm tougher than you think.'

'I know you are Jack, but – '

'We make a deal,' he said. 'A deal, right?'

Annie nodded hesitantly.

'You get yourself a man, I'll stop drinking.'

'What d'you mean, get myself a man?'

Sullivan smiled. 'The night I can't sleep because you're

pounding the headboard and moaning like a banshee I'll stop drinking.'

'So crude,' Annie said. 'So unnecessarily crude Jack Sullivan.'

'You get yourself someone you feel you can care for, make a go of it, see if you can't make something of a relationship, and I'll stop drinking for good. That's the deal, take it or leave it.'

Annie shook her head. 'I want you to stop drinking because it will kill you Jack – '

Sullivan raised his hand. Annie fell silent.

'And I want you to find someone because loneliness is gonna kill *you*.'

The day unfolded around her and she lost it within its own insignificances. After breakfast Sullivan had gone down the street to meet his friends. Annie stayed home, watched TV, did other things of little moment, and as evening crawled along the sidewalks and whispered between the buildings she sat and read for a while. Like someone who owns a bar drinking so rarely it's barely worth mentioning, Annie read infrequently these days. She thought a little of Forrester, a little of Jack Sullivan, and how each of them had in some way come to represent a part of what her father might have been. But she thought mostly of David Quinn and whether she would ever see him again.

And it was with these thoughts that she turned on her side on the couch, tugged her knees up against her chest, receptive to the silence in the apartment, the vague ghost of wind beyond the walls that was somehow comforting, and closed her eyes; she drifted away; she dreamed.

She sits at a table. Sullivan faces her. He has one eye closed, and from the other a thin stream of smoke issues. It slips from between his lids with a gentle sound of exhalation, and as he breathes the smoke is caught in curlicues and arabesques. She watches them without a word and she is somehow enchanted by the patterns they make.

'Operations Malheur, Hickory and Rolling Thunder,'

Sullivan is saying, with his one eye closed and his other exhaling thin gray smoke. 'Dragon Head . . . and Cedar Falls when the Yanks and the ARVN destroyed the Iron Triangle twenty kilometers north of Saigon. And then there was Operation Junction City . . . and you know twelve thousand civilians were killed in the Tet Offensive crossfire alone?'

'I didn't know that,' Annie hears herself saying, but her lips haven't moved, and the sound doesn't come from inside her head, it comes from outside.

'Something else,' Sullivan says. 'From January '68 to January '69 there were fifteen thousand wounded . . . '69 to '70 that figure jumped to ninety-six thousand, but we still kicked their commie asses in Khe Sanh, Gio Linh and Con Thien . . . '

'Why are we here Jack?' Annie asks, and she wants to smoke a cigarette more than anything in the world.

'Made a deal, didn't we?'

'A deal?'

Jack Sullivan smiles. He opens his smoking eye, there's a mirror inside, and when she looks at it she can see her mother's face. Her mother is crying, mouthing some silent word.

Annie peers closely.

Chance, the mouth says. *Chance . . . Chance . . .*

'Yes . . . we made a deal Annie O'Neill . . . and the deal was?'

'I have to fuck someone and you'll quit drinking yourself to death.'

'Ladies and gentlemen, give this girl a Kewpie doll!' Sullivan shouts.

'I don't use words like that,' Annie says. 'Words like fuck.'

'Maybe you should,' Sullivan replies. 'Maybe if you used a word like that every once in a while you might get some.'

Annie reaches out, touches him, passes right through him, and as Sullivan unfurls into arabesques and curlicues of smoke she hears him whispering *Not everything is as it seems Annie O'Neill . . .*

*

And then she woke, and for a moment she didn't know where she was. Her knees against her chest, her face pressed against the back of the couch, and she found it hard to breathe. Claustrophobic, suddenly tense and frightened, Annie began to breathe heavily. She turned and sat on the edge of the couch, placed her feet firmly on the floor as if to convince herself that the here-and-now really existed, and closed her eyes. Reorienting herself, her breathing slowed. She wanted a cigarette, a cup of tea, something.

She stood up, hesitated for a moment to gain her balance. She thought of her dream, could remember little but Sullivan's voice, the voice that had woken her.

She made it to the kitchen, prepared tea, and as she poured water into the cup she lost her grip and scalded herself.

'Fuck!' she said, her voice bitter and sharp, almost like someone else's.

She stopped, frowned. 'Fuck?' she asked herself, and realized that this was a word she never used.

She shrugged, reached for the tap and put her scalded hand beneath the cold running water.

'Fuck,' she said again, and even as the word escaped her lips she knew she was letting go of something. Or something was letting go of her.

'Fuck, fuck, fuck,' she repeated emphatically, and reached for the towel to dry her hand.

A little later, seated there at the same table where she'd shared breakfast with Sullivan, she thought of David Quinn, of Robert Forrester, of the reading club she was to attend the following evening. Something had changed, and if Sullivan was right it was all down to her. Perhaps – finally – she had decided to reach for life, and in deciding such a thing found that life was now reaching her. She was uncertain, a little afraid, but what was it that Sullivan had said?

If you never actually live a life then you'll wind up more bitter and twisted than if you get kicked a few times. She smiled, and in the same moment she cursed Jack Sullivan. Until now everything had been fine. Life *had* been fine. Or had it?

She closed her eyes, felt the warmth from the cup between her hands traveling through her fingers, her wrists, up her arms, and she wished . . . somehow she wished her father was there for counsel.

SIX

Monday morning it was raining heavily. *Raining straight down like stair-posts*, Annie's mother would have said, and then laughed her laugh, a laugh that said more about the woman than any words could have done. Annie's mother had tried to live a life after her husband had gone. She'd tried hard, so very hard. But tough though she was life had somehow been tougher than her, and the face she'd worn for the world was one of grim determination hidden beneath a shadow of easy contentment. You didn't have to look long to see the real Madeline O'Neill; didn't have to look long at all.

Annie switched off the alarm clock and stayed right where she was, buried inside the quilts she'd piled around her, savoring those moments of sleep-drenched semi-wakefulness when the night had not yet fully emptied itself out, and the morning was still hurrying on its way. The narrow hiatus between the two was perhaps where she found herself most secure. It was early, there was no rush to be up, and somehow the urgency to be at the store, to ensure that everything was in order, that the sign was turned just at the right moment, seemed unimportant. So many things seemed unimportant in that moment, and yet later – standing beneath the shower as water rushed enthusiastically across her skin – she could place neither the moment nor the event that had changed her perspective. Had it been the letter from Forrester? The sheaf of papers she had read with Sullivan? The words she'd shared at the store with David Quinn? Their chance meeting outside the coffee shop uptown? A dream she vaguely recalled from a thousand lifetimes ago?

Perhaps all of these things. Perhaps none.

She made breakfast – coffee, wholemeal toast with bitter ginger preserve – and then she dressed warm against the rain, collected the sheaf of papers Forrester had given her, and left the apartment.

David Quinn was there when she arrived, doing his best to shelter beneath the narrow eave above the door. He was soaked, his hair plastered in thin streaks down his forehead, streaks that served to angle the rivulets of water down his nose and cheeks.

'David?' she asked, almost as if questioning his identity.

'One and the same,' he said, 'and you're late.'

She glanced at her watch. Her father's watch. It was seven minutes past nine.

'Seven minutes,' she said as she reached the door and started to unlock it. She felt a momentary irritation.

'I wasn't complaining,' David Quinn said.

Annie opened up and walked into the store. She removed her coat and let it fall in a sad, wet puddle behind the door. David followed her inside but didn't take off his drenched overcoat.

'Take your coat off,' she said.

'You're not going to ask me why I'm here?'

Annie stood for a moment, looked down at the floor. She didn't like games. People played games because they had nothing better to do; either that or they were a little crazy. She wondered which kind David Quinn was.

'Why are you here David?' she asked.

'Because I'm a little crazy,' he said, and then he laughed – a sort of nervous sound that said something about his vulnerability in that moment.

Annie smiled to herself. At least he wasn't here because he had nothing better to do. She looked at him and frowned, and in that second her irritation dissipated. He looked a little sad, a little lonely perhaps, and she felt a kind of empathy for him.

'A *little* crazy?' she said.

'Well, maybe a lot crazy,' David replied.

'Don't tell me,' Annie said. 'You read all the books you bought and you want some more?'

David shook his head. 'I wanted to talk,' he replied.

'To talk? About what?'

He shrugged. 'Anything . . . everything . . . nothing perhaps.'

Annie started towards the kitchen at the back, where she kept a towel for days like this. 'Now you do sound a lot crazy,' she said. She turned as she reached the end of the floor. He was still standing there by the front door, his eyes at once looking at her, and then in the next second surveying the shelves and stacks surrounding him. Did she feel threatened? Was that what she was experiencing? She could not tell, for moments such as these were no common occurrence.

'What is it?' she asked.

He shrugged again, and then he raised his hand and started massaging the back of his neck. 'I think I'm lost,' he said. 'I don't know why I came here . . . maybe – ' He looked directly at her. 'Maybe it would be best if I went.'

He turned and reached for the doorhandle.

Annie took a couple of steps forward and raised her hand. 'Don't – ' she started.

David stopped. He didn't turn to face her.

'Don't go,' she said, her voice softening. 'Tell me what you mean.'

'What I mean?'

'You said you were lost . . . what do you mean, lost?'

David looked down. His hair was still stuck to his forehead. He looked like a child who'd suffered a football game in the rain and just wanted to go home.

'Moving here . . . everything changes, you know?' He turned and looked at Annie. He raised his hand once again and massaged his neck. 'I was settled . . . at least I thought I was settled, and then I decided to change everything . . . don't know why I decided that – '

70

David smiled, and then the nervous laugh once more – a short, dry sound.

'S'pose I was looking for something . . . or running away from something?' he said, and the question was directed at no-one but himself.

'So you have no-one to talk to?' Annie asked, and again she took another step or two forward. She felt emboldened, as if here she was in her own territory and someone had come seeking help.

'Sounds pathetic, right?'

Annie shook her head. 'Not at all. Life is people. Starts and ends and there's nothing but people in between. You don't do this stuff alone.'

'You seem to manage,' he said.

'You don't know anything about me,' Annie said, but there was nothing defensive in her tone. 'I could be out living the life and partying 'till three every morning.'

'You could,' David said, 'but somehow I don't think so.'

She smiled. 'You want some coffee?'

'Could kill for coffee,' he said.

'Then washing cups wouldn't be too much to ask?'

He smiled. It was a warm smile, a human smile, and there was something altogether *right* about the moment.

'Come,' she said, and turned towards the kitchen at the back.

David Quinn nodded, followed her, removing his coat as he walked.

For the best part of two hours they talked. There were no customers, and only when Annie went out to fetch sandwiches from the deli across the block did she realize that the store sign had not been turned. Another first. A very first.

They talked of his life, how his family had once been scattered like buckshot across New York, into Connecticut, Rhode Island and Pennsylvania, but then soon after his tenth birthday he had been orphaned. A house fire. Fast, brutal. He had lost his parents and a younger brother. There were two

71

older brothers, one he hadn't seen since 1992, another since 1989. He'd lost his mother and father simultaneously. Left for school, spent a handful of hours learning the names of the presidents and the chemical formulas for water and salt, and then returned home to find his life had changed irrevocably. After that, what was left of the family had drifted apart, gone their separate ways, as if to meet again would merely serve to open wounds that they knew could never heal. He had lived with an aunt until he reached his teens and then he'd walked away. Walked away from the past and never looked back. He spoke without anger, without any apparent emotion at all, and Annie could tell how deeply such a thing must have been buried for him to speak of it so bluntly. Her heart went out to him. There was something that connected them in some small way, and for this – despite its brutality – she was grateful. And Annie told him of her life, a small life though it seemed; the death of her parents, the ever-decreasing concentric circle of her existence.

'What did you want?' he asked her.

'What did I want?'

'As a kid, growing up you know? What did you dream about?'

She laughed briefly. 'You mean like running away to the circus or something?'

'Whatever,' David said.

She was quiet for some time, pensive, casting her mind backward through events and people, names and faces and places, in some moments the edges blending together, seamless and without divide.

'I wanted to write,' she said eventually. 'I seem to remember wanting to write . . . the great American novel or something.'

She looked up from her thoughts, and found David watching her. He wasn't looking at her, he was *watching* her. She felt momentarily unnerved, a little disturbed perhaps. There was an intensity, a *passion* in his eyes, that she found disconcerting.

'What?' she asked, suddenly self-conscious.

He shook his head and smiled. 'Nothing.'

'*What*?' she repeated.

He seemed awkward, off-balance. 'It's . . . it's just that – '

'Just *what*?'

'You really are quite extraordinarily beautiful Annie O'Neill.'

She was lost for words. How did you respond to such a comment? She couldn't ever remember anyone saying such a thing. She waved her hand in a nonchalant and dismissive fashion.

'I mean it,' he said. 'A little Madeline Stowe, a little Winona Ryder – '

'Enough,' Annie said, her voice sharp, unforgiving. She didn't wish to be complimented, for such things seemed unnecessary and inappropriate.

'I'm sorry if I – '

Annie cut him off with another wave of the hand. 'Forget about it,' she said, and though she knew she would not, and neither would he, there was something that was now *out there*. He had crossed the line, turned what could have been an honest and meaningful friendship into something that implied sex and carnality and physical desire. Why did men always have to do that? Why couldn't they just let something be what it was without introducing something awkward and ungainly into the proceedings? Hormones? Necessity?

Annie turned towards the window. She wished he was outside, she wished it was the first moment she'd met him. She wished whatever she'd said or done to make him feel she was approachable could be turned back and folded within itself, packed away neatly with all the other could-have-beens and might-have-dones that seemed to populate her life with such familiarity.

'I've upset you,' he said, 'made you feel awkward . . . I'm sorry.'

She shook her head, and then she thought better of it. So easy to dismiss it all, to cast it aside. Who was it who'd said that all the problems you didn't face were finally the ones that buried you?

'Why?' she asked, aware of the tone of her voice, the emotion she was feeling. It was a new feeling, something closer to anger than irritation. 'Why d'you have to say something like that? Here we were, getting along fine, just talking . . . whatever – '

'I didn't mean – '

'Didn't mean what? Didn't mean to make me feel embarrassed? Well David Quinn, you did make me feel embarrassed . . . as simple as that. How come men have to throw things into the arena that really have no place there?'

He frowned, seemed dismayed. 'What is it?' he asked. 'What are you so afraid of?'

Now she *was* angry. How dare he! 'Afraid? You have the nerve to ask me what I'm afraid of?' she snapped.

'I just said you were beautiful . . . did no-one ever tell you how beautiful you were before?'

She looked at him, looked right at him, and in that moment there was such honesty, such a genuine question in his eyes, that her anger seemed to collapse within itself and disappear. It left as quickly and unexpectedly as it had come. She shook her head. 'I don't think anyone . . . ' She paused, her words lost in some indefinable territory around her heart.

David reached out and touched her hand.

She instinctively withdrew.

He left his hand right where it was, palm upwards now until, with some trepidation, she lowered her hand once more and rested it on his. His fingers enclosed hers; she felt the warmth of his skin.

'I'm sorry,' he said, his voice almost a whisper. 'I'm sorry if I hurt you or made you feel awkward or embarrassed . . . '

'It's okay,' she heard herself say, her voice sounding as if it came not from her but from some other place in the room. It was almost as if she were watching herself. The angles and corners she'd felt were softening, merging a little, and she believed that if she'd been able to step outside herself she would have looked back and seen someone vague and blurred at the edges.

'We go backwards,' he said. 'Rewind half an hour or so and start again, okay?'

She nodded in the affirmative, but knew that what had been said was still *out there*. He'd said she was beautiful, sounded as if he'd meant it, and there was something about such a thing that would never, ever be forgotten. How could such a thing ever lose its sense of moment?

'We were talking about your family,' he said, 'and then we were talking about the great American novel you were going to write.'

She smiled as the memory returned.

'How old were you?' he asked.

She shrugged. 'Twelve, thirteen, I don't remember exactly.'

'And why did you want to write?'

'I think I wanted to make people feel things . . . make people feel emotions that were new, have thoughts they hadn't had before, something like that.'

He nodded, understanding reflected in his eyes. 'What's the most important book you've ever read?'

She smiled. 'The most important book I've ever read? How is it possible to answer a question like that?' she said, and then it came to her, came to her so easily, and she started to smile wider, her face relaxing, her tension easing so comfortably.

'Which one?' he prompted.

'A book called *Breathing Space*,' she said. 'My father left it for me . . . one of the few things he left for me.' She touched the face of the watch on her wrist, and in that moment she recalled an image of her father, vague and indistinct, standing there in the hallway of their house. It had been raining then also. She could remember the sound of the water hitting the deck beyond the kitchen, and there was a smell in the air like cinnamon, and something else unidentifiable. He was leaving, always leaving it seemed. She couldn't have been more than five years old, perhaps six, and had she known then that he would be alive for no more than a year or two she would have rushed towards him, thrown her arms around him, told him she loved him, that she didn't want him to leave again. She tried to concentrate on the image, tried to focus, but there was nothing more than a feeling.

There was a tightness in her chest, her throat felt constricted, and when she blinked there was moisture around her eyes.

David squeezed her hand, and only then did she become aware that he had never let go. A lifeline. Tenuous, fragile, but nevertheless a lifeline. To what she didn't know, and in that moment it didn't matter. She was not alone. That was the main thing, and she appreciated it.

'You okay?' he asked, his voice sympathetic, gentle.

'Fine,' she said, but there was a reserve in her tone that said she wasn't so fine at all.

'What did he do?' David asked.

'Do?'

'Your father . . . what did he do?'

Annie didn't speak for some time. She tried to recall something, anything. She tried to picture him leaving with a bag, a holdall perhaps, some kind of uniform? She could remember nothing at all.

'I don't know,' she said. 'I honestly don't know what he did.' Her voice conveyed her uncertainty and confusion. She found it hard to believe that this thought had never really crossed her mind before.

'And your mother never told you?' David inquired.

Annie shook her head.

'You never asked?'

Annie was still for a while. 'I must have done,' she said quietly. 'I must have asked her . . . and she must have told me.'

There was a silence between them, as if here in this moment some deep secret had been unearthed, something that even as she considered it brought a sense of potential alarm. How

76

could she arrive at thirty years of age and not have the faintest clue as to her own father's profession?

'Perhaps he was a spy,' David said, and he smiled, and the tension was broken.

'Perhaps,' she replied, and tried to engage in the levity he was attempting. It worked, just a little, but nevertheless that aura of mystery prevailed.

'The mysterious Mister O'Neill,' David said.

She was elsewhere for a moment, and then she looked up and saw David once again massaging the back of his neck. It seemed like a nervous habit now, something he couldn't control.

'You okay?' she asked.

He nodded. 'Sure . . . why d'you ask?'

'Your neck,' she said. 'You keep rubbing the back of your neck.'

'It aches sometimes,' he said. 'Just a little.'

Annie glanced at her watch. It was gone two o'clock. There had been no customers, not one, despite turning the sign when she'd left for sandwiches. Perhaps the rain kept them away. Perhaps the unspoken thought that at such a time as this she didn't wish to be disturbed. Sullivan would have said the latter.

'You don't have to go to work?' she asked.

'No,' David said. 'I'm on leave. Work is so unpredictable, and sometimes we're away weeks at a time. They like to give us breathing space every once in a while.'

Breathing space, she thought, but didn't say a thing. The atmosphere had changed, and Annie felt that she'd walked along the edges of something deceptively simple, and yet somehow profoundly complex. Later, thinking back, her single most enduring thought, resonating like a bell in the cool crisp air of a still Sunday morning, was that she did not know a thing – not one thing – about her father. Such a simple question – *What did your father do?* – and she had been lost in a host of half-formed imaginings that had no connection to reality.

And then David said, 'I should go,' and rose from the chair. A while back he had released her hand and she hadn't even noticed. The lifeline was disappearing.

'Are you busy later?' he asked.

She nodded. 'I have someone coming to see me,' she said.

'A date?' he asked, but there was nothing suggestive in his tone.

'No,' she said, and smiled. 'No such thing. Tonight I have my reading club.'

'A reading club?'

'Yes, a reading club, first meeting tonight.'

'And anyone can come?'

'No, not anyone . . . a very select group of initiates, only the very best people – you know?'

David nodded, seemed distracted. 'Then another time,' he said.

'Yes . . . another time. You know where I am.'

'I do,' he said, 'and I'm sorry about what I said.'

Annie smiled. 'I'm not . . . not anymore.'

He seemed to relax a little. 'So another time it is then?'

Annie hesitated for a second. 'Yes, another time.'

David smiled, seemed pleased. 'I'll see you then,' he said, and started towards the door.

She went after him, slowly at first, and even as he reached the sidewalk she was there at the window watching his back as he walked away. He didn't turn, and for some reason she was glad of that. She wouldn't have wanted to appear desperate or lonely – or hopeful. Hope was an over-rated commodity, too over-rated by far.

She thought of the possibility that something might happen here, and for a moment she was caught in a brief question-and-answer with herself.

Should I? *Perhaps, perhaps not.*

Could I? *I think I could.*

Will I? *I . . . I hope . . .*

And then there was Sullivan's voice: *Coincidence my dear, is bullshit . . . Your thoughts are almost exclusively responsible for the situations you get yourself into.*

David Quinn disappeared at the end of the block, and Annie turned to survey the store. For the first time the walls seemed to be closing in upon her: the place seemed so small; so many shadows, so little space.

She shook her head and went to the counter, and there on the surface sat the sheaf of papers that Forrester had left with her five days before. She reached for the telephone and called Jack Sullivan, shared the time of day with him and then reminded him to come down at six before Forrester arrived. He said he would, *promised* he wouldn't drink too much and forget, and she hung up the receiver.

The store was filled to bursting with silence. The rain had stopped and, but for the sound of her own gentle breathing, there was nothing. Nothing at all.

SEVEN

Forrester arrived punctually. Sullivan was already in the kitchen, out of sight. He wasn't drunk, he hadn't forgotten, and if anything he'd been early. Annie was grateful for that, more grateful than he could tell from the nonchalance of her greeting when he appeared at the front door.

'Good day?' he'd asked.

'Quiet,' she'd said, deciding before he'd even arrived to say nothing of David Quinn. Irrespective of whatever doubts she herself may have had about David, Annie O'Neill was considerate enough to take Sullivan's feelings into account. Though there could never be any possibility of a relationship between herself and Sullivan she knew that he held her close in his thoughts. His feelings were avuncular, paternal almost, and if she started to change her patterns too rapidly he would become concerned. His presence at the store before Forrester arrived, the fact that he had made it at all, said all that needed to be said about how much he cared for her welfare.

'So the mystery man arrives at seven,' Sullivan had commented as he passed the counter and made for the kitchen. 'I'll be back here, out of sight, and then if there's any trouble I can leap out and wrestle him to the ground.'

Annie had smiled. 'The guy must be seventy Jack . . . I really don't think there's gonna be any trouble.'

'Charlie Chaplin fathered his last child when he was eighty-two . . . even when we're on our deathbeds we're still up for that.'

Annie had waved him away, and though she honestly believed that Forrester presented no threat at all, she nevertheless felt a sense of security in the fact that Sullivan would be on hand to help her.

And then Robert Forrester arrived, the same topcoat, a similar bundle beneath his arm, and though he merely smiled and nodded towards her as he came in, Annie felt a slight feeling of disquiet invade her thoughts.

Did she dream something? Something about herself and Sullivan and a child? She couldn't remember, but seeing the old man standing there, his character-scarred face, his white hair, she felt the images of the things she'd read come flooding back. The horror of Auschwitz, the ugly killing of hundreds of thousands of human beings in some desolate and godforsaken place . . .

'Miss O'Neill,' Forrester said. 'It is good to see you again.'

'And you Mr Forrester,' she replied, and smiled, and felt that the smile she wore was perhaps the most unnatural expression she'd ever managed.

He walked towards her, set his bundle on the counter, and then asked if there was somewhere they could sit.

'Of course,' she said, and showed Forrester to the small, plain deal table set to the back right-hand corner of the store, the table where she sat late into the night once a month to update inventories and dream her dreams.

The exit to the kitchen was no more than fifteen feet to her left, and though she could not see Sullivan she knew he was there, knew he would at least hear every word she and Forrester shared at this most awkward and strange rendezvous.

Forrester set his package down on the table, removed his coat and threw it across the back of the chair, and sat himself down with an exhausted sigh.

'You want something to drink?' she asked.

'A glass of water perhaps,' he said, and took a handkerchief from his breast pocket. He wiped his face, his forehead, his mouth, and then twisting the handkerchief between his fingers he closed his eyes for a moment and lowered his head.

'Are you okay Mr Forrester?'

He smiled without opening his eyes. 'Yes,' he said, his voice quiet. 'Sometimes I get a little breathless when I walk. I took a later train, had to hurry a little to meet our appointment.'

'You shouldn't have hurried,' Annie said. 'I wasn't going anywhere.'

He opened his eyes. 'We were never late,' he said. 'That was one of the primary rules of membership . . . never late. If you were going to be late you didn't come at all. Better never than late, if you like. Your father was a stickler for punctuality and professionalism.'

Annie sat down. 'I wanted to ask you something – ' she started.

Forrester nodded. 'Could I have some water first my dear?'

'Yes, of course . . . I'm sorry,' she said. She stepped back into the kitchen, filled a glass from a bottle of Evian in the refrigerator, winked and smiled at Sullivan, and returned to the front.

Forrester took the glass and nigh on emptied it with one swallow. He breathed deeply several times, and then set the glass down.

'A question?' he asked.

'Yes,' Annie said, sitting down once more. 'My father . . . what did he do?'

Forrester frowned and smiled simultaneously. 'What did he do? You don't know?'

Annie felt awkward for a moment. 'I feel like I should know,' she said. 'And I can't believe I didn't know when he was alive, or that my mother didn't tell me after he died, but for the life of me I can't remember the damnedest thing.'

'Your father was first and foremost an engineer, a planner. His career encompassed some quite significant jobs that were carried out in New York throughout the '50s and '60s. He was a meticulous man, a perfectionist, and he was employed by some of the most influential organizations in the state. Had he not passed away I think he would have been responsible for some very memorable things.'

'An engineer,' Annie said.

'Of sorts,' Forrester replied, and lifted his glass to drain it.

'More water?' she asked.

Forrester waved his hand. 'No, I'm fine,' he replied. He reached for the bundle of papers on the table, and from it withdrew another single sheet of paper.

'Another letter for you,' he said. 'I have two or three more somewhere, but it takes time to find them among everything.'

He handed the page to her and she took it, once again feeling that sense of tension in her chest. Was this all that there ever would be of her father? A few words from a stranger, a handful of seemingly confusing letters?

Once again, scrawled across the top of the page was the legend *From the Cicero Hotel.*

'You said this hotel was pulled down,' Annie said. 'Was this something he was working on?'

Forrester half smiled – a strange expression. 'In a way,' he said. 'In a way I suppose you could say that.'

Annie waited for him to explain but nothing was forthcoming. Forrester once again performed that small introductory motion with his hand and indicated the letter.

Annie looked down at it.

Dear Heart,
You will hear things. I know you will. Some of them will be true.
Some of them will not. Do not believe everything, and if you are
ever in doubt I would ask you to cast your mind back to the most
special moments you remember of me, and then make your
judgement. What is said by others can never take the place of what
you feel in your heart. I believe it is that simple. Take care of our
daughter. Remember to remind her how much she meant to me,
how much I loved her. And remember this yourself, because you
were – and always will be – everything.
*   Chance.*

Annie felt tears welling in her eyes. There was something so powerful in the words, and though she would never have been

83

able to explain it there was something that touched her more closely than she could have believed possible.

'What does he mean . . . do not believe everything?' she asked. 'What does he not want her to believe?'

Forrester smiled. 'I am not sure I can answer that question as precisely as you might wish Miss O'Neill.'

Annie shook her head. 'Is there something he did? Something that people said he did?'

'He was a good man,' Forrester said. 'A very good man, and though there were people that spoke badly of him there were many more who in some way owed their lives to him.'

'Their lives?' Annie asked, fighting back the urge to cry. 'Whose lives? And who were these people who spoke badly of him?'

Forrester nodded. 'He fought for people. He made life difficult for those who challenged him. Once you earned his friendship there was nothing that could take it away . . . and I am proud to say that I earned his friendship, his trust, and he also earned mine, and from the day we met I never found another human being so deserving of respect.'

Annie looked down at the letter once more. The handwriting was fluid, elegant almost, and she thought to consult a specialist, to have it analysed, to see what she could learn about her ancestry from this small fragment of reality. She set it aside on the table.

'So you read what I left with you?' Forrester asked.

Annie nodded. 'I read it . . . I have it back there on the counter.'

'So tell me.'

'Tell you what?' she asked.

'What you thought . . . what you felt.'

'Fear . . . fear that such a thing could happen to a human being,' she said without thinking, without any sense of self-consciousness. 'And that people don't understand love – '

'Elena and Jozef,' Forrester said. 'A union made in Heaven and burned in Hell.'

84

'Elena and Jozef,' Annie repeated, and was quiet for a time, her mind almost empty of thought.

'And what else did you think?'

'I wondered if it was true . . . a true story,' she said.

Forrester shook his head. 'I'm not sure . . . and I don't know that anyone will ever know all of it.'

'You have more,' she said.

'I have more. I have brought you a further two sections here,' he replied, and indicated the bundle of papers on the table, 'but I don't believe it was ever finished.'

'How much more is there?' she asked.

'Three or four more chapters perhaps.'

'And you have all of it?'

He nodded in the affirmative. 'All that was actually written I think. I wanted to have you read it little by little,' he said, 'and then there would be a reason for us to continue our discussions.'

Loneliness? Annie asked herself. *Is he doing this because he's lonely?*

'Is there anything more you can tell me about the man who wrote it? Did he know my father?'

Forrester shook his head. 'Not well I don't think. Like I said, he was just one of the people who was with us at the time. I knew very little about him, very little at all.'

'He writes of someone else's life as if it was his own,' Annie said.

Forrester nodded. 'He does, but you must read on . . . read all of it and perhaps you will understand more about the man who wrote it than I could ever tell you.'

'And you will leave these two chapters with me now?' she asked, hope in her voice, because somehow – suddenly – it had become important to know what had happened to Haim Rosen when he left the Lower East Side and crossed the river into Queen's in 1952. What was it he had become that Rebecca McCready would never have recognized? Perhaps – and this as an afterthought – there was something in these pages that would show her the kind of person her father had associated with.

'Yes,' he said. 'I'll leave these with you now, and then we will meet again next Monday at the same time.'

Forrester spoke directly and without hesitation. There was nothing uncertain in his tone. He would be here next Monday at seven and there was no doubt in Annie's mind that she would be here also.

He started to rise from his chair.

'You're not staying?' she asked, questions about her father clamoring for attention at the forefront of her mind. For some reason she could not bring herself to ask them. Forrester seemed carefully to pace everything he did, everything he said, and she did not wish to risk any possibility of offending him. To offend him would be to lose his confidence, and to lose that would be to watch her only connection with her father disappear.

Forrester shook his head. 'They were never long meetings,' he said, and started to put on his coat.

Annie rose from her chair.

'Thank you for coming,' she said. 'Thank you for the letter . . . I really appreciate it Mr Forrester.'

'And I appreciate your humoring an old and lonely man,' he replied, and he smiled, and once again nodded his head in that polite European manner. 'Until next week then?'

Annie held out her hand. 'Until next week.'

Forrester took her hand, held it gently, looked at her directly as he did so, and though he did not smile with his mouth there was such warmth in his eyes that Annie felt she should reach out and hug him. She did not, for such things were not done. Not by Annie O'Neill.

Forrester walked towards the door, paused momentarily as Annie opened it for him and then, turning once more, he surveyed the store. He was remembering something. She could see that in his eyes.

'It was a different world back then,' he said. 'People had

more time. There was less importance in being somewhere. People would dress for dinner, we would drink whisky sours and sloe gin, smoke cigars afterwards, and always we would find time to talk . . . '

Forrester took one more look around the shelves and then turned towards the street.

'Take care Miss O'Neill,' he said, and stepped out through the door.

Annie closed the door behind him as Sullivan came from the kitchen to join her. Together they stood in silence and watched the old man make his way towards the junction of Duke Ellington and West 107th. *It could be my father. It could be him walking away*, Annie thought, and again she was invaded by the slow, cool, quiet sensation of nostalgia and loss that always accompanied such thoughts. The wind caught Forrester's hair, the tails of his coat, and for a moment it looked as if he would be caught by a gust and carried up into the sky. He disappeared around the corner and Annie turned to Sullivan.

'Let's read it at home,' she said.

Sullivan nodded, and fetched his coat.

EIGHT

America, 1952: a different world. The war was over, had been for seven years. Truman was president, but would retain his mantle only until November when Eisenhower would win the largest ever popular vote other than Roosevelt's landslide in 1936. The election also served to bring two young politicians into the public arena. A senator called Richard Milhous Nixon, thirty-nine years old, would become the youngest-ever vice-president. Best known for his dedicated and 'patriotic' support for McCarthy's anti-Communist tirades, Nixon would not feature a great deal in the public's collective mind until some years later. And then it would be for something quite different. Perverse prophecy perhaps, but in September of 1952, four months before Eisenhower and Nixon took office, Eisenhower would already have to defend his vice-president's conscience and reputation. Nixon – accused of misusing eighteen thousand dollars of a political fund – was publicly exonerated, and Eisenhower found him 'not only completely vindicated as a man of honor, but, as far as I am concerned, he stands higher than ever before.' Eisenhower, dead in March 1969, did not live to see Nixon's spectacular fall from grace, and thus never had to eat crow regarding his beliefs. On the Democratic front, a young man of thirty-five called John Fitzgerald Kennedy upset everyone by winning the Senate seat in Massachusetts against the Republican, Henry Cabot Lodge. John Foster Dulles was Secretary of State; he was a man who encouraged the mass production of nuclear weapons, but perhaps his most infamous attribute was his relationship with his brother, Allen Welsh Dulles, Director of the Central Intelligence Agency from 1953 to 1961. These were men who thought nothing of destroying the entire island of Eniwetok in the Pacific in a hydrogen bomb test in November of that year: these were the men in charge of America.

This was the America, Haim Rosen told me, that he found vacant and wanting when he arrived in Queens in July. Fifteen years old, wide-eyed and hungry, he began by making his mark in a small community seemingly populated by brash working men with money to lose and over-painted, beehive-haired wives with bad skin and loud mouths. Into this melee of sounds and smells and colors he blended quickly and quietly. Changing his name to Harry Rose, he became a courier for an illegal gambling joint, running tickets and small bundles of cash between the idle wise-ass losers and their bookies. He worked them at their level, he learned the language and the signs, and those that he could not sway with the force of his personality, he swayed with humor and charm. He watched the business flow, the tens and hundreds of dollars exchanging hands with no more than a wink or a nod or a knowing smile. He kept track of how much money passed between the gamblers and the makers in a day, a week, a month, and he saw what that money could buy. He watched the cars and the dames and the kickbacks and the bribes. He watched it all like a hawk, soaking up everything around him like a sponge. He ran a sideline on the small-circuit boxing tables, gathering a few dollars here and there, renting a two-room broken-down apartment on Charles Street, never once crossing the lines, always on time, always exact to the cent and the dime.

He earned trust, and he deserved that trust. And when one of the older bookmakers was hit by a stroke in the spring of 1953, Harry Rose, bold as brass, stepped into the old man's shoes and no-one had a mind to complain. He was always ready with their winnings, consolatory in their losses, and at the end of each month he would send a quart of cheap rye to each of his clients with a little card. *Always another race. Best of luck. Harry Rose*. They appreciated the rye, they appreciated Harry's honesty, and though he was only fifteen he was treated as an equal, a contemporary, a confidant. He knew who was losing what, how often, and why. He knew which gambler's wife was screwing which bookmaker's flunkey. He had his eye on the ball, his ear to the sidewalk, and his heart set on millions.

A month before his sixteenth birthday, taking his balls in his hand and his heart in his mouth, he gambled everything he possessed on Rocky Marciano keeping his world heavyweight title against Roland LaStarza. He took the winnings he made on the fight and threw them at Carl Olsen winning the world middleweight against Randy Turpin. Harry Rose cleaned up good. Came away with more than seven thousand dollars in cash, and with that money he set himself up in a five-room apartment on St Luke. He was king of the country, a teenage prodigy, and his reputation for honest dealing and odds-on favorites was soon known throughout Queens and the surrounding boroughs. Honest Harry Rose he was called, and no-one seemed concerned that he was all of sixteen, fresh-faced and youthful, for they'd look in his eyes and see a man of forty who'd carried the business end of things for two decades.

As Marilyn Monroe married Joe DiMaggio in January of 1954, Harry Rose – a little known Jewish kid from the Lower East Side, a kid who'd successfully hidden his past from anyone who'd cared to know – took a hooker called Alice Raguzzi to his apartment on St Luke and she taught him how to be a man. Alice was a girl out of the backwoods of nowhere, twenty-two years old, brunette and brassy and bold as sunlight. Her mother had been a hooker, her father a pimp, and had she been a boy she would more than likely have followed right into her father's line of work. She was not, and so she followed her mother, and her mother taught her all she knew. And she knew a great deal, Alice did, and she could hold her hand across her hardened heart and swear to God and country that never had a man walked away from her arms unsatisfied. Girl like that could suck the chrome off a trailer hitch, Harry would tell me, give a ninety-year-old guy a blue-steel boner, and when she was breaking a sweat she never forgot to say the guy's name a few times. Made it personal, made it mean something for him, because her abiding philosophy was that no matter what you did you did it as a professional. That was Alice Raguzzi, and she stayed with Harry Rose for two days, and when she left him she took three hundred dollars with her and a small window of soul through that hardened heart of hers. Harry would speak of her later, and he would smile with that wry, sardonic twist to his mouth that said everything without saying a word.

'Girl like that,' he'd say, 'girl like that should run this country. She knows more about the way folks work than any politician or businessman I ever met.'

That told me a great deal about Harry Rose: that he was, above all else, a real human being. Where I came from men were one of three things: they were as stupid as the day was long; park them in an Easyboy, stick a can of beer in their hand, feed them mystery meat three times a day and send them out with a broom to sweep the yard and they never wanted for anything else. Second kind of guy was the one that never grew up. Had been, and would always be, nothing more than a child. Wide-eyed innocence, a belief that all the world was on their side, and then when the shit hit the fan they would look at you with an expression of such dismay, and then they would convince themselves it was all a figment of their imagination and grant the world its perfection once more. And then there were people like me and Harry Rose. We worked the edges and crossed the lines. We lived for the sake of living itself. Where other men wanted one or two of something, people like us wanted half a dozen. Half a dozen girls, half a dozen cars, half a dozen paychecks, even if they happened to be earned by someone else. Life was not cheap, don't get me wrong, but life – like everything else in the world – could be traded.

Harry recognized in Alice Raguzzi something of himself. She was a live one, a real human being, and when she talked Harry

91

listened, and when she listened Harry opened his mouth and his heart and his mind. There was something between them, something other than the sweat they broke on the sheets of his crowded little bed. There was an understanding that if there was something you wanted – well, if there was something people like Harry and Alice wanted, it was up to them, and them alone, to go out and get it. That was the way their world worked, and as far as they were concerned that was the only kind of world there was.

And Alice? She had found this teenage Harry Rose irrepressibly charming, a little slanted when it came to his view of the world, but nevertheless endearing and generous and respectful. No trick had ever called her *Ma'am* before, and she kinda liked it. Made her feel she was providing a necessary public service, instead of just taking it in the ass for a few bucks.

Her mother would have told her to take care of a young man like that. Young man like that had stamina for sure, and there were years of business ahead of him. Young man like that would make it good, and he wouldn't forget those who had taken him seriously despite his age. When he went up in the world, well, she would go up with him, and it wasn't very far from Alice's mind that she would make sure she saw him again. One thing about her industry, it was all repeat business. Whatever it was that made a man's balls fill up, darned, if they didn't keep on filling up despite the number of times you emptied them. Such a thought made her smile, and when she smiled she looked like a million dollars. With some work on her hair, with a little expensive make-up, Alice Raguzzi could have held a candle to all of those Hollywood sweethearts. But Alice was smarter than that. Alice knew the streets and she knew people, and people – real people like Harry Rose – was where you found real life.

Two hours after Alice Raguzzi left that apartment on St Luke she was robbed of her three hundred dollars. Whoever took her money took most of her beauty as well, pounding into her face with a piece of wood until she was barely recognizable. She would never work again, she knew that, and a week later – still confined to a bed in the St Mary Mercy Hospital on the corner of Van Horne and Wiltsey – she broke a small compact mirror in her purse and cut her own wrists. She was found dead two hours later by a hospital orderly called Freddie Trebor. Freddie was a gambler, he knew of Harry Rose, and though he had sworn to Alice Raguzzi that he would never divulge the name she'd given him when she was admitted, he felt such a sense of horror about what had happened that he went to see Harry, told him what Alice had said regarding her attacker. He gave Harry a name – Weber Olson. Harry knew Olson, had dealt with him many times on the racing pitches, and when he told Freddie Trebor to forget anything and everything he had seen and heard, when he pressed a hundred bucks into Freddie's hand and asked if Freddie truly understood what he was asking, Freddie saw something in Harry Rose's eyes that was not – and never could have been – the expression of a sixteen-year-old. Freddie, as nervous as Capone's bookkeeper, gave his word, swore on the deathbed of his mother, gave a promise to the Father, the Son and the Holy Ghost that he had never heard of Alice Raguzzi, Weber Olson or Harry Rose, and left that apartment on St Luke with his heart in his mouth. He never did say a word, even when the police asked questions about Weber Olson's disappearance a little more than a week later, even when they found Olson in a disused basement beneath a tenement on Young Street with his severed penis in his mouth and his eyes in his coat pockets. Freddie Trebor didn't know a thing, and two months later left Queens for Brooklyn in case Harry Rose ever got concerned that Freddie might say something out of turn.

Harry told me about that night later, after we had spoken of many such things and earned one another's trust. Told me like he needed to, like I was his priest and he was a sinner. I took his confession, took it willingly, and there was something important about sharing such things that made us all the closer.

'Found him in a bar,' Harry had said. 'Found him in a bar

uptown, one of those fancyass places where they put bowls of peanuts and pretzels down with your drink. He was sitting there like he was the king of freakin' Persia, and the moment I saw his fat ass on that bar stool I knew that I had to kill him. Wouldn'ta mattered if he'd been the president of the United fucking States, I saw his fat face, the way he laughed while his mouth was all full of chewed-up shit, and I just knew I had to kill that motherfucker stone dead before the night was out.

'I went up there, took the stool alongside his, sat there for a while minding my own business. "Hell of a wristwatch you have there," I told him. "Sure as shit looks like an expensive piece of work." The fat bastard smiled like he had a fifty-dollar piece of ass sucking his dick, and he turned his wrist so I could see the huge gold face, a diamond set right there at the top where there should have been a number twelve. "Swiss," he said, his mouth still stuffed with God knows what. "Twenty-four carat gold through and through." I wanted to take that tasteless ugly piece of crap wristwatch and make the asshole swallow it. Chase it down with a bowl of pretzels and watch the fucker suffocate. I minded my manners, I complimented him on his jewelry, and then I offered to buy him a drink. The fat fuck took my drink, took another two or three, and he must've been busy in there for a couple of hours before I even arrived because by that time he was talking like a man underwater and I knew I could get him out of that place without even raising an eyebrow.

'I told him I knew a good place down on Young Street. "Pretty girls there," I said. "Real pretty girls . . . you ever hear of it?" The cocksucker didn't know shit from shinola, he just followed me like a lost puppy dog, and I walked him out of that bar and across two blocks to Young Street. It was late, some of the streetlights were down already and no-one saw us . . . and hell, if they had, they wouldn't have thought twice about it. We were just two drunk fucks staggering our way home, sharing a joke, having a good time. Halfway down the street I stopped near the top of a flight of stone steps that ran down the side of a building and through into the rear yard. Olson didn't know where the fuck he was, and so I just told him to head on down those steps. I followed him, stayed behind him all the way so there was no chance of him escaping. At the bottom and to the left was a broken-down doorway. I got behind the fat asshole and gave him a damned good shove. The door just collapsed in beneath his weight, and Olson went sprawling across the floor in all this rat shit and fuck knows what kinda garbage. He was so drunk he was still laughing, and I let him laugh, laughed with him, and the fat murdering bastard kept right on laughing until I let fly with one almighty kick to the side of his head. I felt the toe of my shoe impact against his cheek, felt his teeth cave in, and then he was on his hands and knees, screaming blue murder, hollering like a fire siren, blood and teeth foaming out of his mouth like a running faucet.

'I had to shut the fucker up, and so I raised my foot and stamped down on the back of his head with every ounce of strength I possessed. Figured for a moment that I might have killed him stone-dead, but I knelt down and pressed my ear against his chest. He was still breathing, his heart thundering like a train, and I thought for a moment that he might get up and walk away from this thing in a few hours and come looking for me.

'Figured he wouldn't recognize me if he couldn't see, and that's when I had the idea to take his eyes out. And once I had him on his back, once I had my knees on his chest and one hand around his throat so he couldn't move . . . once I had my knife out and was pushing that blade beneath his eyeball and feeling it give, it was then that I thought he should pay in kind for what he did to Alice.

'Two, three times I had to bang him in the side of the head with the butt of the knife handle. Fat fuck kept wriggling and screaming, but I stood up at one moment and kicked him in the head again, and he lay still, still like a corpse, and I finished what I'd started. Then I cut his pants open, took his shorts off, and after hacking at his groin for a couple of seconds his Johnson came off right in my freakin' hand.

'Afterwards I sat on the floor beside his body. I looked at my clothes, the way the blood had spattered all across the legs of my pants, and it was like I'd become someone else. I looked at the fat fuck lying there and it was almost like I'd been watching someone else do this thing. Like I went into some black hole where nothing counted for anything, even someone's life counted for nothing, and when I came out of it he was already dead. I couldn't connect with the thing I had done, not for a while . . . not for a long while. That was the end of Weber Olson, and I had done it to him. Left him there with his eyes in his pockets and his dick in his mouth. Figured he wouldn't be screwing any more hookers . . . figured he wouldn't be screwing anything ever again, the fat useless sack of no good crap.'

And that was Harry Rose, all of sixteen years old; christened in blood now, and set to make a mark.

Folks knew Harry Rose, and they knew a kid who could do such a thing for the sake of some cheap no-good two-bit hooker, was either crazy or desperately loyal. Harry Rose didn't kill Weber Olson for the money, or because it gave him a rev. He killed Olson because of principle. Nothing more nor less than principle.

Word went from mouth to ear to mouth once more, and those who had a mind for such things contacted Harry through runners and consorts. Harry Rose was where the big money could be made, where the wagers in excess of a grand or two could be carried, held back, run three times over at three different fights, and never a moment's delay in payback. And then there were poker games – fat sweaty men with five-cent stogies in smoky back rooms behind bars and clubs, bets starting at two hundred, sky's the limit. All these things, and more besides, and more beyond that if the mood took someone to gamble their life away. And they did, and Harry Rose let them, watched them deal their lives away through the pages of a California prayer book, and though he was always willing to pay his dues he was just as precise in his collections. And collect he did, handfuls of dirty money, used bills and clean, never banking a cent but keeping his earnings in boxes beneath the floorboards of his rooms. Some said there were thousands, others said millions, and no-one but Harry ever knew the truth.

September of 1954 saw Rocky Marciano slay Ezzard Charles in Rocky's forty-seventh consecutive victory; October saw Harry turn seventeen years old, and on the eve of his birthday he threw a party the like of which Queens hadn't seen too often. Rumors said there were more than two hundred people, and when the police broke it up they found more liquor than in Prohibition times and they arrested Harry Rose for under-age alcohol violations. That was Harry's first run-in with the law, and the law listened, and they understood, and they took some dollars and let him go. They even drove him back to his apartment on St Luke and said he should call if there was ever any trouble. Harry said he would, and he learned a lesson: everyone was a hooker. Everyone was up for fucking someone else for money. As long as the rules were understood there wasn't anyone beyond a price. While other kids were heading for colleges and straight-As, Harry Rose – still fresh-faced and youthful – carried a hundred and thirty grand in cash and turned more bets than all the bookies in Queens combined.

He ran cigarettes and silk stockings out of Idlewild until the Italian airliner crash of December '54. Security tightened like shoelaces and Harry, understanding the rules as well as any man in the business, moved his operations out of there and opened a bar. The bar became three, then six, then eight, and while the dope-freak jazzers smoked their mighty mezz and snorted H and C through tightly rolled ten-dollar bills, while the hookers plied for trade along the boardwalks, while the drunks rolled each other for as much long green as they could find, Harry lived the high life.

Honest Harry Rose was The Man. He carried a name. He was

always there at the business end of things, and business always seemed to find him.

Folks said there was a light in his eyes like a devil. But then most folks had loose tongues and looser minds. Truth was Harry was a businessman, a born entrepreneur, and where one man would see an obstacle, Harry would see a stepping-stone to something bigger, better, faster, higher. Seemed to me he saw everything as a challenge: and one small story perhaps illustrates how he worked.

After Idlewild closed down and after the law got real interested in all the shit that had been running smooth in and out of there, Harry found himself as unemployed as a boat-builder in Texas. Another man might have seen it as a setback, but not Harry Rose. 'One man's accident is another man's coincidence,' he'd say, and he'd smile with that little devil-glint lighting a spark in his eyes. He took what money he had, walked into the city with his pockets stuffed, and he stopped at the first bar he found on East 26th. Walked right in like he already owned the place, asked to see the owner, some wiseass, wide-mouthed inbred Polish-American faggot with a name all made up of Zs and Ws.

'Got a crew,' Harry Rose told him. 'Got a crew of Irish and Italians, maybe twenty-five or thirty all told, and then there's all their cousins and brothers and sisters if you wanna include them too. Well, me and my crew took a liking to your little establishment here and we wanted to make you an offer.'

'Ain't for sale,' the wiseass replied.

Harry smiled, maybe winked as well, and he told the guy: 'I understand that it might not be for sale right now this minute, but you gotta hear me out. Good businessman always listens to a proposition whether he's planned for it or not, right?'

The wiseass smiled and nodded, like he knew the difference between a good businessman and a flatfish.

'So here's the deal. I got some cash in my pocket, a whole bunch of cash, and I've taken those dollars and tied them together in bundles of a grand apiece.'

Harry reached into his inside pocket and took out a wad of greenbacks. He laid them on the table ahead of the wiseass.

'There's a thousand dollars there, and it's good money, and what we're gonna do is sit here while I put another grand on the table, and then another one, and when you think there's enough to buy this place outright you stop me.'

Harry paused for a moment and looked at the wiseass.

'Only thing is this . . . at some point I'm gonna stop, and I ain't gonna go no further. You don't know how many thousands I'm gonna put on the table, and I ain't gonna tell you. If we get to that point and you ain't agreed to a sale already then I'm gonna leave. And then tonight, maybe tomorrow night, maybe in a week's time, you're gonna find my crew of Irish and Italians outside with a Molotov party, and we're gonna burn this piece of shit joint to the ground with you inside it.'

The wiseass started laughing. He got up from his chair and pointed at the fresh-faced teenager, and he carried on laughing and he carried on pointing until Harry took a .38 from his pocket and pointed it right at the guy's gut.

'This here,' Harry said, 'is my friend Maurice. Maurice is an ugly little motherfucker who gets mad and spits lead at folks who joke around. Now sit your fat ass down and play the game you ugly sweat-stinking piece of crap.'

The Polish guy sat down, heavy like a bag of cement, and he watched as Harry Rose slowly removed the second bundle of cash from his jacket pocket.

The wiseass wriggled like a stuck pig. He sweated a bucket and a half before Harry even got to five grand.

The deal was done for six. Six thousand dollars all told. Bar and chairs and bottles and pool tables, the juke box, the refrigerators, the freeze-boxes and outhouse. Six thousand dollars.

The wiseass hightailed it out of there because he saw the devil-glint in the kid's eyes, because he couldn't be sure how much money the kid was going to offer, and he sure as hell didn't have a clue that there were no Irish and no Italians to come down and burn his place to ashes.

He got out of there with six grand and his life, and that – as far as he was concerned – was the best deal he was gonna get. Who could he have turned to? The Police? The Mob? Make a call to Poland and ask for his big brother to come over and kick this smart-mouth little kid six ways to Sunday? Hell no, that wasn't the way it worked. He knew that he could have died, and while a bar could always be started over again a life couldn't.

That was the thing that made Harry Rose special. He could bluff it with the best of them, and when he told you something there was nothing in his eyes that suggested what he was saying was anything but the gospel truth. That was his magic, that's why everyone thought he was honest, but Honest Harry Rose wasn't honest at all. Honest Harry Rose could tell a lie that would make the devil blush with shame.

At the time, still a teenager and with the whole world out there waiting for him, it seemed to be a blessing, but later, when a great deal of bloody water had flowed beneath a lot of burning bridges, it would perhaps be his undoing.

NINE

Sullivan turned the last page over and leaned back in his chair. 'Jesus Christ,' he said. 'Jesus Christ Almighty.'

He turned to Annie. She looked back at him with a kind of vacant, washed-out expression. 'No more,' she said, her voice almost a whisper. 'I don't think I can read any more of this right now.'

Sullivan nodded. 'Another time,' he replied. He took the sheaf of papers and straightened them, set them on top of the others that lay there unread.

'One helluva story,' he said. 'It goes from the history of Poland and the liberation of Auschwitz to Goodfellas,' to which Annie nodded and frowned, and then changed the subject entirely.

'Stay,' she said, 'just for a little while. I'll order some Chinese, have it brought up, okay?'

She didn't wait for his response, but walked across to the phone and called the take-out.

She felt shaken, a little over-emotional. It was not the events in the story that had disturbed her, more the fact that she now believed it was the story of a real man, a real human being, and how in the first sixteen or seventeen years of his life he'd lived more of life than ten people put together. Later, folding take-out cartons and putting them in the refrigerator, she looked from the window into the darkness behind the glass, and caught her own reflection. *Like a ghost*, she thought. *I could live my entire life here, could die one of those anonymous New York deaths where no-one knows you're dead until the smell offends the neighbors, and no-one would be any the wiser. How many people would come to my funeral? Sullivan, David Quinn perhaps, John Damianka and his new girlfriend? And what would a priest say? She owned a bookstore. She was a nice person. She thought about taking a stray cat in one time but decided against it.*

Annie shook her head. It was not a life to be proud of. It had not – if she was honest – been much of a life at all.

Sullivan stayed and talked a while – things of little importance – before wishing her goodnight, and though he proffered his customary and routine invitation to a game of cards and a drink with his friends at McKintyre's on Schaeffer and 105th, an invitation Annie always customarily and routinely declined, this time her refusal was a conscious choice. She wanted to be alone and, in the familiar shadows and silences of her four-room apartment, she sat and listened to the wind as it carried rain west from the coast, rain that would paint the city with its own indiscriminate pattern.

She thought of Robert Forrester, of Harry Rose; she thought of David Quinn and Jack Sullivan; she thought of Elena Kruszwica and Jozef Kolzac . . . and they all seemed as real as one another, and all – disquietingly – a little more real than herself.

And then she thought of her father, the engineer. Frank O'Neill, a man who wrote letters that stirred emotions and made memories come alive, a man who had given her life and vanished after seven years. Why? Why so little time? And why had her mother told her so little of the man that she'd loved with such passion and who had broken her heart? These were new questions, and alongside them – as close as shadows – were new emotions: grief, loss, heartache, nostalgia, passion, promise, hope. And desire? A desire to live life? A desire to feel something . . . perhaps some*one*?

There had been times, of course there had been times, when she had gotten close. She was thirty years old, she was not altogether unschooled in the complications of men. High school there had been Tom Parselle, bookish and studious, reciting poetry to her, trying his utmost to court her, but Tom had neither the passion nor the nerve to seduce her, to sleep with her. Their relationship had lasted seventeen months, and never once had they passed first base.

Eighteen years old, her mind windswept with literature, she'd been carried away by Ben Leonhardt, altogether the antithesis of Tom. Ben had been an anachronism much the same as herself, and perhaps that sense of isolation and individuality was what drew them together. That was how she'd felt: *drawn*. Ben was from a wealthy socialite family, his father a financier, his mother a perpetual organizer of charity functions and theme dinners, and Ben had rejected the values and veneer of his background with vigor. Within a week of their meeting she had been seduced, slept with, swept off her feet, and yet for the two years they were together she felt there was always something missing. Her perception was confirmed when Ben took the scholarship to Harvard, plunged head-first into the deep undercurrent of expectation and majored in law. As far as she knew he was down in the financial district right now: Hugo Boss suits, Armani ties, Brooks Brothers shirts tailored to fit, handmade calfskin loafers and weekends in the Hamptons.

After Ben there was nobody until she was twenty-three, and then Richard Lorentzen appeared one day out of nowhere and convinced her that he was indeed *the one*. He was not, but it took the best part of a year for Annie to realize this simple yet irrefutable truth. Richard was intense in a tightened-up Swiss watch-spring manner. Everything possessed significance, and though at first she believed his attention to detail, the endless questions, the schedules and calendars and precise sense of organization were more to do with his own insecurity rather than anything else, she soon realized that Richard Lorentzen was fuelled by jealousy. *Where had she been? Who had she been with? A girlfriend? What was her name? What did they do?* She took it as long as she could, and then she told him that she really had better things to do with her life than report in every fifteen minutes. If she wanted such a life she would join the army. He was obsessive nevertheless, and for a further five months he pursued her, appeared in the street, knew her routine and followed it to the letter. She made efforts to change her routine, to leave at different times, to walk a different way. Finally she told him, on the corner of Columbus and West 99th that if he didn't leave her alone she would speak to the police. He left her alone. He found someone else. She saw them together a month or so later, the poor girl wearing the hunted look of an abused child.

It took two years to recover her sense of participation, to let go of the idea that all men were crazy in some indefinable and yet ever-present way, and then she walked open-eyed and open-hearted into a relationship with Michael Duggan. Michael was everything good about all of them with very little of the bad. He lectured at Barnard, English Language, and thus there was something they held in common. Michael was a writer, a good one, and though he was not published then, and to date had never achieved print, she believed that one day he would make it. Their relationship lasted less than a year, and though Annie believed it had not been of her own doing, nor for her own failings, Michael had had a sufficiently restless spirit to seek the embrace of one of his students. Michael was thirty-three, the student – a brash and unnaturally self-confident nineteen-year-old called Samantha Wheland – had apparently given Michael a blow job in his office. This she surmised from the meandering explanation he had attempted when he'd ditched Annie.

The circumstances of that fiasco had stopped Annie dead in her tracks. She was twenty-seven years old, her mother had been dead seven years, her father close on twenty, and she was alone once more. She had never had sex with somebody in their place of work, never gone Greek or screwed somebody in an elevator. Blow jobs yes, even down on all fours like a Chicago hooker, but she felt such things should be reserved for those guys that meant a little more than a one-off Saturday night lay. And perhaps that was the problem. Perhaps if she'd been a little less *lights-out-missionary* she might have managed to hold onto any one of the men that had walked into and out of her life. But, looking back, she would ask herself if any one of them would have been enough, if any one of them had come even close to what she desired. All but Michael were far wide of the mark, and Michael had showed his true colors when Samantha Wheland showed up. And then there were kids. Kids were the thing, weren't they? Couldn't you tell if you really loved a man when you considered the possibility of having children with him? Sex was but a part of it and, though no small part, it was nowhere near as grand or significant as her friends in college had claimed.

She remembered nights she'd spent with some of her friends, how they'd talk of movie stars and heartthrobs – Kevin Costner and Robert Redford and Jon Bon Jovi et al. What they would do to them. What they *wished* they could do to them. Carrie-Ann Schaeffer had asked Annie who she liked, who she would spend a night with, and Annie – quietly, a little reserved – had said Frank Sinatra. *But he's like . . . like old!* Carrie-Ann shrieked, and Annie had smiled and said she'd want to talk to him, just talk, nothing else. *Just talk?* Carrie-Annie asked, her face folding into something confused and disproportionate. Just talk, Annie had replied, nothing more nor less than that. *Weird*, Carrie-Ann had commented, and then told Grace Sonnenberg how Antonio Banderas could *do her in the ass* if that was what it took.

Again her mind was filled with images of David Quinn, the words he'd released into the hollowness of that moment . . . a man who believed her beautiful. A man who – perhaps, just perhaps – would be the kind of man to think of as her children's father . . .

She undressed sometime before midnight, and lying naked in her bed she imagined someone beside her – a nameless, faceless being; imagined someone holding her, touching her, kissing her perhaps. She closed her eyes and thought of Tom Parselle, of Ben Leonhardt, of Richard Lorentzen and Michael

Duggan, and for the first time in her life she believed that perhaps half of the difficulty had lain with her. They had reached out, but had she reached back with equal desire, the same passion? Had Richard Lorentzen's demands been fuelled by jealousy as she'd so thoroughly convinced herself, or had those demands been nothing more than his need to get something in return? He had given everything, and she had managed to keep it all at arm's length.

Annie O'Neill opened her eyes. She would not sleep, she knew that, and leaving the warmth of her bed she went barefoot to the kitchen and stood in the shadowed silence for a moment. She opened the refrigerator door and, glancing to her left, caught the reflection of her naked form in a mirror hanging on the wall beside the bedroom door. She turned and faced herself, her body cast in a half-light; overcoming an initial sense of self-consciousness, she reached up and pulled her hair back behind her head. She looked at her face, her breasts, the angle of her ribs as they sloped down towards her stomach, and beneath her stomach the dark triangle of pubic hair. With her right hand she touched her breasts, each in turn, and then with her outstretched fingers she traced circles across the tops of her thighs. She shuddered, closed her eyes, and for a moment listened to nothing but the sound of her own breathing.

Annie opened her eyes, looked at her reflection for a second more, and then closed the refrigerator door. The kitchen was swallowed into darkness. Annie lowered herself into that darkness willingly, silently, and was overwhelmed by a sense of loneliness that obliterated all else. And of all people, she wanted to speak to David Quinn the most. Couldn't have even if she'd had the nerve, had no way to reach him, no way to find him, and that, perhaps, was the loneliest thing of all.

She sighed, a deep and enervating sigh, and returned to her bed, lay there for some time while the rain ghosted through the city and dampened each sound, each color, each image. There were people out there – hundreds, thousands, millions

106

of them – and she believed that fundamentally they were all chasing the same thing. To have someone listen, to have someone understand, to have someone appreciate who they *really* were. For they were all someone, deep down they were, and it was just that no-one seemed to notice these days.

She closed her eyes, she slept, she did not dream.

Too empty to dream perhaps.

TEN

The store opened late Tuesday morning, closed early too. Wednesday it rained more heavily, and out along the horizon a storm threatened New York with angry thunderheads and darkness. Annie stayed home, dressed in sweat pants and loose-fitting tee-shirt and listened to Sinatra and Barry White. She ate left-over Chinese food from Monday night, cold noodles and gelatinous lemon-honey chicken. She read too, bits and pieces of a dozen or more books: by Steinbeck and Hemingway, Francine Prose and Adriana Trigiani. She read poems by Walt Whitman and William Carlos Williams, wandered back and forth between the kitchen and her bedroom. Then she searched out *Breathing Space* by Nathaniel Levitt. She traced her fingers across the legend on the inside flyleaf – *Printed in 1836 by Hollister & Sons, Jersey City. Bound by Hoopers, Camden.* And beneath that – in the same unmistakable hand that had written the letters brought by Forrester: *Annie, for when the time comes. Dad. 2 June 1979.* She read the book through again, and though she had read it a dozen times before there was something about the pace and rhythm of the prose, the simplicity of the story, that touched her in a way that it had not done before. Love lost, and found once more. Like Sullivan said, better to love and lose than never to have loved at all. She held the book close to her face, could smell the age in the pages, feel the texture of the leather cover against her skin, and for a moment she wanted to cry. *For when the time comes* . . . What had he meant? What time? When would it come?

Once or twice Sullivan looked in on her, read the simple

desire to be alone in her expression, and with nothing more than a smile, a nod of his head, made it clear that he was there if she needed him. She did not. She wanted no-one for a while. She wanted to be herself, to find something inside that would explain why these past thirty years now seemed so hollow and meaningless.

On Thursday she returned to the store, early if anything, arriving a little after eight-thirty, and when she'd made coffee, removed her coat and returned to the counter, she stood there among her books, her thousands of worn-out books, and wondered if there really would be anything other than this. She felt disoriented, like a child losing sight of its parents in a crowd, and when David Quinn appeared in the doorway, his familiar silhouette pausing in the light that came through from the street, she believed she'd never been more pleased to see someone in all her life.

She stepped out from behind the counter. 'David!'

He smiled, walked forward. 'You okay?' he asked.

'Sure I am . . . why d'you ask?'

'I came yesterday, the place was closed up . . . I thought you might be sick.'

'I took a day off,' she said. 'First time in years.'

'But you're okay?' he asked again.

'I am – ' she started, and then without the thought forming in her mind, almost as if her lips were taking involuntary control of her words, she added, 'and better now you're here.'

He was dressed the same; the same as last time, and the time before that. There was a comfortable familiarity in the way he looked, his expression as he came towards her, and when he leaned against the counter and smiled she wanted to reach out and touch him, as if to verify his presence, to ensure he was real.

'Take another day,' he said quietly. 'Let's go buy stuff, go waste some money. I've been wearing the same clothes since the end of last week, and the truth is I haven't even bothered to unpack most of my stuff.'

'So let's go unpack it,' she said. 'I can help you get settled.'

'In my apartment?' he asked, a little surprised.

'No, in the 7–11 David . . . where the hell d'you think I mean?'

'You want to come and help me unpack my stuff?'

She nodded. 'I want to help . . . I want to do something other than sit in here all day waiting for someone to come buy a book.'

David was nodding slowly, his thoughts running faster than he could catch them, and then he looked up, looked directly at Annie, and said: 'Okay, let's go do that . . . why the hell not?'

She turned the sign, locked up, and from the corner of West 107th they took a cab to the other end of Morningside Park. He led the way, down the street and in through the elevated entrance of a tall sandstone building. Up two flights, down the hall, turning right at the end and reaching a single doorway at the end of the corridor.

'Home,' he said, and produced keys. He unlocked the door, stepped inside and waited for her to follow.

Annie went in slowly – wide-eyed she suspected – and though there was anticipation and excitement contained in the moment, there was also her in-built caution, that walking-on-eggshells sensation that invaded the edges of her consciousness. What was she doing here? She barely knew this man. Nice guy or serial killer? Charming or deadly? She took another step forward and watched as the door seemed to close behind her in slow-motion. The latch hit the striker plate; it snapped home suddenly, and inside she jumped. What in God's name was she doing?

'Take your coat off,' he said. 'I'll make us some coffee.'

She stood in a vast and apparently empty room. A single chair was positioned beside the ceiling-high windows that ran from one end of the floor to the other. This would have been heaven for a painter, the light flooding in through the glass and bathing the entire space with an ambient yellow glow. To the right against the far wall were stacked a half-dozen cardboard boxes, ahead of them a long rolled-up rug, beside it a wooden chest and a small suitcase with the travel tags still attached to the handle.

The room smelled a little musty, unlived-in, and crossing towards the window she stopped by the chair and looked down. The books he'd bought from the store were still in the same polythene bag she'd given him, and leaning down to take a closer look she noticed the till receipt was still inside. He had brought them back, set them down, and more than likely they had remained in exactly the same place.

'Not that much of a reader.'

She turned suddenly, a little startled by the sound of David's voice. Again a quiet sense of anxiety invaded her.

'I want to read, I plan to read, but somehow I don't get it together.' He was walking towards her holding two cups, and when he reached her he set them down on the floor and held out his hand.

'Your coat?' he said.

She nodded, smiled a little awkwardly, and took it off. She handed it to him, and crossing the room he set it on top of the boxes behind the rug. He picked up a folding chair from beside the boxes, crossed back towards her and set it down.

'Sit,' he said, and she did, and for a moment felt a degree of tension inside her that was new. All of this was new. She was here with a man, a man she barely knew, and there was something so *close* about him that it unnerved her.

'This stuff,' he said, indicating the boxes against the wall, 'has been here since I moved.' He looked to the right, a door in the wall. 'Through there is the bedroom, the door over there is the bathroom, and the kitchen's through there.' He nodded back towards the way he'd walked with the cups. 'I unpacked some sheets, a quilt, my alarm clock, a few items of clothing, and that was where it ended . . . the relationship I have with my possessions. I think it has to do with my hotel mentality.'

Annie frowned. 'Your what?'

He smiled. 'My hotel mentality. Spent so much of my time in hotels I've forgotten how to take care of myself.'

Annie reached for her cup. She sipped. The coffee was strong but good. She savored the smell, the heat through her skin, and over the rim of the cup she watched David Quinn as he surveyed the hollowness of his home.

Perhaps, she thought, *this man is as lonely as I am, but in a different way*.

'So when will you work again?' she asked.

He shrugged. 'I wait for a call. As soon as they call I have to leave. Could be anywhere. Newfoundland, Alaska, somewhere on the Pacific Coast. Furthest I ever got was Southampton in England.'

'You've been to England?'

'For a little while,' he said.

'What's it like?'

'It's good . . . the people are good, different.' He paused, as if remembering things – images and sounds. 'It's a dark country, claustrophobic almost, rains a great deal. They are tough, the English, a really tough people. They aren't faddish or insubstantial. They know what they want and they'll do everything to get it. They have persistence, and they don't take any crap from foreigners.'

Annie laughed. She liked this man, this David Quinn. He seemed real and unpretentious. He seemed to be the sort of man who would possess a thought and voice it. A man who liked the truth.

'So why did you come here?' Annie asked. 'Why not stay in East Village?'

David shrugged. He drank his coffee. He emptied the cup and set it on the floor. From his jacket pocket he took a pack of cigarettes, lit one, and then proceeded to use the empty cup as an ashtray. 'I think I wanted a change, but I'm too conservative to go the whole nine yards and move state. I wanted to stay around Central Park, and one day I took a cab up here and there was something about the atmosphere of the place, something learned and academic that appealed to me. Seemed everywhere I looked there were bistros with students eating brioche and drinking cappuccinos and reading Whitman and William Carlos Williams – '

Annie looked up, struck by the sudden coincidence of what he'd said.

'– and I just felt a strange sensation . . . sort of like when you've been away and then you come home.'

'But you've never lived here before?'

David shook his head. 'No, always and forever an East Villager.'

'You like it here?'

'I do,' he said. 'It makes me feel like I have more substance. People look at me and I believe they think I'm a Barnard lecturer, or someone taking a season at Columbia.'

'You ever thought of going back to school, doing something else?'

'You know, I have,' David said, and in his voice was an element of surprise, as if he was puzzled why someone would ask such a thing. 'I *have* thought about it, but never followed it through. I need some English blood perhaps.' He smiled, smoked his cigarette, and for a little while neither of them said a thing.

Later, alone, Annie would wonder why she'd broken that silence with a question. Perhaps she had been uneasy, aware of the vast emptiness around her and needed to fill it with something. She didn't know why, perhaps would never understand her own motivation, but nevertheless she asked the question.

'David?'

He looked up at her.

'You ever get lonely?'

He smiled, again that warm and genuine smile that said more about him than any words. 'Endlessly,' he said, his voice quiet, almost a whisper.

113

'And why don't you go out, meet people . . . how come you don't have a girlfriend or something?'

'Or something?' he asked. 'And what kind of something would that be?'

'You know what I mean,' Annie said.

He nodded. 'I know what you mean. Defence through humor, eh?'

'So how come?'

He shrugged. 'Fear?'

'Fear?' she repeated.

'Yes, fear,' he replied. 'Perhaps anxiety is a better word, but that's just a harmonic of fear anyway, isn't it?'

'Fear of what?'

'Of the something you end up with being worse than the nothing you had before. Fear of rejection, of losing whatever you might find, of others' opinions, fear of discovery – '

'Of discovery?'

'Someone discovering that you're not the perfect human being they first imagined you to be . . . that you have bad days, that you have irksome habits and idiosyncrasies.'

'But surely those things are all part and parcel of making a relationship, even a friendship, work?'

'Sure they are,' he said, 'but they're also the things that you're most afraid of when you walk blind into something like that.'

'But you have to accept the fact that whoever you're with has the same doubts and reservations, and you have to take as well as give.'

'Sure you do,' he said, 'but it's always there at the beginning isn't it? It's the first days, the first hours even, when all you think about is what that person might think of you.'

'Isn't that a little egocentric?' she asked.

He shook his head. 'I don't think so . . . more like hoping that someone likes you as much as you like them, and hoping as well that you're not going to say or do something that drives them away. We all have our monkeys to carry, and sometimes those monkeys jump without warning.'

'I think somewhere you have lost your basic faith in human nature.'

He shook his head. 'No, I think somewhere all of us fear the unknown, the uncertainty that comes with meeting new people, guessing what they're like, whether they can be trusted or not.'

'You don't trust people?'

'Do you?' he asked.

'I think I do,' Annie said.

'You think?'

'Yes,' she repeated, 'I think I do.'

'You trust me?'

Annie looked at David Quinn, looked at him directly. 'I don't know you well enough to answer that.'

'That's exactly my point,' he said. 'That's exactly what I'm talking about. This could be the start of a friendship, right?'

Annie nodded. 'It could.'

'So we have a little time here and there to get to know each other, to ask questions, to hear the answers . . . not only the words that are said, but what might really be meant by those words, and we make our judgements. You had to have trusted me somewhat to suggest we come here, agreed?'

'Agreed,' Annie said.

'So you must trust me.'

'Okay,' she said, 'I trust you.'

'How much?'

'How much do I trust you? I don't know . . . how d'you measure trust?'

David leaned back in his chair. 'You want to do an experiment?'

'What kind of experiment?'

'A measure of trust experiment.'

Annie frowned.

David stood up, walked across the room and went through

115

the door into the bedroom. He returned a moment later, in his hand a scarf.

'Sit back,' he said. 'Relax, close your eyes.'

Annie shifted uneasily in her chair.

David leaned towards her, looked right at her. 'Trust me,' he said.

'You're a doctor, right?'

He smiled. 'Grace under pressure Annie O'Neill.'

She leaned back, closed her eyes, couldn't imagine what she was doing, or why.

David took a step behind her, and brushing the hair back from her forehead with his hand he placed the scarf over her eyes and tied it loosely at the back.

'What are you doing?' Annie asked.

'Blindfolding you,' David Quinn said, and then Annie felt his hands on her shoulders. She tensed physically, and in her mind she was shouting at herself. *What the hell are you doing? What the hell do you think you're playing at?*

'So this is the experiment?' she asked, and even in her own voice she could hear a sense of trepidation and anxiety. She wanted to pull the scarf from her face, but there was something in the simplicity of how he had captured her in this game that made her want to see it through.

But what if he kills you? What if he really is a deranged sociopath? Who knows you're here? Does anyone actually know where you are?

'You have to sit there for one minute straight,' David said. 'I'll time it, exactly a minute, and for that minute you cannot move, you cannot say a word, okay?'

'And what will you be doing?' she asked.

'I'm not going to tell you.'

'You're not going to tell me?'

'Right, I'm not going to tell you . . . you just have to trust me, okay?'

Annie was quiet for a moment.

'Okay?' he asked again.

116

She nodded. 'Okay.'

'So we start the minute now,' he said. 'Three, two, one, go.'

Annie felt the desire to move immediately, but she didn't. She sat stock-still, every muscle in her body tight like whip-cord. She tried to imagine what it was that had possessed her to suggest she come here in the first place, and what in God's name had made her agree to this ludicrous game.

And then she thought of David. She was aware of the fact that he'd been behind her when he tied the scarf, but where was he now?

Was he still behind her or had he moved?

For a couple of seconds she held her breath in the hope that she would hear his breathing and determine his position, but there was nothing, merely the hollow vastness of the room and the awareness that she was seated by the window. Alone in a stranger's apartment and blindfolded . . .

Surely a minute must have elapsed by now, she thought. *What is he doing?*

And where is he right now?

She turned her head to one side, tried to sense the difference in light between the window and the walls. She couldn't see a thing. It was pitch-black.

How many seconds have gone now? she asked herself, but there was no way she could tell. She should have started counting when he tied the blindfold. *Hell, why didn't I think of that?*

Perhaps a minute had passed, perhaps two, and he was leaving her there in silence just to unnerve her.

She smiled. He wouldn't do such a thing . . . would he? How the hell could she know? It was too much; this was just too goddamned much!

She wanted to say something, anything. She started to move her lips, and then she stopped herself. What if this was nothing more than a simple parlor trick? What if only half a minute had passed, and she was folding up? Was this some way to test her resolve? Was there some other reason for this than David had told her?

117

She couldn't help it, the tension had built inside her chest until she could hardly contain her breathing. She wanted to scream, wanted to say something, to hear something . . . anything.

'Da . . . David?'

She heard the sound of her own voice, like the voice of a lost and frightened child. And that was all she heard.

'David?'

Did she hear something then?

She tilted her head to the right, could feel the restraint of the blindfold.

Was that the sound of breathing?

Was he closer to her . . . closing in on her?

And then she felt angry, abused even, somehow invaded and ridiculed. She felt color rising in her cheeks, felt tightness in her chest. But still there was that sense of disturbing unease that seemed to edge along her spine and settle at the base of her neck.

'David!' she snapped.

Again there was silence, nothing that in any way indicated where he was, if he was even there.

The sensation was like pins and needles, but cold, constantly moving, making her skin crawl upwards. She could feel muscles tensing in her shoulders, her neck, and there was a feeling of nausea building in her throat.

'David!' she snapped again, her voice edged with fear. 'David . . . where the hell are you?'

Silence.

Swollen black silence.

She reached up her hand and wrenched the scarf away.

David Quinn was seated facing her, exactly as he'd been when they were talking.

'Thirty-seven seconds,' he said, his eyes still fixed on his wristwatch.

'No way!' she said. 'There was no way that was only thirty-seven seconds.'

'Thirty-seven exactly,' he said.

She balled the scarf up in her hands and tossed it to the floor.

'What were you thinking?' he asked.

She shook her head. 'Nothing much – '

'Tell me,' he said. 'It's part of the game . . . you have to tell me what you were thinking.'

'I don't know,' she replied, suddenly a little embarrassed.

'You were afraid?'

'I was afraid,' she admitted.

'Of what?'

'Of what you might be doing.'

'Like I was going to strangle you or suddenly plunge a knife into your chest?'

'Something like that . . . hell, I don't like this David, this isn't fun.'

David smiled. 'I'm sorry – '

'It's getting to be a habit,' she said.

'What is?'

'You apologizing to me.'

He nodded. 'You're right, it wasn't fair. It's a little bit of a harsh way to illustrate a point.'

'And the point was?'

'That we all imagine the worst,' he said. 'It seems to be basic human nature, to imagine the worst. I think it's been influenced by the media, by films, by TV . . . led to believe that around every dark corner someone might be lurking with malevolent intent.'

Annie frowned.

'How old are you?' David asked. 'Twenty-seven, twenty-eight?'

'Thirty,' Annie said, pleased a little that he'd placed her younger.

'Always lived in New York?'

'Yes,' she said.

'So, thirty years in New York, a city that's reputed to be one of the most dangerous cities in the world, right?'

Annie nodded in the affirmative.

'So how many times in the past thirty years have you personally witnessed an act of violence, someone being killed, someone being mugged?'

Annie thought for a moment, and then she started to smile.

'What?' David asked, smiling in unison.

'There was a time when I was younger, a teenager, fifteen, sixteen years old, and my mother and I were walking down through Central Park and this guy was playing a guitar. He was just sitting there minding his own business playing guitar, singing a few songs, and people would stop for a little while and toss dimes and quarters into his guitar case. Suddenly this other guy appears, a guy in a business suit for Christ's sake, and he grabs the guitar from this guy and starts whacking him with it.'

Annie started laughing, couldn't help herself as the image came. A guy in a business suit attacking some poor hobo busker with his own guitar.

David was smiling.

'So this guy just keeps whacking this guy with the guitar, and every time the guitar hits this guy there's this sound of the strings. Wha-daang! Wha-daang!'

Annie started laughing harder, a little uncontrolled, and before long she and David Quinn were fit to bust, tears streaming down their faces.

'And what happened?' David asked eventually.

'The poor guy just runs away, leaves behind his coat, his money, his guitar, and the guy in the business suit just drops the guitar on the ground, straightens his vest and jacket and walks away. He comes past us, my mother's looking at him with this shocked expression on her face, and this guy turns to her and says "Fuck the Beatles!", and then he just walks off down the path and disappears.'

'Fuck the Beatles?' David asked.

'Fuck the Beatles, that's what he said.'

Annie was still laughing, settling down a little, and then she looked up at David and believed that perhaps there was nothing to be afraid of here, nothing but what she herself might imagine.

'And that is the sum total of your experiences regarding first-hand violence?' David asked.

She nodded. 'It is.'

'Not a hell of a great deal considering this is one of the most dangerous cities in the world, eh?'

She shrugged. 'I s'pose not.'

'See what I mean then? Most of what we fear is within ourselves, what we imagine, what we consider might be there if we look hard enough into the darkness.'

Annie watched David as he spoke. He was speaking to *her*, not to himself as so many men did. He was not speaking so passionately because he believed he had something worthwhile to say, nor because he liked the sound of his own voice. He was speaking about something in which he believed, and there were so few people these days who believed strongly about anything that she found it in some way admirable.

'So whatever you thought I might be doing while you were blindfolded – ' David started.

'Was all three inches behind my forehead, right?' Annie interjected.

David nodded. 'Right.'

She looked at him, at the intensity of his expression, and in the silence that unfolded she felt that tension, the sense of presence around them, and yet where there had earlier been a feeling of trepidation and anxiety, there was now something singularly . . . something undeniably sexual?

She felt her cheeks flush.

'Okay?' he asked.

'I'm okay,' she said. 'A little warm perhaps.'

'So take off your sweater.'

Annie instinctively tried to remember what she was wearing beneath. A tee-shirt, a blouse? It was a tee-shirt, a long-sleeved cotton tee-shirt, and as she tugged the sweater over her head her predominant thought was whether or not it was clean.

The sweater came off, she folded it neatly and set it on the floor, and then she looked down to straighten her shirt, to check that she looked presentable.

'You want some more coffee?' David asked.

She shook her head. 'No, I'm fine.'

Again there was a moment of silence, a moment she broke when she asked, 'So, I thought we were going to unpack your stuff. Is that what we're going to do?'

David smiled. 'Is that what you want to do?'

She smiled back. 'Not particularly.'

He leaned a little closer. 'What do *you* want to do Annie O'Neill?'

She felt her cheeks flush again. She shook her head.

'Tell me,' he prompted. 'What would you really like to do, right now?'

She looked back at him. 'I want . . . I want you – '

'To what? What do you want me to do?'

'I want you to kiss me David Quinn, that's what I want.'

He closed his eyes for a second, just a split second, but within that second every thought and feeling, every emotion and sensation and desire she could ever have experienced rushed through her body like a freight train.

He came down off the chair and onto his knees, eyes open, and reaching with his right hand he touched the side of her face.

Annie closed her eyes. She sighed. Human contact.

She felt the warmth of his skin, the pressure of his fingers against her cheek, and then his hand was moving gently around the side of her face and over her ear. His fingers were in her hair, and then she felt the slightest pressure as he pulled her slowly forward. She kept her eyes closed, but she sensed his face approaching hers, and then the tip of his nose touched her cheek, and for a moment it seemed that he was breathing her in, inhaling her whole. She could smell him, something like leather and cigarette smoke, and beneath that something warm and pleasant and musky.

His lips grazed hers and she shuddered. For some reason she wanted to cry, and then she felt the pressure of his mouth against hers, and at first somewhat resistant, tentative, and then slowly relaxing, she opened her mouth a fraction and felt the tip of his tongue trace a fine line across her lower lip. She opened her mouth a fraction further, and then she felt him close against her, could feel the pressure of her breasts against his chest, and then his left hand was touching the side of her waist, and she felt bound up in something so powerful she could so easily have forgotten to breathe.

She kissed him. She kissed David Quinn, her tongue finding his, her mouth yielding, and the way he kissed her was so gentle and sensitive, and yet somehow so passionate that she felt she would lose her balance completely and come crashing to the hardwood floor. But he was there, there ahead of her and somehow beneath her, and she raised her hands and closed them around his face, pulled him tighter, tighter again, and when she slid from the chair to her knees it was as if everything was in slow-motion. The sounds, the smells, the colors behind her closed eyelids, and she couldn't ever remember feeling so close to something.

Eventually, and against her desire, he released her. He leaned back, and she imagined she was standing at the far end of the room watching these two people on their knees, their hands around each other's faces, their eyes open, their mouths silent as they looked back at one another and didn't know what to say.

At last she did say something.

Thank you.

He smiled, pulled her tight, and for some eternity of silence he just held her.

Annie O'Neill believed she'd never felt so safe in her life.

ELEVEN

Alone again later, she could not remember how the subsequent two or three hours had really disappeared so quickly. They had talked – that much she knew – but when she lay in the bath in her own apartment, the warm water enfolding her, giving her a feeling of security, she could recall neither the words used nor the subjects discussed, or how the minutes had passed. He did not press her further, he did not lead her quietly to his bedroom, and though she would have gone – willingly and without resistance – she also felt there was something so right in the fact that he had taken her request for a kiss and complied with that and that alone. He had granted her simple wish, and for that she was grateful.

Perhaps, had Sullivan been home, she would have told him about her day, that she had gone to David Quinn's apartment, that he had kissed her. But Sullivan was out, and she was faintly relieved. Some things, perhaps, should be reserved simply for one's self.

When it had been time to leave David, he had called a cab with his cellphone. He had walked her down to the street, paused for a moment facing her, never said a word, and then he'd opened the cab door and closed it behind her. Watching him in the cab's wing mirror, standing there on the sidewalk, she had fought the temptation to look back, to watch him until he disappeared – he'd stood there patiently until the cab had turned the corner, and then she'd leaned back and sighed.

By the time she arrived home it was dark, sometime after eight, and she ran a bath and undressed. She tied her hair back and stared at her face in the mirror above the sink for a while.

She felt naked, not just unclothed but truly *naked*. Her features – her eyes, her nose, her mouth – all these things could be read. The details not only of the last few hours – her desires, her longings, her anxieties and the feeling that she had walked close to the edge of something, peered into a chasm and then slowly stepped back – but the entirety of her life, could be open to scrutiny. Is this what David had meant when he'd spoken of fear of discovery? He had discovered something within her, and truth be told she had discovered something within herself: she was lonely, she was *wanting*, and in the moment that he had reached out and made contact she had given more of herself than she could remember doing for a decade. She had surprised herself with her openness, her willingness to be led, but led only so far: to the edge, but back again. Temptation and passion had risen to the surface of her being, but she retained a quiet reserve that would have allowed her to walk only a certain number of steps before pausing, holding her breath, judging the moment, and then retreating. Was this love? Was she – after all – now *rising into* love?

She smiled at the thought, watched the small crow's-feet and laughter lines around her eyes and mouth as her expression changed, and wished that her father were there.

How goes it Annie?

It's okay Dad . . . how goes you?

Oh, you know? Can't complain. But let's talk about you . . . how was your day?

I met a man, Dad, a man I think I could fall for.

Is that so? Tell me about him.

What's there to tell . . . he's passionate about things, intelligent, sensitive I think, but there is something about his eyes that tells me you wouldn't want to cross him.

I knew people like that.

Tell me Daddy . . . tell me about your life, about what you did, who you were, why you went away so suddenly.

I can't sweetheart . . . I would if I could, but I can't.

Why not?

There are rules honey, there are rules.

Rules? What rules?

The dead never tell on the dead . . . that's the simplest rule there is.

Annie O'Neill saw her smile fade. She turned and stopped the faucets on the bath. She slipped off her robe and sank into the water. She leaned back and closed her eyes, but try as she might she couldn't blank out the image of David Quinn's face. He looked back at her from behind her eyelids. His smile. The way he massaged his neck. And then she could smell him as he came nearer – the musk, the coffee, the tobacco, together in some warm cloud of masculinity. And something else: a quiet ghost of anxiety perhaps; a question about his motives, his intentions towards her. What did he want?

Annie sighed. The water was deep. She wanted to stay where she was. She shrugged her thoughts away, thoughts without substance. She was not going to talk herself backwards this time. This time she was going to walk forward, and if David Quinn chose to walk with her then so be it. She felt safe, secure. She was *wanted*.

She lay there until hunger called her from the bath to the kitchen. She dried her body and wrapped a towel around her hair. She slipped on a pair of panties and, naked but for these, went through to the kitchen and set about preparing some salad, lit the oven to warm a baguette, took cheese and smoked ham from the refrigerator.

Standing there beside the counter, the window to her right, she caught something in the corner of her eye. Looking through the glass she noticed lights on the floor facing hers in the building opposite. There had been no lights there for weeks. The apartments had been emptied out for renovations by some city property developer who had bought the entire block and was set to upgrade the floors one by one. Perhaps they had started. But this late?

Curious, she looked more closely, and noticed someone, barely visible across the distance – a man. He did not look her way, his attention was focused on what he was doing, and for a moment Annie stood there, her naked upper body fully visible in the window. Her attention momentarily distracted – a thought perhaps – she glanced away, and then looked back at the upper windows of the block facing her.

The man had stopped.

He was there at the window.

Looking at her.

Looking right *at* her.

He moved a little to the left, and with the back of his hand he wiped his brow. Annie could sense him squinting towards her, perhaps disbelieving what he saw. There was a naked woman at the window no more than thirty yards from where he stood, and she wasn't moving.

Annie – suddenly aware of her nakedness, the rush of color that flooded her cheeks, her acute sense of embarrassment – stepped to the left, took three steps backwards and switched off the light. Hurrying to the bedroom, barely able to contain her humiliation, she pulled on a sweatshirt and some pants, tugged the towel from her hair and sort of hugged it to her chest as she stood there. She was breathing heavily, the hot flush of embarrassment only now beginning to subside. What had she been thinking of? What had she done? Fearfully she made her way back into the kitchen and stood to the right of the window. Looking carefully, sure the man would not be able to see her, she peered through the window. He was still there. Did he shake his head just then? Was he incredulous about his luck, or was he even now thinking that he must have hallucinated?

Annie stepped back, inwardly cringing once more, and then she stopped. Did she really feel so humiliated? Was she really a closet exhibitionist? She smiled to herself, and thought of telling Sullivan everything, of her rendezvous with David, that she had stood naked before the kitchen window and given some guy a cheap thrill. And what would Sullivan have said?

Go for it sweetheart . . . always told you you should loosen up a little.

And then he would have laughed coarsely and suggested he apply for a job with whoever was working across the street.

Annie opened the refrigerator door, left it ajar, made the rest of her meal in the pale glow from the refrigerator's light, and carried her food through to the front room.

She sat at the table, a table she only ever remembered sharing with Jack Sullivan, and wondered if she should invite David Quinn here to her apartment. Did she want this man in her life? Was he *the one*?

Could he really be *the one*?

And what would he have thought if she'd told him about flashing her breasts at the guy across the street?

She laughed to herself, ate her salad and, to be honest, found she didn't care.

An hour later, perhaps a little more, she heard the faintest knock on her door. She rose and walked to open it, but before she reached it the handle was turning. Sullivan appeared, his face ruddy, and he stood silent for a moment.

'You okay?' he asked.

'Sure I am,' Annie said, and thought for a moment to tell him about how she'd stood naked in the window for some guy across the street.

'You want some company?'

Annie nodded. 'Sure Jack . . . come on in.'

'I was gonna go in and watch some TV, but then I thought maybe we could read that thing that the old guy brought; you know, the second bit.'

Annie hesitated. The time she had spent with David had taken her mind off the book and now, as soon as she thought of it she felt as though a dark cloud was nudging up against the edge of her consciousness. She wanted to tell Sullivan *No*, that she'd had a good day, one of the best days she'd had for a very long time and she did not wish to ruin it by walking back into something that now seemed so dark and horrifying.

But there was some fascination there also, something almost mesmerizing about reading of such terrible things, and though she thought *No* she found herself saying 'Yes, okay . . . come sit down with me and we'll read it.'

Another thought struck her then: that this was her way of making sure that Sullivan did not feel excluded. Was this how it would feel if her father had come, if he'd wanted to talk to her of something serious when she was in no mood for such things? Was this what you did for people you really cared for? You made time for them, you made allowances for them?

Yes, she thought. *This is something my mother would have done. Give just as much as you take, she would have said, and she would have been right. Right enough to love my dad. Right enough to make time for those she cared for even if it meant disrupting her own life.*

Sullivan came in. He offered to make tea and Annie let him. He carried it through, and together they sat side by side on the sofa, Annie leaning against his broad shoulder as if it were an anchor back to reality.

She had carried the pages from the edge of the table and set them next to where she sat, and once Sullivan was settled she reached for them, turned them over one by one, glancing through them as if to remind herself of how it had all been.

'You ready for this?' she asked Sullivan.

'As I'll ever be,' he said quietly, and as one they turned their eyes towards the page and started to read.

TWELVE

It was in early 1955 that I met Harry Rose. At that time I went by the name of Johnnie Redbird, and though I was from Staten Island, a foreigner by all accounts, there was something about me that stopped Harry Rose in his tracks. I was down at the stoop ahead of a backstreet gambling joint, minding my own business; seem to remember I was counting a handful of dollars I had taken on a race. This kid comes by, and though he was a good head shorter than me there was something about him that made him big. Can't say I know of any other way to describe it. He had on a tailored suit, hand-stitched collar an' all that, hair cut short in the back and kind of hanging forward at the front down to his eyebrows. He looked at me, kind of nodded his unspoken acknowledgement as he passed and went up the steps to the house, and there was something in his eyes, something silent and brooding and almost melancholy that made me think he carried some weight of pain beyond his years.

When he came back down again, couldn't have been more than fifteen or twenty minutes, he nodded once more. He paused at the bottom of the well, stood right there beside me, and then he said: 'Easy come, easy go, eh?'

I had my cigarettes in my hand, was just gonna light one up, and so I offered this kid a smoke and he took it. Remember the way he didn't look away when I lit it for him. Eye contact, all the while there was eye contact, and there was something in the way he looked that made me – Johnnie Redbird – a little unsettled. I came with a reputation, I had set a few to sleep in their cold-meat boxes, didn't turn a hair when I took the fingers off a gambler who owed me thirty-five bucks. Took them off with a box-cutter: seven fingers, five dollars a piece. But standing there in my dark suit, white shirt, silk tie, packing a .38 in the waist of my pants, face like someone had chiselled me out of Arizona sandstone . . . me, Johnnie Redbird, whose picture you'd keep to scare up your kids and make them eat their greens and get to bed on time, well, hell if I didn't feel that there was someone here who would give me a run for my money.

Watch the little ones, an old friend of mine used to say. Watch the little guys who look like a streak of piss wrapped in a suit. They're fast. They got stamina. They're all wired up inside like you could flick a switch and they'd go off like a roman candle. Watch those guys, 'cause the little ones have had to fight all the harder for folks to take them serious.

'Lost some bucks?' I asked the kid.

The kid laughed. 'Lost some, won some, all the same shit to me.'

'You placin' or runnin'?'

'Little of both,' he said, and then he smoked some of his cigarette and looked up and down the street.

'You keep to your own turf or you cross the lines?'

'Flexibility,' the kid said, and then he turned and smiled at me, a weird kind of smile that moved his mouth but didn't reflect in his eyes. 'Secret of success is flexibility.'

I nodded. 'Is that so?'

'Sure is,' he said, and then he smoked his cigarette again.

'You a lone operator, or you got a crew?'

The kid turned. He looked at me askance with his sixty-five-year I-seen-it-all-go-to-hell-and-back eyes. 'You gotta whole suitcase of questions there mister, or you just short of folks to talk to?'

I took a step sideways. I could feel the pressure of the .38 in the waist of my pants. 'I got a mind to be conversing,' I said, 'and there ain't nothing more to it than that.' I figured I could pop the kid right where he stood before he even knew which way the wind was blowing.

The kid shrugged. 'Seems to me people spend an awful great deal o' time talking these days, time they could be spending doin' things a great deal more useful.'

'Such as?'

'Such as making the dollars, you know?'

I nodded. Couldn't disagree with him.

'So you makin' enough dollars?' he asked.

I laughed. 'Is there such a thing as enough?'

The kid laughed too. 'Name's Harry Rose,' he said. 'Maybe you heard of me?'

I shook my head. 'No more heard of you than I heard of your sister.'

The kid frowned. 'I ain't got a sister.'

'See, that's how much I heard of you then.'

The kid didn't take offence at the dig I gave him. 'So you were asking about a crew?' he asked.

'I was,' I said. 'Asked whether you were a loner or running a crew.'

'Sometimes a little of both, but I'm the kind of guy who figures that there's many a deal where two heads are better than one. Yourself?'

'Looking for a partnership,' I said. 'Looking to kick the ass of this neighborhood, shake it down some, you know?'

Harry Rose nodded, and then he turned and looked directly at me again with those painfully old eyes of his. 'Figure we could share a fifth of something dangerous and see whether there might be something mutually beneficial for us.'

The kid was okay. Had some balls. I nodded. 'Figure we could.'

'We'll walk a block or two, find some place and have a sit-down, okay?'

'Okay,' I said, and I started away from the stoop.

Kid's hand had been in his pocket all the time, and as we moved away he withdrew his hand, and there within it was a long stiletto blade. He folded the blade back into the handle and tucked the knife back in his pocket.

'You'd have had that through your eye before you ever reached the .38,' he said quietly, and though I thought he was kidding himself, though I thought that such an idea was both a wish and a prayer, there was something about the kid's cojones that impressed me.

We walked. Johnnie Redbird, six-foot tall, wide like a wall, dark-haired with two helpings of face, and Harry Rose, a good five or six inches shorter, fair hair greased back against his skull with bangs hanging down in front, handsome kinda kid if you didn't look directly at him, the pair of us like some mismatched circus act in sharp suits and cordovan wingtips, ugly hearts and ugly minds, and a darkness inside that resonated like a bell. Walked three blocks and sat in a bar, and we talked like there was little time to talk, all full of ideas and scams and twists and turns, all fired up with liquor and ready to kick everyone else six ways to Sunday if that's what it took to get what we wanted. We fell in like brothers, and just as there had been that unspoken and unidentifiable something between Harry Rose and Alice Raguzzi, so there was also something between me and this teenage kid from out of no-where.

And me? Well, I had my own story altogether. I was twenty-two years old, hailed out of Staten Island, but that was not my place of birth. My mother was a prostitute, kind of prostitute with a meter ticking under her skirt, from out of Cabarrus County, North Carolina. My father was an unnamed and forever unknown trick my mother often referred to as 'no better than dog puke', and the room I grew up in was a sweat-smelling, peeling-wallpaper, damp-floorboard honky-tonk where whore-hoppers and junkies came to alleviate the tensions of the world by knocking a hooker around and then fucking her in the ass. How many times did I hear my mother screaming? I lost count. Perhaps in some way there were similarities between my own childhood years and those of Harry Rose. Granted, my room was not in Auschwitz, and my mother did what she did for money, not for fear of her own life or the life of her son, but there were similarities enough for us both to have our view of the world twisted upon its axis and set on its head. People used people. Everyone was a prostitute, up for fucking someone else for money. Perhaps I believed that was the way it was meant to be. I don't know, and now I don't honestly care. My mother died when I was twelve, and that was the end of that.

Three months after her death I was held over by the Cabarrus County Sheriff's Department for stealing hubcaps from an auto shop. Truth be known I liked the way they looked. Truth be known I have no idea why I stole them, but I did, and I got the crap kicked out of me for my trouble. That was the start of a long and meaningful relationship with the law. I knew where they were at, and they knew where I was coming from, and so I left, hightailed it out of North Carolina as fast as I could and arrived in New York. Why Staten Island? Because that's where the train ended up, the train I hitched a ride on. I traveled with vags and hoboes, watched them rob their own traveling companions while those same companions slept, watched them drink their canned heat and sleep on Pittsburgh feathers, and dodge the harness bulls who came looking for them as the train hurtled into the darkness of an unknown future. I went into that future knowing nothing, wide-eyed and hungry just like Harry Rose, and believed that the America that waited for me could only have been better than the one I'd left behind.

There were days I didn't eat. Not a mouthful. There were days I stole more food than I could carry and gorged myself sick. And then there was the day I killed a man for seventeen bucks and change in a narrow back alley near Woodroffe's Poker Emporium. Seventeen and change was a lot of money, seemed reason enough to kill a man, and besides he was fat and he stank bad and he was just like the kind of full-of-shit wiseass who came down to the honky-tonk to take my mama for a ride. Killed him with a tire iron, beat his skull to pulp. Kicked what came out of his head around the alleyway and believed there had to be no better feeling in the world.

Later, when Harry told me about Weber Olson, there was something so similar in the way that we had felt, something that made us connect I s'pose. It wasn't that life counted for nothing, Harry had said, but that a life could always be traded. At that time a life was worth seventeen dollars and change to me. For Harry the life of Weber Olson had been about pride and honor and doing what was right. We saw things the way we saw them. Harry Rose saw them like some wide-eyed and terrified kid whose mother got herself beaten and tortured by some Nazi asshole. I saw them in a different light, but somehow that light came from the same spectrum and cast the same kind of shadows.

And out of that alleyway near Woodroffe's Poker Emporium I ran like the devil. Ran and hid. Knew there'd be questions, knew there'd be interest from the law, but I knew the law, and they knew me and my kind, and so I crossed the Bayonne Bridge into Jersey City and slept rough for a week in Liberty State Park. Made it as far as Hoboken, where I got caught robbing a newspaper vendor on Bergenline Avenue. Sent to Juvy. Helluva place. Thousand and a half crazy kids banged up with a bunch of pedophile screws. Lasted three weeks. Did a runner. Couldn't take any more shit from any of them. Place was a sprawling compound of low-rise buildings, high razor-wire fences, lights and towers and God only knew what. Screws didn't carry guns, hell we were just kids, but they managed their billy-clubs well, practised after lockdown, could throw a club like that and bring a running kid to the ground without even thinking about it. Went in that place with my eyes wide open. Could see the loopholes and the gaps within a few days. They would divide us into chain gangs, work parties of ten or twelve, all of us hooked up together with ankle shackles. We'd walk out of that place at five in the morning, take a hike for a mile, maybe a mile and a half, and then we would set down for a drink of water before we started work. Had us cleaning loose stones and gravel from the hot-top before the maintenance men came down to lay new bitumen. Smoke like Hades, fires

135

setting off in the scrub and bush as they pasted that shit down, and we were there to run with buckets of water and douse the edges down before things got out of hand and the National Guard had to come down.

It was hard work, sweated like a locomotive engineer, but it was during those times that they had to take our shackles off. Remember standing there at the side of the road, all mayhem breaking loose as a tree caught ablaze. Screws were hollering like banshees, smoke and filth shuddering out of the road, and all ten or twelve of us charged down there, yelling and hauling pails of water to put the fire out. Took a good hour to get things under control, and by that time I was black from head to foot, and before they had a chance to gather our crew together and do a tally another tree caught up on the other side of the road and everyone went off like a hare at the track.

I dropped to the ground, lay there for a moment while the side of the road cleared of kids and screws, and then I took handfuls of that black bitumen-soaked ash and started rubbing it into my skin, onto my clothes, my hands, my face, my shoes. Dropped back into the edge of the undergrowth and stood there for a while like a cigar store Indian. Could hardly breathe, not only because I didn't want to make a sound, but because I had that filthy shit in my eyes, my nose, my mouth. Nearly fainted from the heat, and because every pore of my skin was clogged with that mess I thought for a moment it might dry up and I would be stood like a statue until they came and found me upright and suffocated.

The fire went out of control, and in the chaos I took my chance to cut loose. I could move – it was hard work, but the more I ran the faster I got, waded through a river and cleaned off much of the shit that was covering me, and I just kept on running, running into tomorrow and another life.

Crossed the North River into Manhattan and hid out in a derelict tenement a stone's throw from Yankee Stadium near Webster and Tremont. Late nights could hear the crowds roaring. Knew what it was like to be alone. Whosoever knows the sound of loneliness, there's a man I can look in the eye. Whosoever knows the pain of hunger, three days of the sweet-fuck-all kind of hunger, there's a man I can talk to and gain some kind of sense. Perhaps these things, these little things, were other reasons me and Harry Rose connected on the same wavelength so many years later.

So I robbed and tricked and conned and gambled some kind of survival out of nothing at all. Run-ins with the law became a stock-in-trade, an occupational hazard, and by the time I finally collided with Harry I ran a booking sheet the length of the Constitution and a reputation second to not very many at all. I was bad news. It was good to be bad news. I had accomplished something. I had made a mark. I was dangerous. My reputation for willingness to go the extra mile preceded me, and I figured that anyone who crossed me was a man carrying stainless steel cojones. But stainless steel cojones are heavy, and when they drop they drop with a sound like thunder.

I told Harry these things, and Harry told his things back. We connected. We came together like two halves of the same bad penny. Could've been brothers. Could've been twins. Figured we could be anything we wished, and we wished for a great deal.

Like I said, it was early '55, a heady time, a prosperous time. The war was done with, those who survived were home, and America was convincing itself it was sophisticated and wealthy and cultured and great. We figured her for an overweight, varicose-veined, dipsomaniac widow, ready to lay down for any young stud who showed her the slightest interest. We possessed the interest, figured we'd fuck anyone for enough money, and America seemed as ready as anyone we knew.

So Harry, he took a girl, a centerfold sweetheart working out of a speakeasy on Vine, a girl who looked like heaven but couldn't have carried a tune in a bucket, and the three of us moved into the St Luke apartment and made it our home. I ran protection for Harry Rose, ran it well, like a professional, and when the boys came back short on change, when the dollar counts didn't square, I would make it my business to kick them from hell to breakfast until the books were straight again. Harry never asked me for details, I never gave them, and for all the years we would live and work together Harry would never hear a word of my methods – those things you perhaps would care to know, and perhaps some day I will tell you. Those are things I will speak of face to face, for to put them in writing would perhaps turn you away from me. I write only of things that I feel you need to know, and I need you to know about Harry Rose. Bear with me a while longer, this is all I ask.

Harry's girl, the singer, was called Carol Kurtz. 'Indigo Carol' to the regulars who trawled the gin-joints and speakeasies looking for easy lays and cheap laughs. She came from New Jersey, had left home for California three years before, made it back as far as New York and never took another step. Perhaps, had events conspired to find Harry Rose in some other bar on some other night, she might have eventually made it, but Harry saw her, and Harry got what he wanted, and what he wanted was Carol Kurtz. Some said she looked like Marilyn, others like Veronica Lake. To Harry she looked like paradise in cheap nylons and fake fur. He took her out of the life, he gave her money and freedom, he gave her a name and a face and a sense of belonging. She belonged to Harry Rose, and any man that cast an eye or two in her direction would find themselves sharing words with me and a snub-nosed .38. I figured Carol was Harry's way of finding Alice Raguzzi again. They couldn't have been more different in the way they looked, but in spirit they could have been twins. She was a smart girl, she knew which way her bread was buttered, and she treated Harry with the degree of respect he deserved. Harry treated her the same way back. He treated her like a human being, someone with a heart and mind and feelings. She was as quick as he in the way she figured shit out, and Harry liked that. She could tell a dirtier joke than any man I'd ever met, and if she set her mind to drinking you down she would go all the way. Never seen a girl put away so much liquor and still keep a tight tongue in her head.

I cared for Carol too, but not in the biblical sense. Carol was Harry's girl, Harry's all the way, and sometimes I'd see them together and recognize that I was a third wheel. I was business, Carol was pleasure, but that didn't make her any less than family. She held her own, I held mine, and Harry liked it just the way it was and I wasn't going to spoil it.

We did well – Harry and Carol and me – coming on like gangbusters down the sidewalks and streets of Queens, rolling out money like we owned the presses, like the Federal Reserve sat in our back pockets and the world was our mall. We drove limousines and Cadillacs, ate at De Montfort's and Gustav's where the busboys were called 'garçons' and the Rothschild came at forty bucks a bottle and never stopped flowing. This was the high life, the way it was always meant to be, and never a word was shared regarding Harry Rose's past, the years that came before, the horrors he had witnessed as a child and the color he carried in his heart.

And then it all changed: 1955 saw the death of Charlie Parker; a civil war in some godforsaken hellhole called Saigon; Ike laid up for seven weeks after a coronary, and James Dean committing vehicular suicide at twenty-four years of age. Sugar Ray took back his middleweight title in December, and Christmas was upon us once more. It was a cold season, bitter and resentful, and me and Harry took our business uptown for a few days to collect the dues on those who'd figured Carl Olsen would keep his belt. We were gone less than a week, five days in fact, but when we returned – all of seventy thousand dollars richer – Carol Kurtz had gone.

I was despatched, was gone three days, and when I carried the news home it was with a heavy heart and a blackened mind. I'd been the one to identify Carol Kurtz's raped and strangled body down at the city morgue, and I'd been the one to turn a few tongues when it came to naming names and sharing truths. Karl Olson, Weber's brother, a racketeer out of South Brooklyn, a man who was as tight as Kelsey's nuts with his dues and pay-offs, and thus hadn't earned any friends in Harry Rose's patch, had come down here with vengeance on his mind. *Out for revenge, you dig two graves*, the Sicilians said, *one for your mark and one for yourself.* Me and Harry Rose went out to Brooklyn, drove a plain sedan, inconspicuous in our dress and manner, and we soon found where Karl Olson had holed himself up.

Night of 23 December 1955, rain hammering on the sidewalks, lightning fracturing the darkness, we broke in through the basement windows of the Chesney Street Hotel, south side of Brooklyn. We took rope and hammers and a screwdriver. We slugged two of Olson's kickers, woke him up and tied him to a chair. We jammed his mouth with his own underwear before I smashed each of his ten toes one by one with a hammer and Harry Rose screwed holes through the guy's hands with the driver. When he passed out we woke him up again, and then we tortured him till he passed out once more. Finally his heart gave out, but Olson was a big man, a horse, and he'd lasted the best part of two hours before the pain got the better of him.

Me and Rose committed first-degree murder, vengeance yes, but murder all the same, and though Olson was never free with his dues when it came to his winners, he was nevertheless as prompt as a schoolma'am when it came to the law. Those who'd talked to me sang the same song for the law, and on Christmas Eve, snow falling on the roof of the St Luke apartment, the police busted wide the doors and took us both down. Backhanders aside, there was little that could be done for either me or Harry Rose; the gambling, the liquor, the fights and the hookers, the speakeasies and juke joints, the nose candy and mighty mezz passing beneath beer-stained tables in backstreet diners – these things could be forgotten for an extra hundred a month to the Widders 'n' Orphans, but not murder. Murder was as murder is, and there wasn't a way to see it any other how.

So I took the fall, not out of choice, but out of some sense of retribution for history. The cops were all too quick to nail me. There was word about the other things, the things from my past, and it seemed those things had caught up with me. Hell, they still had a ticket on me for running from Juvy, and they wanted to punch that ticket just so they could straighten their books and keep the house in order. Harry had been the one to grease their palms, not Johnnie Redbird, and when it came to a choice between nailing me or Harry there was in fact no choice at all. They wanted my head, they wanted their Johnny the Baptist, and hell if they didn't take it. Harry greased more palms than he ever had before, and with the right attorney and a paid-up judge they let it run on a second degree. I skipped the chair and took a lifer. Sent me out to Rikers Island to grow old in an eight by eight. And Harry Rose packed up St Luke, sold the leases on his bars and juke joints, and took his business south; disappeared for a handful of years, did all he could to help me survive through visits and dollars and favors owed. Loyalty was his strong point, had been his downfall in some respects, but Harry Rose would always remember the man who took the stand and swore the oath and bowed his head when sentence was passed.

On 25 April 1956 Rocky Marciano retired undefeated. Forty-nine wins out of forty-nine fights, and only five opponents had ever survived to hear the final bell. Rocky Marciano recognized when a good thing was done, and he got himself out.

Much like Harry Rose, a small kid out of someplace called Hell who'd only ever wished to be free. When we found each other we had pretty much next to nothing, and when we parted we parted much the same way.

'Easy come, easy go,' Harry Rose would say, but with Harry – as always – you could never tell how much of that was the truth.

There was silence for a little while after they'd finished reading. Annie had rested her head on Sullivan's shoulder the whole

141

time through, and it was only as he turned the last page that he realized his shoulder had gone to sleep.

Annie moved slowly and let him up. He stood there without words for a second, and then he smiled.

'Why do you think the old guy wants you to read this?' he asked.

Annie shrugged. 'I don't know Jack. I've been thinking about it, and I haven't liked what I've been thinking.'

Sullivan didn't respond.

Annie shook her head. 'When he first came there was something unsettling about him . . . like there was a way he would look at me as if he knew me.'

'You think – '

Annie stopped him. 'Let's not go there Jack . . . I don't even wanna know what you were gonna say. All I know is that we're not gonna be going there tonight, okay?'

'Okay Annie,' Sullivan said quietly. 'Okay.'

Sullivan stayed until just after midnight. Later, lying in her bed, Annie heard him talking to himself through the wall. It was a little while before she realized it was the TV. She was relieved; all she needed now was for Sullivan to lose the plot on her.

A half-hour or so earlier it had started raining again, and from the warm darkness beneath her quilt she had listened as the rain scattered its footprints across the roof above her. There was something so infinitely reassuring in that sound, something timeless and unique. She wondered if such a sound had been there through her childhood, and if she'd felt the same way. She remembered so little of those years, the handful she must have shared with her father. He must have come to her at night – all fathers did, didn't they? And he must have tucked her in, perhaps read her a story and then, turning out the light, he must have leaned close and kissed her forehead.

Good night Annie.

Goodnight Daddy.

Sleep tight . . . make sure the bugs don't bite . . .

I will Daddy . . . I will . . .

And then sleep would have come, and she would have remembered the security and strength of his presence. Perhaps he had smelled like David Quinn: leather and coffee and tobacco, a haunt of musk, but paternal, benevolent perhaps.

All those memories must be there, she thought as she drifted into sleep . . . *but for some reason I can't remember a single one . . .*

THIRTEEN

Another change of pattern. Seemingly insignificant to others, but in some way life-changing to Annie. She woke at her regular time, and though she had expected to think immediately of what she had read the night before with Sullivan it was not until she stood beneath the shower that the images came back to her. Strangely, they came with less intensity and emotion than previously. Was she becoming numb to what she was reading? In the place of discomfort and disturbance she found herself thinking of these men, Harry Rose and Johnnie Redbird, and wondering how it would have been to lead a life like that. A life so full of every human emotion, good and bad, terrifying and exhilarating, that there would be no room for worry and confusion. Life would come at such a pace you would merely have to ride with it, or get crushed beneath it.

She left at the same time on Friday morning, but walked the other way, just walked – without purpose or direction – down Cathedral Parkway onto Amsterdam, continued all the way to West 97th and turned left towards Columbus. The store was now four blocks behind her, her apartment seven or eight. She thought of John Damianka appearing at lunchtime with a mayonnaise-drenched sub, looking through the closed door of The Reader's Rest and wondering if Annie was sick. This was so unlike Annie, so unlike her completely.

She found herself smiling at the thought, and continued walking. At 96th she decided to take the subway, the 59th Street/Columbus Circle route, and when she boarded she found the train all but empty. Ordinarily she would have chosen a seat away from other passengers, but this time she sat down without thinking, looked up as the train pulled away, and noticed a young priest facing her. He was dressed in dark pants, a black shirt and white dog-collar, and over this a worn leather jacket. A suede bag, tassels on its lower edge, hung from his shoulder and protruding from the top of the bag was a mass of folded papers and notebooks. He was reading something and, peering at the book as inconspicuously as she could, Annie recognized the cover of *The Human Stain* by Philip Roth. She frowned, a little bemused, and then questioned her own preconceptions as to why a priest would not read such a book. Not that she had read it herself, but that he would be reading anything except the Bible or 'Notes Regarding The Book Of St Luke: Part One'.

She looked up. The young priest was looking back at her and he smiled, a warm and genuine smile, which she returned. He couldn't have been more than twenty-two or three, dark-haired, his face muscular and well defined. His eyes were a startling blue, and from the way he sat, his carriage and demeanor, he looked like the sort of man who would take care of himself physically. Break a sweat in the gym two or three times a week, perhaps play basketball, quarterback for the monastery?

He was handsome, that was for sure, and Annie found herself wondering what such a young man would do with all his hormones.

She blushed at the thought, and silently scolded herself for entertaining sexual thoughts about a priest.

'You have read this?' he suddenly asked.

Annie looked at him, surprise evident in her expression.

'Er . . . no, no I haven't read it,' she replied.

'It's quite something,' the priest said.

'Is that so?' she said, wondering what kind of conversation she would now have to endure with a priest.

'It's about a man of seventy-one who has an affair with a cleaning woman half his age. He sees her mopping the floor in

145

the post office one day, and he winds up having an affair with her. What d'you make of that, eh?'

Annie shrugged. Was he asking her about her moral standpoint on age differences? Or the fact that it had been an affair? She opted for the safest response she could think of and said, 'I haven't read it . . . I really couldn't say.'

The young and handsome priest obviously wanted to engage in conversation, because he smiled and said, 'I don't mean the book per se, I mean the idea of a seventy-one-year-old guy banging a thirty-four-year-old woman.'

Annie's mouth visibly dropped open. Had she heard him right? Did he say *banging*?

'I . . . I suppose it's all down to individual needs and desires.'

The priest winked at Annie. 'Sins of the flesh,' he said in a deep and serious voice. 'And why the hell not? You only live once, and if you get it right you go to heaven, though I can't say that even I know how you get it right all the time. If you screw it up you go burn in an everlasting pit of sulphur for eternity. What's there to lose? I'm getting off two blocks from here and you'll never see me again.'

The young priest laughed, shifted his tasselled suede bag from his lap and leaned forward. 'So whaddya reckon?' he asked. 'Would you get it on with a guy twice your age?'

Annie thought of Jack Sullivan, and then there was a fleeting image of Robert Forrester . . . She stopped at that thought, and it was not that his age seemed to present an inhibition, but that there was something almost *incestuous* about the thought. It would have been like having sex with her uncle . . . or her father? And then she spoke: 'I suppose it would depend on who it was, and whether or not I found them attractive.'

'Good enough,' the priest said, and then he leaned back in his chair and smiled a winning smile.

'Can I ask you something?' Annie said, feeling a little more confident, a little relieved that this conversation would only continue for a few minutes more.

'Shoot,' the priest said.

'Are you talking to me about sex because you can't ever have sex?'

The priest smiled, and then he started laughing, and the sound of his laughter seemed to fill the entirety of the carriage, drowning out the sounds of the wheels on the tracks beneath them.

'Of course I can have sex,' he said. 'I had sex this morning as a matter of fact . . . damned good sex if I might add. Figure I'll marry this girl . . . helluva girl who can have wild sex with a priest and not get into the moralistic guilt-ridden bullshit that seems to drive so many people out of their minds.'

Annie shook her head. This couldn't be a real conversation. This couldn't be a real priest. I mean, what was it with the book? What was the tasselled suede bag all about? What possible notes could a priest need to write down and carry around that would justify a shoulder bag?

Must remember to have intensely provocative conversations with single young women on the train. Must remember to mention the fact that not only can I have sex, but I can have damned good sex with a girl who doesn't do guilt trips. Say four Hail Marys and three Our Fathers after I jerk off in the chapel bathroom. A quart of milk, a dozen eggs, a tube of vaginal lubricant and three packs of Trojans. Oh, and don't forget to tell Father O'Reilly that Sister Martha's got a vibrator.

Annie smiled weakly, couldn't think of anything to say, and for a moment she looked to her left out of the window and wished that the priest would go away.

'I'm sorry,' he said quietly. 'Did I embarrass you?'

She shook her head. 'No, you just caught me a little off-guard.'

The priest sighed. 'I'm constantly being reprimanded for my outspoken views, you know?'

Annie eased back in her seat. She didn't want to look at him. Her mind was crowded with what kind of wild sex he might have had that very morning before he put on his shirt and collar, donned his leather jacket and shoulder bag, and walked down to the train.

But then who was she to judge anyone? Only last night she had stood naked at the kitchen window and watched a man across the street as he gawped at her. Perhaps, she thought, she should tell the priest.

Forgive me Father for I have sinned. I have never attended confession in my life, but I felt I should make an appearance because last night I stood naked in front of my window and let a complete stranger stare at my breasts. And to tell you the truth, after the first moment of embarrassment and shame, I actually felt something like an epiphany, a catharsis perhaps, like Paul on the road to Damascus. Oh, and another thing. When you first looked at me I thought about you sweating in a gymnasium, and I kinda figured you might be in pretty good shape under the collar and crucifix . . .

She didn't think so.

The priest glanced at his book once more, and then said: 'Reading this thing you can't help but think of the seventy-year-old guys you know, and it just seems crazy that the drive would still be there at that age.'

'Charlie Chaplin fathered his last child in his eighties,' Annie said.

The priest nodded. 'He sure did, you're right there . . .' he said. And then: 'My stop,' as the train drew to a halt. 'Take care,' he said as he rose from his seat and passed her. 'Remember that it's not a sin unless someone else gets hurt, eh?'

Annie looked up. The winning smile. The startling blue eyes. Beneath the shirt and collar a body that would sweat in the gymnasium. Wild sex with a guiltless girl first thing in the morning. She smiled weakly. 'I'll remember,' she said, and silently upbraided herself for her wicked thoughts.

The train moved away. She closed her eyes. She thought of David Quinn, and asked herself if anyone would get hurt, if she was merely living this thing called life, or if she was pushing the walls of the envelope a little too far. What would she do if she found herself in another close situation with David Quinn?

If he made an advance towards her that was anything more than an advance of friendship? Yes, she had kissed him, but she had kissed men before, kissed them more than once, but it had gone no further. It was her decision now, for she sensed that David would not hesitate, either that or she had read everything wrong. She could make it go whichever way she wanted. Would she back away? Would she ever so politely refuse his attentions? Or would she seize the moment? She believed she could not answer that question until the moment came, *if* it ever came, and even the thought of such a moment sent butterflies through the base of her stomach. The anxiety . . . no, the *fear* was there, but wasn't it this very same fear that had forever denied her what she really wanted? And how would one overcome such a fear? By living life perhaps? By doing the very thing that one was afraid of? She believed so. She actually believed it might be so. And then she asked herself why she'd ended up taking this train, why she'd sat facing the priest, and how he had possibly imagined she would want to discuss such a subject with him.

Your thoughts are almost exclusively responsible for the situations you get yourself into, Sullivan would have reminded her.

And of this she didn't wish to be reminded. It was Friday, she wanted the week to end so she would feel somewhat less guilty about leaving the store closed. She wanted some time and space. That was it: some time and space to be herself, to collect her composite parts together and gain some understanding of what might be happening to her. Something had changed, and though she could not clearly isolate the point of change she surmised that it had to be the effect of several factors. Her concern for Sullivan and the deal they had made, David Quinn of course, and then there was Forrester. He would return Monday evening, perhaps bring another letter, a fourth chapter of the book, and it was this story that had intrigued her. Haim Rosen a.k.a Harry Rose, a young man who had seemed to tear off handfuls of life and devour them before he even reached twenty. She wondered what might happen to him, what might happen to his friend Johnnie Redbird – even now imprisoned somewhere for the rest of his life for a killing that seemed altogether justified. Someone had been hurt then. Someone had died. But had it been right? She wondered what the priest might have said about that. Was it wrong for Elena Kruszwica to have killed the SS officer? Was there such a thing as justifiable homicide? Did it make it okay if killing someone balanced the scales of injustice, or prevented the loss of further life? She thought that perhaps it did, that God would understand such a thing. Johnnie Redbird and Harry Rose had killed Karl Olson because Olson had brutally murdered Carol Kurtz, and then Johnnie had taken the punishment for both of them, and thus Harry owed his life to Johnnie. What would happen to these people? She wished for them to be fictional characters, but then again somehow representative of all that was involved in being human. Love and loss, faith and passion, jealousy, anger, hatred, and finally death. These were heady and intoxicating themes, themes that played through her mind as the train sped through the theater district towards Chelsea. She figured to get off in Greenwich Village, to spend a couple of hours wandering without any real sense of purpose, and this – at that moment in her day, perhaps her life – seemed the most purposeful thing to do.

NYU Books, Barnes & Noble on Broadway, north-east into the antiques district, back along Fifth past Mark Twain's house towards Washington Square . . . somewhere in her wanderings the day dissolved, and as evening drew in around her, as her feet started to ache, she made her way back to the subway and went home.

There was something so familiar in the smells and sounds of the block as she walked up the stairs. Here was home, and home, after all, was surely the residence of the heart. Years ago, back in her childhood, she must have felt this way coming from school. Must have done. Couldn't remember. Had for some unknown reason folded all those memories neatly and stowed them in a hope chest never to resurface. Why had she chosen to forget? Was there something back there so frightening it had been safer to wipe all of it away with a single sweep? She didn't know, and at that moment didn't care. She was tired mentally and physically, and all she wished for was silence and warmth, perhaps the company of Jack Sullivan for an hour or so before she slept.

She knocked on his door but there was no reply. He was either dead drunk or out. If he woke or returned she would hear him, she'd invite him over, but that was later – after coffee and some TV, after taking time to think of nothing for a while.

She closed the apartment door behind her and threw her coat and scarf across the back of a chair inside the doorway. From the kitchen window she could see the lights across the street. There were several people over there. Perhaps the guy had invited a few friends over, bought a couple of six-packs and some pizza, see if the brunette with the towel on her head would get her clothes off again.

She smiled to herself, switched on the coffee percolator, and returned to the front room.

FOURTEEN

Annie?

She could hear breathing, and then there was the faint smell of alcohol and cigarettes.

'Daddy?' she murmured. 'Daddy?'

Annie . . . wake up . . .

She felt a hand on her shoulder, and though there was something pulling her firmly but so gently into a deeper recess of sleep, she fought it, fought to open her eyes, and saw Sullivan leaning over her, smiling, opening his mouth to say something else.

She raised her hand, silenced him. 'Give me a moment,' she whispered.

Turning somewhat awkwardly on the couch she sat up straight. She looked at Sullivan, her eyes unfocused, a taste in her mouth like sour copper, and she closed her eyes once more and breathed deeply.

'Coffee?' he asked.

She nodded. 'Please Jack.'

He was away a few minutes, and as he busied himself in the kitchen she adjusted herself to the here and now.

'Time is it?' she called out.

'A little before ten,' Jack replied, and appeared in the doorway carrying a small tray with cups and cream and sugar.

He set it on the table. 'You want it black?'

She shook her head. 'A little cream please.'

He pulled a chair over and sat facing her, handed her the coffee which she held for a while before she drank.

'You okay?' he asked, and there was that tone – the paternal tone he sometimes assumed when his concern for her welfare overrode his simple friendship.

She nodded. 'Fine,' she said. 'Tired maybe.'

'I can see that. You open the store today?'

'No, not today.'

'Where'd you go?' he asked.

'Downtown, Greenwich Village.'

'Any particular reason?'

'No, no particular reason.'

Jack smiled. 'And that's sometimes the best reason, is it not?'

'Sure . . . the best reason.'

Jack leaned forward. 'You want I should go? You wanna be alone?'

She shook her head. 'No, stay. Tell me a story.'

'A story?'

'Sure, tell me a story, but nothing gruesome . . . can't handle gruesome tonight.'

'Okay,' he said, 'let me think of a story.'

Annie settled back on the couch, pulled her knees up to her chest, held the coffee cup beneath her face to savor its warmth and aroma, and then closed her eyes. She imagined she was a little girl, that it was snowing outside, the wind howling back and forth across the front porch like some angry ghost demanding entry. Her father was here, keeping her safe, keeping her close, and he was telling her a story until she slept. Another thought entered then, tiny but significant: she sensed her father's presence, and even as she did so she pictured his face, and the face was that of Robert Forrester. She pushed the thought away, but it was tenacious and unforgiving. She forced herself to concentrate on the sound of Sullivan's voice to the exclusion of all else, and that sound enabled her to focus her mind.

'March of 1969,' Sullivan said. 'It was March of '69, four months after returning from Vietnam, and I went to Haiti. Haiti is a republic in the West Indies, part of Dominica, used to be part of the Spanish colony of Santa Domingo, and then the

153

French came, brought African slaves with them, and they worked sugar plantations in the north. Until the rebellion in the 1780s they were one of the world's richest coffee and sugar producers, and then the French and British interfered, there was war between the blacks, the mulattos and the white Haitians, and it wasn't until 1804 that the blacks secured their freedom and they became part of the Americas. They were raised on a diet of Catholicism, but always there was voodoo. Behind every part of the social and cultural fabric was the ghost of voodoo. They practised obeah – sorcery – a mix of Catholic symbolism, alongside the magic and spells of the shamans who came with the French from Africa. The religious beliefs that came from Africa were called Gine, and the Haitians believed that spirits called Iwa traveled with the shamans, and the Iwa could assume right of possession over someone's body and communicate through them. There were people called the Medsen Fey, the leaf doctors, and they believed they could commune with the spirits of plants.

'We came in at Port-au-Prince. I was shell-shocked, still recovering from the things I'd seen and heard in Vietnam, and there was an older man with us, a journalist from England called Len Sutton. Len had been everywhere a man could go, he was maybe fifty or fifty-five, and there was this thing he kept doing, like there was something inside his chest, some-thing that made his body tense up and started him coughing. He'd been to every doctor, people in Harley Street in London, but according to the medical guys there was nothing wrong with him. You could see him double up sometimes; looked like a man in the middle of a coronary seizure and there was nothing anyone could do.'

Annie shifted slightly, tugged her knees up again and rested her head on her folded arms.

'We checked in to a hotel on the outskirts of Port-au-Prince,' Sullivan went on. 'Len was with me, we shared a room, and twice in the four or five days we were there I saw him seize up. These seizures would last anywhere from ten minutes to half

154

an hour or so, and he would just lie there in agony, couldn't speak, could barely move, and then it would pass as sudden as it had come. I happened to mention this to one of the guys downstairs, a black Haitian called François L'Ouverture, and he said he would call his sister. Is your sister a doctor? I asked him, and François starts laughing, laughs like a horse, and then he tells me that his family line went all the way back to Toussaint L'Ouverture, the man who led the slave rebellion in the early 1800s and secured freedom for the blacks. We have a powerful line, he told me. We are Medsen Fey. What? I said. Medsen Fey, he said. The leaf doctors. And we can cure your Englishman if his spirit is open to obeah.

'I told Len about this guy and what he'd said, and Len told me he was open to anything and everything if it would handle the pain. So I spoke to François again, he went to get his sister, and this little girl comes. François calls her LouLou Mambo – couldn't have been more than twelve or thirteen, but there's something about her, something in her eyes that makes me feel like I'm talking to someone who's eighty years old and has seen everything there is to see. She tells me and Len that they have family Iwa, zanset yo' she calls them, and these are ancestral spirits that have followed their family line since they came from Africa. She tells us that the ancestors understand human pain because they were once human themselves, and they are touched by the power of the Iwa and can heal people directly through the Medsen Fey.

'So this little girl, she sits beside Len Sutton. She touches her hand to his forehead, and then she tells him that an angered spirit is inside him. It is one of your own ancestors, she says. One of your ancestors was killed by a bullet through the chest. Len Sutton's mouth drops open. His eyes wide like a jack o'lantern. My grandfather, he says. My grandfather was shot in the chest in the war. 1901, the Boer war. My father was thirteen years old when he died, he says. And then the little girl proceeds to tell Len Sutton the name of his grandfather and how he died, that he was a good soldier, but that he fought for the wrong reasons, and it was his belief that he was fighting for these reasons that killed him. He felt guilty, the little girl says, and as such he brought his own death upon himself. So what can I do? Len Sutton asks her. The little girl smiles. Do? she says. What can you do? It is not what you do Englishman, it is who you are. You are here for the wrong reasons, and there is a fear inside you that you have spent your whole life doing things for the wrong reasons, and when you accept this truth and live your life for the right reasons your pain will cease.

'Len looks like someone's slapped him across the head. François comes closer, and he tells us that his sister is a powerful Medsen Fey, that she is speaking the truth, that her met-tete, her master of the head, is responsible for guiding her from birth to death. He tells us that each Medsen Fey is born as a child of a particular Iwa, and that the Iwa lives in the blood and is their guide and protector. He says her Iwa has guided many people back to health and away from madness, and that if the Englishman wants to suffer no more pain he should follow LouLou Mambo's advice.

'I'm into all of this, I believe every word that's being said, but Len isn't so sure. He's a journalist, has been all his life, and this little girl's telling him he must give up his life, do what he knows to be right, and his pain will go away. François leaves then, takes his sister with him, and Len tells me he thinks it's all crazy bullshit, and just as the words are leaving his mouth he gets hit with this seizure, such pain that it rolls him off the bed and onto the floor. He's howling in agony down there, and I'm standing over him like a retard ready to piss myself, not knowing what to say or do. I think about what the little girl said, and then I lean over Len and I'm shouting at him. Give it up! I holler. Give up your job! Call the newspaper and tell them you quit! Okay! he's shouting back at me . . . Okay, I quit! And as soon as the words come out of his mouth the pain stops. Just like that it stops, and Len Sutton's eyes open wide, and he starts to cry.

'Later I asked him why he became a journalist. He tells me he doesn't know, never understood it because he hated the job really. I asked him what he wanted to do with his life, what he felt would make him happy, and he told me that he'd always wanted to work with animals, train dogs or horses or something . . . maybe buy a farm in England and grow stuff. I told him he should do that, that he should do what LouLou Mambo told him to do, and he said he would.

'Three days later he left, went back to England, and I never heard of him again.'

Annie smiled, her eyes still closed, her knees still up against her chest.

'But,' Jack Sullivan whispered, 'I'm sure he lived happily ever after.'

'True story?' Annie asked.

'True as daylight,' Sullivan said.

'You've had some life haven't you Jack,' Annie said, a statement more than a question.

'Some life,' he replied, 'but not all the life I would have liked.'

Annie opened her eyes. She leaned forward and straightened her legs. 'What do you miss?' she asked. 'What would you have done differently?'

'A family,' Sullivan said. 'Always wanted a family, but I didn't think it was fair to put a family through the torment of never knowing where I was and if I was okay.'

'But you did what you did because you felt it was right.'

'Must've done,' he said.

'Must've done? What d'you mean?'

Sullivan leaned back in his chair and sighed. 'You get to my age and you look back at things. You look at what you did and what you said to people, you ask yourself if you got your priorities right, if there was something else you could have done to make things better, and after a while you come to the conclusion that it was what it was, and even if there had been something you could have done differently there's no way you can go back and change it. It's a kind of philosophical

157

resignation if you like. So you deal with it, and kind of hope that you might come back again a little wiser and get another chance.'

Annie smiled. 'It's a nice thought.'

'There is one thing though,' Sullivan said.

Annie raised her eyebrows.

'I can honestly say that I haven't had a "what if . . . " life.'

'A what if life?'

He nodded. 'Sure, you know what I mean. The kind of life where you look back and ask yourself endlessly what if you had done so-and-so, what if you had said yes instead of no, and having spent so much time with people who were dying I can tell you a single, simple truth. When people know they're gonna die, when they really know they're gonna die, you know what they talk about?'

Annie shook her head.

'What they talk about is what they didn't do, all the things they didn't do. They don't talk about what they did, where they went, who they knew . . . they talk about the places they didn't see, the girl they should have married, and if you believe a twelve- or thirteen-year-old Haitian girl called LouLou Mambo then the only things that ever really hurt people are the things they knew were right, and then they compromised.'

Sullivan assumed a serious expression. 'Like you,' he said.

'Like me?' Annie asked, frowning.

'I said something the other night, a deal . . . and I want to hold you to that deal.'

'You'll stop drinking if I get serious with someone?'

Sullivan shook his head. 'I'm not talking about serious . . . serious never worked for me. I'm just talking about something with substance, something that has some kind of meaning for you.'

Annie smiled.

'What?' Sullivan asked. 'The three-book guy?'

'The three-book guy,' she replied.

'You saw him again?'

'I did.'

'And did you . . . you know?'

'Did I fuck him?' Annie asked.

Sullivan started to laugh. 'Jesus Annie O'Neill, I can't ever remember hearing you use that word.'

'Well I did. There we go. Fuck. Fuck and fuck and fuck. And to answer your question, no I didn't . . . but there's time.'

Sullivan nodded approvingly. 'Good enough,' he said.

'So don't be buying any more fifths of Crown Royal, okay? I think you got enough in your apartment to keep you going.'

'You're keeping the deal?'

Annie smiled. 'It was your deal Jack Sullivan . . . you're the one who has to keep the deal.'

'Right,' he said. 'You make it through this, make it work Annie, and I'll never drink another drop.'

Sullivan reached out his hand. Annie took it, held it for a moment, and then she smiled.

'You're a good friend Jack,' she said. 'Best friend I ever had.'

'Likewise,' Sullivan said, and then he reached up and touched her face, held his hand against her cheek for a moment. 'So when d'you see this man again . . . what was his name?'

'David, David Quinn . . . and I don't know when I'll see him again.'

'You have his number?'

She shook her head. 'No, no number.'

Sullivan frowned. 'This doesn't sound too promising.'

Annie smiled. 'He'll show up Monday or Tuesday at the store.'

'If you show up yourself.'

'I'll be there Monday . . . I have another reader's club meeting, right?'

'Right,' Sullivan said. 'Another meeting. Hell, you're getting something of a whirlwind social calendar, young lady.'

'I am,' Annie said. 'Following your advice, right?'

'Take care huh?'

'I'm not a little girl any more Jack.'

Sullivan was silent for a moment, and then he looked directly at her. 'Sometimes you are,' he said, and though there was nothing critical or offensive in the way he said it Annie felt a momentary irritation.

'I can look after myself,' she said, her tone a little sharp.

'I know you can,' Sullivan replied. 'But I wanna make sure someone else does too.'

'I'll be fine Jack.'

Sullivan smiled. 'I'm here if you need me . . . always here Annie.'

'I know you are Jack Sullivan . . . my ancestral guiding spirit, my Iwa.'

'Your Iwa,' he said, and smiled. 'Anyway, I'm outta here . . . got a good five or six bottles to drink before you get laid.'

Annie dragged a cushion out from behind her and threw it at him as he reached the door. He ducked it, opened the door, and closed it behind him, laughing.

'Howl like a banshee so I know when to stop drinking,' he shouted from the hallway.

'Asshole!' she shouted back, but Jack's door had slammed shut.

FIFTEEN

Annie opened the store Saturday morning. Late, but nevertheless she opened it. She went not out of obligation or desire, but
because she hoped David would come. Closing the door
behind her she saw a plain envelope on the mat, she picked
it up, turned it over, and there in a neat hand was written
Annie.

She knew what it would say before she opened it.

Friday 30th.

> *Dear Annie,*
> *Got a call. Have to be away. I think for just a couple of days.*
> *Should be back in the early part of next week. Take care.*
> *Love, David.*

She read through the note again, her eyes finding the last two
words and concentrating on them: *Love, David.*

Was this merely the routine salutation found at the end of so
many informal notes . . . or did it mean something else?

Love, David.

And did it matter what it meant? This was a hard question, a
question for the heart, the soul perhaps. Did it really mean
anything to her?

The question was asked; the answer came swiftly. It did
matter. It did mean something, or rather she *wanted* it to
mean something. There were no perfect human beings, men
or women, and there was enough about this man David Quinn
for her to feel that something could be built here. Wasn't it

161

always a risk? Wasn't there always some chance of losing? Of course there was. Surely – *surely* – that was life.

She returned the note to the envelope, held it in her hand for a moment, and then tucked it into the pocket of her jeans. She had worn jeans today for a reason, jeans and a tee-shirt. Today she possessed a figure, a form, some contours. Today she was not a shapeless sweater and calf-length woollen skirt. She felt more like a woman than she had in some considerable time, and she resigned herself to feeling like this alone.

She logged stock, she updated her inventory, but for some reason she paused with each battered paperback in her hand, read the flyleaf notes, in some cases the acknowledgements and tributes.

This book is dedicated to Martha, who was always there.

This book was written for many people, many of whom I cannot name, but safe to say that they all possessed their own sense of magic, and for this magic I owe them much more than I could ever repay.

For Daniel, Kelly and Frederick.

For my agent, LeAnnie Hollander.

For my editor at Huntseckers, Gerry Liebermann.

Most of all to my wife Catherine, who made me believe I could.

Annie traced her finger over the names, and imagined who they might be, what they might have said, the times they listened, advised, criticized, applauded. She gave them faces and mannerisms, quirks of character and idiosyncrasies. Gerry at Huntseckers wore Homer Simpson socks with a Brooks Brothers suit. He smoked cheroots that smelled awful, and he insisted on having his office window wide even when it was five degrees outside. These were people with lives, *real* lives, and so real were their lives that they possessed sufficient reality for it to overflow and affect the lives of others. They had dreams, and in some small way both David Quinn and Robert Franklin Forrester had opened a door to her own dreams.

This time she was determined to walk through it, head held high, eyes wide open, teeth gritted, fists clenched, and take on whatever came her way. Too long in the background, too long skulking in the shadows waiting for someone to call her name and have her come forward. If you wanted it, you had to go and get it. Surely this was the case? Both Harry Rose and Johnnie Redbird seemed to have such a belief as their guiding philosophy. And Sullivan would have agreed with them on that point if nothing else, and Sullivan was perhaps the closest she had to a real friend. If you could not trust your friends, then whom could you trust? David had showed her something – his experiment, his parlor trick – but there was something of substance in what he had done. And then she had asked him to kiss her, and kiss her he did, no more, no less. She had trusted him, and he had not violated that trust. A small thing, but didn't everything begin with something small, and then grow? And Forrester. Was he to be trusted? She knew nothing of either of them, but each in his own way – David with his words, Forrester with letters from her father and a story that touched the edges of her imagination – had served to strip away some of the façade, the face she had worn for the world for as long as she could recall. It was not her own face – it was a composite of all the things she'd ever believed people wished her to be, like a suitcase, and dependent upon the event there was always an identity within that suitcase that she could wear for the occasion. Sometimes they suited her, sometimes not.

She considered these things and a great deal more besides, and with each passing silhouette beyond the door she wished the bell would ring, that someone would enter her store, her *life*, and bring with them a little of the outside world in which she could share.

But the morning disappeared without visitors, and she wondered how much of this disconnection she had created for herself.

A little before one Annie locked up and returned home. She sat for a while watching some old black-and-white movie on the TV, defeated a pint and a half of cappuccino ice cream, and when she was done she wandered across the hall to call on Sullivan.

He wasn't home, more than likely in a bar down the street, and considering the possibility that she might walk down there and join him she stood on the landing in the silence of the house.

There was a sound below. The street door opened, slammed shut, and then there was the sound of footsteps on the risers.

They were not Sullivan's footsteps. His footsteps she had heard several times a day every day she'd lived here. This was someone else, and as there were only two upper floor apartments – her own and Sullivan's – the person now hurrying up the stairs had to be a stranger.

A taut sense of apprehension invaded the skin across the back of her neck. She glanced to her right, the door to her own apartment, and even though the impulse to hurry inside was there, to close and lock and deadbolt the door behind her, there was also something that forced her to stay right where she was.

What are you doing Annie?

Her mother's voice.

Get inside girl, get inside . . . you're inviting trouble . . . you don't know who it is . . .

Annie clenched her fists involuntarily.

She took a step backwards, almost as if she wished to fold silently into the shadows at the head of the well. She took a second step back, a third, and found the wall behind her. It was cool and hard and unyielding.

She had felt like this before. This was not a new sensation.

The footsteps gathered speed, gathered sound, and soon there was nothing she could hear but the hammering of those feet on the risers as they turned the last corner and came up towards her.

A sound escaped her lips.

Where had she felt this?

And then it came. David's apartment. The trick he had played on her.

She looked at her door, cursed herself for not rushing inside it and closing it tight behind her.

She felt her skin go cold and tight. Again that sense of rushing nausea building in her chest. She started to breathe – fast and shallow – and when she closed her eyes she saw that same depth of blackness she'd seen when she was blindfolded.

She saw the shadow of the intruder . . .

Perhaps the guy from across the street had come to check out where his showgirl has gotten to . . .

And then she found herself sliding down the wall to her haunches, her knuckles white, the fingernails of her right hand embedding themselves in the flesh of her palm.

She closed her eyes, she held her breath, she waited for the intruder to make himself known, to do whatever he had come to do . . .

The sound of footsteps was like a frightened heartbeat . . . her own heart even now trip-hammering in her chest, getting louder, faster, and hearing the blood rush in her ears . . .

This was just like David's apartment . . . just like it, but worse, because this time she could hear someone coming, and this time they were coming to get her . . .

They were seconds away, less than seconds, less than the heartbeat that was even now deafening her . . .

'Annie?'

The sound that escaped her lips as she opened her eyes was almost a scream. A sound of shock and surprise. A release of bottled emotion.

She looked up.

'Annie . . . what the hell are you doing down there?'

'David?'

He took a step forward, was standing over her with his hand outstretched.

She took it, her eyes wide, the color drained from her face, and when she stood she could do nothing but let his arms enfold her and pull her tight.

'What are you doing here?' she asked. 'What are you doing here David?' Her voice was tinged with fear.

'Jeez, you're shaking,' he said. 'Let's go inside Annie,' and then he stopped, hesitant, looking both left and right in turn.

'This one,' she said, indicating her apartment, and without pausing he hurried her into the apartment and closed the door behind them.

'I got your note,' she said, fumbling to retrieve it from the pocket of her jeans even as she was speaking.

'The job was canceled,' David said. 'I think they had someone closer . . . I got a call and they canceled the job.'

He stood for a moment, his eyes on Annie, and then looking around the room he started to nod his head. 'This is one hell of a place Annie . . . this is really something. Did you do these colors and things yourself?'

She nodded, surprised and bemused that he would notice such a thing at all, even more so that he seemed to have forgotten how shaken up she was.

He looked back at her. 'Christ,' he said. 'I really gave you a shock, didn't I?'

'A little,' she said, and then she started to smile. She cut the smile short, she frowned, tilted her head to one side. 'Anyway, how come you're here . . . how did you find out where I lived?' A fleeting moment of disturbance, the sensation of being threatened, invaded. She had not known this man when she had gone to his apartment, and now he was here, here within her sanctum sanctorum, and truth be known she knew him no better.

'The phone book,' David replied. 'You're the only "A. O'Neill" that lives in this suburb.'

Annie nodded. She was still shaken, visibly so.

'I can go,' he said. 'I went down to the store to see if you were still there but you'd closed up. If you want me to go I can go right now. I'm sorry if – '

Annie raised her hand. 'It's okay . . . I don't know what happened. I went out to check on Sullivan and then I heard someone coming up the stairs, and for some reason I just stood there like a halfwit.'

'Sullivan?' David asked. 'Is that . . . is that like your cat or something?'

Annie started laughing. 'Sullivan is nothing like my cat David . . . Sullivan is my neighbor.'

'Oh, right, your neighbor . . . so where's the cat?'

'The cat? I don't have a cat.'

David frowned.

Annie laughed again. 'No cat David. Just a neighbor. Neighbor's name is Sullivan . . . end of story.'

David nodded, still frowning. 'So you don't want me to go?'

'No, I don't want you to go.'

'Which means that you want me to stay, right?'

Annie shrugged. 'What is this . . . stupid day or something? Yes, I would like you to stay. Take off your coat, sit down, make yourself at home. You want some tea, some coffee?'

David took off his coat. 'Some tea, yes, that would be good.'

He set his coat down on the chair inside the front door, looked around once more, and then crossed the room. He sat at the table where Annie and Sullivan had spent so many hours shooting the breeze, unfolding their thoughts for one another and airing them in that same mellow current.

Annie paused in the doorway to the kitchen, and standing there for a moment she was surprised at how different the entire room seemed to appear with someone new inside it.

David looked up at her. 'What?' he asked.

She shook her head and smiled. 'Nothing David . . . relax, take it easy okay?'

'Okay,' he said. 'Sure . . . I'll relax. You okay now?'

She nodded. 'I'm fine, just fine.'

Annie left him there amongst her co-ordinated colors and tell-tale possessions while she made tea. She was no more than a few minutes, but when she returned she found him looking through the CD rack.

'Sinatra,' he said.

'You like Sinatra?'

He turned and smiled at her. 'I *love* Sinatra.'

She looked at his face. It was genuine. David Quinn loved Frank Sinatra.

'Put some on if you want.'

David took the CD from the case, turned on the player, the amplifier, and within a moment Frank was joining them in the room with his inimitable rendition of 'I've Got You Under My Skin.'

'Los Angeles, 30 April 1963,' David said.

Annie frowned and sat at the table. 'What was?'

David walked across the room and sat facing her. 'This record.'

She shook her head. 'You know that? When and where it was recorded?'

'I do,' David replied. 'Do you think that's really pathetic?'

She smiled, laughed a little. She was touched. He had shared something with her, something personal. 'You're asking me if I think that the fact that you know when and where this track was recorded is pathetic?'

'Uh huh . . . a bit, maybe?'

She frowned and looked serious. 'David, it's possibly the most pathetic thing I've ever heard.'

For a moment he was speechless, and then Annie started laughing, and then David Quinn was laughing too, and it seemed that Frank was looking over them and crooning 'I've got you deep in the heart of me . . .' like it had been written especially for this moment.

And then there was no-one making a sound but Frank, and though Annie O'Neill had lived in the apartment for the best part of seven years, though everything in it had been chosen by her, though each cushion and drape, each chair and lamp had been purchased after considerable thought and consideration, there was something entirely strange about her surroundings.

She looked across the table at David Quinn, a man she had met only eight days before, and there was something so meaningful in the fact that *he* was there. Richard Lorentzen had been here, as had Michael Duggan, but they had never served to change the way she felt inside her own home. David Quinn had been there all of five minutes, and something *had* changed. Something definitely *had* changed.

'Thank you for coming,' she said. 'Despite how pathetic you are, I appreciate your coming.'

David smiled, reached out his hand, and closed it over hers. He leaned forward.

'Kiss this pathetic little man would you Annie?' he whispered.

The moment was there, right there in front of her. It was the moment of which she'd thought on the train after the priest had gone. It was this moment that required her decision, because now she could choose – to stay with it, or to let it go.

She looked at David, looked at his eyes, looked *through* them to see what lay on the other side, and tried to hear the language his expression was speaking. There was no way to tell such things, but it would always be like this, and if she turned back now there would be the 'what if' life that Sullivan had spoken of. She would look back at this moment, and she *would* regret it.

She felt butterflies in her stomach. The palms of her hands were sweating. She felt the grip of tension through every muscle in her body. She closed her eyes slowly, opened them, took a deep breath. She asked herself one last time if this man was a blessing or a threat . . . but the answer didn't come, and she knew that had she waited for eternity there would always be silence out there.

And then Annie O'Neill leaned forward, touched his face, closed her palm over his cheek, opened her fingers and ran them through his hair, and then she pulled him towards her.

The sensation was somehow different, and yet somehow the same as before – the time in his empty warehouse apartment. This time it was *her* home, here amongst *her* things. And simply because it was here it was somehow more meaningful, and when her lips touched his, when she felt the pressure of his face against hers, when she sensed the rush of emotion and feeling that came with it, it was all she could do to restrain herself from tearing his shirt from his back and dragging him to the floor.

Eventually – a lifetime, perhaps two – she withdrew from him.

He continued to hold her hand, and when she rose he rose with her, and when she walked he followed her without question, and leading him past the kitchen towards the door on the far side of the room there was nothing in his expression that questioned what she was doing or why.

And once through the door, her bed behind them, clean clothes scattered across the end of the mattress and over the deep armchair that stood beside it, she pulled him close once more, could feel the pressure of her breasts against his chest, the ache that had started in the base of her stomach, the tension in her throat . . .

His hands were on her waist then, his fingers pressing into her, and then he slipped his thigh between her legs and she closed her legs around him, and seeming to float backwards she felt the backs of her shins touch the edge of the mattress, and with her right hand she swept the clothes off the bed onto the floor and collapsed.

He collapsed with her, and she could feel his weight over her, but somehow weighing nothing, and then his hand was sliding from her waist to the top of her leg, and with his fingers he was tugging her tee-shirt free from the waistband, and when it was free he seemed to lift it from behind, and with one swift motion she felt her tee-shirt slide up over her head and vanish. She found his shirt buttons, slid them free from their eyes, and then he was helping her, and she could feel the warmth of his skin, the rough texture of hair on his chest . . .

Her jeans, her bra, his pants, his shorts beneath, his shoes, his socks, her socks, the clean clothes from the mattress, and something up close and personal amidst all of this, and breathless beneath his weight for a second, and then released but enclosed, and feeling the weight of his head on her stomach, his hands over her breasts, her nipples swollen, her back arched, and then his tongue tracing a fine line from her navel downwards, downwards . . .

And a warm rushing sensation inside her, like a slow-motion flood of something indescribable as his mouth touched her, as his fingers brushed against her, found their way inside her, deep inside her . . .

And then she was turning, and she could feel the muscles in his thighs tensing as she touched him, as she closed her hand around him, as she kissed his stomach, his back as he turned, and then sitting up she closed her mouth around his nipple, and she could feel him sigh without sounds, and then lowering her head she took him inside her mouth, and it meant something, more than it had ever meant before, and never had she felt so close as this to someone . . .

From the edge of the mattress he turned her onto her back, and then he was over her, his hands around her, gripping her waist now, and leaning up he pressed himself against her leg, and then sliding sideways he entered her, and she could feel him within her, deeper, ever deeper now, and there were tears in her eyes, and she was laughing she seemed to remember, and then there was motion, and within that motion there was something that could only ever have been described as love . . .

At least she believed this was love, for she had never felt something like this . . . could never *remember* ever feeling something like this.

And it seemed to go on forever. And she didn't want it to end.

More than anything in the world, she didn't want it to end.

But it did, and then there was silence but for their breathing, and out beyond the window rain began to fall.

She didn't make a sound, didn't wish to fracture the atmosphere for a second. She closed her eyes, pressed her face against his chest, and lay silent as he ran his fingers through her hair.

SIXTEEN

An hour passed, perhaps more, before she stirred. She turned slightly, looked up at David's face. His eyes were closed, his breathing deep but gentle. He was sleeping. Here among the mid-afternoon ghosts of something they had shared, he was sleeping.

She slid out from beside him, slipped on his shirt, and tip-toed to the kitchen to pour a glass of juice from a bottle in the refrigerator. Standing there, in front of the window, the rain sheeting down against the glass, she was conscious of a smile creeping across her face, taking over her whole expression.

This was something new, something different she believed, and though their lovemaking had been spontaneous, im-pulsive, she also felt that it had perhaps been the rightest thing she had ever done. She was not *in love*, not so naïve as to consider such a thing, but she truly felt there was enough about this man that she *could* love him. He made her feel important, and – truth be known – she believed the feeling was reciprocated. They were both odd ones out, anachronisms within their own lives. She knew almost nothing of him, a little of his family and what he did for a living, but beyond that very little. It didn't matter, such things would come in time, for wasn't falling in love – or *rising into* love – all about creating the here and now and building from that into the future? The past was the past. The past was gone, best forgotten, and for now she believed that the past had been worth it: it had given her this, and this was something which could make her truly happy.

Somewhere beyond the far reaches of her thoughts she heard

the street door open and close. Footsteps on the stairs. Sullivan, unmistakably. And when he reached the landing she heard him pause, and then – perhaps sensing the need to leave Annie undisturbed – she heard his apartment door open and close. She closed her eyes and smiled again.

Another sound. A sound behind her.

She turned, the glass of juice in her hand, and saw David standing there. He was naked, and for the first time she saw the shape of his body, the way he looked in the late afternoon light, and she felt herself react to his nakedness, the feeling inside her that she wanted to feel that same nakedness close against her once more.

'Fuck me,' she whispered. 'Fuck me again David.'

He turned.

Annie set the glass on the counter and followed him, un-buttoning her shirt – his shirt – and letting it fall to the floor as she went.

This time it was different. Passionate. Heated. Angry almost.

She remembered clawing at his back, his stomach, digging her fingernails into his thighs as he thrust himself into her time and again.

She remembered feeling the headboard smacking against the top of her head, but she didn't care, didn't care at all, for the pain she felt was drowned out by the sound of her own voice as she moaned beneath David's weight. At one moment he turned her over onto her hands and knees, and then he was behind her, and with his one hand finding her breast, the other gripping her shoulder, he pushed himself into her and kept going until she felt she would collapse.

Sweat ran down her forehead and into her eyes. She bit her own lip until she tasted blood. She clenched her fists until she felt her fingernails would puncture her skin, and then the sound from the base of her throat was like some animal lost in a wilderness of emotions and feelings and sensations.

And then she did collapse, and David rolled sideways, and

still holding her from behind he thrust back and forth in slow motion, his thighs against her buttocks, sweat adhering to their skin, his hand between her legs, stroking her, massaging her, kissing her neck, her shoulders, his fingers finding her nipples and pinching them until the pain was almost more than she could bear. And then there was that warm release inside her, every muscle tensed, every nerve and sinew rushing with electricity, and as he moaned she moaned with him, and the sound was like one voice echoing up against itself and then separating into two.

'Oh Christ, oh Christ,' he was gasping, and rolling onto his back he withdrew from her, and turning to face him she held his hand, pressing it then between her legs, using his fingers to touch her, pushing them inside her. She rolled onto her front, and then kneeling up she straddled his chest, leaning forward and kissing his face, holding handfuls of his damp sweaty hair, and then she felt his hands around her waist, pulling her forward, her own arms outstretched until she felt the cool surface of the wall behind the bed against her palms. Pulling her forward again he leaned back, and with one final movement she felt his face between her legs, his mouth beneath her, his tongue finding its way inside her. Looking down she watched him, his eyes closed, his expression intent, and before long she could watch no more, aware of nothing but the feeling inside her, the sensation of everything within rushing to escape from between her legs. She screamed, a scream of ecstasy as she hurtled over the edge of anticipation into orgasm. He kept going, his tongue pressed up inside her until she couldn't bear any more. She rolled sideways, collapsed beside him, and turned to hold his face between her hands. His skin glistened with her sweat, with her passion, with everything she was, everything she had become within these moments.

She smiled. She closed her eyes. She pressed her lips against his. His arms enclosed her, pulled her tight.

And then they slept once more.

When Annie woke it was dark outside.

The rain had stopped, but still she could hear the wind playing around the edges of the building and against the windows. She pulled herself closer against David. He stirred, murmured, shifted slightly, and then relaxed. He did not wake, and for this she was grateful.

Lying there in the semi-darkness, the room warm, the gentle rising and falling of David's breathing beside her, she asked herself why she had so long divorced herself from such a life as this. This was real, this was what life was all about – the knowledge that there was someone there, someone who wanted you as much as you wanted them. She gazed at his profile and wondered if it was her decision alone that had brought him into the store that day, a day only a little more than a week before. If we were all responsible for the actions and events of our lives, then David was responsible for this as well. He must have wanted something such as this as much as she had. Such a thought comforted her: she had not been alone in her desire, her longing, her loneliness. Now there was someone with whom to share her thoughts and feelings, and believing that this beginning – this perfect and timeless beginning – could only be the start of something infinite, she closed her eyes.

She thought of Sullivan and smiled: there was a deal to honor, and honor it he would.

SEVENTEEN

The sound from the street was just as bold, floating up with the breeze like a bright-colored streamer, and from the sidewalk vents the smoke and steam crawled like tired ghosts from the underground below. And yet the sound was somehow different, and leaning against the frame of the bedroom window, her nose against the cool glass, Annie watched the people below as they emerged into morning.

Sunday morning, the first day of a new month, of a new life perhaps, and turning as David stirred she watched him surface from sleep, his eyes flickering open, a momentary hesitation as he adjusted his thoughts to where he was, and then he smiled as he located her, as he stretched out his hand towards her, as he opened his mouth and slurred: 'Come back . . . come back to bed Annie.'

'Breakfast,' she said. 'I could chew the ass out of a moose.'

'Christ Annie,' he said, hauled into consciousness, 'that's the grossest thing I ever heard.'

She laughed, standing there naked and aware of herself, but without any self-consciousness, and then she crossed the room and sat on the edge of the mattress beside him.

He snaked his arm around her waist and tried to pull her down, but she resisted.

'Seriously,' she said, leaning forward and kissing him. 'I am famished.'

She ran her fingers through his hair, over his ear, his cheek, and leaning once more to kiss his forehead she said: 'You want something to eat you get your carcass out of bed . . . otherwise you can lie there and starve.'

Annie stood up, David grabbing the air behind her, and from the chair beside the bed she took her panties and tee-shirt, slipped them on, and walked out of the bedroom to the kitchen.

Standing there, eggs cooking, filling a jug with orange juice, spooning coffee grounds into the filter, she heard a sound. Stepping back into the front room she heard the sound again, a sound like glass clinking. It came from the hallway beyond the front door.

She crossed the room, unlocked the door, inched it open, and there on the mat she found three bottles of Crown Royal, two of them full, one a third empty. She started laughing, laughing out loud, and within a moment David was beside her dressed in just his jeans, his hand on her shoulder as he looked down and saw the bottles.

'Your milkman?' he asked. 'Hell, I should've moved into this neighborhood.'

'Sullivan,' she said.

'He leaves bottles of liquor on the doorstep for you?'

Annie shook her head. 'We had a deal.'

'A deal?'

'I can't tell you,' Annie said as she gathered up the bottles and closed the front door behind her.

'Can't tell me what?'

'About the deal.'

'Trust,' David said. 'Trust means no secrets, Annie O'Neill.'

'But this is personal – ' she started.

'And what happened yesterday wasn't?' he asked.

He was goading her, teasing her, for she knew that if she held her ground he would not push her.

'Okay,' she said. 'But if you say a word of this to Sullivan I will be so mightily pissed.'

David nodded. 'Not a word,' he whispered, and pressed his fingers to his lips.

'He drinks too much, far too much,' Annie said. 'Sullivan was a journalist, Vietnam, Haiti, Cambodia, El Salvador, all

178

those places. He's seen some terrible things . . . he has ghosts, you know what I mean?'

David nodded, and in his eyes she could tell that he understood what she was talking about.

'So he drinks too much, and we made a deal . . .'

Annie looked at David Quinn. David's expression was hesitant, anticipatory.

'Not a word,' she reminded him.

He shook his head. 'Won't even think about it.'

'The deal was that when I got myself . . . you know?'

David raised his eyebrows. 'What?'

'You know . . . When I – ' She waved her hand as if to fill in the missing words.

'When you . . . ?'

'Christ David, when I got laid, okay? When I got myself well and truly laid, then he would stop drinking. That plain enough for you?'

David smiled. 'Very plain Annie, very plain indeed. So evidently he felt that whatever happened last night was well and truly enough.'

'Evidently – ' she started, and then, 'Oh hell, the eggs!'

She pushed past David and rushed into the kitchen, found the place filled with smoke from blackened eggs in the pan, opened the window and started wafting a towel to clear the air.

David came in behind her. 'Coffee's good enough for me,' he said. 'Let's have some coffee and go back to bed . . . perhaps we can make enough noise for Sullivan to send a case over.'

Annie put the burned pan in the sink and filled it with water. She poured coffee, handed a cup to David, and they walked back to the bedroom.

The coffee wasn't drunk. It went cold after a while. Hell, coffee was the last thing on Annie's mind that Sunday morning.

Later, an hour, perhaps two, she lay beside David, his arm around her, her face on his shoulder, and with her fingers she turned tiny circles in the hairs on his chest.

179

'When was the last time?' she asked him.

'Katherine Hellmann,' he said. 'August two years ago in New Jersey.'

'That's very specific,' Annie said, a little surprised.

'And you?' he asked.

'A man called Michael Duggan about three years ago . . . here in fact as far as I recall.'

'What was he like?'

'Very different from you,' Annie said. 'What was Katherine Hellmann like?'

'She died.'

Annie leaned up, her expression one of concern. 'She died?'

David nodded.

'How'd she die . . . if you don't mind me asking, that is.'

'I don't mind. She died in October of the same year . . . came off the back of a motorcycle and was hit by a car.'

'Oh Jesus,' Annie said. 'Not your motorcycle?'

'Nope. Her brother's.'

'And her brother was riding it with her?'

'Yes, he was riding it with her.'

Annie was speechless, couldn't think of anything appropriate to say.

'Let it go,' David said.

'Let what go?'

'The image of someone coming off the back of a motorcycle and being hit by a car.'

She closed her eyes tight, tried to think of something else, *anything* else – an elephant, a stained-glass window – but still the fleeting horror pressed against the edges of her mind.

'Tell me about Michael Duggan,' David said, reaching for his cigarettes and lighting one.

'Michael? Michael was an English Language lecturer at Barnard. We went out for a year or so. He was thirty-three years old, and our relationship ended when one of his students gave him a blow job in his office.'

David smiled, started laughing.

'What's so funny?' Annie asked, a little surprised at his reaction.

'Christ Annie . . . it's a bit clichéd isn't it?'

'Mister fucking sensitive aren't you?'

'I'm sorry,' he said. 'It's just that – '

'It's just a bit clichéd, you're right,' she interjected. 'Anyway, that was the last man in my life and that was how it ended.'

'And what do you want now?'

'What do I want now . . . want from what?'

'A relationship,' David said. 'What is it you want from a relationship?'

'*A* relationship or *this* relationship?'

'Okay, this one,' David said. 'I didn't want to be presumptuous.'

'You had no problem with presumptuousness yesterday, David Quinn.'

He smiled, leaned forward and kissed her. 'So tell me,' he said. 'What do you want from this relationship?'

She was silent for a time. She believed she'd never been asked such a question by a man. There were deep waters beneath the glassy surface, undercurrents of consideration that she appreciated. 'A friend predominantly . . . an ally, a confidant. I want trust and loyalty. I want someone who can be serious when seriousness is required, but the rest of the time someone who can take things easy, relax a little, do things just for the hell of it, you know?'

'I do,' he said.

'And you?' she asked. 'What do you want?'

He said nothing for a time, and then he turned slowly, and looking directly at her, his eyes bright, his face inches from hers, he said: 'You Annie O'Neill . . . I want you.'

He leaned forward and kissed her, and she knew such a question could have been answered no better way than that.

Why she told him about Forrester she didn't know. It was early evening – five or six – and they had risen, dressed, and were at

181

the table in the front room eating cold chicken and potato salad. She had opened a bottle of wine, and there was a stillness between them, a hiatus, and into that she brought Robert Forrester as a topic of conversation.

'He just turned up at the store?'

'Uh huh,' she said. 'Just turned up out of the blue, said he'd known my father many years ago.'

'Your father never mentioned him?'

'I was seven when he died.'

'And your mother?'

Annie shook her head. 'My mother barely spoke about my father, let alone anyone he might have known.'

'And you think he's straight up?'

'I do,' Annie said. 'I don't know why he's come around now . . . but then he could have come around anytime and it wouldn't have made a difference. I get the idea he's just a lonely old man who wants some company.'

'And he said he'd just moved here?'

'He didn't say he'd moved anywhere . . . just that he was here for a few weeks, perhaps a few months, and that he wanted to revive the tradition he'd started with my father.'

'The reading club?'

'Right, the reading club.'

'And he brought letters from your father?'

'Two so far, and I get the idea he will bring one every time he comes.'

'How did he end up with letters your father wrote to your mother?'

Annie shook her head. 'I'm not exactly sure. From what I can work out they must have lived together for a while, and when my father died they were still with Forrester.'

'So your father could never have sent them, or he wouldn't have still had them in his possession.'

Annie frowned. David was right. 'I don't know,' she said. 'I don't know how it happened.'

'When does he come again?'

'Tomorrow night,' Annie said.

'And what do you read?' David asked.

'He brought a story . . . well, several chapters of a story . . . said that it was something written by one of the original members of the club.'

'Any good?'

Annie smiled, shrugged. 'Good? I don't know that it's the sort of thing that falls into the category of good or bad. It's like a biography of someone, a guy called Harry Rose.'

'And what does Harry Rose do?'

'He was an immigrant out of Auschwitz, he was brought here at the end of the war by an American soldier, and when the soldier died he became a gangster.'

'You have it here?'

Annie looked up.

'The story?' David asked. 'You have these chapters here?'

She nodded. 'Yes . . . why?'

'I wondered if you'd let me read them.'

Annie was silent for a moment. Uncertain, a little anxious perhaps. Why, she didn't know. It seemed that there was something so personal about the letters, the chapters also, that she was unsure of letting anyone see them. But then hadn't Sullivan read them? Sure he had. But Sullivan she'd known ever since she'd moved in.

'If you don't want me to it's okay,' David said, perceiving her hesitancy.

Annie shook her head, asked herself what she was worrying about. Wasn't this new viewpoint all about letting people in, stopping herself excluding all of life in the belief that life would be better alone? Sure it was.

'It's okay,' she said. 'Actually I'd like you to read them . . . after dinner, okay?'

David nodded. 'Sure, as long as – '

'I've decided,' she said. 'You can read them after dinner.'

Which is what he did, there on the couch, Annie beside him,

and she read them for a second time over his shoulder. He asked no questions, he read quickly, and when he was done he turned to her and said: 'It's one helluva story.' He smiled and shook his head. 'This Johnnie Redbird guy is some character.'

Annie nodded. 'I get the impression he'll figure more and more as the thing goes on, but I'll have to wait and see, won't I?'

David flicked through the pages once more. 'You think this thing is about real people?' he asked.

'I do,' she said. 'That's the way I felt when I read it, and then maybe I tried to convince myself that it was fiction.'

'Convince yourself, why?' David asked.

Annie frowned, hesitated. 'I don't know,' she said. 'Maybe because it made me feel uncomfortable. I got to thinking about why Forrester wanted me to read it, and after that I started wondering whether there was some connection between the story and my father. Like Johnnie Redbird was my dad or something.'

Annie looked at David as if for an opinion. Did she really think that? That someone so brutal could have been her ancestor, her blood? And then there was the other question, the question that had been raised when Sullivan told her the story and she had imagined her father was there. In that moment her father had worn the face of Robert Forrester and she couldn't shake it off. She was confused, none of it made sense, and yet there was something compelling about it. It was now not just her interest in the story itself, but the fact that she felt she *had* to find out what happened.

'Hell of a life though,' David said. 'Even though it was horrifying, it still makes me feel that I could have spent my time doing a great deal more.'

Annie smiled to herself, could hear herself saying exactly the same thing. Maybe that was it; maybe that was where the real truth lay: she had attempted to convince herself it was unreal because she would feel her own life so much less challenged. Her life had been empty compared to these things.

'So you're going to meet him again tomorrow night?'

'I am,' Annie said. 'I want to find out what happens.'

'Can I read it too?'

'Sure you can . . . but you'll have to come over.'

David smiled, put his arm around her shoulder and pulled her tight. 'I was figuring on staying for the duration,' he said.

'Staying here . . . while I'm at work?'

He shook his head. 'I'm joking,' he said. 'I need to get my things sorted out at the apartment.'

'Stay tonight,' Annie said. 'You can do that?'

'Of course. I wanted to stay tonight.'

'I'll go into the store, and then maybe around eight or nine tomorrow night you could come over and read the next chapter.'

'That's a deal,' David said. 'I'll bring something to eat. What d'you like? Chinese? Thai?'

'Chinese is good,' Annie said. 'Noodles and fried rice, and get some ribs and things.'

'Especially the things,' David said.

'Right, mustn't forget the things,' Annie replied.

She tidied the pages together and set them aside on the table.

'So what now?' David asked. 'You wanna watch some TV or something?'

Annie shook her head. 'Or something sounds good.'

'Kinda something?'

'You know exactly what kind of something, David Quinn.'

'The well and truly kind of something?'

Annie rose from the couch, took his hand and pulled him upright. She put her arms around his waist and laid her head on his shoulder.

David moved suddenly, unexpectedly, and before she knew it he'd picked her up and was carrying her towards the bedroom.

She started laughing, tugging his shirt out from his

185

waistband at the back, then struggling to unhook the belt around his jeans.

'Easy tiger,' he whispered.

'Fuck easy,' Annie O'Neill replied.

EIGHTEEN

Monday morning it was raining again, the sky almost dark. They rose, David showered, and after she'd watched him stand in the bathroom drying his hair with a towel she was struck by a thought.

She went into her bedroom, opened the lower drawer of her dresser, and from beneath the clothes she took a book. Searching hurriedly to find some paper she felt somehow excited, as if she was doing something that meant a great deal more in spirit than it did in action. She wrapped the book carefully and then returned to the front room.

She called a cab for David, and as he stood ready to leave she handed the book to him.

'What's this?' he asked.

'*Breathing Space*,' she said.

'Breathing space?'

'The book I told you about . . . the book my father gave me.'

David smiled, shook his head. 'I can't take this Annie – '

'Just to read,' she said, 'not to keep. I want you to read it.'

'You're sure?'

'If I wasn't sure I wouldn't give it to you . . . but take care of it David, and make sure you give it back.'

'I will,' he said. 'Of course I will.'

He held the book for a moment, and then he leaned forward and kissed her. 'Thank you,' he said.

And then he left, and after she'd seen him down to the street and watched the cab disappear at the junction, she went upstairs. She stood for a while in the kitchen considering what she had done. She had given perhaps her most precious possession to this man. It had been an impulse, a momentary reaction to what she had been feeling, but in hindsight – despite her fleeting reservations – it had nevertheless seemed right. It was part of her life, part of whatever her father might have meant to her also, and perhaps in some strange fashion this was her way of sharing this relationship with her father. Though the book in and of itself possessed no great significance or meaning, it nevertheless *was* a part of her. And she had shared it. This *had* to mean something. What, she wasn't sure, but it had to mean something.

Annie made some tea, and then went to look in on Sullivan. He was sleeping and she did not wake him but returned to her apartment to get ready for work.

A half-hour later she looked in on Sullivan again, found him seated at his kitchen table in a robe.

He smiled at her – such warmth, such a sense of self-satisfaction – and then said, 'You got my present?'

'I did . . . and I must say you are a man of your word, Jack Sullivan.'

'And you, Miss O'Neill, are a woman of tremendous vocal capacity.'

Annie felt herself blush.

'It's good Annie, don't hide it. I'm very happy for you.'

'And I am happy for me as well.'

'So tell me, what's he like?'

Annie sat down across from Sullivan. Her expression was thoughtful, her words slow and measured. 'I think . . . I think he's okay Jack, you know? For a little while I felt kind of threatened . . . I don't know, maybe *threatened* is too strong a word. I think in some ways he's very similar to me.'

'A sad lonely old lush – '

'I'm being deep and meaningful, cut it out,' she interjected.

Jack Sullivan nodded, didn't say another word.

'I think he's had some difficulty relating to people . . . at least that's the impression I get. His job takes him away from any kind of stability.'

Sullivan raised his eyebrows.

'Marine insurance investigation . . . all manner of barren and desolate places for weeks at a time. Stayed in hotels a lot, that kind of thing.' Annie leaned forward. 'I went to his apartment a couple of days ago, up near St Nicholas and 129th. I think he's been there some weeks, and it looks like someone's literally just moved in, everything in boxes stacked against the wall. He had his bedsheets and a few items of clothing, stuff to make a cup of coffee, you know? Exactly what you'd find in a Holiday Inn or something.'

Sullivan was nodding. 'I've met people like that . . . hell for years I was a person like that. Everything's always on the move, nothing ever stays still, and you get restless if you've got nothing to do or nowhere to go. Some people never grow out of it.'

'I think he's trying,' Annie said. 'I get the impression he wants some stability, something he can go away from and come home to.'

'And that would be you I guess?'

Annie shrugged.

'Do you want it to be you?'

'I don't know Jack,' Annie said, and smiled. 'It's a little early to tell if this is going to be anything of substance.'

'But it feels right?'

'Yes,' she replied. 'It feels right.'

Jack Sullivan reached and closed his hand over Annie's. 'I want it to be right,' he said. 'Sometimes I feel like you should've been my kid, you know? And if there's any trouble – '

Annie started to smile. 'Trouble? There won't be any trouble. I'm all growed up now, Pa.'

'Hear me out,' Sullivan said. 'If there's trouble . . . if anything doesn't seem right you come tell me, okay?'

'Okay,' Annie said, and her smile was gone. There was a flash of anxiety in her eyes.

'Don't read anything into it,' Sullivan said. 'I don't know the guy from Adam, and hell, if there's anyone's judgement I trust it's yours. If it feels right then that's good enough for me. Forget I said that, okay?'

Annie smiled again. 'Okay.'

'So go to work, and try to think about earning a living for a little while.'

Annie rose. She leaned forward and kissed Jack Sullivan's forehead.

'Take care,' she said. 'And thank you.'

Sullivan nodded. 'Go,' he said.

She reached the door, turned back. 'Forrester comes this evening. You wanna come down there?'

'Hell I forgot . . . I made an arrangement to see someone.'

'It's okay. He's harmless enough. I didn't think it was necessary for you to come anyway.'

'Sure?'

'Sure,' Annie replied. 'Later, alright?'

'Later.'

Annie slipped out and closed the door behind her. Sullivan looked marginally better, but she knew that give him a couple of hours he'd be clawing the walls for a drink. Nevertheless she knew him well enough to know that he wouldn't, not now he'd agreed. Sullivan would no more break a promise than run naked through a shopping mall.

The route she took was the same as ever, but the attitude with which she walked it was different. There was a light at the end of the tunnel, and behind her the dark passageway back into loneliness seemed to be closing up faster than a bullet. People looked different, they sounded different, and when she stopped at Starbucks for a mochaccino there was a tangible reluctance to leave the warmth, the gathering of people, the sound of humanity within.

Once inside The Reader's Rest she busied herself with reorganizing the stacks of hardbacks near the door. Those stacks had always bothered her, as if they presented an auto-

190

matic barrier as soon as someone stepped inside. She made good headway, more than she had in weeks, and the place began to lose a little of its claustrophobia. John Damianka came down at noon, surprised her by making no comment regarding her absence, an omission that was explained when he told her how well things were going with Elizabeth Farbolin from the International Center of Photography.

'Had lunch together pretty much every day last week,' he said. 'And seems the more time we spend together the more time we *want* to spend together.'

'That's the way it should be,' Annie told him.

'Never has been before,' John replied.

'There's always the *one*,' she said. 'Maybe you've been lucky enough to find her.'

'Nothing to do with luck,' he said. 'Sheer bloody-minded persistence if you ask me.'

She smiled, she nodded, she thought of David, and she managed her way through half the mayonnaise-drenched sub John had brought before finally conceding defeat.

The afternoon dragged, and by the time the hands of the clock crawled around to five she was wishing away the next two hours until Forrester's arrival.

She turned the store sign but left the front lights on, retreated to the back kitchen where she made fresh coffee and sat thinking of where her relationship with David would take her.

A little after six there was a sound out front. She got up and went to see who was there. She figured perhaps it was David, and she couldn't help but notice that her heart rose a little.

See, she thought to herself. *It should be rising into love.*

But it was not David. A young man in dark blue pants, a windcheater and a baseball cap with a red-and-white logo stood in the lee of the door. In his hand he clutched a large envelope.

'Miss O'Neill?' he shouted through the locked door.

She nodded.

'Package for you.'

She frowned, opened the door, and after signing for the envelope she closed and locked the door behind the courier.

She went to the counter, turned the envelope over, and there in bold letters was printed her name, the name of the store, and the date beneath.

She opened the envelope, upended it, and from within slid a sheaf of papers and a handwritten note.

Written in the same block capitals was a simple message:

MISS O'NEILL. APOLOGIES FOR MY ABSENCE. BUSINESS CALLS ME AWAY. IN ORDER TO NOT DISAPPOINT YOU ENTIRELY I HAVE ENCLOSED THE NEXT PART OF OUR MANUSCRIPT. I SHALL SEE YOU IN A WEEK. YOURS, FORRESTER.

Our manuscript? she thought. *When did it suddenly become our manuscript?*

She straightened the sheaf of pages, a little relieved that she wouldn't have to wait another hour but at the same time a little disappointed by the fact that she wouldn't see another letter from her father. Disappointed also that she wouldn't see Forrester. She had warmed to him, sensed his desire to involve himself in something, and was somehow pleased that he had chosen her. But then it had never been a matter of choice. He had known her father, and for whatever reason he had decided to seek her out and share with her something that he felt she might appreciate. They had founded a reading club, this man and her father, though she couldn't help but think there was something very unusual about the way it had been organized.

Tempted to start reading immediately, she refrained, collected her coat, her scarf and gloves from the back kitchen, turned out the lights and left for home.

The rain had eased off, but the streets were still wet. Already some of the stores were preparing their windows and frontages for Thanksgiving. Christmas would follow faster than ever, and she felt a deep sense of relief that this year she would not be spending it alone.

Sullivan was out, evident in the silence and lack of lights from his apartment. She let herself in, tossed her coat, scarf and gloves onto the chair behind the door, and before settling to read she made some tea.

From the window she could see shapes moving in the building opposite. She figured she would have to get a curtain, and then thought *To hell with it, just don't make a habit of wandering around naked.*

She sat at the table in the front and began reading.

NINETEEN

So after I went to Rikers Harry Rose left Queens, stayed a little while in Long Island City, and then moved once again into Astoria. His reputation – whatever it may have been in Queens – did not precede him into a new city, and despite the money, despite the history, Harry found himself starting all over again. He was eighteen, and as far as the dealers and cardsharps, the bookies and runners were concerned, he was just another wiseass kid trying to make it good in a grown-ups' world.

Astoria was different from Queens in many ways, neither better nor worse, merely different. There seemed to be more money, and thus the money he carried bought Harry less influence. He took a three-room apartment on Shore Boulevard overlooking Ralph Demarco Park, and late at night, leaning from the back window of his bedroom, he could see the North and South Brother Islands, and he knew that had he been able to lean a few feet further he would have seen around Bowery Bay to Rikers where I was holed up. Through May and June, even into the early part of July, Harry couldn't face the prospect of going down there, and he set his mind to working his way back into the world.

He was now alone, and though alone was never good it nevertheless gave him some freedom. He could be where he wanted to be when he was needed, and he took advantage of that flexibility. He started the card games and running bets, establishing a small operation from a single bench in Ralph Demarco Park where those with greenbacks to spare could pay them over and place their odds. He paid on time, always to his word and bang on the nickel, and the reputation he had forged as a younger man came back – slowly, but it did come back, and within five or six weeks he was turning around ten or twenty thousand dollars a week. He ran a sideline in recommendations for some of the more up-market hookers, and from them he earned a commission and a blow job whenever he needed one. He became a face, the face carried a name, and people started to remember him and count him as one of the players.

By the start of the summer Harry was back on form. He bought a car, and with that car he traveled further afield, used some of the money he was earning to invest in gambling houses and bars. He let the crazies smoke their weed and shoot their shit out back, but he charged them rent by the hour to sleep it off and put a man at the top of the alley to shout when the cops came cruising. He was safe, he was quiet, he kept his word and shut his mouth, and when he felt that he had arrived he started once more to think of me.

He convinced himself that I didn't need him visiting, but he knew it was a lie, and finally – his nerves steeled against whatever he would find – he made the trip. It was a bitter day despite the season, and from the East River through Hell Gate the wind came like a tornado of razor blades and cut into his face as he stood on the deck of the ferry, his heart like a dead man's fist in his chest, his nerves ragged, his mouth dry.

The sounds and smells of the penitentiary were as bad as he had imagined. The bitter-sweet taint of cheap disinfectant mixed with the cloying stench of a mass of men crammed into tiny cells, all living out of each other's pockets. Harry could smell the fear, and inside of that the frustration, the interminable boredom, the hatred and resentment, the guilt and the innocence. All of these things rolled together and pumped through the building by a noisy air-conditioning system that probably carried more dust and infection than anything else.

Harry came into the communal visitation room, a long bank of tables back to back with a ceiling-high sheet of toughened glass separating them. Some of the tables were taken. Beaten-to-fuck cons muttered as their wives nagged, as their children itched and wriggled and squirmed to leave; a young man, possibly no older than Harry himself, sat cowed and despondent as an elderly woman – presumably his mother – endlessly berated him about the lack of heating in her apartment, and how everything would have been fine had he not gotten himself 'all mixed up with bad sorts.' Harry listened without hearing anything at all, he told me, and when the far door opened and I appeared in denim jacket and jeans, my hands cuffed to a wide leather belt around my waist, he got up from where he was seated and felt the urge to push right through the glass, to throw his arms around me, to swallow me whole and carry me out into the real world. These things he would explain to me as best he could, but I knew whatever he might feel, however this place might challenge his sanity and his reason, it was nothing compared to what I was feeling. I had lost my life, and though I understood that being in Rikers was as much my own fault as ever it was Harry's, there was nevertheless a deep-seated seed of resentment. I did not water the seed or tend it with any care, but I could feel it, and it was growing.

We talked for a little while, exchanged words of little consequence. I had lost weight, and down the right side of my face a wide bruise was fading. Harry asked me about the bruise, how it came to be there, but I did not tell him. Even at that point I felt Harry Rose was tormented enough, and I did not want to fuel the fire of that Hades. I told Harry that he could bring money, as much as he wanted, but to be aware of the fact that whatever he brought I would receive only half. The remainder would be split between the duty guard at visitation and the block warden. Money is good in here, I told him. With money you can get a better cell, be a little more selective about who you might share it with, and when it comes to food there's a few little extras that can be obtained by the man carrying greenbacks. Harry told me he would bring more money next time, and from his overcoat pocket he took a roll of ten-dollar bills amounting to little more than three or four hundred. I turned and nodded at the duty guard, the guard sauntered over, and after a few brief words with me the guard nodded at Harry and walked away. He'll take it when you leave, I told him.

Before Harry had a chance to say any of the things he had planned and rehearsed, the half-hour visit was over. I stood up and, looking directly at Harry, my eyes cold and emotionless, I said, You take care Harry Rose. Someday I'll beat this thing, and I want you to remember what I did for you, okay?

Harry told me he would remember, told me that he would never forget, and with that I turned and walked to the door.

Harry stayed there – motionless, unable to think of anything – and though he hoped that I would turn and look back as I went through the door, he also hoped I would not. There was a look in my eyes, he told me later, not of a man defeated, but of a man fighting against tremendous odds to maintain his sanity. I went silently, I didn't turn back, and when the door closed Harry Rose was left alone and confused in a strange room filled with lost lives and broken hearts.

He came back to see me the following week. Brought a thousand dollars with him, three cartons of cigarettes and a bottle of bourbon. Won't see the smokes or the bourbon, I told him, but the money'll be good. Leave it a while now. Stay away for a month or two. Things're looking up. Got myself moved into a better cell. Got some quiet guy with me who minds his own. I'll be okay. Could be worse.

Could be one helluva lot better, Harry wanted to say, but he didn't say a thing.

Harry went back on the ferry, bitter wind like sheet ice cutting through him. Buried his hands in the pockets of his overcoat and wondered how often he could come across here. Seemed like every time he came he died a little inside. We'd both killed Olson. Both of us were guilty. Harry felt he was paying for his sins in some bitter hole of personal torment, but my fate had been much worse. I would be in Rikers for the rest of my life.

Or so I believed.

I can talk about things now, things I would not have realized then, and even had I realized them I would not have shared them with the world. Killing is in the commandments, but killing remains to be the one commandment that the vast majority of us never see from the inside out. How is it to kill a man? I'll tell you how it is. Necessary. That's how it is. Sometimes something happens that catches you someplace inside, someplace within the shadow cast by your own heart that you didn't know existed. Someone does something that is beyond anything even close to forgiveness. What was done to Carol Kurtz was such a thing. Maybe we saw it the same way, me and Harry, like raping some poor schmooze was like raping our own mothers. Some bullshit psychology theory the head-shrinkers would have loved to share with us. Time and again I replayed the moment I stood in the county morgue basement looking down at that girl. She was naked, a paper tag tied to her toe. The big toe on her right foot. Paper carried a number. That was all she was to the world by that time. A number. But before she was a number she was a life. A real life, you see. She had a name and a heart and a voice to sing with; she had folks someplace outside the back of nowhere; she was pretty and smart and funny and crazy in some small kind of way, and hell, maybe she would never have amounted to anything more than Harry's girl, but that would have been enough. Enough for her at least. Maybe that's what she had always wanted: to be *somebody's girl*. And then she wasn't even that. She was a rape victim, a killing, a corpse and a number. Assholes down there didn't even know her name. I didn't tell them. They didn't deserve to know. But I knew. That was enough for me. Went out of there touched in some place I'd never been touched before. Guy I killed for seventeen bucks and change wasn't someone I'd known. Hadn't known him from Adam. But Carol I did know. And when I found out who had done this thing to her it became necessary to see them wind up the same way. Blue and cold and stiff and silent with a paper and a number tied to their toe; big toe on the right.

Seeing the asshole die was justice, a catharsis, a balancing of the scales. Killing him was just as simple as that.

You look back on it in hindsight, look back on it from the inside of a Rikers eight by eight, and you don't regret the killing. No, you never regret the killing. You just regret the getting caught. Like they say, you know the thing about the eleventh commandment: Thou shalt never get caught. Fucked the dog on that one. Fucked it good.

I hung in there. Fingernails on the precipice. You shut down your mind, your thoughts, your feelings. You walk the walk and talk the talk and color inside the lines. They say 'Jump!' and you say 'How high boss?' Either that or you wind up in the cubes. Don't go to the cubes, they tell you when you get inside. The other cons. Don't get yourself in the cubes kid. Cubes are blackpainted, no windows, hole in the door through which comes your food. Once a day kind of food. Bucket in the corner to dump your guts and take a piss. Live in the stench of your own shit for a week at a time. Come out, you can't see. Lights are bright, too fucking bright. Eyes can't handle it. Come out once a week, stumble around like a punch-drunk bareknuckle prizefighter for fifteen minutes until your head screams to turn off the lights, and then they shove you right back in again until next Tuesday. Went there once. Three days only. Short shift. Long enough for me. Badmouthed the boss. Told him I saw his mother chasing a troop train with a mattress on her back. Model citizen after that. No shit boss. Didn't tell Harry Rose about these things, not then. Told him another time, a long time after. Just gritted my teeth, clenched my fists, tightened my ass and followed the lines. Like a good kid. Momma's boy.

Time passed, slow and painfully.

August of '56 saw John Kennedy beaten by Estes Kefauver in

his hope for the Democratic vice-presidential nomination. Eisenhower and Nixon were nominated by the Republicans to run for re-election. Harry Rose worked out of his apartment on Shore Boulevard, taking bets, collecting what was owed and paying what was due with the same sense of exactness that had always been his trademark. It wasn't the same however, and when he was approached in September by a man called Mike Royale, 'King Mike' to anyone who knew him he said, he was presented with a proposition that would take him out of Astoria, away from the stench of the Bowery Bay Sewage Treatment Plant and the ghost of Rikers Island on the other side of the channel. Harry Rose – always on the lookout for a route to greater things – listened very attentively to what the man had to say.

Hookers, King Mike told him, sitting there with his gut busting out of his vest and his shirt collar tight enough to choke him. Wide face, teeth like stumps of broken chalk, hair slicked back with pomade so's it looked like it'd been spray-painted on his head. Everything about him was fat, even down to the stubs of his fingers, and on those stubs were jammed rings that looked like they'd stem all possibility of blood-flow to his fingertips. That's where the money is these days, he said, his voice a little breathless like his neck was too swollen for the words to get out properly. And I'm not talking your five-dollar alleyway hand-job hookers, face like a bulldog licking piss off a poison ivy . . . no siree, I'm talking uptown, class-A, clean girls who work out of respectable hotels, a manager and a couple of heavies to take care of the miscreants. That's the kind of thing I'm talking, you know? Where your blue-collar Joe Public can come and spend an hour or so in the company of a girl he'd never have a hope in hell of getting if he was out on his own. We got a coupla places sorted out already, and we're looking for some investors if you know what I mean. You seem like a smart kid, and from what I've heard you carry a little money and your word's as good as it comes. Heard you ran a three-way for Benny Schaeffer a month or so ago, heard he hit for you for three big ones, and neat as paint you showed up at his place and paid up. Even told him thank you for his business and you were hoping to do more business with him real soon. That so kid?

Harry told him it was so. Didn't mention the fact that Benny Schaeffer was one of the stupidest gamblers Harry had ever met, and in the previous fortnight alone Harry had taken back the three big ones and a couple more besides.

So this is the kind of thing we're talking about, King Mike went on, and seems to me you're the kind of guy we'd want to have come down and see our places. If you like what you see we can cut you in for a ten-percent share, okay?

The cost? Harry had asked him.

A businessman, King Mike said. I like that kind of attitude. Straight as an arrow and right to the point. You come down, you check it out, and if you want in we talk figures. Deal?

Deal, Harry said, and they shook hands.

The following day King Mike sent over a car, and they took a trip across the Triborough into Manhattan.

Harry felt at home almost as soon as he set foot on the sidewalk. Franklin D. Roosevelt Drive, Rockefeller University, the Cornell Medical Center, the Whitney Museum and Jack Jay Park. Names that meant something, places he'd heard of before, and when they stepped up to a tall brownstone building, a discreet sign in the window that read Gentleman's Hotel & Bar, Harry felt he had perhaps lucked into something that carried a little more class than Benny Schaeffer and his cohorts.

Inside, the walls were covered in velvet-embossed paper, the floors were wooden, the recliners and chaise-longues out of something by F. Scott Fitzgerald. There were fresh flowers in crystal vases, an antique grandfather clock ticking like a gentle heartbeat and echoing down the corridor, and when they turned the corner at the end and entered the reception lounge Harry took in his breath and held it like it was his last.

The girls were right out of *Harper's* and *Vogue*. Tall, blonde,

201

elegant, brunette, slim, olive-skinned, redheaded, legs that ran all the way to their waists, bodices and bustiers, silk stockings and suspenders . . .

King Mike appeared with a throng of half a dozen women and walked towards Harry. He was grinning, seemed in his element, and when he clapped Harry on the shoulder and shook his hand Harry felt as if he'd been led into paradise by Hasan-i Sabbah himself.

So this is one of three places we run, King Mike told him, and before you take a look around we figure it would be appropriate to sample the goods, so to speak. Go meet the girls, take your pick, two or three of them if you like, and then we can look at whether or not you want in.

So Harry met the girls – Cynthia, Mary-Rose, Jasmine, Louella-May, Claudette, Tanya, others whose names he couldn't remember. But the afternoon he did remember, would have remembered it for the rest of his life regardless of what else had happened, and when he came down again to talk with King Mike in a small office to the right of the reception lounge, there was little he could do but listen and nod and confirm that yes, he would be very interested in some kind of investment plan.

Tend to turn over somewhere in the region of fifteen to twenty grand a week in each hotel, King Mike told him. We have three right now, hoping we can set up another three before the end of the year. That's something like forty-five to sixty grand a week, and with an initial investment of a hundred grand we can cut you in for ten percent for the first twelve months, and then depending on the number of places we have going we can renegotiate further investments for the future and work out new profit-sharing schemes. You like that? Profit-sharing schemes. Got ourselves a real honest-to-God accountant here and everything.

Harry was in, up to the hilt, and the following day the same driver came with the same car, and Harry went to the Gentleman's Hotel & Bar with a hundred grand in cash.

Claudette gave him head while King Mike counted the bills, and once they were done they shook hands. First payment will come in a week, King Mike said. But if you wanna come down and party with any of these ladies you feel free. Investors have an open ticket seven days a week.

Nothing to sign? Harry had asked him.

Sign? King Mike said. What the hell would you wanna be signing anything for? This is as big an operation as you're gonna find in Manhattan, and the less that's on paper the better. You figure any of the families around here want us to be taking the best part of three mill a year?

Harry understood. They shook hands again, and the driver took him home to Astoria across the Triborough Bridge.

A week passed. No-one came. Harry left it another two days and then he couldn't take it any more. He went out there, crossed the river into Manhattan, and after a little unwanted sightseeing tour of the lower end of Yorkville, he found the street, found the Gentleman's Hotel & Bar, the front door unlocked, the hallway empty, the reception lounge nothing more than an empty shell of nicely painted walls and a broken packing crate in the middle of the room.

He kicked his way into the small office where he and Mike had done their business, and he found the same thing – an empty room.

Panicking, his heart thundering in his chest, he charged up the stairs, burst through the door of each of six rooms on the second floor, and found the room where he had been entertained on his first visit – the only one decorated. The rest were empty, not even a rug on the floor, and then he sat on the top riser of the stairwell and buried his face in his hands.

He'd been taken for a hundred grand by a fat guy and half a dozen hookers.

Harry Rose was gutted, mentally and emotionally devastated. He sat on the stairs of that house with his head in his hands and he cried – not out of self-pity or grief, but at his own stupidity. Stupidity that had made him blind to everything but the way those girls had looked, and the way they'd taken his teenage dick and sucked it dry. He'd let his balls rule his head, and that had been the biggest mistake of all. He thought less of the hundred grand and more of the work that it had taken to make that hundred grand. He thought of how that money had been his future, and now it was nothing more than a memory. Had he been a weak man he perhaps would have drunk himself to death, or sucked a .38 and blown the back of his own head off. But he was not a weak man. He had survived Auschwitz, had seen his own mother beaten and tortured and raped, had killed a man with his own bare hands and carried the light of that man's eyes in his own.

Harry Rose believed he'd learned a lesson. Manhattan wasn't Queens, and it sure as hell wasn't Astoria. Manhattan was where the big boys came to play. Wanted to play up this side of the park then you came with the same artillery and the same intention. Didn't matter a fuck who you were before, it was who you were now that counted. It happened to be King Mike Royale, but sure as shit it could have been anyone. Harry had been taken for all he had, and now he was back to the beginning again. Broken down he might have been, but he'd been down on his bare ass before and made it back. He would do it again. If anything, he had learned resolve, a willingness to fight against whatever came his way and make it through. The scam with Mike Royale had made him stronger, he had to believe that, for to believe anything else was to succumb to fate and destiny. Such things did not exist in Harry Rose's vocabulary. Destiny was what you made it, good, bad or indifferent, and fate was something the weaker guy blamed when things went belly-up and bad.

A fortnight later he left his apartment on Shore Boulevard. He didn't take a trip out to Rikers Island, didn't tell me where he was going. He just vanished. He took with him eleven thousand dollars – all the money he possessed in the world – three suits, a pair of loafers, a good pair of hand-made cordovan wingtips, two white shirts, a collection of ties, and a .38 caliber snubnose with four shells that once belonged to me. He put some money down on a small apartment in midtown, moved in the same day, and when he sat down at the beat-up kitchen table, a bowl of chicken soup and a half-dozen crackers for his evening meal, he made a resolution. The day would come when he'd find King Mike and his pretty girls, and once he'd hung the fat bastard out to dry he'd fuck Claudette in the ass while he choked her with her own silk stockings. That was the way it was going to be, and that was the real deal.

November came. Ike was re-elected. Christmas was around the corner, the New Year of 1957, and in the year that would see Humphrey Bogart dead; all the shit that went down in Arkansas when Faubus mustered State troops to stop nine little black kids going to school; a year that would see Eisenhower floored by a stroke and Elvis enlisting in the army, Harry Rose started watering the seeds of an empire. Muscle counted for shit in Manhattan. Muscle was okay for Queens and Brooklyn, may have worked the trick in Harlem, but here it was smarts and quick-thinking, the better plan, the faster sleight of hand that gathered the greens and kept you one step ahead of the competition.

He started once again with what he knew best – the gamblers and bookies – and by the time Sugar Ray took the middle-weight championship for the fifth time in March of 1958 Harry was in his stride. He kept the small apartment, never told a soul where he lived, and from there he started working the lines, changing lanes when he had to, gathering a few compadres in the NYPD who would roll over a leech or a late payer for no more than twenty or thirty bucks a time. Manhattan was as dirty as any place Harry had been, but there was a certain class to the Manhattan style of corruption, a layer of airs and graces that veneered over the surface of what was nothing more than a crew of cheap hustlers and lousy drunks. Harry was six months or so from his twentieth birthday, he grew a mustache and looked twenty-five, and when he started to cut into some of the heavier deals and transactions that were run by the Jewish families and some of the Italians that were brave enough to edge their way out of the Lower East Side, he was taken seriously. Harry Rose was earning back the kind of credentials and reputation that he'd possessed back in Queens. Harry was a good guy, Harry paid on time, Harry was a man you could work with but you wouldn't want to cross. Rumor had it he'd killed a man, and though the rumor was never substantiated it was safe to say that anyone with that kind of reputation earned a degree of respect from his associates.

The hundred grand came back hard: he broke sweat and talked his mouth dry. He ran hookers and drugs, he hit the protection circuit and oversaw a crew of six thugs who looked after the nightclubs and bars in the rougher neighborhoods. He took what he earned and he rigged fights and races, card games and football games. He played hundreds of dollars on the college circuit, and once he got the machine going the money started crawling back through blood and sweat and tears. The second hundred grand came easier, and for a young man who lived in a scarred tenement on East 46th, no more than a hop, skip and a jump away from Broadway and Times Square, things were coming back to battery. Harry had fought to get his life back, and retrieve it he had, and from one Christmas to the next he didn't think of me.

I, however, thought a great deal about Harry Rose. I didn't bear a grudge, didn't harbor resentment or bitterness towards Harry himself. I had expected him to vanish from the face of the earth, would have done the same myself, and I knew my old sidekick would be out there taking on the world, harvesting those greens in fat, ripe handfuls, and that all I had to do – *all* I had to do – was find some way out of Rikers and I would own the world again.

And that's where my mind went as the decade drew to a close. I heard about Ingemar Johansson slaying Floyd Patterson in Yankee Stadium in June 1959. That fight gave the world heavyweight title to a non-American for the first time since Primo Carnera in 1934. I also knew – if Harry Rose was still the same Harry I'd known and loved all those years before – that such a fight would have given him God only knew how many thousands of dollars, a significant percentage of which were rightfully mine . . . for hadn't I risen at the stand, given my name, and taken the fall for us both? Sure I had. I knew that, and Harry would know that too. Time would come when dues had to be paid, and Harry would pay them. Sure he would.

That thought – and possibly that thought alone – kept me out of trouble on Rikers Island through the next seven years.

TWENTY

As Annie turned over the last page a thought seemed to hover at the edges of her mind. She tracked it, felt it skirt around Forrester and settle somewhere between David Quinn and Jack Sullivan. She was uncertain; perhaps it was nothing.

Annie glanced at her watch: it was a little after seven-thirty. David would be over anywhere between eight and nine that evening, as far as she recalled. She looked at her watch again, touched the face with the fingers of her right hand and imagined her father wearing it. Dead twenty-three years. Times were he would look at this self-same watch, perhaps late for an appointment. An appointment where? Engineering things perhaps. What things? Annie sighed and shook her head. She had no idea. Her disappointment at Forrester's failure to appear that evening surely had less to do with Forrester and more to do with the fact that there were no further letters. There had been no more questions asked or answers given regarding who her father was, what he did, what became of him.

Annie frowned.

Christ, she thought. *I know so little about him. My own father, and I know almost nothing . . .*

A momentary sadness overcame her, slow and quiet and almost intangible. Seven years old, and he was gone. She couldn't even remember being seven, let alone the moments, the hours, the days that she must have shared with him. Or the feeling she must have had when she knew he was coming home. Thanksgiving. Christmas. Her sixth birthday. These were things she *should* remember, and yet try as she might to send her mind backwards she found nothing. Had there been something so painful that she would not allow herself to remember?

I don't know, she thought. *I just don't know.*

And then she thought: *Sullivan.*

She felt a surge of anxiety, electricity skittering through her nerves. The hairs on the nape of her neck stood to attention.

Sullivan could find out something. Why didn't I think of this before?

Because you didn't want to know, a voice answered.

Hell, of course I wanted to know.

Maybe now you want to, but not then . . . not before . . .

Before what?

Before someone came and reminded you that there might be something you were missing.

And who might that be?

Forrester of course. Robert Franklin Forrester. He brought you the letters. He told you about the reading club. He reminded you that Frank O'Neill existed somewhere back then, that he possessed a life just as real as anyone else's, and that you were never really old enough to become part of it. That's who. He reminded you that you were once somebody's daughter . . .

Somebody's daughter. I was somebody's daughter.

Annie looked at the watch-face again. She closed her eyes, her fingers still touching the smooth glass surface, and holding her breath she could hear the sweep hand ticking, the tiny metronomic movements encased in something that had once encircled her father's wrist.

She thought she was going to cry, but she did not. She breathed deeply, and then rose from the chair and went to the sink in the kitchen, a vantage-point on the world beyond the window. She wondered if there was anything in her line of sight that her father might have built. If indeed he had built things at all.

If . . .

She decided to ask Sullivan to look into it. Perhaps there were people he could ask who would look up obituaries, personal records . . . perhaps he might even locate a photograph and she would find out how much like her father she looked . . .

The idea scared her, yet excited her. Like the high turn on the county fair rollercoaster, stomach all tightened up in a ball of frightened muscle, feeling like your breakfast was rushing ahead of you, eyes wide, teeth gritted, fists clenched . . . *Here I go Ma . . . top of the world!*

Annie smiled to herself, switched off the kettle, and made some tea. She wanted David to come. Wanted him to read the next chapter. Wanted him to feel the way that she felt: that Johnnie Redbird was a real human being, that he was holed up in Rikers Island while Harry Rose lived the high life in Manhattan and pretended that he didn't owe his life to someone who would never forget. These were dangerous people living dangerous lives. Murder, intrigue, passion, money, scandal: these were the elements of their everyday existences, and she felt certain these would be the things that found them in the end.

Leaving the kitchen she returned to the couch, and just as she sat she heard the street door open and slam shut. Footsteps on the stairwell. Not Sullivan's. David's, she felt sure, though she was not yet familiar with the sound of him arriving. His was a new sound, a different sound, and when those footsteps reached the third floor and she heard him knock she believed she'd never been so pleased to have anyone come to her home.

'David?' she called.

'Bearing ribs and rice and things,' he called back. She unlocked the door and let him in, barely allowing him to set his bags down before throwing her arms around his neck. He'd had a haircut, wore a clean pair of jeans, a white open-necked shirt and a tan-colored cotton jacket. He looked good, he smelled good, and when he returned her greeting with a breath-squeezing hug she felt everything she ever could have hoped to feel about being close to someone.

'Whoa,' he said. 'I only brought Chinese.'

Annie let him go. She stepped back and surveyed him. 'You look good,' she said. 'Good haircut . . . it suits you.' She reached up and touched the side of his face, pulled him towards her and kissed him. She felt his hands around her waist. Strong hands. Sensitive fingers. She felt like getting laid.

'Eat first,' he said.

'First?'

He smiled. 'Your face is a book, Annie O'Neill.'

She laughed, took the bags he'd brought and fetched plates.

They ate. They talked a little while. Annie made coffee and watched him smoke a cigarette.

When he was done she rose from her chair, pulled her tee-shirt up over her head and took off her bra.

She started towards the bedroom, tugging the button free on the waistband of her jeans. 'Come get it,' she said when she reached the doorway.

David was up out of his chair and had caught her by the time she reached the bed.

They made love. Furious almost. Hungry, as if they were out for revenge. And when it was over they lay naked and breathless, sweating on the bed beside one another, not touching, no contact, waiting for nothing but inner silence to return.

'You see Forrester tonight?' David eventually asked. He rolled over and leaned up, supported his head on his hand.

'He couldn't come . . . sent a courier over with the chapter.'

'Can I read it?'

Annie rolled over to the edge of the bed. 'Now?' she asked.

'Sure . . . if you don't mind.'

She smiled. 'I don't mind. Why would I mind?'

David shrugged and shook his head.

Annie sat up and started towards the door. She glanced back, saw David watching her as she moved.

'What?' she asked.

'Stunning,' he said.

'What is?'

'You are.'

'Stunning? That's a little strong isn't it?'

He smiled. 'Not from where I'm looking it's not.'

'Tease,' she said, and slipped out the door into the front room.

She brought his cigarettes back with her, sat on the edge of the bed and lit one for him. She took a mouthful of smoke and blew it out without inhaling.

'You don't want to start that,' David said.

'Practise what you preach,' she replied, and handed him the cigarette.

David took the pages, sat upright, his back against the headboard, and for the time he took to read it Annie just sat and watched him.

Strange, she thought, *how someone looks one way when you meet them, and as you get to know them they look different each time. Maybe as you get to know them what they're really like comes through . . . you begin to see what's under the skin, behind the face they wear for the world. Like the really attractive ones, at least attractive when you see them, and then when you get to know them you find out they're complete assholes and they become uglier and uglier.*

She smiled at the thought, smiled and watched David, who could sometimes look a little like Kevin Costner, and yet again looked like no-one at all but himself. She wanted to reach out and touch him, perhaps lay her head on his stomach and feel the rising and falling of his chest as he breathed, but he was reading – his attention rapt – and there seemed to be something so important in sharing this thing with him that she didn't want to disturb his concentration. They were sharing people's lives, and it didn't matter if they were real lives or not, didn't matter if it was all a figment of someone's imagination or The Gospel of Rose and Redbird. What she had read she could *feel*, and in feeling it she *wanted* to share it, and at this

212

moment it felt so much more important to share it with David Quinn than anyone else she could think of. Even Sullivan. Even Jack Sullivan – the man she'd once believed would be the closest she would ever get to a real honest-to-God friend. Annie felt she could spend the rest of her life with such a man as this and never want for anything else. For some reason – unknown, intangible, non-specific – it felt *that* right.

'This is some story,' David said as he turned the last page. 'This is really something. This intrigues me, intrigues me greatly.'

Annie nodded. 'Me too,' she replied. 'I am actually fascinated by the whole thing . . . who they were, how this all happened, what will happen to Redbird, if he'll ever get out of Rikers Island.'

'The suggestion is there that he will,' David said. 'This line: "That thought – and possibly that thought alone – kept me out of trouble on Rikers Island through the next seven years" – certainly gives me the idea that something happens to change things for him.'

'Who knows?' Annie said.

'Forrester knows,' David replied, and then setting the pages down on the bed he turned and looked directly at Annie. 'Aren't you interested to find out more about who he might be?'

'Who, Forrester? Or the guy who wrote this?'

'Forrester,' David said.

'I am,' she said. 'But there's something else that seems more important to me now.'

'And that is?'

'My father . . . how this thing might connect to my father.'

'Your father?'

'Forrester has given me two letters . . . both of them written by my father to my mother. They're addressed from somewhere called the Cicero Hotel . . . you ever heard of it?'

'Can't say that I have, but there's gotta be hundreds of hotels in New York.'

213

'If it was New York at all,' Annie said.

'Right, if it was New York at all.'

'The whole thing has made me curious. The fact that I barely remember anything about him, that my mother never spoke of him, that I don't really know what he did for a living. The letters have made me think about what he might have been like, and I was thinking of asking Sullivan to make some inquiries, try and find out how he died, stuff like that. And then there was the thing you said the other day, how Forrester had the letters amongst my dad's things, and so the letters could never have reached my mother.'

'It would be good to know,' David said. He rolled over and pulled Annie close. His hands were warm, and he started to trace tiny circles across the top of her thigh.

Shivers ran through her leg, and pushing the pillows up behind her head she lay back and folded the length of her body against David's.

'How did you end up with the store?' David asked.

'How did I end up with it?'

'Yes, how did you get to own a store like that?'

'When my mom died I sold the house we lived in and bought the lease. Why d'you ask?'

David closed in tighter to her. 'I just wondered.'

There was silence between them for a minute, perhaps two.

'You okay?' Annie asked.

'Sure I am,' David whispered. She could feel his breath on the back of her neck and it made her shiver pleasantly.

'What're you thinking?'

'Closure,' he said quietly.

'Closure?' she asked. 'What d'you mean?'

'Like when you don't know something it seems to stick to you, and then when you find out the truth you can feel it let go . . . even if it's the worst thing you could imagine, it still somehow manages to help you let go.'

She nodded without speaking.

She moved her left hand up close to her face, and there was

her father's wristwatch again, its face no more than six inches from her own.

She could hear it ticking, and it seemed to follow the beating of David's heart. She could feel the pressure of his chest against her back, the warmth of his skin, the sense of security and stability it gave her. Like an anchor. A safe port in a storm. She pushed herself closer against him, felt him respond and then, closing her eyes, she sighed so deeply she felt she would empty out and vanish.

'You alright?' he whispered.

'Never better,' she whispered in return.

She felt him kiss the back of her neck, her shoulder, the sound of his breathing mere inches from her ear, and within the depth of whatever it was she was feeling – an emotional freedom that was rare and heady and addictive beyond measure – she felt herself slip soundlessly into sleep.

David slept with her – front-to-back – their bodies pressed together as if one entity, and though the wind pushed against the windows of her third-floor apartment, there was nothing she could hear but silence.

The silence of loneliness tip-toeing its way out of her life for keeps.

TWENTY-ONE

The way the early morning light seeped through the window, the way it outlined David's form as he slept on the bed, the warmth from the sunlight as it touched her skin – all seemed timeless, eternal, unforgettable.

Annie closed her eyes, opened them for a second, and then closed them again as if taking a photograph. Her mind was a camera. She would hold this image forever, and at any time she could replay it, see it there behind her eyelids and remember how she'd felt right at the second it was taken.

A Kodak moment for the heart.

She left him sleeping, *wanted* to leave him sleeping, because she could barely remember the last time she had done that: gone away and come back again to find someone in her bed. The feeling was one of completeness, coupled with anticipation for what this might bring and an urgent need to discover all that could be discovered in a relationship that worked. And beyond and beneath all that, she was aware that loneliness was already something she could barely remember as significant.

Annie put on a tee-shirt and jeans, slipped out of the apartment and crossed the landing to Sullivan's. She tapped on the door, waited a handful of seconds, and stepped inside as the door opened.

'Good to see you,' she told Sullivan, and hugged him.

He was dressed, had more than likely been up since dawn. He did that sometimes, and then other times she couldn't rouse him until after lunch. There was something around his eyes, not so much the shadows of insomnia, but more the mental and physical tension he must have been fighting. It was not easy to stop drinking, she knew that much, and Sullivan had a battle on his hands.

'How're you doing?' she asked.

'With the drinking, I'm actually doing okay Annie. I figured it would be tougher, kinda cursed myself for making a promise, but I'm actually doing okay. And you?'

Annie smiled. She knew he was lying for her. She would have said something, but she didn't know what to say, and in this moment she believed she could not have submerged her sense of well-being beneath anything.

'I'm doing good enough,' she said. 'David's still sleeping . . . I came over because I wanted to ask if you'd do something for me.'

Sullivan walked into his front room and sat on the couch. Annie took a seat at the table facing him.

'My father,' she stated matter-of-factly.

'Your father?'

She nodded. 'I wondered if you could do a little investigatory work, find out what you can about him . . . I figured you might have some contacts in the newspapers or something.'

'And why would I be doing this?' Sullivan asked. 'First time in the five years we've known each other that you've asked me to do something like this.'

She shook her head. 'Thought about it many times, but I think the letters from Forrester made me look at it more seriously. I could never get the nerve up, you know what I mean?'

Sullivan frowned. 'Because there's something you think you might not like?'

'No, I don't think so. More because I thought it might make me sad that I never got the chance to know him.'

'I can check it out,' Sullivan said. 'Pass me a pen and paper from over there.' He pointed to a chest of drawers against the wall. 'Tell me his date of birth, where he lived, anything like that.'

'I think he was born at the end of the '30s, but I'm not sure.

217

Mainly lived here in New York as far as I know, and Forrester said he was some kind of engineer.'

'Anything more specific than just a kind of engineer?' Sullivan asked. He took the pen and paper and jotted down what Annie told him.

Annie shook her head. 'That's as good as I've got. I know it doesn't help much but I thought you might be able to find out something.'

Sullivan shrugged his shoulders. 'You never know,' he said. 'But for this kind of work it's a hundred an hour plus expenses.'

Annie smiled. 'I appreciate it Jack, I really do.'

She turned suddenly at the sound of someone knocking the door.

'Come!' Sullivan hollered.

The door inched cautiously open and David's head appeared.

'David,' Annie said, rising from her chair. 'Come and meet the cat.'

Sullivan frowned.

Annie winked at him. 'A short story,' she said.

David walked towards them, held out his hand as he reached Sullivan.

'David Quinn,' he said.

'Jack Sullivan.'

They shook hands.

'You want to stay and have some coffee with me?' Sullivan asked.

'I'd love to,' David said, 'but I just got paged. I wondered if I could use the phone, Annie.'

'Use mine,' Sullivan said.

David looked awkward for a moment. 'My pager's back inside,' he said. 'The number's on it . . . I might as well call from there.'

'Go ahead,' Annie said. 'I'll be back in a moment.'

David nodded, smiled. 'No hurry,' he said, and turned back towards the door.

'He seems okay,' Sullivan commented when he was once again alone with Annie.

'Yes,' Annie replied. 'He really is okay, Jack.'

'I'm happy for you.'

She reached out and touched his face. 'Thank you,' she said.

'So go and be with him, not with the old drunk opposite, eh?'

'Ex-drunk,' Annie reminded him.

'Drunk, ex-drunk, whatever . . . go be someone's girlfriend.'

Someone's girlfriend, she thought as she closed Sullivan's door behind her. *Long time since I've been someone's girlfriend.*

Stepping back into her apartment she found David standing there, his expression intent. He held the pager in his hand.

'Something up?' Annie asked.

'Boston,' he said. 'I need to go to Boston for a couple of days.'

Disappointment was evident in her face before she said a word. 'Right now?'

He nodded. 'Right now.'

'You get that little warning?'

'Sometimes, yes,' he said, and then – almost as an after-thought – 'but I have an idea.' His expression suddenly lost its intensity, became animated. He started smiling.

'What?'

'Come with me . . . come up to Boston with me.'

'Go to Boston? What the hell am I going to do in Boston?'

'You ever been to Boston?'

She shook her head. 'No.'

'So there's always a first time for everything.'

She frowned slightly. 'You're serious aren't you?'

David came forward and took her hand. 'I am, yes. Why the hell not? I've got to see a couple of people, check out some-thing, but possibly only for a few hours. We could go out to Nantucket Island . . . hell, we could even see Cape Cod and Martha's Vineyard. It's a good idea Annie, a couple of days out of New York, change of environment, you know?'

David was enthused, passionate, almost insistent, and there

was something about the proposition that seemed both exciting and romantic.

'There are these little hotels overlooking the harbor . . . you can get up early in the morning and go down to see the boats come in. It's a beautiful part of the country, it really is.'

Annie was still undecided. She started to shake her head. 'I don't know David, it seems a little premature.'

'Christ Annie, I'm not asking you to marry me . . . I'm suggesting we go up to Boston for a couple of days and have a break from the city. What the hell is there to lose?'

What the hell is there to lose? she asked herself. *Miss out on a couple of sales at the store? What am I so worried about?*

'So?' David asked, his tone insistent again.

'Fuck it,' she said. 'I'll come.'

'Great! Hell, that's great!' He threw his arms around her waist, pulled her close and hugged her. 'It'll do us both good.'

Twenty minutes later he left for his apartment to collect his clothes and other necessaries. Annie stuffed a few things in an overnighter, took her toothbrush and hairdryer from the bathroom, went across the hall to tell Sullivan that she was being uncharacteristically spontaneous and impulsive.

Sullivan seemed pleased. 'Send me a postcard,' he said.

'I'll send a fish,' she replied.

'A fish for the apartment cat, eh?'

She laughed with him, hugged him once more and left.

She felt nervous, like a child standing in line at the ferris wheel, tall enough to take a ride for the very first time. It was all too new, and it seemed to be happening too fast, but there was something about it that seemed to pull her along whether she wished to be pulled or not.

Standing in the kitchen, pouring half a carton of milk down the sink, she asked herself what she was doing.

Falling in love? Simply taking a running leap at something in the hope that it will all work out? Trying to live ten years of life in a fortnight to make up for all the time you've lost?

She smiled at her vague reflection in the window, smiled and shook her head and told herself to stop reading significant meanings into everything she did. She was simply going away for a couple of days with David. *And who was David?* Well, he just happened to be some guy she'd met the best part of two weeks before. *And was it all happening a little too fast?* Hell, how fast was it supposed to happen? Wasn't there such a thing as love at first sight? Sure as hell there was. That would be the kind of thing that could be considered too fast, and that certainly hadn't been the case here. There was nothing complicated in this. This was just how life went sometimes . . . and judging by the way she felt it seemed that this was more like the way life was *supposed* to be. Something to look forward to, something to be excited about, something to leave, something to come home to . . .

The phone rang.

Annie snapped to, turned and stared at it as if it were some small and intrusive animal.

Jesus, she thought. *And how long is it since the goddamned phone rang in here?*

She came out of the kitchen, crossed the front room and picked it up.

'Hello?'

Annie?

'David?'

Are you nearly ready?

'How did you get my number David?' she asked.

Christ Annie, I just used your phone to call Boston. Your number is right there on the phone . . . now are you ready or what?

Annie nodded. 'Yes, I'm ready David . . . five minutes or so.'

I'm coming in a taxi . . . we'll go out to the airport. Got us a flight that leaves in about fifty minutes, okay?

'Okay,' she said, a little surprised at her reaction to his calling. This was new, all of it, and she had to get used to the fact that now there was someone else in her life. And did she want that someone? Sure she did, and therefore there was a price to pay. You gave up the loneliness, and in return you lost

221

a little of your privacy. Was that such a bad deal? She figured not.

See you in five.

'Right,' she said. 'See you in five.'

She hung up the telephone and hurried the last of her things into the overnighter. She checked the appliances were off, turned down the thermostat, bundled a few items of clothing into the washing basket behind the bathroom door, and left the apartment.

She checked in on Sullivan on her way, found him on the internet.

'Checking on lists of engineering trade organizations,' he said. 'Have a good time . . . and remember that too much screwing makes you blind.'

She laughed as she closed the door behind her, and then hurried down the stairs.

TWENTY-TWO

There was a moment as they came in to land, a moment when the sea was right beside her, water stretching all the way to the horizon and over the edge into the unknown. It was early evening, and the setting sun caught the sea on fire, and beneath her it seemed like a great roiling ocean of sulphur; and suspended there in mid-air with the sensation of being buffeted by the wind, she tried to recall the last time she had felt as free as this. She could not remember, and in the moment that the aircraft's wheels touched the runway she gripped David's hand – not out of fear or tension or anything such as that, but in sheer exhilaration. She looked at him and he smiled.

'Too long in New York,' he whispered.

'Too long alone David,' she whispered back.

He squeezed her hand.

Annie closed her eyes as the runway rushed beneath them, and when the aircraft taxied to a halt, as people gathered their bags and made their way off the plane, she realized that she had somehow managed to extricate herself almost completely from life. These people, the people she'd flown with, were the same as those who came to browse in The Reader's Rest. Six degrees of separation and all that.

David hurried them across the airport concourse and out into the wind and rain of this Boston evening. He hailed a cab, gave the driver the name of a hotel, and as they pulled away Annie looked back towards the airport. Bright lights, a hundred thousand different people criss-crossing their way through the lives of a hundred thousand more, and all of them weaving back and forth, intermingling, associating, living their lives the only way they knew how: ahead of, behind and beside one another. This was people – good, bad, indifferent, inconspicuous, extravagant, idiosyncratic, profound, stupid and beautiful. All of them together, and Annie O'Neill saw how she had lived on the edges of life, and only now was discovering that the only way to survive was to turn and reach outwards once more.

'How're ya doing?' David asked as the road unfolded before them.

'I'm good David . . . how are you?'

David put his left arm around her shoulder and pulled her close. He took her hand with his right and squeezed it reassuringly. He didn't say a word. Didn't need to say a word.

They drove for little more than ten minutes, and when they pulled up ahead of a small hotel on the outskirts of Boston, when David came around the back of the cab and opened the door for her, as he paid the driver and carried her bag inside, Annie following, feeling something new with each step she took, she realized it was enough to *feel* in those moments. That was the only way she could later describe it: it was enough to feel.

The booking was in the name of Mr and Mrs Quinn.

'Nothing prophetic,' he whispered to her as he signed the register.

'Cash, check or credit card?' the receptionist asked him.

'We'll be paying cash,' David told her.

'And you're staying just the one night?'

David nodded.

'If you could make a deposit of seventy-five dollars,' the receptionist told him, 'and then settle the remainder when you leave?'

David paid the money, took their bags. Annie took the key and they were shown up a curved stairwell and along a wide corridor to a room on the right-hand side.

The room was homely, warm – almost too warm; Annie took off her coat and sweater, stood there surveying the bed, the chairs on either side, the table upon which sat a small colonial-style lamp, the wide bay window beyond which was nothing but deep blue peppered with streetlights and the passage of cars on the freeway in the distance. David was in the bathroom, unpacking his toiletries, and when he appeared in the doorway he looked at her askance.

'You look like you've never been in a hotel before,' he said.

'Many years ago,' she said. 'My mom took me away for a long weekend when I was thirteen.'

'That was the last time?'

She nodded.

'Hell Annie, you really should get out more.'

'I am . . . I have done,' she said, and then she held out her hand and David walked towards her.

'Hungry?' he asked.

'Famished.'

'They have a good restaurant here,' he said.

'You've been here before?'

'A couple of times . . . one of our offices is here in Boston. That's where I have to go tomorrow.'

'So let's go eat,' she said.

There was fresh crab and lobster, shrimp and oysters; David ordered Surf 'N' Turf for them both, a bottle of red wine, fresh-baked bran muffins and salad. Annie ate more than she believed humanly possible, and when the meal was finished they sat for a while with their coffee, David smoking, talking about a job he once undertook out near Nantucket.

By the time they left the restaurant it was gone ten. Annie was tired, dragged herself along the corridor, and once inside their room she collapsed on the bed fully clothed.

David ran a bath, called her once he was in it, and together they lay in the deep water, talking a little of things inconsequential, aware of each other, believing perhaps that there was no other place in the world that they would rather be. When they had bathed, she stood naked in the bathroom while he dried her, and then he lifted her and carried her to the bed where he lay beside her for a while before folding himself against her and kissing her neck.

Their lovemaking was languorous and slow, wordless and without sound. Annie felt whatever tension may have existed within her bones, her muscles, her nerves, slip away, dissolving like ink in water until it vanished. And then she lay beside him as he slept, and she unraveled her mind and drifted effortlessly into sleep.

She could hear the sound of the rain, the passage of cars on the freeway, and the sound of David's breathing matching her own.

The ghosts have gone, she thought. *At last – perhaps forever – the ghosts have gone.*

Wednesday morning broke through the windows in bright, cool sunshine. The room was bathed in a lustrous clean warmth that seemed so different from New York.

At breakfast, an hour or so before David was due to leave for his meetings, she mentioned that she had spoken to Sullivan the day before.

'He'll have a look for me, you know?' she said. It was a non-chalant comment, off-hand in a way.

'I've been thinking about that,' David replied, and for a moment the intensity of expression came back.

'What?' she asked, concern suddenly rippling across the tranquility of their breakfast. It had been good – fresh coffee, warm rolls and butter, scrambled eggs, and little porcelain pots of homemade English marmalade.

He shook his head. 'It's nothing.'

'Don't say nothing when there's evidently something.'

David looked at her with a flash of defensiveness, perhaps even *defiance*.

226

Still waters run deep, she could hear her mother saying. *It's always the quiet ones . . .*

'Tell me,' she prompted.

He shook his head. 'I don't know,' he said, his tone a little reserved. 'I was thinking about it on the plane, like if I was in your situation where I didn't know anything about my father, and I was asking myself if I would want to know.'

'And?'

'Well Annie, I kind of had the thought that the past was the past, you know? Whether I'd want to find out things, whether it would really change anything now . . .'

'I should think it would change things now,' she said.

'But for the better?'

She frowned. She was uncertain of the thread he was pulling, where he was going with this thing.

'I mean, for example, say you found out something you didn't want to find out?'

'Such as?' she asked.

'Like he wasn't everything he was supposed to be . . . like he had an affair or something.'

Annie smiled. 'Christ David, is that the worst scenario you can imagine, that my father might have had an affair? You really think that might change my viewpoint now?'

'Everything changes your viewpoint Annie, even the little things.'

She stopped for a moment. She thought of the flight up here, the thoughts she'd had on the plane, as she'd walked through the airport concourse, as they'd pulled away in the cab and started towards the hotel. She'd had many shifts of viewpoint, and they *were* just little things.

'Say it was something worse than that,' David said. 'Like he had done something bad . . . I mean really bad.'

Annie shook her head. 'I think I would have known about it,' she said. 'I think my mother might have said something . . . I mean, if it was that bad then there's no way that I wouldn't have found out something. And what about Forrester? Surely

227

he would have said something if there was really something worth saying.'

'What *about* this Forrester?' David asked. 'How many times have you met him?'

'Twice,' she said.

'Two times you've met him, and spoken to him for literally a few minutes each time, right?'

'Yes,' Annie said.

'So who the hell is he? Where does he fit into anything?'

Annie leaned forward. 'What makes you think he *has* to fit into anything David? I don't understand what you're getting at.'

David smiled, shook his head. 'I'm sorry,' he said. 'I think sometimes I'm a little possessive, you know? Everything has happened so fast, seems it's been no more than a few days and already we're going away to Boston together.'

'It has only been a few days,' Annie said, 'and we *are* going . . . in fact David, we *have* gone to Boston together.'

He laughed, seemed to relax a little. He leaned back in his chair and lit a cigarette.

'Ignore me,' he said. 'This is what I was talking about when we went over to my apartment.'

Annie raised her eyebrows. 'What bit exactly?'

'You know, the thing about pushing the barriers, like when you start to look at yourself and realize there are things that perhaps you don't like.'

'What exactly?'

'The things you don't like about yourself that you hope no-one will ever find out.'

Annie shook her head.

'Jealousy,' David said. 'Let's face it Annie . . . I'm a little jealous.'

'Jealous?' she said, and started to smile.

'No, seriously . . . I don't mean like *Fatal Attraction*-type jealous, bunny-boiling and all that, but you know when you really like someone, when you really care for someone, well I kinda get like I want them all for myself and there's nothing left to share.'

'You're jealous about Jack Sullivan and Robert Forrester? Christ David, I've known Jack for years, and Forrester must be getting on for seventy. I really don't think you have a thing to worry about.'

David smiled, leaned forward and took Annie's hand. 'I know,' he said, 'but we are men, you see? We are different creatures altogether, and once we find someone, I mean *really* find someone, then we kind of go a little crazy.'

'But if I talk to another man you're not gonna do anything nuts, okay?'

David laughed, seemed back to himself again. 'No, I'm not gonna do anything nuts, Annie. I think I'm just over-compensating.'

'Over-compensating for what?'

'For all the years I've believed that being with someone couldn't feel as good as this.'

Annie smiled; she was touched.

'I'm sorry – ' he started.

She raised her hand. 'Enough of the sorry already. Eat your eggs, drink your coffee, go to your meeting, okay?'

He nodded. 'Okay.'

And he did. He ate his breakfast, drank his coffee, and then he rose to leave. She watched him as he pulled on his jacket, leaned across the table and kissed her forehead, and then holding her hand he told her he wouldn't be more than a couple of hours.

'Take in some sights,' he said.

'And no talking to strange men, right?'

'Not just the strange ones Annie O'Neill . . . no talking to *any* men.'

David laughed. She laughed with him. And then he was walking away, and just for a moment a slight trepidation about what she had let herself in for crept into her thoughts.

She brushed it away. It went – effortlessly, silently – and for a while she sat alone in the small hotel restaurant believing that whatever this might bring it was better than what she had – or more accurately, didn't have – before.

TWENTY-THREE

There was something about waiting that unsettled Annie O'Neill.

After breakfast, after David had left for the city, she went back to their room and sat in a chair leafing through a copy of *Tatler* that someone had left behind on the coffee table. Then, already restless and a little agitated, she went to the window and looked out across the green lawns that spanned the length of the building, at the slip-road from the freeway, and the cars that hurried past as if late for their destinations.

She could remember a time, a time that seemed an age ago, when she had accompanied her mother to a hair salon.

A woman had sat beside Annie's mother, a woman she seemed to know, and they had talked for a little while as their heads baked inside their space-helmets.

Secondary melanoma, three, four months and he was dead, the woman told Annie's mother.

He went somewhere out west, to some place where they used Steiner's teaching. Iscador they gave him. That's essence of mistletoe, something about a parasite plant curing parasite diseases, but he just kind of dissolved away. I saw him just before he died, out with some nuns in a convent hospital near Secaucus. His face was all drawn up tight, his cheeks thin like tissue, as if you could just push your finger right through them and feel them pierce like rice paper. Scared me Madeline . . . never so scared in all my life. Little more than forty he was, running every day, didn't smoke, drank less than a Puritan preacher, faithful to his wife, worked for that corporation . . . you know, that big new place out near where the New Jersey Turnpike crosses 280 . . .

And Annie had listened, listened to every word, and though she hadn't understood much of what they were saying she nevertheless understood the emotion. It was something close to fear, and something about waiting for someone to die.

And she'd had a thought, a single thought that haunted her even after they'd left the salon and her mom had taken her to De Walt's and bought her a cream soda float *for being such a good girl while momma had her hair fixed.*

And the thought was: *There you are you old dreamer . . . there you are again.*

Like fear was nothing new. Like waiting for something bad to happen was something she'd experienced before but could not remember. However hard she tried, she could not remember.

In the hour or two after David had gone she felt that same emotional twinge. She was alone, at least on the face of it, having placed her trust in a man who was little more than a lover, hadn't even become a real friend as yet, and here she was, hundreds of miles from home, and he had gone. How long had he said? *Shouldn't be more than a couple of hours.* Well, that couple of hours had already expired, and surely if he was going to be considerably longer than that he would at least call. He *would* call, wouldn't he?

Annie thought to go out, to take a walk, see the sights, but the idea that David might phone kept her in the hotel room until gone noon. He'd left just after nine, but then of course the traffic may have been bad.

By one o'clock she was cursing herself for not asking for the name of the insurance company he worked for. If she'd known the name she could have called, asked if he was there, or had he already left? But even if she'd had the number she wondered if she would have made the call. Would that have irritated him, would he have felt that she was a little obsessive? For God's sake, he'd gone to a meeting, a business meeting with his employers, perhaps prospective clients, and she was panicking that he might not return, that this was some sort of awful practical joke. Find a girl, get her to sleep with you, take her out to Boston and leave her in a hotel.

Annie O'Neill smiled to herself as she paced back and forth from the bathroom to the door of the room; suddenly she stopped in her tracks.

What was she doing?

This was crazy.

She glanced at her watch; it was just twenty after one. She was hungry, decided to go down into the restaurant and have some lunch.

She reached the door and the phone rang.

Right there beside the bed the phone rang. The sound was shrill, piercing the silence of the room. She jumped, startled, and then almost leapt across the bed to snatch the receiver from the cradle.

Mrs Quinn?

Annie frowned, and then – realizing – she smiled and said, 'Yes, this is she.'

A message from your husband. He says he'll be a little later than planned. He suggested you have some lunch in the restaurant, that he hopes to be back by about four or five, okay?

'Okay,' Annie said. 'Thank you.'

She set the receiver in its cradle, and then rising from the bed she asked herself why he hadn't asked to speak to her directly. Perhaps he'd called and she hadn't heard the phone. Had she been in the bathroom or something? She couldn't remember a second when she'd been out of earshot. Perhaps David just wanted reception to relay a message to 'Mrs Quinn', like it was something to make her smile.

It had made her smile.

Why was she getting so wound up about something that really meant nothing at all?

There you are you old dreamer . . . there you are again.

She shrugged the thought away, and headed down to the restaurant.

Annie ate what the mâitre-d' suggested – clam chowder, a

green salad with avocado slices and lemon mayonnaise. The food was good, she hadn't realized how hungry she was. Perhaps the sea air. Perhaps the sex. Perhaps compensation for being alone someplace strange and feeling there was no-one to talk to. Like Elvis.

After lunch she did go out. David had relayed his message, there were at least a couple of hours to kill, and if he called again he could spend a little time wondering where she might have gone. It would serve him right for dragging her out here and then leaving her by herself.

She didn't even know the name of where she was, but for a little while she lost herself in the gift shops and bookstores that seemed to populate the harbor-facing street with alarming frequency. She bought a copy of *Heart Songs And Other Stories* by Annie Proulx, sat on a bench at the end of the street and started to read until the cold was too much for her to bear. She walked back slowly – aimlessly – and by the time she reached the hotel it was almost five.

She stopped at reception to ask if her husband had returned, if there had been any messages. She was told *No, there's been nothing, but we'll let you know the moment he calls, okay Mrs Quinn?*

Okay, she'd said, but it wasn't, and it still wasn't okay when she reached her over-warm room and sat on the edge of the bed.

She took off her coat, used the small two-cup kettle and a complimentary sachet of instant coffee to make a drink. Seated in the armchair she tried to read again, but her mind was elsewhere. She considered going down to the restaurant again and eating an early dinner, but she wasn't hungry, at least not in the nourishment and vitamin department. It was boredom-hunger, that gnawing sense of agitation that makes you feel that anything could be better than sitting waiting for something to happen.

She was angry with herself, angry that she was feeling like this. This was one of those things that David had spoken of in the apartment, when the something you wind up with might not be altogether better than the nothing you had before.

She turned at the sound of footsteps approaching the door.

Her heart stopped.

The footsteps didn't.

She cursed, rose from the chair and tipped the remainder of the foul-tasting instant coffee down the sink. She wanted to throw the cup in there too, to hear it smash, to spend her time collecting fragments of delicately painted porcelain from the linoleum floor. It would be something to do for God's sake.

She left the bathroom, started towards the window, and even as she heard the door open, even as she saw David appear in the frame, his face ruddy, his hair windswept, the smell of the outside rushing in with him like a long-lost cousin at Christmas, she wanted to challenge him, to ask him what the hell he had been thinking of . . .

But she couldn't.

There were no harsh words, no interrogation about where he had been, what he had been doing, why he didn't call her, visit, send a postcard . . .

There was simply relief that he was there.

She felt that now he'd arrived she could be herself.

'I'm really, *really* sorry,' he said quietly, and then he walked towards her and put his hands on her shoulders. 'I had no idea they would want me for so long . . . there were some people we had to show around, prospective clients, and they had three hundred yards of questions. Jesus, I was furious.'

He pulled her close and hugged her.

Annie let him overwhelm her with his presence, with his person, and for a moment she could think of nothing to say.

'It's alright,' she said eventually. 'I had some lunch, went out for a walk. I even bought a book.'

David was shaking his head. 'I really didn't mean to leave you here all day,' he said, and then he let her go, and without taking his hands from around her he looked right at her.

There was something in his eyes, something that suggested

exhaustion, and when he moved to the edge of the bed and seemed to drop she asked him if he was okay.

He shook his head, smiled as best he could, and said he was fine. *Just fine Annie.*

'I think we should go out,' he suggested. 'Go take a look around, have a drink or something. What d'you reckon?'

'A good idea,' Annie said. Her eagerness was obvious. She felt like she'd been trapped inside all day. The world beckoned.

She gathered her coat and purse, and together they left the hotel. They walked, she held on to his arm, and everything seemed back to rights to her – the sounds and smells of this place, the faces of people walking by, the muted colors of early winter invading this territory.

'I've been thinking,' David said at some point.

Annie glanced sideways at his worn-out face.

'I've been thinking that we should do something different.'

'Kind of different?'

He smiled, put his arm around her shoulder and pulled her close. 'I don't know, something spontaneous . . . like pack everything up and go somewhere for six months, maybe Europe or someplace.'

She laughed suddenly, a little awkwardly. 'And how the hell could we afford to do something like that?'

David slowed but didn't stop walking. 'I've got a little money saved, you know? I mean, maybe we could put whatever money we have together and do something like that.'

'You might have a little money, but I've got about enough to pay the rent and eat for the next three weeks. I don't exactly make a great deal from the store.'

David frowned and shook his head. 'You haven't managed to save any money at all?'

'This is real life,' Annie said. 'I am fortunate to have bought the lease on the store from the sale of my parents' house, and thankfully the apartment I live in is in a rent-control area. The money I make from the store is just about enough to get me through from one month to the next.'

David nodded understandingly, but his disappointment was palpable. There was little he could have done to disguise the expression he wore. 'So no six months wandering around Europe then?'

She smiled and shook her head. 'I'm afraid not David. Six months away from the store and I'd come back to nothing at all.'

'So maybe I should sort out my apartment, decorate it, perhaps look for some other line of work. I feel I should stay put for now, that I should get used to being in one place for more than a week at a time.'

His voice trailed away.

She knew he didn't wish her to say anything; he wasn't done with his line of thought.

She glanced at him again. He was smiling. He turned towards her. She smiled back.

'I was thinking that when we get back to New York you could help me . . . if you wanted, of course.'

She nodded. 'I would like to help,' she said.

'Good,' he said quietly. 'That's good.'

They didn't speak again, and after crossing a junction at the end of the street David pointed to a bar on the facing side. The place was jammed with people, the sound deafening, but there was great warmth in that sound, an overwhelming feeling of life, of *being alive*.

They jostled with people – people laughing, people shouting orders – and only when she stood there, the counter-top ahead of her, David to her right, strangers all around, did she think *Why am I here? Why have I come out here when what I really want to do is stay behind in the hotel with David?*

Then a woman was asking Annie what she wanted, what she wanted to drink, and Annie was caught for words, for thoughts perhaps, and she hesitated.

A man pushed past her, his elbow jamming into her side and causing her some degree of pain.

She turned suddenly. 'Hey!' she said.

'You gonna make up your mind or what?' the man snapped.

'Patience . . . have patience,' Annie replied.

'Aah, get a life why don'tcha?' the man sneered.

Suddenly David was beside her, there between herself and the man.

'You know this woman?' David was asking him.

The man frowned, decided not to answer, and at the same time didn't know where to look.

'Hey!' David said. 'Do you know this woman?'

Annie felt immediately uncomfortable; confrontations did not suit her, especially those connected to herself.

The man shook his head.

'Well, let me tell you something – ' David started.

'What the fuck is this?' the man interjected.

Annie wanted to shrink back into the crowd and slip silently into the street. She was tense, scared even, and she wanted to pull David's arm, to tell him *Never mind, it doesn't matter*, but there was something in his face, something about the way he was standing that told her not to interrupt. That something was passion, the passion with which he'd first spoken to her in his apartment.

David seemed to tower over the man even though they were of the same height. Annie could feel people watching them.

'What is it? I'll tell you what the fuck it is,' David continued, his voice getting louder. 'You tell her to get a life . . . get a life? What the fuck d'you know? Tell me what the fuck you know?'

David seemed to round on the guy, seemed to corner him mentally, and the guy just stood there wishing to hell he hadn't said a word.

'You come here thinking that because she gets in your way then she owes you something . . . that you gotta say something, you gotta be the big man. And now you feel bad because I have something to say about it, and maybe you feel a little guilty, a little embarrassed, right?'

The man stood expressionless, lost for words.

'You tell me that, and then you tell me that your life means something more than anyone else's.'

The man stood immobile, rooted to the spot.

David leaned close to him, whispered right to his face. 'Sorry to the lady?'

The man glanced at Annie, a weak smile playing at the corners of his lips.

Sorry, he mouthed.

Annie smiled, nodded in acknowledgement, at the same time feeling sympathy as well as a strange sense of satisfaction. She couldn't remember anyone ever coming to her defence in such a forceful and challenging manner.

David gripped the man's shoulder. 'Now you,' he whispered, his voice cold and direct. 'You go get a life.'

The man lowered his head and backed away. The crowd that had gathered dispersed in silence, some watching the man, some watching David.

Annie looked up. A woman, leaning against the bar was watching David, her face intent; Annie sensed the woman's attraction, her interest in David.

Mine, Annie heard herself think. *He's mine*. And then: *What is this? Jealousy?* She surprised herself with the intensity of this emotion, an emotion that was new, another sensation, another viewpoint.

She shrugged it off, gripped David's arm, and then they were walking through the crowd, walking towards the door, out into the street, the cool air, the space, the sound of life, unaffected by what had happened here.

It was only as they reached the junction that she realized David was laughing to himself.

She nudged him with her elbow. He turned, still laughing, and this became contagious, virulently contagious, and she was laughing with him . . . these two people, these strange people, standing there at the junction while the cars waited for them to cross.

*

Back at the hotel, after they'd eaten, after they'd once again made love and there was nothing but silence, she'd asked him why he'd reacted the way he had in the bar.

'Because people are sometimes so blind and self-centered,' he said. 'Sometimes you look at someone and there is just nothing in their eyes . . . like they're hollow, you know? Sometimes you see someone like that and you want to do something to wake them up.'

Like what you did to me in your apartment? Annie wanted to ask, but she didn't.

And then *Is there something else going on here David? Is there something else you're not telling me about? Were you really mad at that guy, or is there something else you're fighting?*

But she didn't say a word.

She just pulled herself against him and closed her eyes.

Tomorrow would be another day.

TWENTY-FOUR

He saw her home. Drove all the way from the airport with her, had the cab wait while he walked her up to her apartment, and then he kissed her, held her for a while, and he left. He had work to do he said, reports to prepare for the clients he'd seen in Boston. He needed a day or so, that was all, but unless he was alone he would never get it done. And besides, he'd added, Annie should perhaps go back to the store or her regulars might give up on her.

From the front window overlooking the street Annie watched the cab pull away, and then she turned and walked through her apartment as if this was some place new. Some place she'd never been before. She touched her things – her books, the ornaments lined up like soldiers on the chest of drawers, and from the front she stepped into the bathroom, opened the cabinet above the sink and looked at the jars of anti-ageing cream, moisturiser, herbal shampoo, the *Have A Hollywood Smile* toothpaste, other such things that really seemed to mean nothing at all the way she felt now. And how did she feel now? A little disturbed perhaps, a little ill-at-ease after the scene in the bar the night before? No, that wasn't it. David had not mentioned it, not another word about why he had turned on the man the way he did. Perhaps he didn't feel there was any need to justify or rationalize his behavior. And Annie, wanting to say something, had restrained herself. She hadn't wanted to grant it any more importance than it deserved. And was it important? Perhaps, in a way, it was. It had meant something to her, that someone had stepped forward to defend her, to place her well-being above their own.

The man could so easily have become violent, abusive, could have justifiably attacked David for what he said. But he had not. He had backed down. And for that and that alone Annie had been immeasurably relieved. Weeks ago, days even, such a scene would have horrified her. She would have walked from the place terrified, trembling, and it would have been hours before she would have returned to battery. But no, she had walked half a block and laughed with David about the situation.

Something had changed. So many things had changed. And they had all come from within.

Annie smiled to herself and walked into the kitchen. Looking to her right, she opened the cupboard door above the counter and reached for the tea. Her hand went left a few inches, back again. She looked up, frowned. The tea wasn't there. She moved aside a box of packet soups, and there – beside them and to the rear – was the container in which she stored tea-leaves. She reached it down, set it on the counter. She shook her head.

A place for everything, and everything in its place, her mother would say. That was one particular characteristic she had inherited from Madeline. Annie O'Neill was neat and predictable beyond reproach. She always knew where everything was, and everything went right back there when she was done.

She shrugged. *The male influence*, she thought, and switched on the kettle.

Sitting at the table in the front she looked through the pages that Forrester had brought. She was ready to know more, and once again a vague thought started to nag at the edges of her mind. It was Thursday, Forrester wouldn't come again until Monday: disappointment and frustration seemed to lie ahead in the gap between.

And then she remembered.

Sullivan.

Her father.

She got up, left her apartment, and knocked on Sullivan's door. Nothing.

She glanced at her watch, it was a little after ten, and she tried to remember if Sullivan had anything arranged for Thursday mornings.

She returned to her front room, sat once again at the table, and began to leaf through the manuscript. It all came back – Jozef Kolzac and Elena Kruszwica, the horrors of Auschwitz and Wilhelm Kiel; Sergeant Daniel Rosen carrying this ghost of a child back through liberated Europe and onto a boat bound for New York; Rebecca McCready accepting the child into her home, the child becoming a teenager, leaving after Rosen's death and disappearing into New York. From there the rest unfolded like a Martin Scorsese movie: the gambling and the drinking, the killings and robberies, all of it filling her mind with the images and sounds and colors of an age past. She thought of Johnnie Redbird holed up in Rikers Island for Olson's murder, and how Harry Rose had left him there, left him to pay the penalty for something they both had done.

And when she turned the last page she really wanted to know, *really* wanted to find out what had happened seven years later.

Annie fetched the telephone book, searched until she found listings for *Forrester* . . . *A, B, G, K, O, P* . . . and then dozens of *R. Forresters* scrolling down the page like a taunt. There was no way she would find him. Not this way. Such an idea was hopeless.

She turned and looked at her door. Where the hell was Sullivan?

As if in answer to her thoughts she heard the street door open and close.

She got up, hurried out onto the landing and called down.

'Jack?'

From the bottom she heard his voice. 'Jesus Mary Mother of God you gave me a fright Annie O'Neill . . . what the hell are you doing?'

243

Sullivan came around the last turn on the stairwell and stopped, looked up at her, stood there catching his breath like he'd been hurrying.

'When did you get back?' he asked.

'This morning, just a little while ago.'

'And what is it that's so important you're hollerin' at me from the top of the stairs?' Sullivan started walking towards her. He was already breathless, his face strained and tired. He looked far the worse for wear than she'd ever seen him. His body was fighting, she knew, and for a split second she regretted the promise he'd made. The regret vanished as she realized what he was doing. He was no longer drinking.

Have to be cruel to be kind, her mother would have said.

'I wanted to know if you'd found anything out,' Annie said, and in her voice she could hear the sense of anticipation and expectancy.

Sullivan shook his head. He walked to his apartment door, produced his key and unlocked it. He was inside, Annie following him, before he answered.

'Your father,' he started, 'as far as I can tell – '

'What?' Annie prompted. 'As far as you can tell what?'

Sullivan shook his head and frowned. 'Your father . . . well hell, Annie, it seems that your father has no records.'

She laughed, a short nervous laugh. '*What?*'

Sullivan crossed the room and sat down. 'I've gone through every engineering trade association and organization record I could find. I've been on the internet. I went down to the library yesterday and scoured most of their engineering and architectural sections. References, indexes, everything I could think of. I didn't find a thing, so I called up some friends and had them go through newspaper microfiche records for obituaries, and then when that proved fruitless I went to the Department of Public Works, and when I couldn't find anyone named Frank O'Neill who even came close to the dates you gave me I went to a bar on 114th and had a club soda and a bowl of peanuts.'

'A club soda?' Annie asked.

Sullivan nodded. 'A club soda, Annie O'Neill. Jack Ulysses Sullivan sat in a bar on 114th drinking a club soda, as God is my witness.'

Annie sat down beside Sullivan. 'I don't understand,' she said. 'I don't understand how someone can't exist.'

Sullivan smiled, took her hand and squeezed it. 'Of course someone can't not exist Annie. Your father existed as much as you and me . . . but for whatever reason I haven't found any records. It really isn't that big a deal – '

'Perhaps not to you Jack, but it is to me.'

'Okay, okay Annie . . . perhaps that didn't come out the way I meant it. People can live their whole lives and never really – '

'Amount to anything?' she interjected.

'You're putting words in my mouth, Annie,' Sullivan said. 'All I'm saying is that I'm sure your father did whatever he did, and I bet he was fucking good at it . . . but he never really figured from a social record point of view.'

Annie was silent for a time.

'I mean, apart from a few newspaper photos no-one will ever know I existed, except the people that knew me,' Sullivan added.

'I don't know,' Annie said. 'I can't say that I'm not disappointed . . . I'd hoped that you'd find out something about him.'

'Tell me,' Sullivan said. 'Tell me why it's become so important all of a sudden.'

Annie shook her head. She looked away for a while, away into the middle of the room. 'I can't say,' she eventually said. Her voice was quiet, a whisper almost. 'I was thinking about it a while back, a few days ago. I think this thing with Forrester started it up, the fact that there was someone else apart from my mother who knew him. It made me look at the fact that he had a life too, he had friends, people who knew his name, perhaps someplace he'd go and have a drink when he felt down.' Annie paused, was once again silent for a few seconds.

'He was my father, a real honest-to-God human being, and there's absolutely nothing left of him but this wristwatch and a book he left me.'

'And the store,' Sullivan said. 'You have the store.'

'Yes, I have the store,' Annie replied.

'And what do you think it would give you . . . if you found out?' Sullivan asked.

'Christ only knows Jack. A sense of belonging I s'pose, a feeling that I came from somewhere.'

'Seems to me it's an awful lot more important to know where you're going than where you came from.'

'Except if where you came from could determine where you're headed,' Annie said.

'And where d'you think you're headed?'

Annie smiled. 'I want to go on feeling what I've felt with David, like there's someone to come home to, someone to go see – '

'And someone with whom you can exercise your tremendous vocal capacity,' Sullivan added with a wry smile.

'Yes Jack . . . that too.'

'So just live life Annie O'Neill . . . 'cause the fact of the matter is that life will go on whether you live with it or not. And I'll tell you one thing for free. You sure as hell seem happier these past few days than I've ever known you.'

'I am,' Annie said. 'I am happier Jack.'

'So forget about your father. I know it's easy for me to say that, but whoever he was, whatever he did, those things don't hold anywhere near as much importance as what you're doing now.'

Sullivan squeezed her hand again.

'Seems to me the one thing that fathers always want, mothers too for that matter, is for their kids to be happy. Comes down to it they always come to terms with decisions their kids make as long as they're happy, right?'

Annie nodded. 'I s'pose.'

'So make this thing with David work, and spend whatever

time you want with Forrester; hear what he has to say but don't give it any more importance than it deserves. Stories are really nothing more than stories, okay?'

Annie leaned forward and hugged Sullivan. 'Okay,' she whispered. 'Okay Jack.'

She held him for a moment more and then released him.

'You got plans tonight?' Annie asked.

Sullivan shook his head. 'Figured I'd eat half a box of Excedrin and try and sleep off the DTs.'

'Sounds like fun. Why not come over and have some dinner with me.'

'Sure I will,' Sullivan said. 'That would be good.'

'We'll eat and watch a video or something okay?'

'Good enough for me,' he said, and smiled.

Annie left his apartment and crossed the landing.

That evening, while preparing food before Sullivan came over, she looked for a particular CD in the rack system. She found it no problem, but it was out of its alphabetical sequence.

She recalled David looking through the CDs when he'd first come by. That must have been it. *Have to educate the man*, she thought, and considered it no further. But then, moments later, having thought of David, she wanted to call him, wanted to hear his voice, and realized that she still had no number for him, no way to reach him if she wanted, or needed, to.

And then Sullivan came across and they ate, and after that they sat beside one another on the couch and watched *The Philadelphia Story*, and Annie fell in love with Cary Grant all over again.

Sullivan didn't stay long once the movie was over, and Annie – more tired than she believed possible – went to bed, tugged the quilt over her, and fell asleep.

She did not dream.

Her mind was empty.

As empty as the memory of her father.

TWENTY-FIVE

It was the envelope that did it. The envelope which the courier had brought with the last section of the manuscript. It was there on the counter at the store on Friday morning when she let herself in, when she walked into somewhere that seemed alien to her, altogether different.

She picked it up, turned it over, and there on the back was stamped SPEEDEE COURIERS and a telephone number.

She dialed the number, was greeted by Al who asked her politely if this was to order a delivery or a collection.

Neither, she told Al. An inquiry.

Shoot, Al said.

She explained who she was, gave her address, and told him that she'd received a package on the previous Monday night couriered by one of their staff.

Some problem? he'd asked.

No, she told him, but she wondered if it was possible to get a contact number for the person who'd sent it.

Sure, Al said. Hang on there, honey.

Annie waited, watching the street through the window, hoping that she might catch sight of David, fed up with writing reports and feeling like there was nothing in the world he'd rather do than be with her.

Al came back. You got a pen? he asked.

Yes, Annie said, and wrote the telephone number he gave her on the back of the same envelope.

Sent by a Mr Forrester, Al said. That right?

'Yes, Robert Forrester,' Annie said. She thanked Al, hung up, and stood staring at the envelope, a number of scenarios racing through her mind.

Hi there, it's Annie . . . I hope you don't mind but I got your number from the courier company, and I was wondering if you wanted to move our next club meeting to tonight.

Mr Forrester. It's Annie O'Neill here. I hope you don't think I'm being presumptuous, but I really missed seeing you Monday evening and I wanted to thank you for sending over the manuscript. I wondered if there was any possibility you might be able to bring over the next chapters . . .

She felt awkward, a little confused, and no matter how she worded it, no matter what phrasing she used, it sounded artificial and rehearsed.

She reached for the receiver. Lifted it. It felt extraordinarily heavy in her hand.

She looked at the number she'd scrawled down and when she began punching it in it was almost as though she were driven: she didn't want to do this, but she couldn't help it.

The telephone rang at the other end. Once. Twice. Three times. A rush of trepidation overcame her, she asked herself what in God's name she was doing, and just as she withdrew the receiver from her ear she heard the line connect at the other end.

Yes?

'Hi,' she said. 'I wondered if Mr Forrester was there.'

There was a pronounced pause.

'Tell him it's Annie . . . Annie O'Neill,' she said.

She was aware of the heavy intake of breath at the other end. But, then again, perhaps it was her imagination. She was crediting the person with the same nervousness that she herself was feeling. She heard the receiver being set down, the sound of footsteps, and then the murmur of words being exchanged.

Did those voices sound aggressive?

The voices went quiet. Footsteps again. The sound of the receiver being lifted.

Miss O'Neill?

It was Forrester's voice.

Annie was almost surprised to hear him there, at the other end of the line.

'Mr Forrester. I'm really sorry about this. I got your number from the courier company you used to send over the manuscript Monday night.'

Ah, yes, of course. How are you my dear? I'm very sorry I couldn't come over but there was some business I had to attend to.

'It's fine Mr Forrester, it really is, and I wanted to thank you for taking the trouble.'

It's a pleasure my dear, and I can assure you that I won't be missing the next meeting.

'That's what I wanted to talk to you about.'

There's a problem? You have another engagement?

'No, nothing like that Mr Forrester. It's just that . . . well it's just that – '

What my dear . . . out with it.

Annie smiled, almost embarrassed. 'Well, I was wondering if there was any possibility that I might – '

Get the next chapter before Monday?

Annie didn't say a word.

Forrester laughed at the other end. It was a warm and engaging sound.

It's quite a story is it not? I really think that it might have had a chance of being published had it ever been finished.

'It wasn't finished?' she asked.

No, unfortunately not . . . but there's still quite a bit of it left.

'And d'you think that – '

You could have it for the weekend?

'Yes, I was hoping that I might see it before the weekend. I know that there were rules and everything, but – '

But rules were made to be broken Miss O'Neill . . . that's what you were hoping, I believe?

'Yes,' she said. 'I was hoping that there might be an exception made.'

Well, I think it's only fair considering I was absent from the last meeting. I'll have someone bring it over for you. What time will you be there until today?

'Well, I'm usually here until about five or five-thirty,' she said.

I'll have it there before you leave . . . but I still wish to hold our next meeting on Monday if that's alright with you?'

'Of course,' Annie said. 'Yes, of course.'

Very well then, Miss O'Neill. I'll send over the next section, and I'll see you again on Monday. Take care, and have a pleasant weekend.

'Thank you Mr Forrester, I really appreciate it.'

Not at all my dear, not at all . . . goodbye.

The receiver went dead in her hand, and slowly, gently, she set it back in the cradle.

She breathed deeply. That had been fine. Forrester hadn't seemed upset about her finding his number. Hadn't seemed bothered at all. She shrugged her shoulders and asked herself why she'd gotten so worked up. There really was nothing to be concerned about. He'd probably appreciated the fact that someone had called him. He was just a lonely old –

She stopped mid-flight.

Someone else had answered the phone. Another man. Younger by the sound of his voice.

And was there something about his tone that made her feel he was surprised by her call? Or had she imagined it?

Hell, it didn't matter. Job done. Purpose served. She would get to read the next part of the manuscript that evening.

The day expired in slow-motion. Four customers. *See Under: Love* by David Grossman; *Acts of Worship* by Yukio Mishima; *The Dust Roads of Monferrato* by Rosetta Loy and, finally, a copy of De Lillo's *Americana*. John Damianka didn't appear with the customary mayonnaise-drenched sub, and for this she was grateful. She felt content dealing with anonymity, people she had never seen before, people she would probably never see again. And if she did – perhaps on the subway, perhaps walking ahead of her on the street – she would not recognize them anyway.

She had enough to contend with. David Quinn had filled her thoughts for the past few days, and now she was trying to balance their burgeoning relationship alongside whatever she was feeling about her father.

At one point she thought of calling Forrester again to ask if there were any further *Dear Heart* letters that he might send over.

She decided against it. You can push the walls of envelope only so far.

The courier came a little after four. Different guy, same company. She gave Stan – his name according to the small machine-stitched tag on his breast pocket – a ten-dollar tip. She wasn't paying ten dollars for his trouble, she was paying ten dollars because she was so grateful to receive the package before the store closed. Forrester was a man of his word. Whoever or whatever else he might be, he was at least a man of his word.

She closed up. Twenty-five after four. She turned out the lights, locked the front door, and hurried home.

Had Sullivan been in his apartment she would have said *Hi*, though as she'd entered the building she'd decided not to speak to him of the manuscript she carried.

This time – for reasons she could neither isolate nor fathom – she wanted to read the pages alone.

TWENTY-SIX

Rikers Island was born from the mind of a vindictive guilt-ridden man.

Rikers Island sits in the East River between Long Island and Manhattan, and from its outermost face you would have seen the North and South Brothers, Port Morris, and the vast expanse of the Conrail Freight Yard. To the left was Lawrence Point, the Consolidated Edison Company site and, over Steinway Creek, the Bowery Bay and the ripe haunt that forever ghosted across the channel from the Sewage Treatment Facility. Though Manhattan would grow, stretching skyward with steel and concrete fingers, though the suburbs of Astoria and Steinway would forever beckon with streetlights and the sound of New York evening parties, Rikers Island would always stay the same.

It was built by unreasonable men to keep the vicious and undesirable in check. And this it did, with decisive and unquestionable authority.

Within its walls were housed the worst of the unwanteds: men who had killed for love, for money, for revenge, or for the sheer joy of killing itself. These were men who carried not only their own pain, but the pain of those they had tortured and maimed and robbed, the screams of women they had raped and beaten and abused, the children they had fathered and deserted and never given another thought for, the mothers whose hearts they had broken, the fathers whose dreams they'd destroyed. And in among these men were the innocent, the lost, the confused, the victimized, the crazy, the defeated and the near-dead.

And in amongst all of those was me.

Seven years I was there, and of those two thousand, five hundred days, and within those sixty thousand hours, there was not a minute nor a second that went by when I did not imagine that this was where I would die. But under this certainty lay a vague and tenuous hope that somehow Harry Rose would engineer a means by which I would be freed – freed to share in the wealth and wonder that was rightfully as much my own as ever it was Harry's. I was a patient man, patience of Job it seemed, and though the hours unfolded like days, the days like weeks, I held myself in check. I never raised my voice or my fists in anger or retaliation, because I knew that once I crossed the line at Rikers there was no going back. I had gone to the cubes once, and once was enough.

From my narrow cell I heard America cry through her growing pains. I heard of the racial tensions, the shooting of blacks in Mississippi, saw Kennedy receive the Democratic presidential nomination, listened to the wireless as he was inaugurated in January of '61.

And I waited.

Through the freedom rides, the Marines in Laos, the death of Marilyn Monroe, white mobs storming the University of Mississippi, the Bay of Pigs, the blockade of Cuba; through a thousand arrests in Alabama, the shooting of Medgar Evers, Valachi's testimony to the Senate Committee on Organized Crime, Kennedy's assassination; through the declaration of martial law in Saigon, the killing of Malcolm X and the bombing of Hanoi – through all these things, these monumental swathes of history daubed across America's canvas – I, Johnnie Redbird, would remember little of anything at all.

Perversely, I would most of all remember teeth.

Incisors, molars, pre-molars, canines, crowns and roots, dentine, cementum and enamel. Infected gums, wisdoms, root canals, fillings, extractions, abscesses and gingivitis.

Through my association with one Oscar Tate Lundy, teeth would become my life, and ultimately my salvation.

'Doc' Lundy was not a real doctor, not even a dentist. Doc Lundy was a retired auto mechanic from Brooklyn Heights, a man who took it in his head to supplement his meager life's savings by holding up a jewelry store in broad daylight with nothing more than a two-foot length of copper pipe packed with sand. He'd been sixty-six at the time, and though he'd managed to run from the store with a handful of cultured pearls and three diamond engagement rings, a lifetime of smoking and heavy drinking caught up with him after four blocks. As did the store manager, two store assistants, a customer, and an off-duty cop who just happened to be looking in the window at the time.

Doc appeared for his arraignment thirteen minutes late. He told the court clerk to 'go fuck himself in the ass' when he was asked whether he was pleading guilty, and when the judge suggested there might be a slim possibility of a contempt charge to go with his robbery, Doc Lundy stood up, unzipped his pants, took out his cock, and told the judge to 'come suck this you faggot motherfucker'.

Some said Doc Lundy handled his court appearance with such delicacy and tact because he was plain and simple crazy.

Some said he wanted the longest sentence possible because by the time he got out his life's savings might actually see him through.

I figured he was a lonely old loser who never amounted to anything much in life, and Rikers Island seemed like a country club after the disappointments he'd suffered.

So Doc Lundy came, and he made it his business to be useful. There weren't one helluva lot of cars to fix, and so he went to the library – religiously, like a full scholarship out of Queens into Harvard – and he studied teeth.

After a year and a half of prodding and probing, painful extractions and saltwater gargles, the Block warden gave Doc Lundy his own cell. They brought in hypodermic needles and painkillers, tongue depressors and paper cups. They painted the walls white and put a little dividing wall between Doc's berth and his 'surgery'. Even the screws came down there to get their checkups, and when Doc fixed a rotten molar that had been plaguing Tony Cicero's brother for the best part of five years, that old man earned himself a place in the hearts and mouths of Rikers Island.

By the time Doc was seventy-four he was getting too old and frail to be fixing teeth. His hands were unsteady, his eyes failing, and though option for parole had been given three times in the previous four years, he had never taken it. Rikers had not only become his place of work, it had become his home, and he'd long since decided that he'd been an awful lot more useful to humanity there than he had ever been on the outside.

So Doc Lundy took an apprentice, and the man he chose was me.

I didn't read so good, at least not then, and so I learned all I needed by watching, by listening, by practice and experience on the mouths of some of the most dangerous men in America. Doc insisted that I study, however, sent me down to the library and punished me through hours of texts. After a while, some months perhaps, I started to crave understanding. I read voraciously, not only about teeth, but anything I could get my hands on. There was a world there, a world within worlds, and through the pages of books, through stories and articles and biographies and technical manuals, I gained the education I had never received. Knowledge is power, Doc told me, and I believed him. He made me write as well, made me practice writing for God's sake, and he would go through sentence after sentence correcting spelling, grammar, punctuation and tense. He made all of these things a condition of my apprenticeship, and I bore them without complaint. It will serve you well one day, he said, and even though I did not believe him then, I do believe him now. Had I not learned then, I would not be writing these lines. At that time such things had no purpose, but in time – as I now know – they became the most important purpose of all.

After a year I knew all that Doc Lundy had ever known about teeth. Teeth became my reason for being, and with the assistance of the local medical facility I started making up dental records, taking patients down for X-rays, some of them in waist-shackles and under armed guard. I took my job seriously, like a real professional, and even as I worked, even as I filled and scraped and injected and rinsed, I began to understand the significance of teeth.

Teeth were as telling as fingerprints. Teeth survived fire and acid. Teeth were as characteristic as retina, as unique as DNA.

It was the birth of an idea, and when Doc Lundy finally died, when his body was cremated and his ashes scattered in Rikers Island Channel, I went before the governor and insisted that the dental facility be maintained. I calculated the amount of money that such care would cost the detention system, and when the governor saw the facts and figures presented he agreed. I would become the new Doc.

It was early 1966. The US launched the most significant offensive of the Vietnam War, sending eight thousand troops into the Iron Triangle; Buster Keaton died in the same month as Admiral Nimitz; Mrs Gandhi came to Washington to talk with Lyndon Johnson, and I started lancing abscesses at Rikers without Doc Lundy over my shoulder.

With access to medical and dental records I found my man. Henry Abner Truro was a three-times guilty child-molester from Staten Island. Posing as a fairground worker, he'd lured three little kids into a narrow tunnel behind the ferris wheel engineer's platform and done his worst. Why he did it no-one knew. Truro didn't give a single word in his defence, merely stared – dumb and angry – at the jury, the prosecutor, even his own lawyer. The trial was swift and perfunctory. Truro went to Rikers Island for ten to fifteen, and when he came to see me he had an infected molar in the right lower quadrant and the worst case of body odor I'd ever had the misfortune of experiencing. Any man who smelled that bad deserved to die. Henry Truro was also the same height, almost exactly the same weight, the same build and shoe size as me.

Truro was in a cell alone, a precaution often taken with sex offenders, and a week after treating him for the first time I went down to that cell during exercise period and doused Truro's mattress with cleaning alcohol. Odorless, highly flammable, Truro didn't figure a thing when he went back into his cell that same afternoon and lay down on his cot.

I went back to my own cell, the cell I had inherited from Doc, attended to a broken crown and an incipient abscess, and then I asked for access to the dental records. I was walked down there by a warder, left to my own devices, and took a moment to exchange my own dental records for those of Henry Truro.

Then I went back to see Truro, offered the man a cigarette as he lay on his cot, and when I was done lighting it I dropped that match onto Truro's horsehair mattress and stood back. I watched the flames envelop him, suddenly, like a wind that had rushed in to swallow him. The expression on his face was one of disbelief and confusion, and I smiled to myself as I thought of the kids' lives he had ruined. He started batting at the flames with his hands, but the fire was hungry like it wanted to devour him, and there was little he could do. At one point he tried to get himself up off the bed, but I raised my foot and kicked him back against the mattress. He opened his mouth and I knew he was going to start screaming, so I raised my foot once more and leveled a kick at his face with all the strength I could muster. He fell back stunned, his head impacted against the wall, and though he was not unconscious he was dazed and disoriented. He was looking at me through eyes that could barely see, his clothes on fire, his skin burning. I could hardly begin to imagine how excruciating the pain must have been, but I wanted him to feel that pain. He was someone I didn't know from Adam, but I wanted him to hurt. Never women or kids, me and Harry always used to say. We never do women and kids, and this asshole had done the worst of the two. He tried to get up again, and this time I let fly with a sideways kick to the middle of his body. Blood erupted from his mouth and I knew I had shattered his ribcage or somesuch. Still he was conscious, his hands clawing desperately at the air, his body fighting the agony he was in. I kicked him once again in the face, and this time he did fall unconscious, and I managed to drag his body away from the burning mattress and smother the flames with a blanket. The smell was like a roasting pig on some Sunday church barbecue. That, combined with the burning horsehair, filled the cell with a dense and acrid smoke. Standing in the corridor beyond you would have seen nothing, would have been unable to enter because of the atmosphere. I tore off my own shirt, and soaking it in the john I wrapped it around my face. I could barely see, my eyes were streaming, and any other time I would never have been able to manage a second in there, let alone several minutes. But my life and my freedom were at stake; if there was any second that I thought I could bear it no more I only had to think of Harry Rose's face as he took yet another bundle of dollars from some poor sucker and tucked it into his jacket. The money was out there. My money. I wanted my goddamned money, and that was all that kept me going.

After the flames were out I took a scalpel from my pocket and slashed Truro's face several times. By the time the other prisoners and half a dozen warders appeared, I had already dragged Truro from his cell onto the gantry, had bound a towel tightly around his face, and was struggling to carry him down to the medical facility. I went with him all the way, assisted in the bandaging of Truro's head and hands, the areas worst affected by the fire. They sedated him with morphine, laid him in a bed, and telephoned the mainland for hospital clearance and the ambulance ferry.

I told the medical facility orderly to check on the state of the cell fire, and I was left alone with Henry Abner Truro for a little more than thirty minutes. In that time I stripped Truro naked, injected him with enough morphine to kill a horse, unravelled the bandages from his hands and face, used a lighter to sear the tips of the man's fingers, and then set about beating his face to an unrecognizable pulp with the heel of his own boot. I dragged him into a small annex room where they kept the medical supplies and locked the door. I bandaged my own hands and face, dressed in Truro's clothing, and was laid up in bed by the time the orderly returned. I could hear my own heart beating, could feel it thundering in my chest. I could smell my own heated breath against the bandages that surrounded my face. I could see almost nothing, and when the orderlies came and checked on me, when they took my pulse and listened to my heart, I felt the tension growing inside me like something alive. This was it. This was the moment I would make it out of Rikers. I believed I would, I had to believe I would, and if a second passed when I did not think of Harry Rose and what he owed me I could not remember it. I could see Harry's face, I could sense the way he smiled as he took yet another fat wad of greenbacks from some poor schmooze . . . and I knew that half of those greenbacks were mine. It was my money. Had always been my money, and hell, I had earned it. Earned it with all these years of my life behind me in Rikers.

It was that passion and promise that kept my nerve. It was that feeling of redemption and justice that kept me from crying out in anger as the warders and orderlies asked one another whether they should unwrap my face and see how badly I was burned. It was the feeling that there might be a future for me if I kept my mind together that stopped me reaching for one of them, holding a scalpel to his throat and using them as a hostage to get myself out of there. The moment had been a long time coming, seven years coming, and there was nothing I would do to jeopardize the possibility that I might make it.

At one point one of the medical orderlies decided to take a look beneath the covering of my face. I sensed his hand approaching me, I could feel the pressure of his fingertips through the bandages, I was aware of how he gingerly started to peel it away. I was beneath that thing. Not Henry Abner Truro. Me, Johnnie Redbird.

I held my breath for one second more, and then I moaned out loud as if suddenly experiencing a moment of unbearable and excruciating pain. Someone said something: 'What the hell're you doing there? Don't touch him. For God's sake don't touch him!'

I blessed that man, whoever he might have been, and I believed for a second there might have been a God.

An hour later I was carried out of Rikers Island on a stretcher and ferried across the channel. From the ferry I was transferred to a state hospital ambulance and rushed to the nearest adequate medical facility.

By the time I reached the St Francis of Assisi complex on Brautigan Street, the governor and senior warden of Rikers Island had found Truro's body. Owing to the insular and independent nature of the Rikers Island system the discovery was not reported along official lines. The face was unidentifiable, and owing to the severe nature of the burns on the fingers they could not fingerprint the cadaver. So they X-rayed his teeth, matched the records to mine, and tried to figure out what had happened. The governor was a clever man, and though it was a couple of days before he figured out that he did not in fact have my body in his medical facility, he nevertheless did figure it out. Rikers Island carried a reputation second only to Alcatraz. There had been no previous escapes on his watch, and with his own retirement due in less than three years, he did not intend to leave with anything but a flawless record. Henry Abner Truro was cremated on the grounds of Rikers Island, and in the death records he appeared under the name Johnnie Redbird. They closed the book, and had no intention of opening it again.

As for myself, I made it hotfoot out of the back of that state hospital ambulance as soon as it drew to a halt against the sidewalk. Passers-by saw a man dressed in burned and bloodied denims, his face and hands bandaged, high-tailing it down Brautigan Street. They saw me once and once only, and that was the very last they would ever see of me. I disappeared. Vanished like smoke.

It took three weeks for me to find Harry Rose. Found him in a bar no more than walking distance from the beaten-to-shit tenement on East 46th Street. He was sitting minding his own affairs, drinking a straight-up Jack Daniels, a beer chaser, and I sidled up and took the stool beside him without a word.

Harry Rose near choked to death when he turned sideways and saw me. We said nothing for a good thirty seconds, and then I smiled like it was the new fashion down this way, asked if there was any hope of getting a drink.

We stayed in that bar three hours, retreated to a small corner table and consumed liquor like we'd seen the sign *Drink Canada Dry* and taken it as an instruction. Harry listened as I regaled him with the horrors of Rikers Island, and never once reminded him of how he owed me, of how seven years of my life had vanished and I'd come for my dues. He told me of himself then, his life, his beginnings, all the things I write of here, the things he hadn't told me at the start . . . as if he wished to balance the scales, to show me how his life had been as hard as my own. I listened, listened well, and even though there was no thought at that time that I would ever write it down, it stayed with me – every detail, every word, as if my mind had become a sponge and I would now soak up everything that ever happened to me to compensate for the years I had lost.

Harry didn't need reminding of his debt to me, and once we dragged ourselves from the bar and made our way back to East 46th, Harry showed me how much money he was keeping in shoe-boxes beneath the floor. It was like no time had passed at all, and though there was a dark shadow around me, a shadow I'd carried all the way from the Island, there was still something about me that could never change. I was Harry Rose's sidekick, his compadre and friend. We were as good as brothers, and though a great deal of water had flowed beneath a great many bridges, there was still a fundamental agreement: we were in this thing together, always had been, always would be.

So Harry told me about the hundred grand scam. He told me about King Mike Royale, about Cynthia, Mary-Rose, Jasmine, Louella-May, Claudette and Tanya. He told me about the ease with which the fat motherfucker had taken him for all he'd possessed, about the sweat he'd broken to get it back. And it had been our money. Money that both of us had worked for before Carol Kurtz, Karl Olson and the hell of Rikers Island.

So I went back to work, did what I did best. I dressed like a plain-clothes cop, carried a badge and a tone of authority, and I trawled the bars and speakeasies, the juke joints and strip clubs until I got a fix on Mike Royale and where he was at. King Mike had ploughed his money into an upmarket bordello off of Edgewater Avenue between Cliffside Park and Fairview. Hell of a place, hell of a clientele, and the girls he worked out of that joint were some of the classiest broads a man might ever see off celluloid. Senators, congressmen, police captains, bankers, mobsters, councilmen and city officials; they were all down there to sink the pink torpedo, and the money they turned around dwarfed anything me and Harry Rose had ever imagined. Some said they pulled upwards of twenty-five grand a week, others said such a sum was an understatement of magnitude, but – truth be known – Harry and I didn't so much as care for the long green as we did for King Mike's head.

The only complication was that I had gotten myself a girl, a sweet little redhead from Hudson Heights who figured me for Gary Cooper. She hung around me like a bad cold, and though I cared for the girl, though I treated her well, I never saw myself as the settling type. Strange as it may seem now, there was something in the back of my mind that told me I could've been a father. Maybe I was crazy, because I sure as hell knew that the life I led was not something that would take a child. But nevertheless it was there, the thought was there, and there was little I could do to deny it. When she got pregnant I told her the truth I wanted her to hear; that there was no future here, that I was no more a father and a husband than I was a Tuscaloosa milkmaid. I gave her five thousand dollars, told her she could keep the kid or not – her decision and her decision alone – and then I made her leave. I lied to that girl, and I lied to myself, because there was that something inside of me that said I should do it, that I should let her stick around, that she could look after the kid while I did my day's work. She squawled like an Apache tribal burial, but she went. There was one thing she understood from her time with me: I was a man who said only those things I meant, and what I meant was as good as law. It was only later, much later, that I thought about her again and whether that child had ever taken a breath. And when that thought came I would work so hard to convince myself that I had made the right decision for all concerned, but if I'd looked in the mirror I would have seen a man with a lie behind his eyes. Where she went and what happened I didn't want to find out at the time; my mind was set on balancing the books with King Mike Royale.

It could have been a scene from a bad gangster B-movie, and perhaps we had intended it that way. Hugging the edge of the sidewalk in a dark sedan, me and Harry waited four hours one night until King Mike exited his bordello and started home. We followed his Cadillac Towncar across three miles of the city, and when he pulled up outside a sprawling adobe mansion on the outskirts of Fort Lee where Lemoine crossed I-95, we pulled up also, let the engine die quietly, and we waited. Waited two hours while lights went on and off inside that house, and when there was nothing but darkness we broke in and went upstairs.

The fact that King Mike's bedroom reeked of alcohol, the fact that he barely stirred as we stripped back the covers and bound his hands and feet, gave us some idea of how much the man had drunk. Miracle he made it across town in one piece, I said as I started to slap King Mike's face and poke him in the eye.

King Mike Royale, a man who had never had to walk a yard in his adult life, a man who ate and drank the best Manhattan had to offer, a man who believed himself not only above the law but more than likely above God, woke to find a stranger peering down at him with a paperclip in his hand.

There was very little explanation. There was a lot of pleading of course, and I hushed King Mike up to ask Harry why it was always the fat guys who moaned the worst. Seems the fatter they are the more they cry, I told Harry, and Harry laughed, and held King Mike's head still while I straightened out the paperclip and pushed it through the fat guy's eyelid.

He screamed louder than a fire siren, so we took the corner of the bedsheet and jammed it into King Mike's mouth until it seemed he would choke. His one good eye did all the pleading then, and Harry and I took it in turns to rabbit-punch him, to hold a lighter to his testicles, to piss on him, to score deep bloody grooves in the flesh of his belly with a metal comb. After an hour we were bored, and King Mike, still remarkably conscious, was relieved of the bedsheet and told he could ask one question before he died.

Who are you? he gasped and gagged and spluttered.

Harry looked at me, I looked back, and then – laughing as if sharing some private joke – we told King Mike that he'd asked the question and now he was going to die.

Didn't say we'd answer it did we, you fat motherfucker? Harry told him, and proceeded to tear the bedsheet into long strips which we used to lash him to the frame.

You want the money? King Mike asked us. Is that what you want? Take the goddamned money and leave me alive . . .

Harry sat beside King Mike as he sweated and bled and moaned.

What money would that be? Harry asked him.

The money in the bank, King Mike said. I got the best part of three hundred grand in a safety deposit box . . .

In a bank? Harry said. What the fuck use is money in a bank?

King Mike's remaining one good eye widened and stared at Harry Rose. Was there a flicker of recognition there? Perhaps, perhaps not. Harry imagined that the last thing in the world King Mike would ever wish to do was remember the faces of those he had scammed. Besides it had been more than seven years since Harry had given this fat asshole a hundred grand.

You want the money in the bank? Harry asked me.

I tilted my head to one side and sort of half smiled. I shrugged my shoulders and said, You want it?

Means we'd have to keep this asshole alive while he took us there, wouldn't it?

Reckon it would, I said. Whaddya think?

Harry shook his head. Naah, he said. Fuck it. Rather see him burn.

A wad of bedsheet went back in King Mike's mouth. We tied him tight and fast to the frame. We packed pillows and blankets beneath his body until he looked like a bloodied prizefighter laid up in hospital after eight rounds with Primo Carnera.

From the dresser on the other side of the room we took two bottles of 1929 Armagnac and soaked the sheets, the pillows, the blankets and King Mike's overweight form.

Then we lit him. And then we ran.

We started the car and drove to the end of the street, and when we saw flames through the upper-floor windows we looked at one another and nodded.

Vengeance is sweet, Harry Rose said.

Sweet as sweet can be, I said, and pulled away.

We hid out for two days in the apartment on East 46th, and it took only two days for us to realize the kind of trouble we'd caused.

King Mike Royale had been a connected man, as good as made in some circles, and there were those in positions of influence who were more than a little concerned that an investigation into his death might bring to the surface other facts that should never see the light of day. Harry and I talked. Talked a great deal. And when word on the street suggested there might be some possibility that one or two Italian families would lose on their investments in King Mike's business, Harry suggested that I lose myself for the meantime, said he would stay behind and take care of our interests for a while, make sure the dust settled. Harry told me he was a known face, that if he suddenly disappeared people would ask questions, make some noise.

Mexico, I said.

Mexico, Harry agreed.

Take twenty or thirty grand with you, Harry said, and I'll send more in the New Year. When you settle yourself contact me, let me know where you're staying, and I'll take care of things.

I was reticent, and there was something in my eyes that told Harry there was more going down than I was saying.

Rikers? Harry asked me.

I nodded. Rikers, I said. You were gonna take care of me while I was down there, Harry.

Harry nodded. He knew I was right. I lost all that money, Harry told me. The fat bastard we torched took all the money I had, and I figured it would be better to make the money back than to stay in Queens and be a shit-heel.

I nodded. Harry was right. And, besides, I still trusted Harry Rose, knew that a man such as Harry would always and forever maintain his principles. Like the thing with Carol Kurtz. Olson died because he killed a girl that Harry had cared for, wouldn't have mattered if she was a two-bit hooker or Princess Grace of Monaco.

So I went, took twenty or thirty grand, and made it to Mexico, place called Ciudad Juarez over the Rio Bravo del Norte. Bought myself the top floor of a four-storey hotel, and after a month or so I sent a message to Harry Rose. Here I am, I said. Down here Mexico way, where the tequila runs free and the senoritas run freer. Come down and visit me sometime. Money I don't need for a while. Seems you can buy a month of the high life for a Lincoln and change. Let me know when things cool down. Let me know if you ever hear my name in the same breath as Rikers Island or King Mike Royale. Take care an' all that.

Harry got the message, and in his heart of hearts he knew he'd let me take the fall once more. There was nothing to keep Harry in Manhattan, and the fact that my escape from Rikers was never reported in the papers made Harry think that the two of us could have headed down to Vegas and been kingpins once more. But Harry had become a solitary man, a man alone, and in the years that I had been away he'd earned himself his own reputation without me at his side. In some ways it had been good to have me back, but then again . . .

So Harry Rose moved once more, out of the tenement on East 46th, to an altogether more upmarket place across the Bergen Turnpike near Columbia Park. He was thirty years old, he had money to burn, and there was something inside of him that made him feel that his life had turned a corner. Two men he'd killed – out of principle, for revenge – and the only true friend he'd ever had was hiding out in Mexico. So when he met Maggie Erickson one Saturday morning in the apartment block elevator, when he helped her carry her bags across the hall to her parents' apartment on the floor beneath his, when she turned and thanked him, told him that gentlemen seemed to be a dying breed these days, Harry Rose felt something inside of himself that was not only alien as an emotion, but somehow magnetic in its pull.

He backed up to the elevator, held it open until she'd opened her own front door and stepped inside, and when she turned and smiled at him, fluttered her eyelids like she was a little embarrassed or coy, he came right back out of the elevator, and in his most charming manner asked her if there might be a possibility she would share a cup of coffee with him one after-noon at the corner delicatessen. Blushing once more, Maggie

Erickson said she would like that very much, and they set a date, a time, and a meeting place. Maggie was not the kind of girl who would ordinarily agree to such a thing, but there had been something about the man, something about his manner, his forthrightness, that had appealed to her. For all of her twenty-eight years she had lived with her folks – good people, Christian people – but there was something inside of Maggie that made a fire in her belly. She wanted more, knew that more was out there somewhere; it was waiting for her, and perhaps she'd agreed merely because such a thing was different. Sometimes different was enough it seemed, and maybe here she had experienced the same kind of magnetism that had so effortlessly drawn Elena Kruszwica to Jozef Kolzac. Maybe it was a facet of Harry Rose that had been inherited from his own errant and inimitable father. Whatever it was, Maggie didn't speak of Harry to her parents, considerate enough not to give them any cause for concern, excited enough to feel that here was someone they might disapprove of. Perhaps that was another reason: the forbidden, the taboo, the frowned-upon. Her education and upbringing taught her that such meetings were always chaperoned, that there were polite and conservative introductions to be made between parents and potential suitors before any such rendezvous, but she'd seen the spark of fire in Harry Rose's eyes and it had matched the fire in her belly, and the idea of that man sitting drinking tea while her parents spoke of politics and church and family picnics made her cringe with embarrassment. Maggie Erickson was no Alice Raguzzi, but she sure as hell was no Shirley Temple either.

And Harry Rose? Harry went back up in the elevator to his own apartment and wondered if he'd gone crazy, if there might be some slim chance he would become a real human being after all.

They did meet. Three days later. Met where they'd said they'd meet. And Harry brought flowers, a discreet little arrangement of roses and carnations, and Maggie Erickson took

269

Harry's arm as they left the apartment building and walked down the block to the corner delicatessen. Harry found her witty and charming, almost intellectual in her grasp of literature and politics, and when he asked her if she would care to have dinner with him one evening, he was as surprised to be accepted as she was to be asked. There was something about this girl, something that belied the appearance she presented. While Alice Raguzzi and 'Indigo' Carol Kurtz had seen all the rough edges and sharp corners of life, while they talked when their mouths were full and used the john with the door open, while they may have known everything about people from the gutters to the stars, there was something missing. That something was class. Maggie Erickson had class, class enough to have plenty to spare, and though she was no wallflower, though she could talk Harry sideways into Sunday and show him how things really were, though she was well-read and educated in a way that Harry would never under-stand, there was something about her that ran a whole lot deeper.

She was quieter than either Alice or Carol, but quiet waters ran deep. Harry knew that for a fact, and when she challenged him about the way he spoke of people, when she made him open doors for her and wait patiently while she finished her meal, Harry began to see that perhaps there was another side to folks that he had never paid any mind to.

Honest Harry Rose started to consider the possibility that there might be some part of life he had missed. The part with class, the part with a certain sense of grace and decorum. Maggie taught him to think of all people in the same light, that there was a reason they were the way they were, that they all carried their troubles no matter their background or up-bringing. 'People are people,' she'd tell him. 'People do the things they do because they believe them to be right even when they're wrong. And people do wrong because they never took the time to figure out a better way to do it.'

And Harry listened. Perhaps for the first time he listened to someone other than himself. He began to think that there might be a way to handle people without his fists or a gun, that there might be a way to close down some of the chapters of his past and start again.

Perhaps . . . just perhaps.

Seemed someone somewhere was stoking the fires, and as sparks became small flames, as smoke started to rise and make its way towards the sky, Maggie also believed that perhaps she'd found an out. Middle-class America was its own kind of prison – comfortable, good food, a warm bed to sleep in and a roof over her head, but a prison all the same. Harry Rose carried a key it seemed, and he knew what was on the other side.

It was the end of a decade – a decade that had seen changes throughout America that were perhaps the most significant of the century. And Harry felt he had changed as well, changed inwardly as well as for the world, and when dinner date followed dinner date, when he took his Maggie dancing to the Regent Astoria off Broadway, when Christmas unfolded into a brand new year, he knew – he just knew – that now he was away from Queens he would never go back.

He had slipped the moorings of his former life, and the boat that had carried him thus far was allowed to drift back into the deep and turgid undercurrents of the past. It was a brand new day, a brand new life perhaps, and the world seemed so much more real and alive to Harry Rose without the pressure of looking over his shoulder. He let go of everything it seemed – Daniel Rosen and Rebecca McCready; the horrors of the war he'd been born out of; the gamblers and losers, the drunks and cheats and liars, the killers and dealers and pimps and hookers; Alice Raguzzi, Freddie Trebor, the Olson brothers and Carol Kurtz, Mike Royale and that last prevailing image of a frightened and overweight man burning alive in his own bed . . .

And me too. I too was allowed to slip away. For the second time Harry Rose forgot the man who had paid his penalties for him.

And he took Maggie Erickson away from her parents; they

moved out to Englewood near Allison Park. Though they never married she did take his name, and Maggie Rose was a girl who knew better than to ask questions where questions were not required. It was 1970, it was a more liberal and permissive age, and when she became pregnant in early 1971, Harry Rose believed that finally he'd arrived. He wanted the child, wanted the child more than he wanted his own life.

For a time, ignorant in his happiness, he would have both.

TWENTY-SEVEN

Later, much later, Annie O'Neill would wonder why she had been so trusting. Hadn't it always gone this way? Hadn't it always been far more complicated than she had let herself believe? Perhaps, perhaps not. It was always in the cold, harsh light of day, as the pieces scattered around her feet, pieces to be viewed in all their bitter and twisted glory, that she saw the signs. Little flags. There were always little flags.

David came to the store on Saturday morning. He said he'd been to the apartment, figured she might not open up, but there had been no answer.

'Sullivan's always out Saturday morning,' Annie told him, and David nodded, smiled, and asked if they could go back to her apartment.

'Insatiable,' she said. 'You are insatiable David Quinn,' and then he kind of smiled, and once more started massaging the back of his neck, and Annie recognized the little flag.

They walked in silence the best part of the way, and though in itself this was nothing significant in the grand scheme of things, and perhaps would not have seemed out of place before, Annie knew something was awry, and there was a cold sense of apprehensiveness that seemed to pervade her thoughts.

And once they were inside, had removed their coats; once Annie had made coffee and walked back into the front room; once they'd sat beside one another and David had been silent for a minute, she *had* to ask him.

And he said it. In one simple statement – four words, each in and of themselves of no great meaning – he said all that needed to be said.

We need to talk.

She felt the emotion welling in her chest before the words had even left his lips. Before they had reached the walls. Before their real meaning had even been confirmed in his eyes.

She felt it.

All there was to feel.

And once those words were *out there* there was no taking them back, no way she could desperately claw them from the air and return them to him. It was done.

'What do you mean, we need to talk?'

He smiled. There was something important about the way he smiled. In that moment she could not be specific as to why, nor what that expression might mean, for all her thoughts were clamoring together at the forefront of her mind and there was no room for any other consideration.

And then he said the second thing.

The second worst thing of all.

And once he'd said the second worst thing Annie knew there would be no going back, that whatever might have been salvaged from this with words and expressions, whatever physical reach she might have made towards him, he was already too far from arm's length to be grasped.

'It all seems to have happened so fast,' he uttered, and looked down at the way his own hands seemed to be fighting with one another in his lap.

'Too fast?' she asked, and there it was – so obvious in her voice, that tone of grief and loss and heartache, of seeing something she'd believed to be constant and resolute slip away so soundlessly.

He nodded. 'Too fast,' he repeated. 'I don't know,' he said. 'Perhaps it's just me . . . perhaps the fact that it's been so long since I was involved with anyone like this – '

'Involved?' she said. 'Is this what you call involved?'

He shook his head. He was already back-pedalling, already

wishing he wasn't there, wishing he was elsewhere, some-where, anywhere at all.

He looked at Annie and smiled once more, but it was the smile one would give a grieving widow at her husband's funeral, a smile one would give a little girl who didn't win the beauty pageant.

It was the smile of a traitor as he withdrew the knife and started to wipe the blood from his hands.

'Let me get this straight,' Annie said, even now creeping towards anger. 'You're telling me that you want to cool this thing off . . . that perhaps we ought to spend a little less time together? Is that what you're telling me, David?'

Annie rose from the couch, unable to bear being next to him, and she started to pace the room, started to feel redness rushing up inside her chest.

David looked down.

'Look at me!' she snapped. 'Look at me David Quinn.'

David, startled by her outburst, looked up at her. It was an involuntary action, a *re*action, his eyes wide, his breath caught in his chest.

'Is that what you're telling me?' she repeated.

'I am,' he said, and his tone was so matter-of-fact, so busi-nesslike, that she could barely believe her ears. He stood up slowly, and for the first time Annie felt a sense of threat, real threat. There was something in his eyes, something cold and distant and aloof and menacing that made her shrink back inside. 'I do not have to explain myself to you,' he said, his voice measured, almost monotone. 'I am telling you that I cannot continue to see you, and if you ask me why I will not tell you. I *cannot* tell you.'

'And where the hell has this come from?' she asked. 'Where the hell has this suddenly come from? We spend two days in Boston together, we're twenty-four hours apart so you can get some work done . . .'

Annie stopped mid-flight. She took a step towards David,

and David – for a moment – seemed to press himself further into the couch.

'You're married, aren't you?' Annie said, her voice cold. 'You're fucking married, aren't you?'

David laughed – a short nervous laugh, the laugh of a cornered man. 'Married?' he said. 'Jesus Christ, no I'm not married.'

Annie took another step forward and put her hands on her hips. 'So what the fuck is this?' she said. 'What in God's name is this? I thought we had something here, something real for a change . . . something that might turn out to mean something instead of some shallow two-week affair with about as much substance as – '

Annie threw her hands up in despair.

She wanted to cry.

She wanted to shout and smash things, and she believed – later – that had she been somewhere other than her own apartment she would have done exactly that.

'You want out, is that it?' she asked.

David shook his head. 'It isn't a matter of choice . . .'

'Choice? Not a matter of choice? Oh for fuck's sake, you people!'

David frowned.

'Men!' she said. 'Spineless, immature fucking teenagers, the lot of you. No more backbone than a fucking . . . oh, Christ I don't know what! You come over here, you fuck me, you take everything you want from me, and then when it gets a little too close for comfort, when it starts to look like there might be some possibility of commitment you all run like scared rabbits.'

David started to rise from the couch.

Annie was aware then of how much taller than herself he appeared to be. He seemed coiled, like a spring, like there was a tension inside of him that could explode at any second. Again she felt threatened, intimidated, and the expression in his eyes was one of emotional deadness, as though he were fighting against something he couldn't control.

She hesitated for a second, just a second, and then she turned on him, her voice even louder. 'So what the fuck is it then? You tell me what the fuck it is David Quinn. We need to talk. It's all moving too fast. You have any kind of idea of how fucking clichéd that is? You asshole . . . You fucking asshole.'

Annie's fists were clenched, and even as she started towards him he stepped back, the backs of his legs reached the edge of the couch, and he fell once more into a sitting position.

She was over him then, her face red, her eyes wide, and when she spoke her voice was determined and angry and cold and vicious.

'Get the fuck out of here,' she said. 'You take your sorry pathetic self-absorbed weak-willed spineless excuses and get the fuck out of my apartment, you hear me?'

David hesitated.

'Now!' Annie screamed at the top of her voice. 'Get the fuck out of here now!'

David got up from the couch and walked across the room. He walked slowly, too slowly, and when he reached the door he turned and looked at her.

There was something then, something unspoken that seemed to issue from him. He looked lost for a moment, and then that feeling disappeared like a handful of smoke. *He wants to stay*, she thought. *He wants to say something, to explain what's happening here. He wants me to understand something but he can't . . . can't or won't?*

She wanted to ask him, wanted to pull him back and make him tell her what was really going on, but once again she sensed the threat that appeared to emanate from him, and in defence of herself, in defence of her pride and her dignity, she canceled out any possibility that there might be anything reasonable about his behavior.

The anger came like a tornado, sudden and unexpected, and

she started across the room towards him, her fists clenched, her eyes wide and desperate.

David made an effort to grab his jacket from the chair behind the door, but Annie was so close behind him, so angry, so violent in her outrage and disgust, that he missed it.

Annie almost pushed him down the stairs when he reached the landing, and though there were a million words in his mouth there was only one that managed to escape.

'Sorry – ' he started.

Annie had his coat then, and when David was half way down the stairwell she hurled it after him. He tried to catch it, almost lost his footing, but he grabbed the rail, picked his jacket up off the floor, and hurried down the stairs.

Annie rushed back into her apartment, and snatching a vase from the small table just inside she went out again.

She threw the vase with everything she possessed, and even as she heard it shatter into a thousand pieces in the hallway below she also heard the front door slam shut.

Like a gunshot it was, ricocheting up the well, turning the corners as it came, and penetrating her heart right where she stood.

And then she collapsed. Fell to her knees, her hands white-knuckling as she gripped the stair-rail for support, and then she was sobbing, and it seemed everything that she'd ever suffered – every hurt, every betrayal, every loss, every weakness – came rushing out of her chest like a tidal wave.

Eventually, after how long she didn't know and didn't care, she dragged herself back into the apartment and closed the door behind her.

For a while she knelt on the floor with her head on the edge of the couch. And then she walked through to the kitchen, fetched a bottle of Sullivan's Crown Royal that she'd secreted beneath the sink, and without a glass, without even so much as a coffee cup, she started drinking.

Straight from the bottle.

Straight from the bottle all the way to her soul.

TWENTY-EIGHT

At first there was the smell. It was not a bad smell, it did not actually assault the nostrils but it was strong. It seemed to be a combination of many smells, each with its own identity, and had there been some possibility of savoring each aroma independently she perhaps would have been successful in identifying each and every one.

But, as it was, they were all folded together in one package, and after a while she became aware that the package contained sounds as well, and a sense of motion perhaps, and then there were voices – non-specific and vague, words that she did not understand, did not care to understand, and also there was a bright light, and the light seemed to be strong enough to pierce her eyelids and illuminate her thoughts.

And the first thought was *Where am I?*

And the second thought was *Oh God . . . oh God . . . David . . .*

And with that she kind of gave up, and let herself fall back into something vaguely resembling freedom, and though that freedom was accompanied by pain and deep waves of nausea that threatened to engulf her body, she believed that this was a better freedom than awareness.

And so she let it take her, and take her it did – willingly, easily – and for a while she was aware of nothing at all.

Perhaps it was better that way.

And then the sounds came back, and she perceived movement beside her, and when she struggled to open her eyes she was blinded by something bright and white and invasive.

'Move it,' someone said, and the brightness was gone.

She tried to open her eyes again, one at a time seemed sensible, and when her vision began to focus she saw a man seated beside her, a man in a white coat, and her first thought was how handsome he was.

'Hi,' he said, and his voice seemed understanding and sensitive. But that was only a front. Annie knew that.

'I'm Doctor Jim.'

'That's your surname . . . Jim?' she asked, and her voice was fuzzy and slurred.

Doctor Jim smiled and shook his head. 'No, that's my first name. Parrish is my surname.'

'And you call yourself Doctor Jim? Where the fuck am I, the children's ward?'

Doctor Jim laughed. 'No,' he said. 'You're in St Luke's Hospital Emergency Room near Amsterdam Avenue. Your friend brought you here . . .'

'Friend? Which friend?' Annie asked. She tried to lift her head. A thunderous pain lanced through the side of her face.

'Aah Jesus Christ, what the hell is that?'

Jim touched her shoulder and eased her down again. 'You had a fall,' he said. 'I think perhaps you went busy with a bottle of something, and your friend found you collapsed in your kitchen. Seems you fell and hit your head on the side of the sink.'

'Which friend?' Annie asked.

Jim shook his head. 'I don't know, some guy.'

'How old?'

Jim shrugged. 'Fifty, fifty-five maybe . . . looks like he hasn't slept for three weeks.'

'Jack,' Annie said. 'Jack Sullivan. Thank fuck for that.'

'Does the bad language go with the drinking, or did the drinking come first?' Jim asked.

Annie started to smile but her head hurt too much. 'Well, you know what they say. If you don't say fuck every once in a while you might not get some.'

Jim Parrish nodded understandingly. 'You make a habit of this drinking and falling over stuff?'

Annie closed her eyes. 'No,' she said. 'I got dumped by the asshole of the millennium.'

'So you figured if you drank enough he might come back?'

'You're a smartmouth asshole too,' she said. 'Go away and let me sleep.'

'That I can do,' Jim said. He stood up. 'You sleep for a while and I'll check on you in a couple of hours. We X-rayed your head and you haven't broken anything, but sure as hell you're going to have one helluva headache for a few days.'

'Thanks very much Doctor Jim,' Annie said.

'I'll be back,' he said. 'I'll come see how you're doing in a couple of hours.'

But Annie O'Neill didn't hear him. Sleep was there like the down-curve of a rollercoaster, and she was all paid-up on the ticket.

He did come back, two or three hours later, and though she could see no windows Annie knew it was evening.

'How goes it?' he asked her.

'As can be expected,' she said. 'When you drink enough to fall over you kind of expect to feel like this.'

Annie hoisted herself up on the pillows. Her head hurt, but it was easing.

'Your friend is still here,' Jim Parrish told her. 'He's waited the whole time. I told him he should go home and sleep but he wouldn't have any of it. Is he sick too?'

Annie frowned. 'Why d'you ask?'

'He looks like he has a fever, his hands shake a lot.'

'He quit drinking,' Annie said. 'He's having a rough time of it.'

Jim Parrish nodded understandingly. 'As you will, if you don't take your most recent experience as a lesson.'

'We can do without the puritan lectures, okay?'

Parrish nodded. 'Okay.'

Annie frowned. 'What day is it?'

'Sunday,' he said. 'You've been here the best part of twenty-four hours.'

'Oh Christ,' she said.

Jim Parrish sat on the edge of the bed. 'He tells me you own a bookstore.'

Annie started to nod, and when she felt the pain she stopped. 'Yes,' she replied. 'I own a bookstore.'

'I majored in Lit.,' Parrish said. 'First and foremost I'm a bookworm.'

'So what's with the white coat and stethoscope . . . or do they just call you in when literary people overdose on Crown Royal?'

'No, I'm a real doctor,' he said. 'Figured I had to do something to pay the bills. I'm not sure what the going rate on sitting around reading books is, but I guess it ain't great.'

'The rate for selling them isn't so good either. If I had to pay rent on the store I'd go under in a week.'

'You want to see your friend?' Parrish asked.

'Sure thing,' she said. 'My port in a storm.'

'Hell you look awful,' was Annie's greeting for Jack Sullivan, and perhaps because he didn't reply, perhaps for some other unspoken reason, there was a moment's silence between them. And in that moment it came back – the reason she was there in the first place, that if it hadn't been for David she would never have gotten drunk, never have fallen down, and Sullivan would not now be visiting her in St Luke's.

The tears came without effort, and they were slow and lazy and fat, and even as she felt Sullivan's arms around her there was nothing she could do to temper the tidal wave of heartache that came rushing to take her.

'Fucking asshole,' she kept saying through the sobs and hitches. 'Fucking asshole Jack . . . just the lousiest good-for-nothing asshole you could ever imagine. Christ Jack, how did I ever get taken for such a fool?'

Sullivan tried to say something – something consoling, words that showed he understood, that he empathized, but

Jack Sullivan had never been a man to translate the sounds of the heart into words, and whatever he tried to say just seemed to make things worse.

'I mean, you meet someone, they seem alright, like a regular human being . . . Goddamnit Jack, do I have schmuck loser tattooed on my face or what?'

No, he was saying. *No, you don't Annie*, but she wasn't listening, she was merely monologuing her thoughts out into the room.

'What the hell d'you have to do Jack . . . what the hell does it take to find someone with anything more on their mind than how they can get you into bed? And once they've done that they just want out. It's always the fucking same . . . always the fucking same.'

And Jack just held her, and after a while she did nothing but cry soundlessly, and he could feel her breath stuttering in her chest, the way she pressed her face against him and didn't want to let go.

So he didn't let her go. He stayed there, and would have stayed there all night, but the duty nurse came back and gave Annie painkillers, painkillers Sullivan himself could have used, and within minutes she seemed to close up inside herself and disappear.

Her last thought, neither fully formed nor vocalized, a thought she would have difficulty even remembering, was for the book she had lent David Quinn. She had given him *Breathing Space* and he had stolen that as well as her heart.

Jack Sullivan left Annie O'Neill sleeping and went down the block to eat, his face unshaven, his tongue like the bottom of a birdcage, his hands shaking and his head swollen with tension. This was not an easy trip, this wagon ride to sobriety, but he'd made a deal, made a promise, and hell, no-one could ever tell Jack Sullivan he wasn't good to his word.

When Annie again woke Jim Parrish was there.

'Time is it?' she asked as she slurred into semi-consciousness.

'A little after four,' he said. 'Monday morning.'

'I'll be able to go home today,' she said.

'That a question or a statement?'

'I want to go home today,' she said.

'Let's see how you're doing in a few hours,' Parrish said. 'Rest some more . . . you've been through something that you don't recover from in a day.'

'But people do recover?' Annie asked. Her eyes were wide, brimming with tears.

Jim Parrish stepped forward and sat on the edge of the bed where Annie lay. He reached out and took her hand.

'Recover?' he said. 'Sure they recover . . . as will you Annie O'Neill, bookstore owner.'

She smiled weakly, and then she closed her eyes and breathed deeply.

'I brought something for you,' he said quietly, and from his coat pocket he took a slim volume. 'You know Hemingway?'

'Ernest or Mariel?'

Parrish smiled. 'Ernest.'

'Not personally, no.'

He held the book in his hand for a moment and then passed it to her.

Annie took it. It was *A Farewell To Arms*.

'You're giving this to me because it's a tragic love story, and you thought that was the kind of thing I needed to read right now?' she asked, her tone a little sarcastic, perhaps a little defensive.

Parrish shook his head. 'No, I'm giving it to you because Hemingway was a drunk, and when he was drunk he was a foul-mouthed son-of-a-bitch and I thought you guys might relate.'

'Jeez, you really have switched on the charm tonight haven't you?'

Parrish smiled, and there was something in his expression that told Annie this was a little more than the standard bedside manner.

She closed her eyes for a moment, and then she looked at him directly, and with as little emotion in her voice as she could manage said, 'Thank you Doctor Jim Parrish. I appreciate that you brought me this, but right now I have a headache the size of Texas, my boyfriend just dumped me, and I really don't think I can handle whatever it is you think I might be able to handle.'

Parrish shook his head. 'Take the book,' he said. 'It's a helluva story, and if you read it and want to return it you know where I am, okay?'

'Okay,' she said. She wanted him to go away, to leave her be. However handsome and sympathetic he might have been he was still a man.

Jim Parrish didn't speak again, merely sat with her for a little while, then got up and walked away. He didn't look back, didn't even glance.

Just like the rest.

Standing at the front entrance of St Luke's, Jack Sullivan propping her up against the rain and wind that rushed towards her as the automatic doors slid open, Annie O'Neill was suddenly filled with the impulse to turn back, to hurry down the antiseptically white corridors, find the bed where she'd lain and crawl beneath the disinfectant-smelling sheets to hide from the world.

The world was rough edges and sharp corners, and sometimes you collided with them, and sometimes it hurt so bad you couldn't breathe, could barely stand, and there was nothing you could say, nothing *anyone* could say, that would make it feel better. *Beautiful, but worthless*, a voice said. *He said you were beautiful, but what he did made you worthless.*

They took a cab – Jack and Annie – and when they arrived at the apartment building it was all Jack could do to bring her from the car to her own doorstep.

'Don't want to go in,' she kept saying. 'Don't want to go inside,' and so he carried her up the stairwell and took her into his place, and he put on the TV, turned it up loud, because Jack Sullivan knew all about the need for noise, the need to have something mindless to drown out the sound of the ghosts inside.

Always recover, she kept telling herself, but she knew it was a lie, and early afternoon came, and then it went, and even as darkness started creeping along the sidewalks and filling the spaces between things, she remembered Forrester.

'Go,' she told Sullivan. 'Go tell him I can't be there,' but Sullivan was determined not to leave her alone.

'I mean it Jack . . . he's a good man, probably the best man I know aside from you. He's too old to want me for anything other than company, right?'

She insisted, insisted more than Sullivan imagined she could, and so he took a cab down to The Reader's Rest and he waited there for Forrester to arrive.

Annie left the TV on, and when it started to drown out her thoughts she turned it off and crossed the landing to her apartment.

She stood silent and immobile for a time. She looked at where David had sat. She stepped through to the bedroom and sat on the edge of the bed. A bed where she had felt safe beside him only hours before it seemed. From there she could see through to the front room, the small table upon which had sat a vase, now a thousand pieces swept up and emptied away somewhere unknown. Like her emotions perhaps. Like her life.

She leaned forward, rested her elbows on her knees, and put her face in her hands.

She was too empty to cry, too hollow, like a clay gourd waiting to be filled. But there was nothing to fill her, nothing to rid her of the sense of absence and longing and heartbreak.

She asked herself what there was now, where she would go, what she would become.

Is this it? she asked herself. *Is this all there will ever be? This apartment, the bookstore, my evenings with Jack Sullivan – wonderful man though he is, he is not my lover, nor my soul-mate, nor . . .*

Nor my father . . .

And then she cried again, because she wished her mother and father were there, wished they would hold her and tell her everything would be alright, because moms and dads didn't lie, did they? No, moms and dads never lied.

And by the time Sullivan returned with the message from Robert Forrester Annie was sleeping, curled up in the middle of her bed like a little child. Sullivan tugged the quilt out and covered her, and because it seemed right and fitting, because for some reason he didn't wish to be alone either, he lay beside her, his arm over her to protect her from things unseen, and he slept too.

The wind crept up to the windows and pressed against the glass, for it was warm inside, and out beyond those windows Manhattan teemed with a hundred million thoughts, each one special, each one unique, and yet all of them – in some strange way – silent and alone.

TWENTY-NINE

'A fascinating man altogether, your Mister Forrester,' Sullivan said.

He was sitting at the table in Annie's front room. It was Tuesday morning, a little after eleven, and when they'd woken earlier Annie had seemed comforted by the fact that Sullivan had stayed with her through the night.

'He said very little about himself at all. He didn't seem guarded as such – '

'You want tea or coffee?' Annie called from the kitchen.

'Coffee,' Sullivan said, and rose from the chair. He walked to the kitchen doorway and stood there watching her for a moment.

'It wasn't as if he didn't want to answer questions . . . more like there was something about him that made you feel any kind of question would have been an invasion of his privacy.'

'And he said he would come Wednesday?'

Sullivan nodded. 'Wednesday, seven as usual.'

She handed Sullivan his coffee and they walked back through to the front.

'When he told me about it, the first time, you know? . . . well, he went through this whole thing about how if you were going to be late you didn't show up at all. He said my dad was a perfectionist, wanted everything just so or not at all.'

'Your father's not there this time,' Sullivan said. 'Maybe he figured things could relax a little. He also said he wanted you to have the last section of the manuscript.'

'The last section?' Annie asked.

''S what he said.'

Annie was quiet for a while. She wanted a cigarette. She wished Sullivan smoked, would have convinced herself that she could have smoked only one and not been tempted again.

'So what do I do about David Quinn?' she asked eventually.

'What d'you wanna do about David Quinn?'

Annie shrugged. 'Hell Jack, if I knew what to do about David Quinn I wouldn't have asked your opinion, would I?'

'Most times people only ask for someone else's opinion to confirm what they've already decided themselves.'

'Well this doesn't happen to be one of those times,' Annie said. 'You want the question again?'

Sullivan shook his head. 'I got it the first time.'

'So?'

Sullivan went silent, then he eased himself back on the couch as if he was settling in for the duration.

'One time,' he said, 'I was on the subway.'

'Good,' Annie said. 'I was on the subway one time as well.'

'You wanna hear what I have to say or you want I should go home?'

She smiled. 'Please continue Jack . . . I am deeply sorry.'

'Too smart for your own fucking good, Annie O'Neill. Anyway, I was on the subway one time and I saw this girl. This was maybe fifteen, twenty years ago. She must've been maybe thirty, thirty-two, something like that, you know real old – '

Annie raised her hand to take a mock swipe at Sullivan.

Sullivan pretended to duck.

'So I saw this girl,' he went on, 'and there wasn't anything particularly remarkable about her, she wasn't what you would have called classically beautiful . . . but there was *something*. She looked right at me, you know, how you make eye contact in a crowded place, like a bar or something?'

Annie nodded. She thought of the priest on the train, and she willed herself not to blush.

'So this girl looks right at me, and I look right back at her, and it's one of those awkward moments when you know you

289

should just look away, like you just happened to be glancing in that direction and they were in the way. But it didn't happen. Neither one of us looked away. And though it was just a second, perhaps less than a second, I knew.'

'Knew what?'

Sullivan smiled. 'I knew she was the one.'

'The one?'

Sullivan nodded. '*The* one.'

'And how the hell did you know that?' Annie asked.

'I don't know . . . well, I do know actually . . . ah hell, how the fuck d'you explain something like that? I just looked at her and I knew that I should go talk to her.'

'So what did you say?'

'I didn't say anything,' Sullivan replied.

'Nothing . . . not even hi, or hey there babe, how goes it?'

Sullivan laughed, but there was something in the sound of his laughter that was forced. Even now, so many years later, he was looking at one of the small regrets of his life.

'No, I didn't say a damned word . . . I just sat there, every once in a while glancing in her direction, but she'd realized by then that I wasn't going to say anything. And I knew how she felt.'

'How did she feel?'

'She felt the same sense of loss as me.'

'How could you tell?' Annie asked, intrigued by Sullivan's story, a small part of this man's strange life that had reached beneath the surface.

'Because she got off at the next station.'

'Maybe she meant to get off there.'

Sullivan shook his head. 'No, she didn't.'

'How could you tell?'

'Because when she got off she took three or four steps to a bench and sat down, like she was just gonna sit there and wait for the next train. And as the train pulled away I was looking at her, and you know what she did?'

Annie raised her eyebrows.

'She held up her hand, you know, like when someone waves but they just raise their hand . . . it was that kind of wave, like she was saying goodbye.'

'And she was looking at you?'

'She was.'

'That's really fucking sad Jack . . . hell, that's gotta be the saddest thing I ever heard.'

'Saddest thing was there was a moment to take and I didn't take it . . . that was by far the saddest thing.'

'So what does this tell me?' Annie asked. 'That I should go down the subway and ride the trains until I connect with someone?'

Sullivan nodded, his face serious. 'That's *exactly* what it tells you Annie. Any time, night or day, every waking hour you should be down those subway tunnels trawling the carriages for single men to make eye contact with. Figure it'd go better if you dressed up a little, you know, a really short skirt, some fishnets with a hole in the back, silver stiletto heels an' all that.'

Annie nodded, and then she smiled. 'Seize the moment, seize the day, right?'

'Carpe diem and all that goes with it.'

'So what should I do?'

'Fight for it Annie. That's what I think you should do. Take a look at what you felt, how you felt when he was around compared to how you felt when he was gone. Weigh the two up, and if one feels better than the other go fight for it.'

'It felt better when he was here.'

'So go find him.'

'Jeez, I wouldn't know where to begin Jack.'

'Marine insurance, that's his business. Whoever he works for is bound to have an office in New York and an office in Boston, right?'

'Right.'

'So I'll check out how many firms deal with marine insurance that run an office in both those places, and then we'll make some calls.'

Annie nodded, and then she looked sideways at Jack Sullivan.

'What?' he asked.

'Figure the subways might be a better bet.'

'Humor . . . the last line of defence.'

Annie shook her head. 'No, I'm just a devout believer in the law of diminishing returns.'

'And what the fuck would that be when it's at home?'

'The theory that the universe is constructed in such a way that you always get back less than you give.'

Sullivan nodded, his face once again serious. 'Well Annie, as far as I'm concerned that's the ripest heap of horseshit that ever assaulted my ears.'

'You reckon?'

'I reckon.'

'You think he was serious?'

'About what?' Sullivan asked.

'About me Jack . . . you think he was actually serious about me?'

'I don't know whether serious is the right word. Seems to me any guy who takes you to Boston for a couple of days has to have some kind of idea that he wants what you got.'

'Would you want what I got?'

'Annie O'Neill, from the first time you hauled your cute little keister up that stairwell I've wanted what you got.'

'And you think there might be a chance if I go find him?'

'There's always a chance. Hell Annie, you gotta get it into your head that men are some of the dumbest and most ignorant creatures that ever walked the face of the earth. They think they know what they want, and when they've got it they go all weak-kneed and spineless.'

Annie laughed suddenly.

'What?'

'That's what I called him . . . a spineless immature teenager.'

Sullivan nodded. 'Asshole deserved it . . . pretty mild if you want my opinion.'

'So, you were saying how men – '

'How men think they know what they want, and when they get it they go all weird and complicated, like they start thinking that there might be something better. Best way to handle them, you know what that is?'

Annie shook her head.

'Tell 'em what they want and don't give them a choice.'

'No choice.'

Sullivan nodded. 'Right, no choice. You just tell them that you're as good as they're gonna get, and if they start that thing with the wandering eye an' all that they're gonna get kicked into touch so fast they'll make light speed look like Sunday chess in the park.'

Annie smiled. 'You're just a leetle beet crazy Jack Sullivan.'

'And you, Annie O'Neill, are just as crazy yourself.'

'Thursday,' Annie stated matter-of-factly.

'What's Thursday?'

'We find him Thursday.'

'Why wait 'til Thursday?'

'Because I feel like I want to finish one thing before I start another.'

'And what would you be finishing by Thursday?' Sullivan asked.

'The story.'

'Right,' Sullivan said. 'The curious Mister Forrester.'

'What did you make of him?'

Sullivan shrugged. 'Seemed harmless enough . . . I don't know, I only spoke to him for a little while, and then he left.'

'He had the other pages with him?'

'He did.'

'Wish he'd given them to you.'

'It matters that much?' Sullivan asked.

'It does . . . don't know why, but hell I've always loved a story.'

'I never read the last chapter,' Sullivan said.

Annie eased herself off the couch. 'Then you should read it now. I'll go get it.'

'And then maybe you an' me could go break a sweat in the bedroom before you get your David Quinn back?'

'Sure thing Jack, you read the story and I'll fetch my fishnets and a twelve-pack of Trojans.'

Sullivan laughed as she started towards the door.

She stopped suddenly, turned and looked at him.

Sullivan raised his eyebrows.

'I meant to ask you,' she said. 'I've been looking every goddamned place I can think for my check book. You haven't seen it have you?'

'Your check book?'

Annie nodded. 'I'm sure it was in the apartment, and then I thought maybe I'd left it in the store or something. You didn't see it anywhere?'

Sullivan shook his head. 'Nope, didn't see it. It'll be around someplace. It'll turn up.'

Annie nodded and smiled. 'So where was I?'

'Fishnets and Trojans,' he said matter-of-factly, his face deadpan.

'Right,' Annie said. 'Fishnets and Trojans.'

She turned and left the room, and Sullivan watched her go, and as he watched her he wished – perhaps for the second time in his life – that he'd been smart enough to get himself a wife.

THIRTY

Wednesday morning Annie O'Neill went amongst the people of Manhattan.

Leaving early, she was acutely aware of them, these people who walked the same sidewalks, who breathed the same air, who took the same cabs and drank the same coffee as she did. Ignoring their existence had been her defence perhaps, and yet now she believed she had something in common with each and every one of them. Pain perhaps, or loss, or nothing more than being touched by life and feeling its presence.

Possibly she had seen these very same people a thousand times as she walked to work, but this day – this bitter Wednesday September morning – it was as if she was seeing them for the very first time.

An old man struggled to make it over the junction before the lights changed; a woman carried bags evidently too heavy, and yet she bore the weight as if it were her lot in life to fetch and carry in such a manner; a child gripped his father's hand, his clothes obviously uncomfortable, his eyes almost brimming with tears as his father droned endlessly about nothing of consequence in some chance meeting at the corner; a young woman, perhaps twenty-five or six, paced back and forth by the service entrance of a department store, cellphone in hand, her expression close to desperation as she attempted to reach someone who wasn't there; a middle-aged couple, politely oblivious of each other's existence, and yet she held his arm as they crossed the street as if letting go would undo the meaning of all the years they had suffered together; a baby in a pram, face smeared with chocolate, staring at Annie as she passed as if to plead for release from its comfortable prison; a teenager, eyes sullen, expression hangdog, earphones jammed in to drown out the noise of whatever parental criticism he had endured that morning; and time slowing down, each second a minute, each minute an hour as Annie looked, as she *saw* into the hearts of these people and perceived a tiny fraction of their lives.

She stopped at Starbucks, and standing there in the queue she grew acutely aware that *she* was being watched. The hairs rose on the nape of her neck, and she sensed that whoever's eyes were burning a hole through the center of her back meant something.

She could not describe it.

No words for such a feeling.

She turned – slowly as though she was having to push the heavy air aside to shift her viewpoint – and saw a man looking right at her.

He was three or four behind her in the line, and there was something in his eyes, something meaningful, something somehow empty, as if by looking at her he hoped she would fall right into that vacuum and disappear.

She felt herself blush.

She looked away, and then couldn't help herself: she looked right back at him.

He still watched her, but there was nothing threatening or invasive about his manner, nothing that suggested anything other than . . . other than *need*?

In that second – that split, hair's-breadth second that spiralled out into something infinite and timeless – she felt something close up against her heart and stop her breath.

There was something.

There *was* something.

Was this the same as Jack Sullivan's subway moment?

She held her head straight, she looked straight up at the counter. The people ahead of her carried away their skinny lattes and iced mochaccinos, their double decaf espressos with whipped cream, and then she was there, and then she heard the sound of her own faltering voice as she answered up for the coffee guy, as he held out the cup, as she felt the warmth through her fingers, as she turned and began walking towards the door.

She was no more than three feet from the man, ignoring him, intentionally ignoring him, but as she reached the door, as she anticipated the rush of cold air that would greet her as she passed out into the street, she turned back.

She couldn't help it.

She turned right back and looked at him.

He was looking right at her. Right *through* her it seemed.

And he smiled.

He smiled.

She felt the color in her cheeks.

The wind caught her unexpectedly, and then she was away, free from the moment, hurrying down towards the junction with her coffee, with her awkwardness, with people all around her.

Her people, she thought.

People just like her.

Arriving at The Reader's Rest she was struck by the seeming anonymity of the place. The frontage was drab, dark in color, and she tried to remember when she'd had it painted. It must have been five, perhaps six years, and whatever had impelled her to choose the deep burgundy she couldn't recall.

Hiding, she thought. *All these years I've been hiding.*

Once inside she removed her coat, set her coffee cup on the counter, and surveyed the interior. She wondered if she could ever bring herself to sell the place. Someone could do something with this. Someone could turn it into a Baby Gap or somesuch. Someone could fill it with parents and kids and noise and laughter, fill it with all the sounds of humanity that these walls had not heard for so many years. Someone, perhaps, could give it life.

But why not you Annie? she asked herself. *Because this is who I was, not who I am now. Who I am now doesn't want to spend the rest of her life enclosed within these four walls, staring day after day at the same images, hearing the same hollow sounds, wishing away the same interminable days . . .*

Who I am wants some other kind of life.

The doorbell rang. She looked up.

'Annie?'

John Damianka smiled at her from the doorway. No, he didn't smile, he beamed.

'You're okay Annie?' he asked as he hurried towards the counter.

'I'm fine John,' she said.

'You haven't been here for a while,' he said. 'I thought you were sick.'

Annie shook her head. 'No, I haven't been sick, just had a couple of personal things to take care of.'

'Well I'm glad you're here Annie . . . I have some news.'

Annie smiled, stepped from behind the counter and met him halfway from the door.

'We got engaged . . . me and Elizabeth got engaged.'

Annie rushed forward and hugged him, threw her arms around him.

When she released him she was beaming too, and for the first time since her fight with David there was a reason to feel good.

'Oh John, that's great . . . that's fantastic! I am *so* pleased for you both. That has to be the best news I've heard – '

'I know, I know, I know,' John was saying, overflowing with goodwill for the world and everything in it. 'It's amazing, I can't believe it. I am so happy, so incredibly happy Annie.'

Annie hugged him again, held him for a while, and felt she was holding onto a real person, a person who – in his own way – had carried all that life had given him, and now, at last, had found some way to unburden those things and move on.

'I'm in a hurry,' he said. 'I wanted you to know, I really

wanted to tell you since last Thursday, and I had to stop and see if you were here.'

John Damianka started backing up towards the door. 'I'll bring her down,' he said. 'I'll bring Elizabeth down to meet you sometime. You should meet her Annie, she's a great woman, a really great woman. Okay, I'll come by . . . I promise I will,' and out the door he went, out into the street, out into the throng that was the people of Manhattan.

Her people.

People just like her.

By mid-afternoon the color of the world had shifted, as if some unseen hand had reached down and pressed against a continent somewhere, slowed the whole thing up, shifted it upon its axis a thousandth of a degree. The sun was enveloped by a bank of thunderheads, and then the rain came – heavy, like spring run-offs, the ice-caps dissolving into Manhattan's streets in an attempt to clean this dirty city once and for all.

Annie O'Neill stood by the front door of her shop and watched the people hurry by, some carrying umbrellas and wrestling with unexpected gusts that caught them unawares, others holding coats over their heads, their feet hammering through the puddles, their clothes wet, their directions focused and channelled and determined. They were all hurrying someplace, perhaps to some*one*, to their homes and businesses, to meetings, to illicit rendezvous in nameless hotels where lovers waited impatiently with wet hair and heavy hearts and too little time.

Where were you? I thought you weren't coming.

I'm sorry, there was a phone call I had to take.

Not your wife?

God no, not my wife . . . it was a business thing.

I was scared you weren't coming.

I'm here now . . . no reason to be scared.

I have to be quick . . . I can only stay an hour. I wondered if we could talk . . .

299

Annie smiled at her thoughts, her small imaginings within this second, and she thought of all the things that turned within that same second.

Somewhere a child was being born; a hundred miles away a man would take his last earthly breath, his widow weeping by his side; a mother would stand at the doorstep of her home and wonder where her daughter was, it was late, she was never this late, something *must* have happened . . .

Sullivan was somewhere, as was Robert Forrester – and David Quinn . . .

And it was with that thought that the tension around her heart returned, the same tension she'd felt when he'd uttered the worst four words that can be uttered.

We have to talk.

Why was it that degrees of love could only be fathomed by depths of loss?

She closed her eyes and breathed deeply, went to the small kitchen at the back and switched on the percolator.

She knew that no-one else would come today, no-one would take the time to stand in the rain and peer through the condensation-ghosted glass into this world within worlds, this small gap out of reality near the corner of West 107th and Duke Ellington.

She wanted out.

No, she *really* wanted out.

But the fear was there, just like David had said: that one would jump only to find one's landing place was somehow worse than one's point of origin.

But better to jump than to die where you stand, she thought, and wished there was some other way.

There *had* to be some other way.

So she made coffee, drank it black because she had no cream, and wondered how many days it would be before she would wake up one morning and find that she could not face the prospect of coming here again.

*

A little before seven, Robert Forrester's arrival imminent, she wanted to call Sullivan to come down to the store. She had tired of being alone, and though she looked forward to seeing Forrester she believed that Sullivan was as much a part of this story as herself.

At the front of the store, the door locked, most of the lights out, she asked herself what a passer-by might think if they saw her standing there alone. But before the thought had time to linger Forrester appeared. Annie knew it was him even as he crossed the street, his worn-out topcoat, his gait, his silver-grey hair, and as he reached the sidewalk he was looking right at her, smiling, pleased to see her it seemed.

A thought struck her then: *If only this was my father . . .*

She opened the door and let him in. The damp wind from the afternoon's rain came rushing in behind him.

'Mr Forrester,' she said, feeling as pleased to see him as anyone else she could think of.

'Miss O'Neill,' he replied. 'I trust you are well.'

'As can be,' she said.

Forrester paused, frowned, and then said: 'Tell me . . . there has been some trouble?'

She shook her head. 'Nothing with which you should concern yourself,' she said.

'But I am concerned,' Forrester persisted. 'Tell me I am wrong . . . it is a man, no?'

Annie laughed uncomfortably, caught unawares. She didn't reply.

'As I thought,' Forrester said as he removed his coat. 'It is always money, men or both, no?'

Annie nodded. 'A man,' she said.

Forrester handed his overcoat to Annie and she set it down on a chair along the wall. He thanked her, indicated the small table towards the kitchen and started to walk across the store. In his hand he carried a manila envelope. The final chapter.

'Tell me,' Forrester said, and sat down.

'You don't want to hear this,' Annie said.

Forrester smiled. 'I do, I do . . . I am most intrigued.'

Annie sat facing the old man. She asked him if he wanted some water, some coffee perhaps, but he declined.

'The man,' he said. 'A boyfriend perhaps?'

'I thought so.'

'And he showed his true colors, yes?'

'He did.'

'And for how long had you known him?'

'A little while,' Annie said. 'In fact I met him the day after I met you.'

'Aah, this is no time at all . . . I cannot imagine that someone could have hurt you after so little time.'

'You have no idea,' Annie said.

Forrester turned his mouth down at the corners. 'Betrayal, loss, heartbreak, I have many ideas Miss O'Neill.'

Annie was quiet for a time, and then she looked at the old man's sympathetic face and said, 'I thought there was something . . . I thought it was the beginning of something important Mr Forrester, I really did. And though it was only two or three weeks it seemed as though a great deal more happened than I imagined could happen.'

'You fell in love?'

Annie smiled. 'Why do they say that?'

'Say what?' Forrester asked.

'Fell in love? Why do they say fell in love, not rise into love?'

'Rise into love?' Forrester laughed. 'I get your point. Love is something one ascends to, yes?'

'I thought so,' Annie said. 'Because when you realize that someone doesn't feel the same way about you it really is like falling. I can see how you can fall out of love, but I really think they should say rising into love.'

'Semantics,' Forrester said. 'I can see it both ways.'

'Anyway, enough of me . . . you brought the last chapter I understand.'

Forrester nodded. 'I did. This is the last chapter.' He leaned

302

back in his chair, steepled his fingers together like a college lecturer, and said, 'So tell me, what do you think of the irrepressible Harry Rose and his friend Mr Redbird?'

Annie smiled nostalgically, as if she was being asked to remember two old friends, friends she had neither thought of nor spoken about for years. 'I think Johnnie Redbird was a man of tremendous personal sacrifice, and I am concerned that Harry Rose will betray him.'

Forrester nodded. 'They lived some life, did they not?'

'Enough for me to question the excuse for a life I lead,' Annie said.

'I don't know,' Forrester said. 'In only the past three weeks you have loved and lost someone, you have shared your time with me . . . and I met your friend Mr Sullivan the other evening and he seems to carry his concern for your happiness upon his sleeve.'

'What makes you say that?'

'You can see it in people's faces, can read what they think of someone when they speak of them. When we spoke of you he seemed very paternal I think.'

'He's a good man.'

'He is indeed, I am sure.'

'And what about you Mr Forrester?'

'Me? What about me?'

'What do you want? What keeps you going?'

Forrester laughed. 'Keeps me going? I don't know Miss O'Neill . . . I don't know that there's any one thing that keeps me going. I think I am waiting for something perhaps.'

'Waiting? Waiting for what?'

Forrester shook his head. 'Equilibrium, a sense that the scales have balanced . . . a clear idea that there has been a purpose and meaning to my life. I think that when we arrive at such a point we can finally let go, you know?'

'Well, if arriving at a clear understanding is what life's all about then I think I'm going to be around for an awful long time.'

Forrester nodded. 'Perhaps, perhaps not. Sometimes things become strikingly clear in a moment, a single heartbeat.'

'I don't think I've lived anywhere near enough life yet . . . if it all came to an end tomorrow I'd be sorely disappointed.'

'As would I, Miss O'Neill, because we would not have the opportunity to discuss the finale of this story on Monday.'

Forrester slid the manila envelope across the table towards Annie.

'Read this,' he said, 'and on Monday, if all is well with you, we shall meet and you can give me your educated opinion.'

Forrester rose from his chair. 'I shall bid you farewell,' he said, 'and I trust that your heart will recover from your recent loss.'

Annie smiled, rose also, and walking to the door she was struck with a question.

'Mr Forrester?'

He turned slowly and looked at her.

'When we are done with this, after we have spoken on Monday, there will be another story?'

Forrester shrugged. 'Let's not jump off that bridge until we get there,' he said.

'You will be leaving?' she asked.

Forrester shook his head. 'My life, Miss O'Neill, is perhaps as unpredictable as yours despite my age. Who knows what tomorrow will bring, eh?'

He collected his coat. Annie helped him put it on, and then she unlocked the door and let him out into the damp, cold night.

'Until Monday,' he said, and raised his hand.

'Until Monday Mr Forrester,' Annie replied, and stood there with the door open until he had vanished from sight.

Sullivan was out when Annie reached home. And for some reason home did not feel like *home* without him. Sullivan was perhaps the closest she would ever come to family, and in that moment – as she stood alone outside her door – she closed her eyes and made a wish.

If Sullivan was right, if all things were ultimately influenced and governed by one's own thoughts, then she would wish this thought with all that she possessed.

That it will change. That my life will change. That it will become something other than a thousand what-ifs.

And then she opened her eyes, unlocked her door, and stepped into the darkness of her apartment.

THIRTY-ONE

Perhaps there were days when Harry Rose thought of me, same number of days I would think of the girl I'd left behind and the child I might have had.

Perhaps there were not.

But I believe those days became less frequent, and as the months unfolded, as his child was born, as he began to understand that there was something more to life than that which could be taken, Harry convinced himself that his decision had been right. I had been a part of some former existence, and in leaving that existence he'd also had to leave me. I belonged *back there*, and back there was something that no longer played any part in what Harry had become.

Perhaps it was difficult for Harry not to draw analogies between his own life and the life of America as a whole. This was his adopted homeland, his refuge, his fortune, and yet he knew that there were those who believed the excesses of the 1960s had now spiralled beyond control. They were reining in, pulling back, counting their losses and asking themselves where they would go from here. As I was too, I suppose. It is hard for me not to think of that time and feel the bitter twisted seeds of resentment and betrayal. They grew, stunted and without flowers, and the roots ran deep into soil that was parched and poisoned. But this earth was all the seeds needed, for the seeds were born of a Judas tree. Harry Rose had taken his pieces of silver, and I had been crucified.

Richard Nixon was faced with the problem of the Vietnam War, how a nation such as America could withdraw itself from such madness and still save face. He directed the national conscience towards those who had fought the war, people such as William Calley and Ernest Medina, those considered responsible for the My Lai massacre. Without ever saying such a thing he was making a clear statement: *The brutality of this war has been perpetrated by men, not by a government. I am innocent. I am a man of my word, a man to be trusted and respected.* And then he had the Supreme Court clear Muhammad Ali of draft-dodging. Nixon was a diplomat, a true politician, and while he whitewashed the world with his right hand, his left gave sanction to the continuing air raids on North Vietnam. He ordered the withdrawal of forty-five thousand men from Vietnam, he announced his intention to stand for re-election, and then he sent seven hundred B-52 Strato-Fortresses to Southeast Asia, and they bombed Hanoi and Haiphong into nothing.

Just a handful of months later five men would be arrested at the Democratic National Committee's offices in the Watergate building in Washington. Nixon would fly to the Soviet Union. Despite his private world exploding in slow-motion Richard Milhous Nixon went on to a landslide re-election victory in November 1972. He would continue to maneuver, scheme, contrive and design for a further nineteen months, all the while believing that he had somehow attained a reputation as the greatest negotiator in American history. He believed in himself long after everyone else had lost their faith. Perhaps this was his greatest attribute.

By the time Nixon's empire fell Harry Rose was the father of a child approaching three years of age. He still did not marry Maggie Erickson, though the house they took in Englewood near Allison Park was most definitely the home of a family. Such a thing was new to Harry Rose; a new feeling, a new reality. There were ties and obligations, trusts and requirements that went beyond the physical. A family was not something that demanded merely money, a family required love and support and ownership. Harry Rose believed he owned something, and recognized also that he was now owned, and thus he established himself as a legitimate businessman. This was the *right* thing to do, and though it at first seemed alien beyond comprehension it was something that grew with him. They were days when he would wake, would turn and look at Maggie's sleeping face, and realize that today, just like yesterday, just like tomorrow, he did not have to be afraid. He loved this woman, loved her as he had loved Alice Raguzzi and Carol Kurtz, and yet with Maggie there was so much more. With this woman beside him he felt complete. There was no other way he could have described it. Where once he had been half a man, he was now whole. Previously he had filled that void with violence and money, with sex and drinking and run-ins with the law. Now that void was filled with serenity, a narrow refuge between the insane fury of the past and the promise of what the future might bring. Maggie Erickson, whoever she might have been before he found her, had brought that with her.

For the first time in his life Harry felt safe, and though he thought of Johnnie Redbird, though images of the past, of the man he once was, sometimes crept into his thoughts, he viewed them as one would view a dream. A bad dream yes, but a dream all the same. The more time passed the more the images faded, and in their place came a sense of security and silence that seemed so much more real than the life he had once led. He had believed for a time that Auschwitz, the things he had seen and heard, were the reasons for his life. He imagined that the years of brutality and torture, the starvation and deprivation had taught him a lesson. The lesson was that life kicked, and if you did not kick back you would die. Maggie had taught him that a man could take a kicking, and though it might floor him, though it might take the very last breath from his lungs, it was the stronger man who would once again rise to his feet without hatred and vengeance in his heart.

And yes, there were the infrequent moments when Maggie would ask him questions, questions that he believed he could never answer, for to see the hurt and pain in her eyes that he

308

knew would surface if he even so much as hinted at his true past, would have been more than he could bear. And then there was the child. The child had become his reason for living, his raison d'être, and to watch the child grow, to see the child become a personality, a human being with real thoughts, real feelings, a real sense of belonging to something, was the greatest emotion Harry Rose believed a man could ever achieve.

Through Gerald Ford to Jimmy Carter, the death of Elvis and Ali's defeat beneath the hammering fists of Leon Spinks, Harry Rose lived his life amidst the people of New York, people who knew his name and his face for what he had become, not what he had been. There were times when he believed it would forever be this way, but somehow he knew, deep inside, that the past would come back to haunt him.

It came back in early 1979. Harry was at home alone, Maggie and the child out walking to school. The radio was on in the kitchen, ex-Attorney General John Mitchell, the last of the Watergate co-conspirators, was being released on parole, and the moment he heard the news his mind turned to prison, and thus to Rikers, and from there to me.

The sound of someone knocking at the door froze Harry where he stood in the hallway. From that angle he could see a silhouette through the frosted pane.

And he knew.

Somehow he just *knew*.

Harry was all that I said when he opened the door.

Johnnie, Harry replied, and stepped back to allow me to enter a house he had once believed would never be visited by the past.

It's been a good few years Harry, I said, and walking past him I made my way to the kitchen, sat down at the table as if this was indeed *my* home, and when Harry came through and sat facing me there was silence for more seconds than he could bear.

Once fool you, twice fool me, I said. Getting to think you might not be the man of your word that you once were Harry.

Not going to try and explain things Johnnie, Harry said. Just gonna say that things are good here and I am not prepared for trouble.

Trouble? I asked. I'm not coming to cause trouble Harry . . . just to ensure that all's well between us, you know? Spent these past years sweating my skin off in Mexico, thinking that maybe next month, maybe the month after, Harry Rose will get a message to me, send me some money, make things right. You know what I mean?

Harry nodded. I know what you mean Johnnie.

So finally I figured that maybe Harry Rose had forgotten about his little friend from way back when, and I thought to paying you a visit.

And so you're here.

I smiled. And so I'm here.

And what kind of payback would you be requiring Johnnie?

Figure I get as much as you did Harry.

Money's gone Johnnie . . . all the money we had is gone. Bought a little business, bought this house . . . earning a wage like a good American citizen these days. Had a family to raise, and when you do things legal nothing comes cheap, if you know what I mean?

I shook my head. I didn't know what he meant. I have lived all these years waiting for my money. Gave up my own family for the life, you know? Coulda been me here with a wife an' a kid an' all, but no, what we were doing was always more important than what I wanted. Seems to me now you didn't share the same sentiment Harry. I came back here just for my money. If I'd known there was no money I wouldn't have taken the time to find you.

Harry looked at me with the face of an honest man. There ain't no money Johnnie, and that's the truth . . . and you made the decision not to have a family Johnnie. That was your decision and your decision alone.

I was quiet for a time. In my mind I was killing him, killing him like I'd killed a guy for seventeen bucks and change a thousand years before.

So if there's no money Harry I reckon you can pay me back in kind, I said.

I could tell that Harry Rose went cold and loose inside. I watched his eyes, and they were the eyes of a guilty man. Seven years in Rikers, all those years in Mexico seeing men hiding from the law had taught me the difference between innocence and guilt.

I have an idea, I said, but this isn't an idea that could be carried by a man alone. Would take two, you know? And you're the best number two a man could ever have wished for. So what I think is that you're gonna help me out with this thing, and then I'm gonna walk away and disappear, and you come home and be dad and Mister Joe Public and whatever the hell else you got going here, and we're done. That's gonna be okay with you, isn't it Harry?

Depends on the alternative, Harry said.

The alternative, my dear friend, is that you might not have a home and family to come home to.

Don't see as there's much of a choice then, Harry said.

No, I replied, I don't see that there is.

In that moment Harry Rose could have tried to kill me, and in killing me he would have killed his past. Murdered it. Vanished it from existence. But he did not, and could not have done, for whatever he may have been faced with at that moment he could never forget that I – Johnnie Redbird – had taken the fall for him twice. He owed me something, owed me all my years of freedom, owed me a fortune in greenbacks and Lincolns, and had we both disappeared to Mexico or Vegas after the King Mike Royale fiasco then Harry would never have met Maggie Erickson, and he would never have been a father. So Harry Rose believed that he was fighting for his family, as well as fighting for himself, and had there been a question about priorities there would have been no question. Despite the agreement we made he believed I could kill a woman and a child just as easily as I could have killed a cop. There *was* no choice. No choice at all. And I could have killed Harry, could have shot him through the head as he sat there at his kitchen table, but I did not, and would not have done. Harry owed me as much money as I could have carried, and I was not going to walk away without it.

June of 1979, a night that would otherwise have promised an hour in the garden playing catch or freeze-tag, a pot roast in the kitchen, later his feet on the coffee table, a can of beer in his hand and the *Movie Of The Week* on the tube, Harry told Maggie that he had some business to attend to. He would not be long. He promised her that. And then he kissed her, kissed his child also, and left the house in Englewood near Allison Park and went out to meet the past.

And I – as much a part of that past as Harry had ever been – was waiting for him. Waiting patiently, like a man owed his dues.

The security truck collected from seven all-night stores and gas stations between Coytesville and Palisades Park. The guy who drove the truck was maybe five-four and two hundred and eighty pounds. A fat useless fuck, a truck-fuck, I said. The guy who carried the money from the gas stations and stores to the back of the truck was maybe twenty-two or three, looked like a college quarterback on a summer job. They both carried hand-guns, and inside the cab up front they had a three-inch Mossburgh Magnum pump action that was padlocked into its retainer. A fuck of a lot of use that'll do them when the shit hits the fan, I said, and then I pulled away from the curb and took a route down Edgewood onto Nordhoff, past The Cemetery of the Madonna towards the Fletcher Avenue overpass.

There was no way for me to know how Harry was feeling, but the fear was in his eyes. Good enough, I thought. Payback time. Now he gets to feel a little of how I lived for seven years in Rikers. Now he gets to smell his own sweat, to feel the

312

pressure in his chest, the dumbstruck sense of terror when you think this might very well be your last living breath. Feel these things Harry Rose . . . feel them and know what it's like to be truly on your own.

How it went down was later a blur, a maelstrom of shouting and struggling, the fat guy fighting to get the shotgun out of its retainer and open the door of the cab at the same time, all the while aware of the fact that he didn't really want to come out. The cab was bulletproof, and there we were, me and Harry dragging his young colleague across the forecourt of the Brinkerhoff Avenue Texaco station, looking crazy and violent and beyond compunction, and there was no way he wanted to get his ass blown off. But hell, this was what he was paid for, and so he did release the shotgun, and he did get out of the cab, and once he'd emptied the gun in our general direction he *did* get his ass blown off.

But even as the fat guy was lying on the stone-cold gravel forecourt, his life ebbing away slowly towards the storm-drain, he managed to get his handgun from its holster and fire three shots. The third – though he would never know this – found its target. In the confusion and melee that followed – as police sirens racketed through the night, as the gas station attendants hurried out to see to the younger security guard who lay dying on the sidewalk – I started away from the back of the truck and hightailed it towards the car. Harry Rose, the bone in his right thigh shattered by a .38 slug, did his best to catch up, but when I saw the flashing red-and-blue cherry bars in a procession down Glen Avenue I floored the accelerator and took off. Behind me, growing ever smaller in the distance, was the sight of four heavy money bags, bags that contained something in the region of three hundred and fifty grand, and beside them, his arm outstretched, as if reaching towards them with one last desperate hope, the security guard.

Harry Rose – knowing that destiny had finally found him – stood in the street, his pants leg soaked with his own blood, in his hand the sweat-drenched balaclava he had worn, and he thought of his child, a few months short of eight years old, and how Maggie would explain where daddy had gone.

He dropped to his knees. The cops encircled him, hollered at him, pointed their guns and made it clear they would shoot him if he didn't comply, but Harry Rose possessed neither the strength nor the will to get up. His life was over, what life he had managed to claw back from the horrors of Auschwitz, and he knew it. There was no coming back from this one. This was three strikes good, the end of the line, and the fat lady had not only completed the aria but the echo of her voice was nothing more than a memory.

In the second that I looked back I saw a broken and defeated man. His life had been smashed with all the force of a juggernaut. Gone was his wife, his child, everything he had worked to provide for them. Gone was his future, his past also, and yet also, in amongst all those things, I knew he felt that the debt he owed me had still yet to be paid. Gone was any hope he might redeem his score with Johnnie Redbird. Perhaps that, of all things, was the hardest thing of all. He knew me well enough to know I would never quit. He knew I wanted the money that was mine, and he knew I would never cease until I got it.

There was no plea bargaining, no second degree, no manslaughter, no justifiable homicide. This was plain and simple murder. The sole extenuating circumstance was that witnesses concurred there were two men. There was no way of telling who had fired the shots that had killed the security guards, and thus the death sentence could not be levied against Honest Harry Rose.

But they could give him life, two terms consecutive, and they sent him down to Rikers like the bad boy that he was.

It was the end of an era, the end of a dream perhaps, and I – looking over my shoulder as I fled – believed that in some small way, in some perverse and circuitous fashion – justice had been seen to be done. Gone was his money, his family, all the things he had worked for.

Same things I had lost. Same things I had never been given a chance to possess.

But I figured that while Harry Rose still carried sufficient strength in his body to breathe there would be a way – there would always be a way – to make him pay his dues.

THIRTY-TWO

Annie could not sleep.

It didn't help that Sullivan was out until the very early hours of Thursday morning, and by the time he did arrive she felt that it would be too much for him to carry her burdens.

She thought of David. A great deal. The *need* to know where he was became a preoccupation, an intensity that almost consumed her. A little after one in the morning she even considered taking a cab out to where he lived. She guessed she could have found it, but the idea of trawling the streets around St Nicholas and 129th in the early hours of the morning frightened her. She was alone, at least for the time being, and she would have to bear it without support.

Eventually, as the sun rose and filled the room with a vague sodium-yellow ghost, she slept, and when Sullivan knocked on her door some hours later it was already past eleven and there was no way she could face The Reader's Rest.

'I need to find him,' she told Sullivan once she'd made coffee for them both and they were seated in the kitchen.

'Need?' Sullivan asked. 'Or want?'

'Need,' Annie stated emphatically. 'I need to find out what happened with him.'

'I can tell you that,' Sullivan started, but Annie was shaking her head.

'I got what you said about fear of commitment and all that, and I'm sure that's part of it, but I want to hear it from him, from David you know?'

'And what about your Mr Forrester? He came last night?'

'He did.'

'And he brought you the rest of the story?'

Annie nodded.

'So tell me . . . what happened with these guys?'

'I want to talk about David,' Annie said. 'I want to go over there, over to his apartment and talk to him.'

'I don't think you should do that Annie,' Sullivan said.

'Why the hell not?'

Sullivan smiled, but beneath that smile there was a flicker of concern. 'What the hell happened to the shy and retiring Annie O'Neill that moved in with me all those years ago?'

'She got pissed off Jack . . . pissed off with being stepped over and walked past and ignored, that's what. I'm going to go over to his apartment and speak to him, and to tell you the truth there's nothing that you can say or do to stop me.'

Sullivan raised his hands. 'Hell Annie, you got fire in your belly today. I'm not going to stop you, not even gonna suggest it, but I think you better be prepared for the worst.'

'The worst? What could be worse than not knowing Jack?'

'Sometimes the truth is worse than not knowing.'

Annie shook her head. 'Not in this case. If it's me I want to know it, and if it's David then fair enough, but I'm not giving up without a fight . . . you said that yourself, right?'

'Suit yourself Annie O'Neill,' Sullivan said. 'Don't let it ever be said that I interfered in matters of the heart.'

Annie rose and walked through to her bedroom.

Sullivan sat quietly while she dressed, called through one time to ask her where the manuscript was but Annie didn't hear him, and when she appeared in the doorway, grabbed her coat from the chair and put it on, he asked her if she wanted him to go with her.

She shook her head. 'Big girl now,' she said. 'I can handle this Jack.'

'You're sure?'

She nodded, reached out and touched his arm as she passed him. 'I'll be fine,' she said.

'The chapter?' Sullivan asked as she reached the door.

'Kitchen counter,' she said. 'Brown envelope. Stay here and read it if you want . . . make yourself at home.'

Sullivan rose from the chair and watched her as she left, even walked to the window and waited for her to appear in the street. She walked without hesitation, her manner purposeful and direct, and he found himself thanking this David Quinn for whatever he had done. Annie seemed so much more certain about what she wanted, and this – however things turned out with David – had to be a good thing.

Sullivan shook his head, sighed deeply, and walked back to the kitchen to find the envelope.

From the junction Annie took a cab, directing the driver towards St Nicholas and 129th. From the back seat she watched the world through the window, watched the people on the sidewalk, people entering and leaving the stores and malls and coffee shops. She watched their faces when the cab pulled to a halt at the lights, watched how they crossed the road, each of them seemingly lost within their own private world, each in some small way a reflection of herself. Here were the lost and confused, the haunted and broken, the loveless, the pained, the angry and exhausted. Here were the black and the white and every shade of grey between. The beginnings and the ends of humanity; the circle. Life was so often a lie, and yet sometimes so true it hurt, and each and every one of these people was perhaps looking for the same thing as herself. It possessed no name, no face, no voice and no identity. It just was. It was too heavy to carry, and yet too light to grasp. It could not be defined and yet we knew so well when we possessed it, and so bitterly when we didn't.

The cab slowed against the curb. Annie paid the driver and let herself out. She walked three blocks before she reached a delicatessen on the corner, and turning left she felt sure she was headed in the right direction.

She tried three buildings before she recognized the frontage, the way the steps ran up through a small covered entranceway, and walking up those steps she felt the tension, the unbearable tension of wanting David to be there at the same time as hoping that she had the wrong building, or that he was out. She hesitated in the lower hallway, looking up the stairwell towards the first floor, and just as she placed her foot on the first riser she turned, startled, as a door opened behind her.

'I can help you?'

A man faced her, an old man, his skin sallow and dry like parchment, his hands bunches of knuckles twisted together.

'Hello,' Annie said. 'I'm looking for someone.'

'Someone who has a name?' the old man asked.

'Quinn, David Quinn.'

The old man shook his head. 'No Quinn here miss. You have the wrong address perhaps?'

Annie frowned. 'I'm sure this is the right building.'

'No David Quinn here,' the old man repeated. 'Had someone here but he gone now . . . up there, first floor.'

Annie turned and looked up the stairs. An indescribable sensation invaded her chest.

'You want to rent apartment?' the old man asked. 'You wanna see apartment . . . good apartment, nice light, big windows eh?'

Annie was nodding in the affirmative. She wanted to see, wanted to know that this was the wrong building, that somehow she'd lost her bearings and was two blocks east or west, or David's building was on a street that ran parallel to this one. That had to be it. It *had* to be.

The old man went up first, painfully slow, one foot on the riser, the other joining it, and then the second riser, the third, the fourth, all the while Annie walking behind him like a funeral procession of two.

Reaching the first floor the old man turned right and started down the corridor. From his belt he took a large bunch of keys, and without asking, without even turning to check that Annie was behind him, he opened the door, threw it wide and stepped back.

'See?' he said, smiling wide. 'Big windows, great light.'

Annie went through the doorway in slow-motion, the light from the room beating against her skin, the air thick, unbreathable almost, and after two or three steps, her eyes scanning the interior, she knew. She just *knew*.

'When did he leave?' she asked the old man.

The old man smiled, shrugged his shoulders. 'I think two, three days maybe . . . I wasn't here. My son you know, he takes care of everything. He went to the market, left me the keys. Good light huh?'

Annie nodded. 'Good light, yes.'

Had there been any question in her mind it would have been swept clean away by the sight of the polythene bag lying on the bare hardwood floor beneath the window.

A bag with books inside. Three books. Thirteen dollars and keep the change.

Sixty lives will connect with what's in this bag . . . makes you think huh?

She walked towards it, leaned down to look inside. There, wrapped in the same paper in which she'd given it to him, was *Breathing Space*. David hadn't even bothered to look inside, hadn't even bothered to open the wrapping.

Annie snatched the book from the polythene bag and stuffed it into her purse. From the moment she'd stood at the door of her apartment that morning and given it to David, except for a fleeting moment in the hospital, she hadn't thought about it. The most important thing her father had left for her and she'd forgotten about it. Despite its importance, finding it seemed now her consolation prize.

She turned abruptly, stared for a moment at the old man, and then she opened her mouth. 'Your son? Where is he?'

'At the market.'

'The man who was here . . . did he say where he was going?'

'Aaach, he's a crazy man. Left like he was headed for a fire. Supposed to give a month's notice or he lose a thousand dollars . . . well, he lost his thousand dollars. Stayed here two, maybe three weeks and he lost a thousand dollars. Crazy people in this world eh?'

'Two or three weeks?' Annie asked. 'He was here two or three weeks?'

The old man nodded, grinned, showed Annie the spaces between his small, child-size teeth. 'So you want this apartment with the good light?'

Annie heard the question but it didn't register. She was across the room and out the door before the old man had a chance to say another word. He raised his hand as if to catch her attention, but Annie was running down the stairs two steps at a time, her heart going faster than she could, and when she reached the front door and burst out into the street she felt as if something dreadful had been chasing her.

'Aaach, crazy people in this world,' the old man called after her, but his voice was like something from someone else's life.

Sullivan slowly turned the last page over.

He sat quietly at the kitchen table for some time.

'Something,' he said to himself. 'Something . . .'

He rose slowly from the chair, put the pages into a neat pile, slipped them back into the envelope, and then he left the kitchen and walked across Annie's front room.

He paused at the door, looked around the room he was so familiar with, a room where he'd shared a thousand days and nights with this woman, a woman who had reached him more deeply than anyone he'd ever known. He closed his eyes for a moment. There was something about those pages, sitting innocuously inside their brown envelope on the kitchen counter.

He shook his head slowly, opened his eyes, and crossed the landing to his own apartment.

He wanted a drink. God, how he wanted a drink. But he'd made a deal, and Annie was even now fighting to keep her half of the bargain.

If this David Quinn hurt her . . .

Sullivan stood for a moment, his right hand rubbing his left forearm, and then he walked across the room and switched on his computer.

THIRTY-THREE

'Gone,' Annie said as she came through Sullivan's apartment door.

Sullivan turned from where he was staring intently at the computer screen. 'What has?'

'David,' she said. 'The apartment is empty. Left behind nothing but the books I sold him the first day we met. And a book I lent him . . . Christ, I can't bear to think how I would have felt if he'd taken that. And there was an old man there, said David had been gone two or three days . . .'

'But he did say David was there?' Sullivan asked.

Annie crossed the room to where Sullivan sat. She balanced herself on the arm of the couch. 'Said someone was there, but the name David Quinn meant nothing to him, and whoever the hell it was he was there for a couple of weeks, that was all, and he left in a hurry and lost a thousand dollars deposit.'

'Private or agency?' Sullivan asked.

'What?'

'The building where he had the apartment?'

'The old man said his son took care of things . . . why?'

'Means it was more than likely private. With private accommodation there aren't references and credit checks, there's just money. Have enough money you can be the Son of Sam and move into a penthouse suite on Broadway.'

'And what's this?' Annie said, indicating the computer screen.

'The last of the insurance companies that hold offices here and in Boston. I've gone through Mutual Consolidated, Trans-Oceanic, Atlantic Cargo Insurance, Providence Shipping

Lines . . . God knows how many. Pulled up their employee listings and there's only one David Quinn amongst the lot of them.'

'And?' Annie said, shifting closer towards Sullivan.

'And that David Quinn is a major shareholder in Trans-Oceanic, fifty-three years old, lives in Baltimore.'

'Which means?'

Sullivan shook his head. 'There must be hundreds of insurance companies Annie, but as far as those who run offices out of New York and Boston your man is not employed in any of them.'

Annie frowned, anxiety entering her myriad other thoughts. 'So who the hell is he?'

'More to the point, who the hell is Robert Franklin Forrester?'

'Forrester . . . what the hell has this got to do with Forrester?'

'Too many coincidences,' Sullivan said, 'and it wasn't until I read the last chapter you have in there that I started to think about it.'

'Think about what?'

'This Harry Rose and his friend Johnnie Redbird.'

Annie shook her head. 'I'm not getting it.'

'Maybe there's nothing to get,' Sullivan said. 'Maybe I'm reading something into this that isn't there, but there's too many things that seem too close – '

'What the hell are you talking about Jack? Too close to what?'

Sullivan looked away towards the window. He shook his head. 'I don't – '

'Too close to what Jack?'

Sullivan turned and looked directly at Annie O'Neill. 'I don't know Annie . . .'

'For Christ's sake Jack, stop saying you don't know. What are you getting at?'

'The way it all fits together, or at least *could* fit together if you look at it from a different viewpoint.'

Annie opened her mouth to say something, then turned and sat on the couch. 'Say what you mean to say Jack Sullivan.'

Sullivan smiled, a kind of embarrassment in his expression. 'Forget it Annie . . . just forget it. It's just that I read this stuff and it really got me thinking.'

'Well you can stop thinking about that and start thinking about how the hell we're gonna find David.'

'Why?'

'Why?' Annie echoed. 'Well, maybe it doesn't matter a fuck to you Jack Sullivan, but it happens to matter a great deal to me. He's more than likely taken an apartment under an assumed name, has swept through here like Hurricane Asshole, taken me for a complete schmuck, and now has the sheer fucking nerve to walk out on me and thinks I'm gonna forget about it. I want to find him just to slap him upside the head Jack, that much at least.'

'Good enough. So where d' you suggest we start?'

'What's with the *we* white man?' Annie said. 'You're the goddamned journalist, the investigative reporter . . . you shouldn't have to even ask where we start.'

'The apartment block . . . I'll go there, speak to the old guy's son, see if he has any idea where he came from, where he might have gone when he left. I'll pick up the books he bought as well – '

Annie frowned. 'The books? What the hell d'you need those for?'

Sullivan held up his hand. 'He'll have touched them, and there'll be prints.'

Annie shook her head. 'Along with about three thousand others don'tcha think?'

Sullivan frowned, shook his head. 'You're right, screw the books. Besides I don't know anyone who could fingerprint them and check them against records anyway.'

'Christ Jack, you're a fucking amateur at this aren't you?'

'Thank you very much Miss O'Neill. You have a better idea?'

Annie cast her mind back to all the times she'd been with David. She thought of the trip to Boston, how everything had been paid for in cash, that they'd registered under *Mr and Mrs Quinn*, that he'd never given her a telephone number where he could be reached . . .

And considering it from that point of view it was unnerving, as if he'd intended to leave no traces, nothing that could ever be used to find him if he decided to vanish. Perhaps he was nothing more than a serial lover. She smiled at the thought, smiled with her lips, but in her heart there was only emptiness and loss.

She shook her head. 'No,' she said, 'I have no better ideas. You're okay to go to the apartment and check this out?'

Sullivan nodded. 'Sure I am Annie, no problem. You have the address?'

Annie looked at him blankly. She shrugged her shoulders. 'Not a clue, but I'd have no difficulty finding it again.'

Sullivan rose from his chair. 'Seems we're out for a little adventure together then, eh?'

'Seems so.'

They left a few minutes later, took a cab across to the other side of Morningside Park, and all the while – with every revolution of the wheels beneath her, with every passing street and block and junction – Annie believed that perhaps she was following a ghost.

Annie waited in the street while Jack went in and spoke with the old man and his son. For some reason she didn't want to go inside. She could not have answered the question had she been asked why. There was just something about it, almost as if within this building someone had made a fool of her and she had no wish to be reminded of that fact.

It was cold, and after a few minutes she went up the short flight of stone steps and stood inside the entranceway. Every once in a while she looked through the glass window in the front door. Waiting was not her forte, and each minute seemed to stretch on forever. She glanced at her watch – her father's watch – and after looking at it for the fourth or fifth time she couldn't stand the suspense any more. She went down the steps and walked to the end of the street, turned back and walked past the building a good fifty yards.

She paced restlessly, agitated by the cold and the situation she had found herself in. She was searching Manhattan for a man with an apparent alias. She had really fallen this time, fallen good. This was not rising into anything.

She turned and started back the way she'd come, and when Sullivan appeared from the entranceway she hurried towards him.

He was shaking his head even before he spoke. 'Doesn't know a thing. Even fifty dollars and he doesn't know a thing. He was more concerned that I might be from Rent Control or something.'

'Did he tell you the name the apartment was taken in?'

Sullivan looked at Annie. There was something in his expression that said all he needed to say.

'Well?'

'David O'Neill,' Sullivan said, and looked down.

'David O'Neill?' Annie asked, incredulous. 'You gotta be kidding Jack.'

'No, that was the name he used. David O'Neill.' He came down the steps and stood facing her on the sidewalk. 'Now tell me there isn't something weird going on.'

'Coincidence,' Annie said, and even as she said it she knew she was fooling herself.

Sullivan smiled, attempting perhaps to be sympathetic. 'And coincidence is what?'

'Bullshit,' Annie said, burying her hands in her coat pockets and sighing. 'Why?' she said, asking herself just as much as she was asking Sullivan.

'Who knows?'

'David Quinn, or O'Neill or whoever the fuck he is, that's who,' Annie said.

327

Sullivan started walking.

Annie stood for a moment, lost in her own thoughts, and then hurried to catch up with him. She put her arm through Sullivan's, and looking at them from the other side of the street they could have been a couple, perhaps a father and daughter, taking a walk, sharing time with one another. They did not speak, did not even look at one another, and three blocks down Sullivan stopped outside a coffee shop and suggested they go inside.

'He did this thing about trust,' Annie said once they were seated.

'Trust?' Sullivan asked.

'When I went to his apartment he did this thing where he blindfolded me and told me to sit on a chair and do nothing for a minute.'

Sullivan frowned.

'He was talking about trust, about how everyone had learned not to trust anyone, that everyone suspected everyone else's ulterior motives and vested interests, and then he told me he was going to ask me to trust him.'

'And he blindfolded you?'

Annie nodded. 'Blindfolded me and told me to sit still and say nothing for a minute and I had to trust him, that he would do something or other and I just had to trust him.'

'And you did it?'

'I did . . . but only for thirty-seven seconds. I couldn't handle it, it was nerve-wracking. You sit there for a minute in complete silence and darkness, trying to figure out what someone might be doing, where they might be from the sound of their breathing, and it really is very disconcerting.'

'And what did he do?'

'Well, he didn't strip naked and stand there with a butcher's knife and a hard-on.'

Sullivan laughed suddenly, spilled some coffee on the sleeve of his jacket. 'Well shit Annie, what a disappointment that must have been for you.'

She smiled, took a napkin and mopped the edge of Sullivan's sleeve.

'No, for real . . . what did he do in those thirty-seven seconds?' Sullivan asked.

Annie shook her head. 'He did nothing . . . absolutely nothing. He just sat there watching me.'

'Just sat and watched you?'

'Yes, that was it. And that was the whole point of the thing. He was basically trying to tell me that whatever I might fear was merely my imagination, that I would sit there and conjure up the worst possible thing, and that my fears were whatever I created.'

Sullivan was nodding his head.

'That was the thing Jack . . . that was part of the whole thing, whatever game he was playing to make me think he could be trusted.'

'And you trusted him?'

'I did . . . trusted him enough to let him take me to Boston, to not pressure him for a telephone number or an address. I think about it now and I actually don't know the first thing about him.'

'So what did you talk about when you were together?'

'We didn't do one helluva lot of talking,' Annie said. 'There were more important things going on most of the time.'

'I'm sorry,' Sullivan said, his voice quiet, tender almost.

'Sorry? For what?'

'That he was an asshole.'

'I don't know for sure that he was an asshole Jack . . . Christ, I don't know anything right now. Seems to me there could just as easily be a perfectly rational explanation for everything that's happened.'

'Like really he was a CIA sleeper living under nine different aliases, and the terrorist cell he was trying to infiltrate got wind of who he was and so he disappeared in order to ensure that no harm came to you?'

'As good as any other explanation I've got,' Annie said.

'You just don't want to face the fact that he was as spineless and immature as the vast majority of men in this city, that it all got a little too close for comfort and he ran for cover before you suggested getting married or something like that.'

Annie shook her head. 'No, I don't want to face that possibility Jack . . .'

Sullivan closed his hand over hers. 'I didn't mean that . . . that wasn't necessary.'

'Sometimes the truth has a way of finding you whether you want it to or not,' Annie said. 'Christ, what I would give for a cigarette.'

'You don't smoke,' Sullivan said.

'I can start, can't I?'

'You start smoking and I'll start drinking again,' he said. He edged his chair back and started to rise. 'Come on,' he said. 'Let's get out of here. Let's go home, watch some dreadful crap on the tube and eat a quart of Ben and Jerry's between us.'

Annie smiled as best she could and rose from the table. She put on her coat, buttoned it, tugged the collar up around her throat, and in leaving the coffee shop she took Sullivan's arm once more.

'Thank you,' she whispered.

He turned, frowned. 'For what?'

'For being there,' she said. 'Just for being there.'

THIRTY-FOUR

Annie O'Neill wondered if there could ever be anything good about losing. She thought of the Joni Mitchell line – *You don't know what you've got 'til it's gone* – but she didn't necessarily agree. She'd had David, at least believed she had, and now he was gone. When he'd been there it had been good, and she had known what it was. It was the start of something, and she'd imagined what that something could have become. Even in Boston, spending those hours alone in a strange hotel room, it hadn't been anywhere near as bad as it might have been because she'd known he was coming back. It was not that she craved company, she believed herself neither insecure nor lacking independence; it was simply that two was better than one. Two was definitely better than one.

In silence she watched a movie with Jack Sullivan. She watched it but paid no attention to what the actors were saying to each other. When it was finished, she could not have told anyone what the movie was called, or who was in it, or what it was about. It was meaningless, because all that mattered to her at that moment were the thoughts inside her head, the feelings in her heart. Her heart was not broken; it was strained. Something had pulled it too far in the wrong direction, and the healing process had not yet begun. Healing needed time, it involved crying sometimes, and waking in the small hours of the morning and asking questions that had no answer. And slowly the healing would do its work; and though it always took longer than you wanted, and though there would be moments in the weeks and months to come when she would be somewhere else entirely – a shopping mall or a

331

vegetable market, her mind considering such things as salad with avocado or parmesan – and though David Quinn would be the furthest thing away . . . even at times like that there would still be moments when she would hear a name, catch a scent, perhaps see something on a shelf that would remind her, and in that split-second heartbeat realize that the healing was not yet done.

Thanksgiving would be tough, Christmas in some ways tougher, but by then more time would have elapsed and, who knows, she might even be in another doomed relationship.

She smiled to herself, a smile of contemplation, of something vaguely nostalgic.

'What is it?' Sullivan asked.

She turned to face him. They were seated side by side on her couch, Annie with her legs tucked beneath her, Jack slouched back with his heels on the coffee table.

'Relationships suck,' she said quietly.

'Sometimes they do, and sometimes having no relationship sucks more,' he said.

'But we always recover . . . apparently we always recover.'

Sullivan nodded. 'Never ceases to amaze me the amount of crap that a human being can tolerate and still come out the other side somewhat sane.'

'Don't know that anyone's actually ever really sane,' Annie said. 'I think everyone's crazy to some extent.'

'But David Quinn has to be the craziest.'

Annie nodded. 'Most definitely . . . David Quinn has to be the craziest of them all.' She leaned sideways until her head rested on Sullivan's shoulder.

He put his arm around her and pulled her close.

'You wanna keep looking?' he asked.

She shook her head. 'I don't know. I'll sleep on it, see how I feel tomorrow.'

'You can't let something like this stop you living life, you know?'

'I know . . . but I think I've come to a point where I've had enough.'

'Enough? Enough of what?'

Annie sighed. 'Enough of doing the same thing day in, day out Jack. Enough of the store, of the stocks and inventories, of battered paperback books that I'm sure no-one ever reads.' She looked up at him. 'You know what I think?'

'What?'

'I think that they buy books to take home and put in a bookcase so people will think that they're cultured and academic and well read.'

'That's a very cynical attitude.'

'I have a right to be cynical tonight . . . at least allow me that much.'

'So what will you do then? Sell the place? Move?'

She shrugged. 'I don't know . . . I really don't know what I'll do. More than likely piss and moan about it for a few days and then go back to the same old routine.'

'It won't ever be the same routine Annie. Something like this happens and you always end up seeing things from another point of view. That much difference at least.'

'But not enough,' she said. 'Never different enough.'

'Maybe we could move together . . . a different city, go out to Vegas or something.'

'Sell the store, take all the money and blow it on the blackjack tables. Stay a week in the presidential suite, and then when the money's all gone we could sleep rough in bus shelters and drink Thunderbird wine out of brown paper bags until we die of liver failure.'

'Sounds good.'

Annie closed her eyes and breathed deeply.

'I'm going home,' Sullivan said. 'You get some sleep . . . we'll talk in the morning.'

'Sure,' she said.

Sullivan eased away from her and got up. He leaned forward

and kissed her forehead, touched her face, smiled, and walked towards the door.

'Sleep tight,' he said.

'Make sure the bugs don't bite,' she replied.

Sullivan left the room and closed the door gently behind him.

Annie lay for a while on the couch before going through to her bedroom. She couldn't be bothered with showering or brushing her teeth; she stripped off her clothes, lay down and pulled the covers over herself.

She lay awake for some time, at one point turning to glance at the clock and then, reaching for it, she turned its face away from her. Time was all she possessed right now, and it was not something she needed to measure.

There are these moments, she thought, *when it all seems so meaningless. Moments when everything you have done, everything you believe you've worked towards comes to nothing. How shallow can it all be? How many lives are spent waiting for something to happen, only to end with nothing happening at all? There must be a hundred million people out there feeling what I'm feeling now. Hollow. Inconsequential. And yet all of us felt at some point that there was something out there for us, that one day it would all come right, that there would be a perfect day when everything started to turn around . . .*

She buried her face in the pillow and closed her eyes. She could feel moisture behind her lids.

Don't cry Annie, she thought. *Crying serves no purpose. You can just lie here and cry yourself to sleep or you can start to plan how you're gonna get yourself out of this hole and make something happen for yourself. Two months' time and you'll be thirty-one, and there isn't anyone gonna come along and hold your hand, tell you it's all gonna be okay and make everything right. That shit doesn't happen. In Hollywood maybe, but not down here in Morningside Park, Manhattan. This is life. Real life. It has sharp corners and rough edges, and sometimes you collide with them and you break bones and bloody your nose and bruise real easy. And what d'you do then? Well, that depends on who you are. If you're a victim of circumstance you lie right where you fell, and you just keep on lying there hoping that the noise will stop. If you're a survivor . . . well, if you're a survivor you survive.*

Are you a survivor Annie O'Neill? Are you?

She hugged the pillow tighter, felt the warmth of her body seeping into the mattress, felt the weight of her thoughts as they tugged her down into sleep.

Just sleep a while Annie . . . maybe when you wake up the world will be a different place. Has to be a different place. Can't take much more of it the way it is. No . . . can't take much more the way it is.

And then she slept, and as she slept the rain started falling, and from the window of her apartment you would have seen a hundred thousand streetlights reflected along wet streets and boulevards and avenues.

And maybe, somewhere out there, someone was thinking of Annie O'Neill and what tomorrow would bring.

An hour or two later, she woke once again. And she cried. And though she cried for David Quinn, or whoever she might have believed was David Quinn, she cried more for herself. She cried for her loneliness, her loss, for many reasons. And she cried for her father. Frank O'Neill. She touched his wristwatch, watched the sweep-hand slowly devour its metronomic seconds, and then she searched out *Breathing Space*, and with her finger she traced the words he had written inside the cover. *Annie, for when the time comes. Dad. 2 June 1979.*

Dad, she thought, and this thought brought more tears, and when her eyes were raw-red she made her way to the bathroom and washed her face.

She stood there for a while, stood there doing nothing but looking at her reflection in the mirror.

Perhaps all of them, she thought, *Perhaps Tom Parselle and Ben Leonhardt and Richard Lorentzen and Michael Duggan . . . even David Quinn, and in a curious way Jack Sullivan . . . perhaps all of them were nothing more than substitutes for him. For Frank. For Daddy.*

Later she cried some more, and then she slept.

Did not dream.

Too tired, too hollow, too broken up to dream.

And when morning came she was still sleeping, and Sullivan – mindful of sleep's curative nature – left her that way. Seemed the best he could do. At least for now.

THIRTY-FIVE

Friday the thirteenth was Annie O'Neill's first thought as she woke.

Her second was *Fuck it.*

The third was neither as portentous nor as angry, it was simply *David*.

It seemed as if the atmosphere in the room had pressed down on her during the night and was challenging her to rise from where she lay. She felt bruised – physically, mentally, emotionally, spiritually – and even as she tried to move the will to do so was not there. She slumped back onto the mattress and tried to sleep again, tried to force her mind to close down and succumb; but there was traffic beyond the window, the sound of life moving on without her, and it beckoned and teased and cajoled her into unwilling wakefulness.

Eventually, resisting every inch of the way, she dragged herself to a sitting position on the edge of the bed. She sat there, naked but for her panties, and looked down at her own body – her breasts, her stomach, the tops of her thighs. It seemed only hours ago that she had permitted this man – this David whoever-the-fuck-he-was – to invade every inch of her, inside and out. It seemed like only last night that he had taken everything she possessed and consumed it for his own entertainment, and then he had walked. Just got up and walked with no intention of returning.

'Bastard!' she said out loud, and then clenching her fist she turned and thumped the pillow repeatedly, and with each impact she hissed 'Bastard . . . bastard! . . . bastard!'

337

She leaned forward and buried her face in her hands.

There were tears, but she would not allow them to come. She would not allow this man to bring her to the edge of grief once more. He didn't deserve it. She was better than that. Annie O'Neill, bookstore owner, was altogether better than that. At least she had strength of character, some backbone, some honor and integrity and a willingness to speak the truth. David Quinn had possessed none of these things, and what he had possessed had been insufficient even to proffer an explanation, an apology.

We need to talk.

It all seems to have happened so fast.

'Asshole,' she muttered under her breath and stood up.

From beneath the rushing shower she didn't hear Sullivan come in. He knocked on the door and Annie jumped, slightly startled, when he hollered 'Coffee?' over the sound of the water.

'Please!' she shouted back, and spent another minute attempting to scrub David Quinn from her body before she came out of the bathroom in her robe. Her wet hair hung in tails around her face.

'I'm gonna wash that man right outta my hair,' Sullivan said as Annie entered the kitchen.

'Don't try the humor,' she said. 'Humor never suited you Jack Sullivan.'

'Coffee,' he said, handing her a cup. She took it and sat at the kitchen table.

Sullivan sat facing her. 'You're gonna get over this,' he said.

'That a question or a statement?' she asked.

'Whichever way you wanna take it,' Sullivan replied.

'If it's a question,' she said, 'then the answer is yes. If it's a statement then sympathetic platitudes are the last thing I need.'

'How does it go?'

'What?' she asked, frowning.

'The emotional rollercoaster.'

She smiled. 'Grief, hopelessness, futility, and then maybe contempt and bitterness. After that you feel angry, hateful, destructive, and after that I s'pose you go kind of numb, and then you find yourself again and you're okay.'

'And where would you be today?' Sullivan asked.

'Contempt and bitterness,' she said.

'So I've got the really fun things to look forward to?'

'You have,' Annie said, and drank her coffee.

'I think maybe I'll go stay with my sister for a couple of weeks.'

'You haven't got a sister,' she said.

'I'll buy one.'

'Smartmouth,' she said.

'Sassy, beautiful, independent, stubborn, hard-headed bitch,' Sullivan replied.

'Thank you,' Annie said. 'You can go home now.'

Sullivan smiled. 'Can I say he wasn't worth it, that you were too good for him?'

'You can,' she said. 'But it will mean absolutely nothing seeing as how you didn't even know him.'

'But I met him once, and there was something weak about his eyes . . . you can always tell what someone's like by looking at their eyes.'

'You can, can you?'

'Sure you can,' Sullivan said.

'Let me see,' Annie said, leaning forward and gazing at Sullivan's face. 'I see a washed-out ex-alcoholic, a lush by anyone's standards, a man who could no more find gainful employment than he could find a girlfriend.'

Sullivan raised his eyebrows. 'Getting personal now, are we?'

'You started it,' she said.

'Okay, truce,' Sullivan replied. 'We start again. You're gonna be okay, right?'

She nodded. 'I'm gonna be okay.'

'So what do we do today? We gonna try and find this guy?'

Annie shook her head. 'Even if I could be bothered I

wouldn't know where to start. What I plan to do is nothing, not today, not the whole weekend, and then after I see Forrester on Monday I'm going to take a holiday.'

'A holiday?'

'Sure, a holiday.'

'Where?'

'God knows,' she said. 'Maybe go up to Niagara Falls or someplace . . . you wanna come?'

Sullivan nodded thoughtfully. 'Sure I'll come. Never been to Niagara Falls.'

'Then apparently you have never lived.'

Sullivan smiled, drank his coffee, thought briefly about asking Annie O'Neill to marry him and then decided against it. Timing wasn't right. Timing would have sucked.

Later, as if an afterthought, Annie asked Sullivan what *he* felt she should do.

'Let it go,' he said.

Annie didn't reply. She seemed pensive, withdrawn.

'You know the old thing about if you love someone the real test is to let them go and see if they come back?'

She nodded.

'Well here . . . well it doesn't exactly apply here, but the point I'm making is that if this guy really had a thing for you he wouldn't have done what he did. He would have come forward with some kind of explanation, right?'

'I s'pose so, yes.'

'There's no s'pose about it. The truth of the matter is that the world is jammed solid from end to end with people who don't have a clue what they want, and even when it's staring them right in the face they still can't decide.' Sullivan smiled. 'You have to let him go, or he'll haunt you.'

Annie frowned. 'Haunt me? What d'you mean?'

'He'll be there, always there at the back of your mind, and you'll more than likely find yourself in some situation in the not-too-distant future where there's an opportunity . . . you

340

know, an opportunity to meet someone else, to start all over, but because this guy is there in your mind you won't let yourself. It may be tough to let go, but if you do you also open yourself up to seeing what's there in front of you when it comes.'

'You'd have made someone a good husband Jack,' Annie said.

'I know.'

'Apart from the conceit,' Annie added.

Sullivan nodded. 'I used to figure I was conceited until I actually realized I was perfect.'

Annie was quiet for a time, and then she said, 'So you reckon the only way out of this is to let it go, to forget all about it?'

'Not forget, no,' he replied. 'Don't ever forget. It's a life experience kind of thing. It's what life is for. The only things that ever really come back to hurt you are the things you never really faced, and the things you forgot about. What I mean is that you imagine it's like an article of clothing that's too small for you, but there's something sentimental about it so you don't throw it out. You fold it up neat, you stow it in the bottom of your dresser, and every once in a while you remind yourself that it's there. It's something you once possessed, and at one time it was perhaps the thing that made you feel best, the thing you felt you looked good in, but that was then, and this is now, and now you have something else that works for you.'

'Homespun philosophy,' Annie said.

'Homespun it may be, but there's a thread of truth in what I say. You don't spend your life looking over your shoulder at what might have been, what could have been . . . you spend your life looking at what you have right now and how you can make it better for tomorrow.'

'Or you go the Prozac and vodka route,' Annie said drily.

'Or the Prozac and vodka,' Sullivan said.

'So today, now, I forget the asshole of the century.'

He nodded. 'Good enough.'

'So what do we do?'

Sullivan smiled. 'I take you to the Italian restaurant on 112th, we eat crab and avocado antipasta, we gorge ourselves sick on fusilli and mortadella and Montepulciano, and then we get a cab home and laugh about how stupid everyone else is but us.'

'Deal,' Annie said. 'You're paying.'

He put on a shocked expression. 'Me? Pay? An old lush incapable of finding gainful employment?'

'You pay or I stay home and sulk about how life is a bitch and how everyone has it in for me.'

Sullivan shrugged. 'So I pay . . . get your coat.'

They walked. It was no more than a couple of blocks, and there on West 112th between Amsterdam and Broadway, was the little trattoria with its subdued lighting, bursting at the seams with Genovese dialects and atmosphere. They took a table near the window, and through the clouded glass Annie watched people walk by in the street. People alone, people in twos and threes, all of them heading someplace with something in mind. She and Sullivan ate, they talked little, and after Annie's third or fourth glass of wine the world appeared to have mellowed a little. The sharp edges were smoother, the rough edges had been sanded down by some unseen and benevolent hand, and as she sat moving a small tiramisu creation around the edges of her plate she felt that perhaps she would recover. There really was no other way. What else could she do – give up?

She looked up at Sullivan.

He smiled. 'It comes, and then it goes,' he said quietly.

She nodded, set down her spoon and closed her eyes for a moment.

'What you doing?' Sullivan asked. 'You forget grace or what?'

She laughed. 'I was just thinking – '

''Bout what?'

'About another birthday in two months' time.'

'What is this? You soliciting for birthday presents already?'

'Sure I am,' she said. 'You can get me a car.'

'This is New York, you don't do cars, you do taxicabs and subways.'

'So buy me a subway, what's your problem?'

They smiled at one another, and things felt okay. Somehow, some way, they felt okay. And then a thought came. Out of left field, out of nowhere. *Wish it was my father here with me. He would know what to say, would know what to do. He would be the sort of man who could make a call and find someone, and drive me there, and stand beside me while I said what I wanted to say, and protect me if things got ugly, and tell me I was right . . . tell me I was right and the rest of the world was so fucking wrong . . .*

She turned to the window as a movement caught the corner of her eye.

David Quinn looked back at her through the glass.

The sound that escaped her lips was a scream, a sudden inhalation, a gasp of surprise, all these things together. She felt she would choke.

She tried to stand up, but somehow the tops of her legs caught the edge of the table and, before Sullivan had a chance to react, the bottle of wine had toppled over and the red Montepulciano was flooding the table, filling the spaces between their plates.

Annie didn't stop, didn't hesitate, and coming out from the table her chair fell backwards, collided with someone who was seated behind her. He started to rise also, and confusion spread like a small whirlwind through the half-dozen or so tables near the window.

Annie's face was white, shocked. Not until she reached the door did she realize she was holding her breath.

'Annie!' Sullivan was calling, confused, unaware of what she'd seen.

He followed her, trying as best he could to settle the people around them, and when he went out through the door, a waiter following – perhaps believing that they were planning to run without paying the bill – he found Annie standing on the sidewalk, her whole body shaking, her head moving swiftly back and forth as she scanned left and right down the street.

'Annie?' Sullivan was asking. 'Annie . . . what is it?'

She looked at him, her eyes wide and brimming with tears, perhaps from the cold he thought, but then she opened her mouth and her tone of voice told him that it was nothing to do with the temperature.

'Da-David,' she stuttered. 'David was here . . . looking . . . looking through the window at me. David Quinn was right here on the sidewalk . . .'

Sullivan stepped forward and held onto her as if she would suddenly turn and bolt.

She looked at him, seemed to look right through him, and then once again she was looking left and right, trying to see between the passing cars and taxicabs to the other side of the street.

'You're sure?' was all Sullivan could think to ask.

'As sure as I could ever be,' Annie said. 'I turned to look out of the window and there he was, right there in front of me looking in at us.'

'It can't have been – '

'It was!' Annie snapped. 'Jesus, I should know Jack, I had the man practically living with me. I don't forget a face, especially a man I've slept with.'

'Okay, okay, okay . . . settle down Annie . . .'

'Settle down? What the fuck good is that gonna do? He was here Jack, right here where I'm standing now.'

'Okay Annie . . . he was here. He's gone now . . . he's gone. Let's go back inside. I gotta pay, okay? I gotta pay and then we'll go home.' He took Annie's arm gently, and started to lead her towards the restaurant. 'Come back inside, sweetheart . . . please.'

The waiter who had followed them seemed satisfied that they were not planning a sudden escape and walked backwards until he reached the entrance. He held open the door as Sullivan took Annie inside and returned her to their table. He asked for the check, stood there while Annie sat shivering, the man behind her turning round, looking at Sullivan, mouthing *She okay?* to which Sullivan nodded and smiled, and then the check was paid, and they were gathering coats, and whatever ambience they may have briefly created, whatever respite they had found away from the sharp corners and rough edges of the world, came back in full technicolor and 3-D visuals. Outside it was bitterly cold, and Sullivan walked beside Annie, pulled her tight, tugging his overcoat around her and holding her hand until they reached the steps of the apartment block and were on their way up.

He saw her inside, went to the kitchen, and poured an inch of Crown Royal into a glass, and though the temptation hit him hard – hard like a Mack truck carrying bridge parts – he resisted. He carried the glass through to where Annie sat, silent and staring on the couch, and handed her the glass.

She took bird-like sips, winced at the taste, the burning sensation that flooded her throat and filled her chest, but she did not complain. She drank the glass empty and set it aside.

She said nothing for some time, seemingly in shock, and then at last she turned and looked directly at Sullivan and said, 'He followed us.'

Sullivan started to shake his head.

'He did Jack . . . he goddamned followed us. You're gonna turn around and tell me that coincidence *isn't* bullshit now?'

Sullivan shook his head. This was one he wasn't going to win. 'You can't be sure,' he said. 'You cannot be sure he followed us.'

'I don't have to be sure,' Annie said. 'I only have to be more than fifty percent on this, and I'm ninety-five percent Jack, ninety-five fucking percent certain that David Quinn followed us.'

'And what the hell would he do that for?' Sullivan asked.

Annie shook her head. 'How the hell do I know? Same

345

reason he seduced me, fucked me, took me to Boston and then ditched me from a great height. You know as well as I do that crazy people don't think the same way we do.'

Sullivan smiled. 'I don't think he was crazy Annie, I just think he was weak and confused and scared to commit to anything more than an uncomplicated relationship.'

Annie sneered. 'Christ Jack, he wasn't even prepared to have an uncomplicated relationship. Two weeks and he ran . . . that sound like an uncomplicated relationship to you?'

Sullivan sighed inside. He didn't know what was going on. There was no way he would ever know if the man who'd looked through the restaurant window was David Quinn, someone who looked like him, or a complete hallucination.

Annie got up suddenly. 'This is bullshit,' she said. 'This is fucking bullshit Jack. I can't live like this . . . I can't spend the rest of my goddamned life . . . aah Jesus Christ, this is a fucking mess.'

Annie collapsed on the couch again, and even before Sullivan had a chance to say anything she was crying.

'I want . . . I want someone,' she said, her voice breaking as she tried to stem the tears. 'I want to have someone around who actually wants me for who I am. Is that too much to ask? Is that really too fucking much to ask? Christ almighty, what does it take to be happy around here? What the hell d'you have to do to find some halfway sane human being who wants the same things you do?'

She looked up at Sullivan. Her eyeliner and mascara were running down her face. She looked like someone had given her a good kicking. Figuratively, Sullivan thought, someone had.

'And where the fuck are your parents when you need them?'

Sullivan frowned. 'Your parents?'

'Yes,' she said, her voice wavering. 'Your goddamn fucking parents . . . your mom and your dad . . . where the fuck are they when you want some sympathy, eh? They're dead, that's what. They're fucking dead, Jack. What the fuck is this? Screw

Annie O'Neill month? Did the mayor announce a special Fuck-Annie O'Neill-In-The-Ass-Month and forget to send me a card?'

She stopped suddenly, her breathing heavy but her sobbing ceasing mid-flight.

'I have to speak to Forrester,' she said. 'He's the only one who knew anything about my family. Some old guy out there knows more about my family than I do.'

She got up from the couch and started rummaging around amongst a pile of papers on the dresser.

'What're you looking for?' Sullivan asked.

'His phone number . . . I have his phone number some-where.'

'You have his number?'

Annie looked back at Sullivan. 'When he sent that chapter down to the store I called the courier company and got his number . . . it's somewhere . . . here!' she said suddenly, and held up a plain manila envelope.

'Call the number Jack . . . call the number and get Forrester.'

'At this time of night?'

'Just fucking call him will you?' Annie snapped, and she thrust the envelope at Sullivan.

He took it, went to the phone, and standing there with the receiver in his hand, asking himself what the hell he was getting into now, he dialed.

Annie was pacing across the middle of the room, glancing at Sullivan as he stood there.

There was silence at the end of the line for a good five seconds, and then a recorded message told him that the number had not been recognized.

Sullivan put the phone down.

'What?' Annie asked.

Sullivan shook his head, lifted the receiver again, and dialed the number once more to ensure he'd dialed correctly.

Once again there was a delay, and then the same recorded message.

'Not recognized,' he told Annie, tension building in *his* chest now.

'Bullshit,' she said, and taking rapid steps towards him she snatched the receiver from his hand, set it down, lifted it again, and dialed the number once more.

Not recognized, the message told her, and she thought *Yes, not recognized . . . just like me.*

Sullivan silently watched the expression of complete confusion register on her face.

'There must be a fault,' she started. 'There must be a fault on the line. I called this number only a few days ago and spoke to him. Call the operator and get them to check the line.'

Sullivan was shaking his head.

'Call them Jack . . . call the operator, get them to check the line.'

Sullivan took the receiver from her, and knowing it was futile, he called the operator. There was no fault. The line had been disconnected.

'Disconnected? What d'you mean, disconnected?' Annie asked.

'Disconnected,' Sullivan said matter-of-factly.

'Why? Why would he have disconnected his phone?'

'I don't know Annie . . . I have absolutely no idea, but I really think that you shouldn't get yourself upset about it. You can speak to him on Monday.'

'And what if he doesn't turn up Monday . . . what if he just doesn't come? What the hell do I do then Jack?'

'I don't know,' Sullivan said. 'I don't know what you'll do.'

'Helluva lot of fucking use you are,' she snapped.

Annie walked back and sat on the edge of the couch. 'I want to be alone,' she said. 'I want to be on my own for a bit Jack. Would you mind?'

'I don't mind,' he said, 'but I think I should stay.'

Annie shook her head. 'I want to be on my own . . . let me think this thing through. I need to figure out what I'm gonna do.'

348

'I don't know that there is anything you *can* do,' Sullivan said.

Annie waved her hand in a dismissive fashion. 'Let me alone Jack . . . just let me alone.'

Sullivan nodded, his eyes downcast. He started towards the door. 'You know where I am,' he said.

Annie looked up, attempted a weak smile. 'Yes,' she said. 'I just gotta come to terms with what's happening, okay?'

'Okay,' he said, and as he opened the door he paused, opened his mouth to say something else, but Annie raised her hand.

'I'll be okay,' she said. 'Go home, get some sleep . . . I'll see you in the morning.'

And Jack Sullivan went, and though he had no wish to go he understood that Annie would not let him stay.

He did not sleep, not for some time, and somewhere in the early hours of the morning, the apartment block silent, he was convinced he could hear her crying.

His heart went out to her, but for the first time in his life he felt there was nothing he could do to help.

THIRTY-SIX

Sunday unfolded like the distant echo of some other day. A day when something meaningful might have happened. There was that same degree of anticipatory tension, and yet as Annie walked through her apartment, as she surveyed the confines of her own color co-ordinated prison, she believed that today – this day – she would spend alone.

She had gone with Sullivan the evening before, and yes there had been a movie, and yes, there had been popcorn and a hot dog with onions and ketchup, but in leaving the theater she felt as if she were a ghost, and the sounds around her became nothing more than a continuous blur, and in looking at faces, a sea of faces, she realized she was looking for one face only. David Quinn. But he was not there. Not in the foyer as she waited for Jack Sullivan, not on the sidewalk as he hailed a cab, not in the lines of people waiting for buses, or the crowds that huddled together as if for warmth outside a club on Cathedral Parkway.

And once home she wanted nothing more than sleep. And sleep came, quietly like a thief, and it stole from her recognition and memory of all that should have been. But wasn't. And never would be.

Sullivan came that morning, shared coffee, spoke little, and then asked if she wanted company.

Annie merely shook her head and smiled.

Sullivan understood, and went to a bar down the street to play chess as was his routine on Sunday mornings.

From the window she watched the silent streets, and could feel her own heart beating, and wished for nothing more than the knowledge that someone was there.

Don't you want somebody to love?

Who had sung that? Jefferson Airplane?

It struck a chord for her. Everybody needed somebody. Until there was a somebody it felt as if this life was only half a life.

Annie ate little; she had no appetite. There was no physical hunger, only the hunger for something emotional, spiritual perhaps. Such a hunger could not be satisfied by anything other than human contact, the knowledge that you were not alone.

She played Sinatra, but the magic wasn't there. Sinatra sounded distant and self-satisfied. Frank *had* someone. This boy from Hoboken, New Jersey, could've had anyone he wished. Today he sounded like that: replete, all filled up, filled to bursting. And so Annie listened to Suzanne Vega and Mary Margaret O'Hara, women who sounded like they'd been hurt, been bruised, and when 'Luca' came on Annie sat with her face in her hands and cried dry tears.

Sullivan returned in the mid-afternoon. He knocked gently, twice, but Annie didn't answer. He got the message and went away. He would not take offence. He never took offence. He would understand. Jack Ulysses Sullivan had more than enough ghosts of his own.

And then evening, darkness swallowing up Manhattan, street-lights illuminated across the city, straight lines of brilliance with random yellow pinpoints filling the gaps in between.

She watched, she waited, and when her body ached for sleep she succumbed, curling up inside the covers, and there she found brief respite from everything.

Tomorrow was another day, a day that would bring For-rester, and Annie – believing that something good must come from all of this – felt that Forrester might tell her a little of the truth about her father.

At least she wished so, for it seemed that wishes were all that remained.

THIRTY-SEVEN

She woke to the sound of a dog barking somewhere, and she thought: *All the years I've been here and I don't ever remember hearing a dog barking.* It was a desperate sound, a pleading monotony, and as she walked to the kitchen window to see where it was coming from, it stopped. Stopped dead. Just like that. Like someone got pissed off and shot it. But there had been no gunshot. Hit it with a shovel perhaps.

She shuddered. *Crazy shit*, she thought. *Your head's full of crazy shit. You're cracking up. Heard it said that people who live alone finally start talking to themselves . . . not out loud necessarily, but inside their heads.*

Like now.

And then she smiled. Maybe crazy would be better.

She planned to stay home much of the day, leave perhaps late afternoon or early evening. She would go to the store just for Forrester. There seemed to be no other reason. And then she thought that possibly all her years at the store had been a precursor to meeting David Quinn and Robert Forrester, and now she had met them, now she had undergone some indescribable change, there seemed no purpose in it. The Reader's Rest was somehow representative and symbolic of her past: empty, full of dark colors and narrow shadows, a place someone went to escape the rain, to find someone who could relate to their own loneliness . . . People like John Damianka. But now even John had found somewhere else to be. He had found someone.

Annie busied herself with cleaning. She hoovered each room thoroughly, scrubbed the linoleum in the kitchen, the ceramic

352

tiles in the bathroom, and in sorting through the drawers of clothes in the bedroom she found blouses and sweaters she hadn't worn for years. She thought of Sullivan, the analogy he had drawn, and she folded them neatly and returned them to where she'd found them.

Sullivan did come and see her shortly after lunch, said he was on his way out to see someone, would be back in a few hours.

'You want me to come tonight?' he asked.

Annie shook her head. 'I want to go on my own,' she told him. 'Don't ask me why but I feel like this is something I need to do on my own.'

He asked her if she was sure.

'I'm sure,' she said. 'But you'll be here and I'll call you if I need you, okay?'

'Okay.'

Annie heard him leave the building a little while later.

She cleaned some more.

When the time came to leave she stood in the doorway and looked around the room. She felt she was leaving something behind or, more accurately, she believed that when she saw this room again she herself would bring something back that would change her perspective. She felt certain that Forrester could tell her things, things of which she was – and had always been – ignorant. And those things were close to the bone, things about her father, about his life before she was born, the few years he had stayed alive as she grew up. Before he had disappeared.

She closed her eyes and took a deep breath. Then she turned, closed the door, and walked down the stairwell to the street.

The Reader's Rest looked almost derelict: soulless, without light, hunkering in the shadows between stores that seemed to have no difficulty telling the world exactly what they were, and why they were there. The Reader's Rest appeared as a

353

somewhat retarded and unwashed third cousin, showing up at a family reunion, reminding everyone present that there always had been some distant aspect of their genes and family tree that had been awry. The family shrub. The undergrowth.

Annie smiled wryly, unlocked the door, and let herself in.

She made coffee, more out of habit than desire, and glancing at the clock on the wall in the kitchen she set herself to wait out the last three-quarters of an hour before Forrester arrived.

She daydreamed, she imagined what Forrester might tell her, and then she hardened herself to the fact that he might know nothing at all, that he and her father had been nothing more than passing acquaintances. The idea scared her, for here she had collided with someone, the only one, who knew anything at all about her family. Other people, regular people, they took their families for granted. Like that song: *You don't know what you've got 'til it's gone*. Perhaps more fittingly, you didn't know what you didn't have until you became aware of the fact that you never had it in the first place.

Such were her thoughts, and in finding some sense of solace in the mere fact that there was silence enough to contemplate such things, she barely heard the door when Forrester knocked on the glass.

She came to suddenly, rose quickly and hurried to let him in.

'Miss O'Neill,' he said as he entered.

He carried no package this time. The story was done, the final chapter had been delivered.

'Come in,' she said. 'Please come in Mr Forrester.'

He did, stepping into the relative warmth of the store, making his way across the floor and taking a seat at the table where they had sat and talked on all previous occasions.

'You would like some coffee perhaps?' Annie asked, knowing that he would decline.

'This evening, yes,' Forrester said, surprising her. 'I would very much like coffee, Miss O'Neill.'

Annie smiled. She was happy to fetch a cup for him, and when she returned and set it in front of him he had removed his overcoat, unbuttoned the top button of his shirt and loosened his tie.

'Your man trouble?' he asked. 'This trouble resolved?'

Annie shook her head. 'No,' she replied. 'He disappeared.'

Forrester smiled, sympathy in his eyes. 'Believe me,' he said. 'I think this young man was running away from something in himself, not from you.'

Annie frowned. 'What makes you say that?'

Forrester shook his head. 'In my experience it is only those who are afraid of responsibility, of the consequences of their own actions, who run away without explanations and apologies.'

Annie smiled. This had certainly been true of herself. And then she stopped midflight. How did Forrester know what had happened? That there had been no explanation or apology? What had she said exactly? That she had met someone, and that perhaps things were not going as well as she would have hoped? And Forrester had asked her something . . . asked her whether this man she was involved with had shown his true colors?

Annie shook her head. She was making no sense. Forrester had merely made an educated guess about what had happened. Perhaps she *could* be read like a book. Perhaps – in her expression, her manner, her body language – everything she was feeling was on display for the world.

'So you have read the story of Harry Rose and Johnnie Redbird?' Forrester asked.

'I have,' she said. 'I found it fascinating . . . I think it would make a great movie.'

Forrester laughed, lifted his cup, sipped his coffee. 'And your thoughts?'

Annie leaned back in her chair. 'Well, truth be known, it ends inconclusively. Harry Rose is in Rikers, and we don't get any idea about what happened to Johnnie Redbird.'

Forrester nodded but said nothing.

'Do you know what happened?' Annie asked.

Forrester shook his head. 'There is a little more to the story, yes,' he replied, 'but nothing that is written down.'

Annie was quiet for a time, and then she looked up at Forrester. 'Can I ask you about my father Mr Forrester?'

'In a little while,' he said. 'First we must hypothesize the end of Harry Rose and Johnnie Redbird, and then I will tell you what I know about your father. Is that agreeable?'

Annie shifted uncomfortably in her chair. She didn't want to speak of some fictional characters in a story, she wanted to speak of her father, Frank O'Neill, but she held her tongue, focused her mind. She believed that here was her only chance to find something of the truth, and she realized all too well that she must be patient.

'So what do you believe might have happened?' Forrester asked her.

Annie shrugged. 'I don't know . . . any number of things could have happened. All I know is that Johnnie Redbird wanted his money more than anything else in the world.'

Forrester nodded as if in affirmation, and then he smiled. 'I shall tell you what I think happened,' he said quietly, and leaned back in his chair. 'I believe Johnnie Redbird went home, back down to Ciudad Juarez over the Rio Bravo del Norte. Went home with nothing to show for his trouble. Went home with a bitter heart and a blackened mind, and the knowledge that somehow Harry Rose had evaded his dues one more time.'

Forrester paused as if in thought, and then he smiled again, a strange smile, somewhat distant and emotionless. 'I think he must have read about Harry Rose and thought things like *An eye for an eye* and *What goes around comes around*, and despite knowing Harry Rose would never say a word about him, for Harry Rose knew that if he spoke a single word Johnnie would kill his wife and his child without hesitation, he still felt the pain of betrayal. He must have had this sense of security, this

356

personal guarantee, but nevertheless he still figured that some-how, some way, he would finally balance the scales and get back what he was owed.'

Forrester looked at Annie as if waiting for a question.

Annie said nothing; her mind was blank. She felt ill-at-ease.

'Harry was in Rikers,' Forrester went on. 'That was perhaps the most ironic thing of all, and if Johnnie had only had the nerve to do such a thing, he might have visited him. The governor and the warders would have changed, many years had elapsed, but he was safe down in Mexico, and that's where he stayed. He must have carried the ghost of his past, a second shadow if you like, and always and forever there would be the sound of Harry's voice, a taunting sound, the sound of a man reprieved . . . and even though he believed he was free of his debt, that justice had been seen to be done, Johnnie would not have concurred. He wanted his money. He wanted all of it, and perhaps he began to think that there must be some way of getting it.'

Annie shifted again. Was it growing cooler? Or was that just her imagination? There was something different in the room, a change in the atmosphere, and she wasn't altogether sure she liked it. She wished Sullivan were there, wished she'd allowed him to come down with her tonight.

Forrester cleared his throat. 'Time passed, years unfolded, and as Johnnie Redbird grew older his thoughts turned to something he had considered time and again for as long as he could recall. He thought of the girl he'd left behind in Hudson Heights, the one who thought he looked like Gary Cooper. He wondered once more if she'd ever had the child he'd fathered, or if the five grand he'd given her had paid for a backstreet abortion and a guilty conscience. For a while he would let it go, but it kept on creeping back, like a stray dog whom he fed at his doorstep and would remain ever hopeful. Harry still owed him the money, and as long as Harry was alive Johnnie believed there must be a way to take it back. He began to think that Harry had lied, that he could not have spent all he had, and he also knew that he had no intention to stay in Mexico for the rest of his life.' Forrester leaned forward, ever so slightly, but he did lean forward. He smiled in that same unnerving fashion.

Annie felt a chill close around her spine and start crawling up towards her neck.

'But you don't kill four men in America and return for your high school reunion now do you Miss O'Neill?' Forrester asked.

He didn't wait for Annie to answer. It was not a question that required an answer.

'So Johnnie stayed in Mexico, and though he tried not to he couldn't help but think of the Hudson Heights girl. Woke one morning and remembered her name. Even remembered her pretty little face and the way she would laugh whenever he kissed her. He was fifty-seven by then, and the child – if ever there had been a child – would have been twenty-two years old. A man or a woman? He had no way of knowing, but he was smart, and he had money, and all it would take was half a dozen phone calls and a scattering of long green and he could find out. Anyone could be found, he knew that as well as he knew his own name, and though he resisted the temptation there was something about growing old that made him feel it was necessary to know; that it was important to know if he would leave anything behind. If there would be anything to show for his life after he was dead. He also felt that if there was a child then the money he was owed also belonged to that child. Perhaps, who knows, he might eventually have let go, he might have become old and tired of thinking about Harry Rose. But he didn't let go, couldn't let go. There was a debt to be paid, and he would keep on believing that until his body couldn't draw another breath.'

Forrester paused, closed his eyes briefly, and when he opened them there was something cold and aloof in his expression.

Annie wanted to say something, wanted to ask him to stop talking, to leave now . . . please?

She opened her lips, but not a sound ventured forth. She believed if she had exhaled in that moment she would have seen her own chilled breath evaporating into the room.

'Not until twelve years later did Johnnie Redbird make the calls. He called people who could be trusted to find a dust mote in a tornado. There had been a child. The child was a man. Thirty-four years old. The Hudson Heights girl was dead, dead of an overdose in 1980, and after her death the boy had been shipped back and forth between foster parents and juvenile facilities until he was eighteen. Now he was out there, had a life of his own, and Johnnie – an old man with a hankering for his roots – thought perhaps the time had come to find him. The child had been denied a father, and in his own mind he believed that the denial had been as much Harry Rose's fault as ever it had been his own. Had he stayed, or had he and Harry gone out to Vegas or Los Angeles together, then perhaps the girl would have come with them, and with the money that was as much his own as it was Harry's he could have provided for them. At least that much. He thought of his son. He wondered about him. He wanted him to understand what had happened, why he had been left alone all these years. He believed it was necessary for his son to know, for in understanding his father's life he could perhaps better understand some aspect of his own.'

Forrester closed his eyes again, but this time they stayed closed.

Annie glanced around the room, felt the urge to get up, to move, to do something other than sit here listening to the old man describing things that sounded all too plausible to be mere speculation.

'And so he started to write,' Forrester said.

Annie looked at him. He opened his eyes suddenly and she jumped.

'Started to write the very words I brought for you. He was

grateful then to Oscar Tate Lundy for making him read books and write the alphabet, for giving him no choice in the matter. Reading and writing had somehow helped him out of Rikers, and now it would help his son to understand his roots. He wrote them for him, so he could read and understand how he had been betrayed, how they had *both* been betrayed by a man called Harry Rose. Harry Rose was their traitor, their own Judas, and for his thirty pieces of silver, silver that had once belonged to Johnnie, he had sold him out to isolation and deprivation and loneliness. It was a new emotion, this sense of betrayal, and there were times he wished for nothing more than to tell Harry what he felt, how angered and tormented and abused he had become. For Harry had possessed everything, and Johnnie had been left with nothing. Not even his own blood. It was his son's right to know who this man was, to see what he had done, and once he understood he could perhaps come to terms with his own sense of loss, and make his own decision to act. Johnnie turned these things over in his mind as he sat in his room in a small adobe house in Mexico. The heat tortured him, and there were times when he would drink and shout into the darkness. A voice clamoring in the desert for justice, for retribution, for equity . . .'

Once more Forrester paused, as if for effect, and then he leaned back in his chair and sighed deeply.

'His son would know,' he said. 'He *had* to know. And if Johnnie could never tell him to his face, then at least he could have him read it, read it and weep, read it and understand that his life had never been his own. Harry Rose had taken his life, and for this – for this crime of the heart – he would pay his dues. And there was another thought. That Harry's child was out there, and maybe they had the money, and if they had the money then perhaps Johnnie could take it back. All of it. These thoughts came out of a shadowed past like ghosts, or like frightened children running for cover and coaxed out again by the promise of something sweet . . . these things kept Johnnie going, kept him alive. The sense that there was a debt to be paid, a balance outstanding, and he – Johnnie Redbird – could always find a way.'

Forrester fell silent. He was breathing deeply, as if his monologue had exhausted him. 'I believe Johnnie would have found the son, a son who would have been somewhat dysfunctional and out of touch. He – after all – did not have a regular kind of upbringing – born with an absentee father, losing his mother at such an early age, and then being shipped back and forth between numerous and sundry foster parents and juvenile facilities.'

'Yes, okay,' Annie said, eventually finding the necessary spirit to say something, anything. 'He's a loner, a man without a past . . .'

She stopped suddenly. She believed, perhaps, that she was referring in some way to herself. 'And then this father he never knew he had shows up, and they are reunited.'

'And the father tells him of himself, his life, shows him what he has written, and the son discovers the real reason that he was left behind,' Forrester said. 'The son discovers the truth about his father and Harry Rose. The son is devastated. His life, the life he thought he had, is smashed to pieces like a car crash. He understands his father's bitterness and regret, he begins to comprehend the depth of betrayal that Harry Rose had perpetrated against them, and he knows that the money Harry took from his father was also taken from him.'

Annie frowned. 'Surely Johnnie would be ashamed of his past?'

'Perhaps,' Forrester said. 'Perhaps not. He gives his reasons in the pages he wrote. There was a lot of money, a great deal of money, and half of it belonged to Johnnie Redbird. He spent many years in Rikers himself, and then again in Mexico, and all the while Harry Rose denied him what was rightfully his . . . he felt his son should know the truth so they could do something about it . . . so they could regain their legacy. They spend time together, a time they never had, and they begin to see eye to eye. They cry together, they talk for hours, they begin to understand that without Harry Rose their lives would have been entirely different. The son imagines how it would have been to have a father. He sees the decisions that were made, how his life has been a war zone because of this man, and he feels the pain and anguish that comes with knowing the truth.'

Annie looked at Forrester. He spoke with such passion and vehemence it scared her. 'So perhaps they would speak to Harry Rose, go see him on Rikers Island?' Annie suggested, glad for a moment to be speaking, to be asking and answering questions. By speaking about these things she could distance herself from them. There was a sense of disquiet that unnerved and disturbed her and she wished that something would happen to make it disappear.

Forrester shook his head. 'Redbird could never go back to Rikers. He was an escaped felon, and though many years had passed there might still be people there who would recognize him.'

Annie was silent, and then she looked up. 'So he sends his son?'

Forrester smiled, nodded agreeably. 'He sends his son perhaps, yes. And the son speaks with Harry Rose to find out if there really was any money, or if Harry lied when Johnnie came to see him at his house.'

'And Harry tells the son where the money is.'

'Or that there is no money, that it is all gone . . . all of it swallowed up in attempting to defend himself and his family.'

'His wife and his child,' Annie said.

'His wife and his daughter,' Forrester replied.

'It doesn't say whether he had a son or a daughter in the manuscript.'

Forrester hesitated, and then nodded in affirmation. 'You're right Miss O'Neill, it doesn't.'

'So the son returns to see his father and he tells him that Harry Rose has no money.'

'And Johnnie Redbird is incensed, angry that he has been

362

betrayed a third time by a man he believed to be his friend, and so he considers how he can save face, how he can hurt Harry Rose for all the wrong that has been done. And then there is another thought, that perhaps Harry is once again lying . . .'

'And the son too . . . he wants retribution?' Annie asked.

'The son too,' Forrester said. 'The son has regained his father, but he has all these years behind him where he went without anything. No family, no roots, nothing. And then he finds out that there was something that should always have been his, and this old man in Rikers Island has denied him his birthright.'

'But they can't hurt Harry Rose any more . . . Harry Rose is in Rikers, and will be until he dies.'

'But they can still reach someone,' Forrester suggested.

'Harry's child,' Annie said. 'They can still get to Harry's child, and the one thing that Harry was always afraid of was that his child might find out the truth about him.'

'And so the son goes back to Rikers – '

'And tells Harry that they will find the child and tell them the truth about Harry Rose, what he did and where he was . . . and see if Harry's child has the money.'

'And Harry's child . . . the child who is now an adult?'

'Will find out the truth and know that Harry Rose has been hurt in return for all the wrong he did Johnnie Redbird.'

Forrester smiled. 'Not only that the father has been hurt, but the father was a crazy man, a killer just like Johnnie Redbird, and is now spending the rest of his life on Rikers Island. The child will find the father, but even as he is found the child realizes that everything they ever imagined was a lie.'

Forrester paused, breathed deeply. 'It seems possible, does it not? Perhaps even possible that Johnnie's son found some way to hurt Harry's child, something deep and meaningful?'

Annie nodded, but felt uncomfortable. She opened her mouth to say something, anything, but nothing came out.

363

She sat forward in her chair. She felt the power of the story, and the way Forrester had concluded it seemed to serve the ends of justice. Johnnie Redbird had been a bad, crazy man, but in his own way Harry Rose had made decisions that were just as bad, just as crazy, and in some ways had been the worst of them. He had given his word, and then he had broken it. Annie tried her best to see it as something separate, something disconnected from herself, but there was a feeling of invasion, emotional and mental invasion, that she could not shake off. She shuddered perceptibly. She wished she was elsewhere. She *truly* wished she was elsewhere.

'So you see,' Forrester said, 'there was some sense of justice in the end, was there not? Johnnie Redbird's son found Harry Rose's child, and though he searched he found no money. But sometimes the knowledge that the scales have been balanced is worth more than all the gold of El Dorado.' Forrester raised his hand, again with that small theatrical flourish. He had concluded something.

Annie sat quietly for a moment. Her mind felt empty.

'And now you want to know about your father,' Forrester said.

Annie nodded. She tried to say something, but already there was an indescribable tension in her throat.

Forrester smiled. 'Perhaps you would be so kind,' he said, and lifted his coffee cup.

Annie took his cup and walked out back to the kitchen. She went through the motions automatically, saw her hands preparing the coffee, but her mind and her heart were back there in the store waiting for what Forrester would tell her. Everything went in to slow-motion. Everything was quiet. At last she held the refilled cup in her hand and was walking back the way she'd come. The distance between the kitchen and the store had never seemed so long. She set the cup down on the table and took her seat once more.

'Your father,' Forrester said, 'was a brilliant man in his own way. There were many people who did not easily understand him, why he was the way he was, but a lot of his idiosyncrasies were down to his background, the things that had happened to him early in his life.'

'Things?' Annie asked. 'What things?'

Forrester shook his head, waved his hand dismissively. 'He was a man of passion perhaps, strong-willed, not afraid to fight for what he believed in. A man of principle . . .'

Forrester paused. He lifted the coffee cup and took a sip. He set the cup down, withdrew his hand, and then he reached for it once more and turned the handle towards himself.

Annie felt the tension rising, a band of steel in her chest.

'And he was an engineer, as I said before, but no ordinary kind of engineer.'

Annie frowned.

'He engineered life Miss O'Neill, made things happen. He had ideas, and then he brought them to life.'

Annie shook her head. She was beginning to understand something, something she knew she didn't want to understand.

Forrester was quiet for a time. He reached up and buttoned his shirt, tightened his tie, and then he leaned forward with his fingers steepled together. 'There was a dark side to your father, and when you believed you understood what he might do he would do exactly the opposite. He was possessed by different moods at different times, but there was always something behind everything he did that was known only to himself. Your father had a remarkable ability to hide inside himself, to let no-one inside, and that – perhaps that alone – was the reason he finally lost.'

Annie frowned, ill-at-ease. The conversation was once again taking a turn that she neither understood nor felt comfortable with. 'Lost?'

'Lost,' Forrester stated matter-of-factly.

'Lost what?'

'His wife, your mother . . . and you.'

The tension in Annie now was suffocating. It seemed

difficult to breathe, as though the air had become suddenly thicker, fluid almost.

'But he died,' Annie said. 'He died back in 1979 . . . why do you say he lost us? We were the ones who lost him.'

Forrester reached inside his jacket pocket. From it he produced an envelope. He held it in his hand as if to let it go would be the end of him.

'I have a picture here,' he said. 'A picture that perhaps may interest you.'

'A picture?'

Forrester nodded. 'A picture of Harry Rose.'

Annie shook her head. She was confused. She *needed* to know about her father, and yet even as Forrester was speaking she knew what was coming, she knew it in her heart of hearts, and she was fighting it all the way.

Forrester opened the envelope, and took out a small grainy monochrome snapshot. He held it for a moment, as if weighing it, and then he slid it across the table towards Annie.

Annie stared down at the photograph, a photograph that showed a fair-haired man standing proudly with a small child in his arms.

'This is Harry Rose?' Annie asked.

Forrester nodded, smiled benignly, as if he were granting a Papal indulgence to the moment. A special moment.

'Yes,' he said quietly, and his voice was like a whisper.

He leaned backwards, and when Annie looked up there was an expression on his face she hadn't seen before. An expression of completeness.

'And this child?' she asked.

'Is Harry's daughter,' Forrester said.

'His daughter?' Annie asked, her voice registering confusion and dismay.

Forrester smiled again. 'Yes, that is his daughter.'

'And he's on Rikers Island?'

'He is, yes . . . and all these years he was housed in a cell in the west wing of the penitentiary, a wing owned and run by the Italian families.' Forrester smiled as if sharing something special and unique. 'So much so that it was often referred to as the Cicero Hotel.'

Annie stared at Forrester, and somewhere inside her a feeling grew, a feeling of being twisted up from within by some unseen hand.

'And the girl . . . the little girl?' she said, and tears were welling in her eyes, and the sense of breathlessness in her chest was enough to suffocate her right where she sat.

Forrester paused. He breathed in and out slowly, as if letting something go. 'The little girl,' he said.

'The little girl is all grown up now,' Annie said, tears rolling down her face, her vision blurred, her hands shaking un-controllably.

'She is.'

'And her name?' Annie asked, her voice trembling, tears filling her eyes.

'Her name?' Forrester echoed. 'Her name Miss O'Neill . . . is Annie.'

Forrester smiled. He bowed his head.

Annie O'Neill, a wave of indescribable anguish overwhelm-ing her for a second, dropped the photograph, sensed it as if in slow-motion as it made its way to the floor, and then tried to rise from her chair.

She could not stand, she had neither the will nor the strength.

Forrester reached out his hand, and closing it around her forearm he pulled her down into a seated position once more.

'Sit,' he said quietly, his voice almost a whisper. His hand tightened on her wrist. She could feel the blood-flow constrict-ing.

Annie looked at him, this Robert Forrester, this man she had trusted, a man who had walked into her life promising some sense of understanding, some sense of equilibrium, and even now had torn everything out from beneath her.

'Your father took my life away,' Forrester whispered. 'He

367

cheated me, he betrayed me time and time again . . . and whoever you may have imagined him to be he was something else entirely. He was a thief and a murderer and a traitor. He was a man who professed to have principles and honor, but he was a common criminal.'

Annie opened her mouth to speak. She could barely breathe. The tears that filled her eyes now rolled in fat lazy streaks down her face.

'You know as much about him as I do,' Forrester said, 'and though I wrote these things for my own son, I also wrote them for you, so you would know, so you would understand what kind of person Frank O'Neill really was.'

No, Annie was mouthing, the word audible inside her head, but from her lips nothing.

No . . . no . . . no . . . no . . .

'Yes Miss O'Neill, and yes again and again and again. Frank O'Neill was an evil man. And now you know, now you feel what I felt when he turned his back on me to let me die a little more each day on Rikers Island.'

She started to mouth the word *But* . . .

Forrester shook his head. 'But nothing Miss O'Neill. You are the daughter of a truly worthless man. And my son – '

Forrester paused, smiled to himself. 'My son understands who your father is also, and he hates you for what you are.'

Annie's eyes widened. She did not want to understand what was happening.

Forrester shook his head, and once again tightened the grip on her wrist. 'He came to get his legacy, the money that was rightfully his, and though you worked on him, though you started to turn him against me, the truth is that you meant nothing to him, will never mean anything to him.'

Annie was shaking her head, and even as her mind was reeling she was looking towards the door, back towards Forrester, trying to think if there was any way she might get herself free of Forrester's grip and make it out and through the kitchen. Was the door deadbolted out there? Was there any way in the world she could make it?

And then another thought, a thought she could barely contain. *Is this it? Is this the point I will die? Is this man now going to kill me as he has killed before?*

In her mind she was screaming, but not a single word left her lips.

'David,' Forrester echoed. 'David who took you to Boston, David who left you in a hotel while he came back here to help me search your apartment for any indication of where your father's money was, David who answered the telephone when you called me that night. The same David who investigated every inch of your life, your bank accounts, your connections, the people you know. The same David who finally convinced me that Harry Rose took all my money and left me without a dime. I told him who your father was, what he had done to me, what your father had done to him, an innocent boy, and who determined to break your heart into pieces just to redress the balance. You almost took him Annie O'Neill . . . for a little while you almost took him from me, but I made him see sense, I made him understand the kind of person you must be. Once again he understands that any child of Harry Rose's is an enemy of ours, an enemy to be despised and hated. And though we have no money to show for this, we also know you have nothing too. You have less than nothing, because whatever you may have believed would happen with my son, you have lost that as well. Your father was so worthless he managed to destroy whatever happiness you might have found without even being here.'

Annie started up again, but once more her legs gave beneath her. Whatever intention she might have had to free herself, Forrester's grip was like a vice. She could feel herself pulling away with all she possessed, and yet she could barely move a muscle.

She collapsed into the chair, couldn't see for the tears that

369

filled her eyes, and as she wiped those tears away she looked at Forrester.

Forrester smiled, and as he did so he rose, and as he rose he released the grip from her arm. He gathered his topcoat, and while he was putting it on, stepping back, making his way from the table, Annie stared back at him with hollow eyes.

'Whatever you may have believed David was, he was not. However you may have thought you reached him, I reached him deeper. You did reach him, I know you did, but in no time at all I turned him back towards the truth and made him see you for what you really are.'

Forrester took another half a dozen steps backward. He was ten, perhaps twelve feet from the door.

'However you might have imagined your father, that he was good and kind and generous and compassionate, he was none of those things.'

Forrester moved again, and this time Annie did manage to get to her feet.

'The life you might have had if your father had stayed with you would have been a life of running and hiding, of stealing and killing and breaking trust.'

Forrester reached the door. His fingers were on the handle, but as he started to turn it Annie was walking towards him, snatching a book from a stack as she passed.

'Your father, Miss O'Neill, was a worthless excuse for a human being, and for his sins he will burn in hell.'

Annie screamed then, screamed and hurled the book at him. Forrester ducked, swung the door wide, and Annie ran after him, grabbed another book from near the counter and threw it towards the man as he hurried from the store. She could hear him laughing, a sound like fingernails on a chalkboard, a sound like rusted wire dragged through a grate, and as she felt the rush of cool wind reach her she knew that there was not enough left inside her to fight any longer.

By the time she reached the sidewalk Robert Franklin

Forrester was across the street. He reached the opposite sidewalk, and for a moment he stood immobile under a streetlight.

Annie took one step forward and stopped dead in her tracks. Forrester was joined by another man, and together they stood side by side, looking back at her.

Robert Forrester and his son looked back at her. They did not move for some time, and whatever Annie O'Neill might have felt in that moment it was swallowed soundlessly when David tilted his head to the left and turned to the side.

Just like in the window across the street a thousand years before.

Just like then.

He had been watching her all the time, watching her as she went about her daily life, watching her while she thought she was falling in love.

And then he moved. David stepped back and turned the corner.

Forrester hesitated for a moment more, and then he turned and vanished also.

And with him – like a shadow, like a ghost – went Johnnie Redbird.

An hour later, the lights in the store still burning, it was John Damianka who found Annie O'Neill slumped in the chair with her head in her hands. He'd been walking home after an evening out with Elizabeth Farbolin. He'd seen the lights on, and the sheer incongruousness had drawn him to the window. The outer door was closed and he beat on it with his fists until she raised her head and looked back at him.

Eventually she rose and walked towards the door, unlocked it and let him in. He called a cab with his cellphone, and almost carrying her as deadweight he got her into the cab and took her home.

Sullivan was there when they arrived, and took her in. He closed his arms around Annie O'Neill and brought her to his apartment. He lay her down on his bed and he turned out the light. He sat with her until he was sure she slept.

There would be no talking that night. Not a word.

Seemed to Annie O'Neill that there was nothing left to say.

THIRTY-EIGHT

It took a week.

A week of tears and hysterics, of Jack Sullivan lying with her night after night until she slept. And often she would wake in the early hours of the morning, and she would start to cry again, and Jack would hold her, pull her tight against him, and say whatever he felt might help. It didn't. There was no way it could.

She knew the truth.

And the truth hurt.

All these years her father had been out there, alive on Rikers Island, and Annie had never known. And her mother carried the knowledge, carried the secret close to her heart for all those years until she herself had died. And never said a word.

And they talked, Annie O'Neill and Jack Sullivan, talked perhaps more than they needed, and they read through the manuscript once more, and Annie faced the harshness of reality, and that reality came with teeth and claws and blood in its mouth.

And sometimes Annie would just ramble, monologuing her thoughts out into nowhere, and the fact that Sullivan was there to hear her made no difference. He could have been anyone at all, and it wouldn't have made a difference. She had been caught up in something that was older than herself, and this man – this Redbird, Forrester, whoever the hell he was – had come for something that she didn't have. He had even brought his son, a son who had used *her* name to take an apartment in *her* city . . . And then she talked of Boston, the way David had disappeared for those hours, and how – upon her return – she had found little things had moved, changed, found themselves out of place, and realized that *they* had been here, invaded her home, invaded her heart and everything about her . . .

And then disappeared.

They had wanted to deliver the truth, and deliver it they had. And the truth was what it was, however she chose to look at it: her father had been a killer; her father would die a killer; he would die in a small stone room measuring no more than eight by eight, and he knew – had always known – that not only was his own daughter out there, but that one day she might find him.

And so it took a week.

Sullivan had made the call. He gave them Annie's name, as much detail as he could, and he requested a visitation order. Rikers Island told him when they could come, that the order could be collected on the day of arrival, and Sullivan started preparing Annie O'Neill to meet her father.

Tuesday morning, 23 September.

It was a bitter day, and from the East River through Hell Gate the wind came like a tornado of razor blades and cut into Annie's face as she stood on the deck of the ferry, her heart like a dead fist in her chest, her nerves ragged, her mouth dry.

She looked back several times, over Jack Sullivan's shoulder as he held her close, back there at the mainland, the lights of Port Morris and Mott Haven. And to her right was Long Island and Astoria where her father had lived all those years before, from where he himself had set out towards the same destination to see Johnnie Redbird. The North and South Brothers were there, and Lawrence Point, the Conrail Freight Yard, the stench from Bowery Bay that seemed to penetrate her very being through the pores of her skin. It was all there, just as it had been written, just as she had read.

Her face was numb with the cold, but better that way – a reason to keep silent. It seemed the tears – whatever tears may have been left – were now frozen in her eyes, and in blinking she could feel them, back there somewhere playing hard to get. Sullivan watched her, watched her intently, her every move, her every gesture, and when the ferry came in towards the docking station – already the sounds and smells of a strange world so far from their own around them – he held her arm tight as she made her way down the steps to the boardwalk that ran the length of the jetty.

They were not alone. There were other people who also knew people within this place. They were cold too, and perhaps a little overawed by what was ahead of them no matter how often they had made this narrow journey before.

And then there were men with uniforms and guns, high fences and razor wire, an endless procession of black walls every which way they looked, walls that seemed to march out into the sea, to reach the sky, their foundations buried in a hundred miles of earth so that no-one might think to leave. But everyone inside thought of little else. Surviving and leaving.

Sullivan was asked his name, gave it, and when Annie was asked, she stayed silent until Sullivan gave her name too.

'And who are you visiting?' the guard asked. He was a wide man, perhaps the widest man Sullivan had ever seen, and in his eyes was a hardness that came from the necessity to do his duty without emotion.

'My father,' Annie mumbled.

'What?' the guard asked.

'Her father,' Sullivan said. 'Frank O'Neill.'

'You visited before?' the guard asked, and with each question he asserted more of his width, his authority, his dispassionate disregard.

Annie shook her head.

'No,' Sullivan said. 'We haven't visited before. There should be a visitation order here for us.'

'Through there.' He pointed to a heavy wire-mesh doorway. 'People on the other side will take your names, go through your things, the usual routine.' The guard pasted a meaningless smile on his face, and as if attempting to bring some humanity into the proceedings, added, 'Like when you go on the plane.'

Sullivan nodded, and they walked on.

The sounds and smells of the penitentiary were as bad as Sullivan had imagined, just as he'd read in Forrester's manuscript: the odor of cheap disinfectant, the clinging stench of a mass of men crammed into tiny cells, living in each other's pockets. He could smell the fear and frustration, the interminable boredom, the hatred and resentment, the guilt and the innocence. And he realized that he was feeling what Annie's father must have felt, first when he came to visit Johnnie Redbird, and again when he came to stay – and knew he would stay for the rest of his life.

Annie was silent, wide-eyed and pale. She stood immobile as a female guard searched her, went through her purse, emptied out its contents and removed a nail file, a hairbrush and a powder compact with a mirror inside. These items were placed in a see-through baggie and labeled. Annie had to sign the label, print her name and the date, and was told in terse monosyllables that she would be able to collect these items upon her departure. Sullivan asked once again about the visitation order, but the guard just ushered them forward and Sullivan took Annie's arm once more.

They were brought to yet another gate, a door beyond, and beyond that a corridor that ran as far as either of them could see towards a tunnel of darkness at the end.

The visitors' group went forward, like a crocodile of scared children.

At some point Annie paused and, without thinking, turned back and took a few steps. Sullivan held her arm even tighter, believed she would be bruised come morning, but Annie seemed to feel nothing, simply stood there white-faced and red-eyed, with an expression so blank anything could have been drawn upon it.

'I can't,' she murmured.

'You can,' Sullivan said. 'You have to.'

And then he was leading her again, and she went without protest or question or choice, and after what seemed like an hour, a day perhaps, they reached another door at the end of the corridor.

Sullivan could smell the people around him; the smell of fear and awe.

The door was unlocked from within. That grating sound of keys and bars and heavy metal cast in such a way as to be challenged by nothing. To Annie, that sound cut through to the very heart of this moment. Within these walls was her past, her present, perhaps some of her future. You could never walk away from such a thing and stay the same.

The light was blinding – too bright, too harsh – and within the brightness a cold and invasive tint of blue like ultra-violet: a light that could see *through* things, see them for what they truly were.

The room extended as far as the eye could see, divided in two by a ceiling-high grating, tables on either side, guards to left and right. They followed the crocodile of visitors to a registration booth, and here they stood in line while names were taken, a phone lifted, a brief and perfunctory call made.

Finally it was their turn. Annie looked at Sullivan, and in her eyes were all the questions she'd ever wanted to ask.

Go, he mouthed, and Annie stepped forward, and Annie opened her mouth and spoke her father's name, and the phone was lifted, the call was made, and on hearing a stranger say her father's name she folded herself sideways into Sullivan; and though she was silent, he knew from the way her body shook that she was crying.

There seemed to be some confusion.

A guard came from the edge of the room and said something to Annie.

'What?' Sullivan asked. 'What is it?'

'This way,' the guard said. 'Follow me.'

They went, unquestioningly, and from the large room they were ushered through another door into a dark ante-room. The light was switched on, and Sullivan stood stock-still while the guard showed Annie to a small table. He nodded at Sullivan, who stepped forward and sat also.

'Is there a problem?' Sullivan asked. 'Is there some kind of problem?'

The guard seemed to smile though Sullivan wasn't sure. 'Wait here,' he said.

He left the room, locking the door behind them, and for a moment Sullivan gained some sense of what it must feel like to find yourself here, perhaps by some dark sleight of hand, and to know that these walls, these sounds, and these feelings were all you would know for the rest of your life.

'What's happening?' Annie eventually asked.

'It's okay,' Sullivan lied, because he knew something was wrong.

'I won't know what to say,' she said, her voice barely a whisper. 'He'll be old Jack . . . really old, and I won't know what to say to him.'

Sullivan closed his hand over hers and squeezed it.

'It'll be okay,' he said. 'You'll know what to say when he comes.'

But there was fear in her eyes . . . no, not fear but terror, abject terror, and for the endless minutes that stretched out as they waited Sullivan believed that in all his life – despite everything he had seen and felt and experienced in all the hellholes of the world he'd discovered himself – there was never anything that could compare to this.

This was a nightmare, a living, breathing nightmare.

'Thank you . . . for coming,' Annie said, and Sullivan squeezed her hand tighter. And then there was a sound, a key in the door, and he instinctively rose to his feet as if preparing to receive his sentence.

He turned to face the door, the widening gap between the door and the frame like something opening up inside of himself, and the man that walked through, the man who stopped and faced them and smiled and took another step into the room where they had waited, could not have been Frank O'Neill.

He was dark-haired, no more than forty or forty-five, and was dressed like a priest.

'Miss O'Neill I believe,' he said, and his voice had that calming tone of reassurance native to those of a religious vocation.

Annie rose, her eyes swelling with tears.

'I'm sorry,' the priest said. 'I'm so sorry, but there seems to have been some sort of mistake.'

'A mistake?' Annie asked, already consumed with emotion and believing she couldn't take any more.

'Your visitation order,' the priest said. 'Your visitation order was for a Frank O'Neill, is that right?'

She nodded. She looked at Sullivan. Sullivan looked back but didn't say a word.

'Well it seems that the person who completed the application registered a Frank McNeal in error.'

Annie was nodding. 'Right,' she said, her voice wavering. 'My father is Frank O'Neill, not McNeal . . .'

The priest looked down, and when he looked up again there was something in his eyes that told her all she needed to know before he even spoke. 'I am sorry to bring this news,' he said, 'but I am afraid your father, Frank O'Neill . . . I'm afraid that your father passed away last June.'

THIRTY-NINE

From the Heartbreak Hotel
27 November 2002

Dear Dad,

Hey, it's me, your daughter Annie.

A few times I've thought about this, writing this letter you know, but I haven't done it until now as I figured it was just another sign that I was losing my mind. But hell, seems I've lost so many things recently one more couldn't hurt.

My friend Sullivan (he lives across the landing from me) tells me that humor is the last line of defence. Well, here I am, down to the last line. The end-zone.

So I found out what happened after all these years. A man called Robert Forrester came and saw me, and he wrote some things. I thought it was just a story, kind of wild really but a story nevertheless, and it turned out that it was true. And he had a son, just like you had a daughter, and he set things up for me to fall in love (or rise into love, whichever way you look at it), and then they took it all away.

I spoke to the people at Rikers Island. They told me that a man called David Quinn came to see you three or four times. They thought he was a friend of yours. And after you died he came again and they gave your stuff to him. They gave him letters that you wrote to mom but never sent to her. They told me you died of a stroke, that your body just folded up and there was nothing they could do to help you. Sullivan told me that sometimes people die to escape the inevitable. Is that true? Did Forrester and his son say they were going to tell me where you were? That if you didn't give up the money I would know everything? Was the idea of speaking the truth so terrifying that death was easier to face? They really believed that you held out on them, that somewhere you had hidden tens of thousands of dollars.

And then there are other things, like finding out that you and mom were never really married. In itself it makes no great difference to me, but it makes me realize there were so many things to know and I didn't know them. Like where you really came from, and what happened when you were a kid. Mom never said a word. I figure you must have made her promise. Well she kept her promise good. She really did. She was like you in that way I s'pose, someone of principle.

The photograph they took from you, the one of you holding me as a child. I'm looking at it now. Your face is a stranger's face, but I can see myself hiding in your eyes. I have the picture. It is mine now, along with the couple of letters that mom never saw. And I have your wristwatch, and the book you left for me. *Breathing Space*. You wrote something inside it. 'For when the time comes.' What did you mean? What time? And when will it come?

It's been just over two months since I went to Rikers. I haven't been able to think clearly. But now I'm getting it back together dad, and I'm gonna read your book again. Maybe it'll read different now. Maybe there's something in it that I'll recognize as a message from you to me. Now I know the truth perhaps I'll see it. Maybe, from this point, I'll see a lot of things differently. I don't know, and in some way I don't care.

I'm thirty-one years old. Had my birthday the day before yesterday. Tomorrow it's Thanksgiving, the family time you know? Well, I have an idea of who you were and what you looked like, and it feels like someone came home. Crazy, huh? I can look at the picture without crying. That's taken a while, but I can do it now. Grit my teeth, clench my fists, and I can do it. You were my dad, Frank O'Neill. You are my dad. I am your child, only one you ever had as far as I know. And you might be dead, but I'm not. I'm here.

Anyway, I've written this letter as a sort of catharsis, a way out of something, and when I'm done with it we're gonna put it in an old Crown Royal bottle (Sullivan's idea), and then we're gonna go over the Triborough Bridge to Randall's Island Park and throw it into the Rikers Channel. Why? Because that's where the Rikers people told me your ashes went. They cremated you and they scattered your ashes into the Channel. So maybe we will get to meet again, you and me, but I'll be a letter, and you'll be a small eddying current that will swallow me up.

More than likely I'll never know, but I gotta hold onto that idea. We gotta have anchors or we float away, right?

Well, I'm gonna go now dad. I've got a life to live. I suppose I could say that I love you, but it would be out of duty, and not from the heart . . . and I kinda get the idea that you'd better understand if I just said I miss you. So here it goes . . . I miss you dad.

Take care.

Your daughter, forever, Annie.

FORTY

There's a way the wind hurries down through the subway tunnels, like it's been trapped there for centuries and still believes it can escape. That wind is bitter, and it always catches you unawares, and with it comes the smell of diesel and oil and dead things. That's the only way Annie O'Neill can describe that smell. Diesel and oil and dead things.

She's glad when the train eventually arrives. She feels nervous, agitated, and is endlessly asking herself why she is doing this, what she hopes to gain. She believes that she will do nothing but embarrass herself, but despite this certainty there is also something that drives her forward.

Up above it is snowing, lightly, but nevertheless it is snowing. It is Saturday, four days before Christmas. There was always something about Christmas in New York, and still is. It feels different. Feels real.

Annie boards the train and takes a seat. She leans back and sighs. She closes her eyes for a moment, and then from her purse she takes the book that he gave her. *A Farewell To Arms* by Ernest Hemingway. Next to it lies *Breathing Space*, and this she carries as if for some kind of emotional support. She has read it again, read it slowly, savoring each line, each word perhaps, in an effort to find the meaning. She knows there is a meaning, she just has to look hard enough.

What she is doing now started three nights before, sitting there in her apartment talking with Sullivan. He had noticed the Hemingway there on the table and had asked her about it.

She told him – about the hospital, the doctor there, what he had said, what she thought he might have meant – and

Sullivan went off on the Carpe Diem speech. He wouldn't leave it be, kept nagging at her. *Go down there*, he'd told her. *Go down there and see the guy. He was cute right?*

She had shrugged. *Sure, he was cute I s'pose.*

So what the hell are you waiting for . . . go down there, take the book back, tell him you read the thing and you're returning it.

For two days Sullivan spoke of it, and finally, perhaps out of the sheer necessity to shut him up, she had taken her heart in her hands and agreed.

She said she would go after Christmas.

Christ Annie, if the guy is half as good-looking and sympathetic as you make out he'll be married with three kids by Christmas. Quit all the maybe-he-won't-like-me, maybe-I'm-not-good-enough crap and get the hell down there and tell him Hi. What's the worst thing that could happen? You find out that he's not into you now you're sober then you'll know he's not the guy for you, right?

By the time Annie reaches Amsterdam Avenue her stomach is in knots. She wants to turn back but she can't. It isn't Sullivan, it isn't that he wouldn't leave the thing alone 'til she agreed, it isn't that she's afraid Jim Parrish will be engaged or married or not interested any more . . . it's none of those things.

The truth of the matter is that she wants to see him, but she's afraid. Afraid that he'll not be who she remembers. Afraid that he'll be someone else entirely, and he will betray her too.

Even as she enters the E.R. she's trying to make herself invisible. She feels what she feels, and yet she doesn't understand what she feels. She wishes her father were there so she could ask him. But he's not. He's dead, swallowed up in Rikers Channel.

She is ten feet from the reception desk, and then she thinks *Hell, if I can handle everything that's happened so far then sure as damn I can handle this*.

'Jim Parrish, Doctor Jim Parrish,' she tells the desk nurse.

The desk nurse doesn't laugh. She doesn't say *Hey girls, here's another lush that's fallen for Doctor Jim and is trying her luck tonight* or *You taken a look at yourself lately lady . . . you figure you stand a chance with someone like Doctor Jim? Ha ha ha!* She merely consults a computer screen and says, 'You're in luck. He's off in about ten minutes. If you take a seat over there you'll see him when he comes out of that green door at the end of the corridor.'

Annie thanks her and backs up, thinking *This is it. Ten minutes to decide whether I stay or leave. I could just give the book to the duty nurse, tell her to return it to him when he comes down . . .*

Annie walks towards the chairs the nurse indicated. She stands for a moment, and then she sits, almost involuntarily. Her mind is driving her away. Her heart is holding her hostage.

The minutes die slowly and she hates them for their tardiness.

She glances at both the clock on the wall and her father's wristwatch.

She thinks of Sullivan's face, the way his eyes lit up when she said she would come down here.

She curses herself for her nervousness, for her sense of anticipation, for her unfounded anxieties. Like Sullivan said, what could be the worst that could happen?

From her purse she takes the Hemingway, and also *Breathing Space*.

She opens the front cover and once more reads the inscription. Was this now the time? Was this what it was all about? Courage in the face of adversity, of conflict, of . . .

'Hi there.'

Annie looks up.

Doctor Jim Parrish stands over her and he's smiling so wide she thinks his face might break in two.

For a moment she doesn't know what to say. Doesn't know what to feel.

'Your book,' she says, her tone sharp, a little brusque.

'Jeez,' he replies. 'It wasn't that bad, was it?'

She smiles. *Relax*, she thinks. *Relax goddamnit!*

385

'So how're you doing?' he asks, and sits down beside her.

She nods, tries to smile, but she's aware of the tension in her face and knows how pained she must look.

She glances sideways at him.

He smiles. It is a good smile. A genuine smile. It isn't the smile of a stalker or a serial rapist.

'You don't remember me from the last time, do you?' he says.

Annie raises her eyebrows, she scans his functionally handsome face, wonders what he could mean.

'Not here at St Luke's,' he says. 'Not when you were the drunk falling over woman – '

Annie frowns. Now she feels embarrassed, really embarrassed.

'I saw you another time as well,' he goes on. 'In Starbucks a while back, and obviously I made a very significant impression on you because you didn't recognize me at all.'

'That was you?' she says, remembering the incident as if it were yesterday, suddenly relieved that something has managed to find its way out of her mouth.

Annie smiles more naturally, a little less embarrassed, though in all honesty she can't think of any reason why she should feel embarrassed. Perhaps because she has earned herself a reputation – at least with one other human being in Manhattan – as the *drunk falling over woman*.

She counters the situation with an artful and spontaneous defence. 'Well, I can imagine you can't remember my name,' she says.

'Annie O'Neill,' he replies.

She is genuinely surprised.

'You have an easy name,' he says. 'It rhymes with Ally McBeal.'

She laughs again. It is a ludicrous moment, and yet somehow oddly life-affirming. There have been other moments like this recently – Sullivan appearing at two in the morning carrying a bucket of southern-fried chicken, a little kid on the porch stoop a week or so ago who asked her if she was looking forward to Christmas as much as he was . . .

'You got me,' Annie says, smiles, nods. 'You get a cigar for that, but only a twenty-five cent stogie, none of those hand-rolled Havana babies.'

Parrish leans back on the seat. 'So did you read the book?'

She shakes her head. 'No, to be honest, I didn't read it.'

'So how come you brought it back?'

Annie doesn't answer the question. She looks at the clock on the wall and feels herself blushing.

There is a stilted silence between them, brief – no more than a heartbeat – but she feels the tension with that moment.

'How's your store?' he asks.

'You remember that as well?'

He nods. 'Sure I remember . . . told you first and foremost I was a reader. Actually planned to come down there and check the place out but never made it for some reason.'

Annie looks at him. There is something else here. And then she remembers the moment she saw him in Starbucks, the anecdote Sullivan had shared with her before. The moment. *The* moment. She shrugs it away.

'So what you got there?' he asks, pointing towards the copy of *Breathing Space* she is clutching.

Annie holds out the book. 'Something called *Breathing Space*.'

'The Levitt one?' he asks, in his tone an element of surprise.

Annie frowns. 'Yes . . . Nathaniel Levitt.'

'Hell, I thought they stopped printing that years ago.'

Annie shrugs. 'I don't know . . . it was something my father left for me. It's very old.'

'You know who he was of course?' Jim Parrish asks.

Annie shakes her head. 'Some guy . . . some writer from the eighteen hundreds.'

Parrish smiles. 'He was Old Hickory's brother . . . Nathaniel Levitt was a pseudonym.'

'Old Hickory?'

'Andrew Jackson, seventh I think . . . yes, seventh president of the United States; served two terms between 1829 and 1837.'

'How the hell d'you know this stuff?' Annie asks.

Parrish shrugs. 'Hell, I don't know . . . maybe I really need a hobby.'

She laughs, holds the book in her hand, turns it over as if seeing it in a new light. 'So this was printed when Andrew Jackson was president of the United States.'

'Well, not actually printed of course, but at least written when he was president.'

Annie shakes her head. 'No,' she says, opening the book. 'It says inside . . . printed in 1836 by a company called Hollister & Sons of Jersey City, bound by Hoopers of Camden . . .'

Parrish leans forward, his face intent. 'No shit,' he says, almost under his breath. 'Can I see?'

'Sure,' Annie says, and holds out the book.

Parrish takes it carefully, reaching for it as one would reach for the hand of a baby.

He looks it over, opens the cover and reads the handwritten inscription, touches the print with his fingertips.

'Your store?' he asks. 'You sell rare and antique books?'

'No,' Annie replies. 'Just your regular paperbacks and stuff.'

'And you know what you have here?'

She shakes her head. 'A book called *Breathing Space* by Andrew Jackson's brother?'

'Right . . . right,' Parrish says, his manner really quite distracted. 'But you know what this is?'

He looks at her, in his hand the book, on his face an expression of such intensity that Annie wonders what is going on.

'So?' she asks, holding out her hand for him to return the book.

'They printed maybe three, four hundred in all,' Parrish says. 'And as far as literature goes it isn't a great deal to write home about . . . but the historical significance.' He pauses for a moment, looks directly at Annie. His expression is like a parent having serious words with a child. 'Don't take this out again Miss O'Neill – '

'Annie,' she says. 'Call me Annie . . . anyone who knows me well enough to refer to me as the drunk falling down woman can call me Annie.'

'Well, don't take it outside your house again Annie, I'm serious. Take it back and wrap it up and go stick it in a security deposit box someplace.'

Annie frowns.

'Six, seven years ago,' Parrish says. 'Sotheby's, here in New York . . . they sold one of these, a first edition by Levitt, for something in the region of a hundred and twenty-five grand.'

Annie looks at Parrish. Looks down at the book. Her mouth is open, her eyes wide.

'You didn't know?' Parrish asks.

Annie shakes her head. 'Give me that again.'

'That book you have . . . a copy of that book sold for a hundred and twenty-five grand at Sotheby's about six or seven years ago.' Parrish shook his head. 'Now? Well now I don't know, but I figure maybe you'd fetch something closer to two hundred.' He smiles, wide like a kid. 'What did your father write in there?'

Annie shakes her head. She looks down at the book.

Slowly, almost cautiously, she opens the cover. She can feel the weight of it in her hand.

Never has it felt so heavy.

Like the weight of my heart, she thinks.

She traces her finger slowly over the words her father wrote – *Annie*

– a father she believed she would never know the truth of – *for when the time comes*

– and now – finally – realizes that the truth has been almost too much to believe.

Dad. 2 June 1979.

She is in denial. Her mind cannot stretch far enough to take this in. She stands up, starts to walk away from the chair where she was sitting, and then she stops, turns back.

'You doing anything?' she asks Jim Parrish.

'Right now?'

'Right now.'

Parrish shakes his head. 'No, nothing special . . . why?'

'Come see the store . . . come see the store and have some dinner with me.'

Parrish raises his eyebrows. He's still got his kid-grin all over his face. 'You asking me out?'

Annie smiles, starts laughing again. 'Sure I am . . . why the fuck not? You only get one chance at this kind of thing, right?'

'I s'pose you do,' Parrish says, and catches her up. 'Okay . . . I don't remember the last time I was asked out, but I'm coming . . . and before anything else is said I want you to know I'm not coming because of the money, right?'

Annie O'Neill starts to laugh, and then he is beside her, and she is putting the book back in her purse, and together they walk out of the E.R. and into the street.

She turns left, Jim Parrish alongside now, Annie smiling, starting to laugh, and the wind that catches her – bitter and resentful though it is – carries that sound all the way down to Cathedral Parkway.